FALL *of the* ARGOSI

FALL *of the* ARGOSI

SEBASTIEN DE CASTELL

HOT
KEY
BOOKS

First published in Great Britain in 2021 by
HOT KEY BOOKS
4th Floor, Victoria House
Bloomsbury Square
London WC1B 4DA
Owned by Bonnier Books
Sveavägen 56, Stockholm, Sweden
www.hotkeybooks.com

A CIP catalogue record for this book is available from the British Library.

HARDBACK ISBN: 978-1-4714-1058-1
TRADE PAPERBACK ISBN: 978-1-4714-1059-8
Also available as an ebook and in audio

1

Typeset by DataConnection Ltd
Printed and bound by Clays Ltd, Elcograf S.p.A.

Hot Key Books is an imprint of Bonnier Books UK
www.bonnierbooks.co.uk

For everyone at Hot Key Books – outstanding companions along the many twists and turns of the Path of Eight Novels.

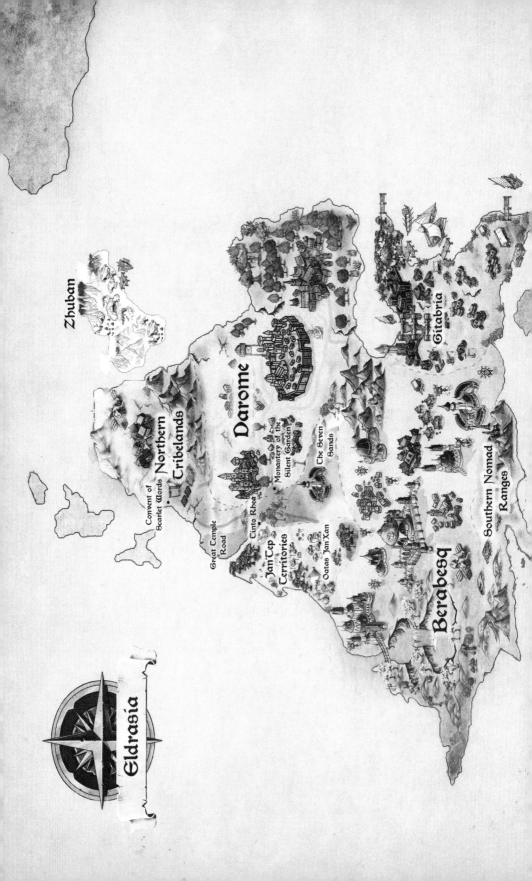

The Boy in the Sand

The child raced barefoot across the desert. The cuts on the soles of his feet were staining the sand a madman's scarlet, but the look in his eyes said that was the least of his problems. Though I didn't know it then, he was fleeing his father, who loved him more than anything in the world, and was now intent on his murder. The same could've been said of my own father, but I'm not ready to tell that story yet.

At first the boy had been nothing but a puff of dust and blond hair in the distance. The sun was beating down mercilessly that day, reminding all living things who was in charge and that deserts were cursed places at the best of times. I had a horse though, which makes all the difference.

'Reckon that's trouble ahead?' I asked Quadlopo, patting his neck.

The horse showed no signs of giving the matter any thought, just swished his tail to keep the flies away. In the five days since we'd fled to the borderlands, Quadlopo had yet to offer an opinion on anything, except perhaps that he would've preferred that I'd not stolen him in the first place. After all, it wasn't like anyone wanted *him* dead.

The grubby whirl of spindly arms and legs ran up the side of a dune, then lost his balance and came tumbling down the other.

He looked like he couldn't have been more than seven. An unseemly age to be running around the desert alone. His pale blue tunic was torn to rags, and the skin of his arms and face shone an angry red that spoke of too many days out in the sun with nothing and no one to protect him. He was limping too, but kept on going, which meant whatever was chasing him troubled him more than the pain.

Brave kid.

When he got within thirty yards of me, he stopped and stared as if trying to work out whether I was a mirage. I'm not sure what conclusion he came to, but I guess he'd been running a long time because his legs gave out on him and he dropped to his hands and knees. That's when I saw the two new figures come shambling through the haze towards us. A tall man and a squat woman, whose unnatural, shuffling gaits made me question whether those labels might be too generous in describing whatever had followed the boy.

For the first time since we'd happened upon this unpleasantness, Quadlopo became restless. He blew hot air out of his nostrils and pawed the sand with his hoofs, trying to turn his head away from the mangled figures lumbering towards the child who was now lying face down in the sand, by all appearances waiting to die.

Most folk in these parts, should they get lost in the desert and run out of either water or the will to live, choose to meet their end on their back, so the last thing they see will be the blue sky above. The boy, though, seemed determined to look away from his pursuers.

Now that I'd gotten a good look at them, I didn't blame him.

Insanity, as I'd learned in my paltry seventeen years, could take all forms, come in all shapes and sizes. I'd witnessed folks of sound mind condemned as lunatics for the crime of being ugly and eccentric at the same time. I'd met well-groomed, erudite gentlemen of means who hid diabolical madness beneath smooth talk and friendly smiles. Then again, when I saw myself in the mirror, I looked sane too, so best not to pass judgement on such matters without strong evidence.

When two strangers come lurching towards you across the desert, naked as the day they were born except for their hides being caked in blood and dirt and fouler things I preferred not to imagine, when those same souls stare out at the world through eyes open so wide they look set to fall out of their sockets, jaws hanging open but nothing coming out except for a snake's hiss, well, times like that call for a different sort of prudence.

I reached over my shoulder and uncapped the long black mapmaker's case that held the smallsword I'd vowed five days ago never again to draw so long as I lived. One of the reasons I'd chosen to flee to the Seven Sands had been to smash the blade into seven pieces and bury each one so far from the others that not even the finest tracker in the whole world could unite them.

The hot desert wind shifted. The blood-soaked pair sniffed at the air like hunting hounds. Their heads tilted to the side like they'd just smelled a vixen for the first time and didn't know what to make of her. Some sort of instinct took hold of them, and they stopped heading towards the boy and came for me instead. At first they plodded, so awkward I kept expecting them to trip over themselves like puppets caught in their strings. But with each step their bare, blistered feet found surer footing. Faster and faster they scurried, and the closer they came, the more their hisses grew into a nightmare's worth of whispers that swirled around me like a dust storm.

I drew the sword from its case and slid off the horse's back, knowing that my oath never again to commit an act of violence, sworn while my foster mother's blood was still slick on my hands, was about to be broken.

The whispers became howls, and the howls turned to shrieks that sent poor, brave Quadlopo galloping away, abandoning me to whatever fate my bad luck and ill deeds had brought upon us. The two feral, manic creatures that came at me must've once been human beings with hopes and dreams of their own. Now their hands curled into claws, and they showed me teeth that had clacked so hard and so long against each other that they'd broken down to ragged fangs. From somewhere deep inside their throats, deranged screeches hid words I couldn't understand and didn't want to hear. Words that proved madness had its own poetry.

My hand tightened on the grip of my sword and I breathed in as slow as I could, preparing to make my stand and wondering whether the awful sounds they were uttering would become the elegy I carried with me into the ground.

My name is Ferius Parfax. I'm seventeen years old. This was the day I first heard the Red Scream.

Arta Eres

The art of self-defence is an illusion. The teysan who seeks to protect themselves and others by mastering the techniques of violence merely perpetuates and justifies that same violence. A true Argosi has no enemy, provides no opponent for another's anger. Ours is a dance and our talent is not in fighting every battle, but in winning every fight.

1

Dancing

The screamers came at me with a speed and ferocity that told me they weren't concerned about the sword in my hand any more than they were the lacerations covering their own ravaged bodies. If I'd taken so much as a moment to ponder what had made them this way, or wasted even a single breath on the panic rising inside me, there'd've been nothing left of my corpse for my foster father to find but a few sun-bleached bones sinking under the desert sand.

But I'd been taught the ways of defence by Durral Brown himself. The 'toughest Argosi dancer the world's ever seen', or so he used to tell me. Still did, if only in my head.

'Arta eres *ain't about fighting, kid. It's about winning.*'

I ran backwards, giving my savage opponents all the ground they wanted, watching to learn how they moved.

'No one can teach you how to defeat your opponent better than they will if you just give them the chance.'

Despite the man being tall and lean and the woman short and stout, they both had a similar style of attack, reaching to try to grab me with both hands even as their necks stuck out to get their jagged, broken teeth closer to my throat. Neither gave a damn about my sword.

'You want to kill someone? Do it in their sleep. It's kinder. Otherwise, figure out what winnin' looks like before you raise your fists.'

I wasn't looking to kill these people if I could avoid it. For all I knew, they were perfectly nice folk caught up in something beyond their ken. Maybe it was a disease from which they could be cured. A poison that would leave their bodies, given a few more hours or minutes. A Jan'Tep mage's spell messing with their minds. If I could knock them unconscious, I could tie them up and maybe find a way out of this for all of us. But that meant I had to understand what it would take to stop them.

I whipped the tip of my blade out to deliver a shallow cut to the woman's outstretched palm. She didn't react at all, just kept up that awful, hissing screech of hers. My free hand reached into the pocket of my travelling coat, thumb and forefinger pinching one of the six steel playing cards I'd stolen from Durral's weapons cabinet back home. With a snap of my wrist, I sent the razor-sharp card whirling through the air and between the tall man's teeth. He too just kept on hissing, spitting blood without even trying to dislodge the card.

'Only a fool tries to wound her opponent believing that what hurts her will hurt them. Pain ain't the Argosi way.'

I scurried back further, then realised I was being stupid and instead turned tail and ran, fast as I could.

'If you worry about how you look when you're dancing, you'll turn yourself into a graceful corpse.'

I could hear that they had sped up and were now running after me, but I was getting away. Once I'd gained a few yards, I spun around to face them and slid the mapmaker's case off my shoulder, letting it fall to the ground so it wouldn't impede my movements. I'd worried that outdistancing my attackers would send them back to the boy, who was on his knees again, staring at me, probably wondering if I was abandoning him. But the blood-soaked pair kept coming for me. They charged like enraged, mindless beasts, yet they didn't get in each other's way at all. So there was still some cunning inside them, along with the unnatural strength and endurance in their limbs.

'*Strength is an illusion. A strong man is strong only in certain angles and positions. If you can't defeat a man face to face, make him give you his back.*'

I shifted a foot to the left so I'd be in the tall man's path. Just as he grabbed for me, I dropped to my knees and dived between his legs, keeping a close grip on my smallsword. As I came out the other side, I drove the heel of my foot to the back of his knee. He buckled and fell onto his right side. But now the woman was coming for me, and I didn't have time to get back up.

'*For every way of fightin', there's a dance to match it. To master arta eres is to become skilled at finding that dance, no matter how strange it may be.*'

I rolled onto my back, feeling the warm, smooth sand beneath me. As the woman rushed me, I put both my feet up at the height of her belly and locked my legs straight out. Sure enough, she kept coming, arms grasping at empty air even as the force of her charge pushed me along like I was a shovel and she was scooping up the desert.

'*Second most important lesson of arta eres, kid: remember to laugh at least once.*'

'*Laugh, Pappy?*'

'*Yep. You learn a lot from seein' how an opponent reacts to laughter. Maybe it'll make 'em angry and reckless. Maybe they'll realise how stupid fightin' is in the first place, and start laughin' right along with you, maybe choose the Way of Water instead of violence. Now that's a proper victory.*'

11

'What if they don't do either? Should I still laugh?'

'Of course, kid. If you're gonna get yourself killed, might as well have a little fun along the way.'

So there I was, sliding on my back with a screaming madwoman trying to reach me with her clawed hands, laughing so loud I was almost drowning out her horrible rapturous shrieks. I kept a grip on my sword, letting the tip trace a sinewy line in the sand. I wondered, if I stayed like this long enough, would the woman end up pushing me all the way south, back to the home I'd fled five days ago?

Now wouldn't that be a fine tale to tell?

Unfortunately the tall man had gotten back to his feet, and he was running after us. I had three seconds before he'd get to me.

'What's the most important lesson, Pappy?'

'What's that, kid?'

'You said laughter was the second most important lesson of arta eres. What's the first?'

It was a year and a half since he'd started teaching me the Argosi talent for defence, but I could still remember the sadness in his eyes, the way his brows rose up at the centre of his forehead, just a little, as if contemplating telling me the answer made him despair at the world we lived in.

'There comes a moment when you know how the fight has to end. Maybe it happens right away, maybe it takes you a while to figure it out. But once you know, then you must follow the Way of Thunder and strike without hesitation, without remorse. Do what must be done, Ferius.'

I bent my knees and slapped my left hand against the sandy ground for balance. As the woman bore down on me, I let her momentum carry her over, thrusting my legs out straight again as I rolled over my back. For just an instant she was upside down in

12

the air, and when she landed on her head, the crunch of her neck breaking put an end to her shrieks.

I rolled up onto my feet, took my sword in both hands and dug my back heel into the ground. The man slammed into me so hard I don't think he even noticed the tip of the blade passing through his open mouth and out the other side of his skull.

That should've been the end of him, but it wasn't. He bowled me over and I discovered the terrible mistake I'd made. I'd assumed that because breaking the woman's neck had killed her, a blade through the head would surely put an end to him. But the human body's a funny thing, and there are stories of soldiers who've had a dagger shoved right through their eye and into their brain who just kept on fighting.

Somehow the sword had slid out and tumbled to the sand. I reached for it, but it was too far away. The man was on top of me now, his teeth clacking as he went for my throat, and when he couldn't quite reach it, tried for my nose. I've always liked having a nose, so I turned my head and squirmed, but there was no leverage to get him off me. I got my arms free and wrapped my fingers around his neck, holding him back as best I could. He wasn't even trying to stop me from strangling him – just kept grabbing at me with his hands, scratching tracks into the sides of my arms and face.

All the while he kept screaming. There was a pattern to it, I realised now. Like a song he kept repeating over and over. The reason I'd not been able to make out the words was that his tongue was gone, though whether someone had cut it off or he'd chewed it off himself, I couldn't say. Probably didn't matter, because my arms were starting to give out, and for the first time I saw something like joy in his eyes as whatever was left of his mind lusted over what would come next.

'What happens if you know you're going to lose, Pappy?'

'You keep dancin', of course.'

'But you said there comes a time when you know how the fight's gonna end.'

'No, I said there's a moment when you know how it has to end, not how it's gonna end. There's a difference.'

Durral loved these occasions – the ones where I thought I'd found a flaw in his teachings and he was holding out giving me a sensible answer. Me? I didn't love them nearly as much.

'Any chance you're going to tell me the difference?' I'd asked.

'Life's unpredictable, kid. A roll of the dice or a draw from the deck. Things start goin' bad, you just keep dancin' until the world sends you a little luck.'

So I did. I fought all the harder, even though I knew I was losing. I bashed my forehead against his nose, shattering it. The man wasn't bothered in the slightest. I wriggled and writhed, forcing him to keep readjusting to keep hold of me. When my forearms got too tired to hold him off, I let them bend, and drove my elbow into his face. I screamed as he left two of his teeth in the skin of my elbow. But I kept striking, kept moving any which way I could. Kept dancing.

Eventually we wound up almost how we'd started, with my hands around his throat trying to hold him off and him using all his weight and madman's brawn trying to drive what were left of his teeth into my neck. Then, just as I felt my sweat-soaked fingers losing their grip on him, the sun disappeared. The two of us were shrouded in darkness for a split second before I glimpsed an iron-shod back hoof smash into the side of the man's head so hard most of it came clean off. I was left holding his shattered lower jaw as his body slumped down onto mine, as if he were falling asleep in my arms.

Disgust and horror lent me just enough strength to roll him off me. I flopped back down and looked up into Quadlopo's big brown horsey eyes.

The first words that came to my mind were, 'What took you so long?' But that seemed inappropriate, given the poor beast had never wanted to be out here in the first place.

'Good horse,' I said instead, as my eyes closed and consciousness slipped away. 'Good horse.'

Arta Loquit

Arta loquit is not the mastery of language, for language cannot be mastered. Words are wild horses whose meanings never submit to the bridle of intention. Do not seek to break those untamed spirits, teysan, but instead listen to them, ride them if they'll let you. This is how an Argosi becomes . . . eloquent in the ways of the world.

2

Listening

I dreamed of my teeth gnashing of their own accord, of creeping madness rising up through my throat until it came hissing out like a puffer snake's venom. The awful creature that had once been me still held a sword in her hand, and though sanity had long fled, still my technique was precise and smooth as I extended my arm, raised my front foot and stretched my entire body out into a long lunge that drove the point of my sword through linen shirt, past skin and muscle, slipping between ribs and deep into –

My own scream woke me. Instincts honed from a childhood of misery that had stuck with me even through those precious eighteen months I'd lived with Durral and Enna sent me springing onto my hands and feet. I rose quickly and glanced in all directions to take in the world from which sleep had briefly released me.

The corpses of the man and the woman were where I'd left them. My own body ached, both from my exertions and from the cuts and scrapes I'd taken in the fight. But I hadn't turned into a shrieking monster.

Quadlopo stood about fifteen feet away, apparently performing an autopsy with his nose on the remains of a dried-brown shrub. A little beyond him the boy sat cross-legged, staring at me.

'Hey, kid,' I said. 'How's it goin'?'

'Hey, kid'? What, am I turning into Durral now?

The boy gave no reply, nor did he answer when I asked his name, where he was from, or if he could understand me at all.

Maybe he's in shock, I thought. *Wouldn't blame him if he was.*

Quadlopo produced a loud whinny, which gave me my own shock. I dived to the ground to grab my grizzly sword that was sticky with the dead man's blood and a decent dose of his brain matter. But when I got back to my feet, there were no attackers or dangers that I could see. The boy hadn't even moved an inch.

He didn't react to Quadlopo's whinny at all. Is he deaf?

I knelt down and scrubbed the blade clean with sand. When it was safely back in the mapmaker's case that I'd retrieved and slung across my back, I found the steel card I'd thrown into the crazy man's mouth and scoured the dried blood from that too. I held it up to the sun to check that the metal was still perfectly flat and hadn't gotten bent or warped from the dead man's teeth. The balance on these things can be finicky.

When I was done, I walked over to Quadlopo and took some cheese and bread from the saddlebag. I then approached the boy, slowly, patiently, expecting him to jump up and try to bolt.

He didn't.

'Hungry?' I asked, and offered him the bread and cheese.

He took both, sniffing the cheese awhile before deciding to gnaw on the bread instead. I sat down in front of him, crossing my legs to match his posture. I tried speaking to him in a few different languages. Pretty much nobody speaks Mahdek any more, which is my own people's tongue. The Seven Sands borders Darome, so most folk in these parts speak a simplified version of that. Having lived as a refugee most of my life, I'd picked up a little Zhuban, some Gitabrian and just enough Jan'Tep to remind me how much I hated hearing their language. None of my attempts got a reaction.

22

After a few more minutes, the boy handed me back the bread. When I took it from him, he tapped a finger once on the soiled blue tunic over his heart and then on his belly.

Is that some sort of fingertongue? I thought.

A few silent languages were spoken across the continent. Most are pretty rudimentary though. Daroman soldiers learn one in order to communicate with each other when they're trapped in enemy territory or need to avoid alerting people to their presence. Professional pickpockets have their own finger chatter that's barely noticeable unless you watch for it. One will use it to signal the other to make a move while the first distracts the mark. The more sophisticated fingertongues are rare, and the only one I'd ever heard much about was created by an order of monks who take a vow of silence.

I glanced back at the bodies of the dead man and woman. Could they have been monks, driven to madness somehow? But what would a child too young to become a novice be doing in a monastery in the first place?

I turned back to him and offered him the cheese a second time. He declined again. I offered it to him a third time, then a fourth, until he got frustrated and tapped his forefinger first to the centre of his chest, then twice to his lips, and ended by slapping it cross-wise against the forefinger of his other hand.

Okay, I thought. *Centre of the chest must mean 'I', lips means 'speak', or in this case, with the double-tap, 'said', and the crossed fingers means 'no'.*

I nodded to let him know I'd gotten the message, then pointed my index finger at him, then tapped my lips once, then touched the centre of my chest.

He watched closely, but did nothing at first, so I tried again. His eyes narrowed, but finally he held out his left hand palm up, rubbed a circle on it with his right hand and then spread them both apart questioningly.

'"*About what?*" *Is that what you're asking?*' I signed by double-tapping my lips, then repeating the gesture of one palm rubbing a circle on the other and finishing by pointing to him.

He pursed his lips for a second, then tapped his chest, wiggled two fingers briefly – which I interpreted to mean either 'am' or 'living' or something like it – and followed it with a series of finger shapes too fast for me to follow.

I wasn't sure how to communicate the idea that I needed him to repeat what he'd said, so instead I performed a terribly mangled version of his finger motions back at him. After a moment of staring at me like I was an idiot, he went through the set of gestures once more. I made him do it a third time, and then surprised him by signing his name back to him perfectly.

Arta loquit is the Argosi talent for eloquence. It's not so much learning a bunch of languages as learning *how* to learn what other people are trying to say and how they say it. Of all the Argosi talents, it was the only one Durral admitted to not being particularly good at, and even Enna – who was good at *everything* – claimed to have never mastered it.

Maybe it's because of my Mahdek heritage, and the fact that our survival depended on travelling from place to place, begging for help from anyone who would give it to us – which meant learning how to follow every subtle signal, from 'Maybe we should help this filthy urchin' to 'Hey, you know what would be fun? Hanging a dirty Mahdek from a rope!' – but I took to arta loquit much more naturally than the other talents.

In the end, it's about listening. Listening with the ears, the eyes, and above all else, the heart.

'*Say more at me about you,*' I signed to him.

24

I'd had to guess at what 'more' might be as a hand gesture, and got it wrong, but he understood my meaning and showed me the correct sign, which was tapping first one finger, then two, then three all in quick succession against the forearm.

As the sun made its journey overhead from morning to evening, I badgered him with poorly worded questions to get him to keep signing, and gradually I picked up more and more of what I was now sure was monks' fingertongue. By moonrise I could make some sense of most of what he said, and speak to him in short, clumsy sentences.

'*You say me your name?*' he asked. I was still having trouble making sense of how his finger gestures conveyed the subtleties of grammar.

Since the word 'Ferius' would've meant nothing to him, I tried my best to use the signs I knew to get as close as I could. After he'd made me show him three times, he laughed. It was a nice laugh, musical almost, and made me wonder if he really was deaf at all, or perhaps hadn't always been so.

'*What –*' not knowing the word for 'funny' I just made a show of laughing, then signed – '*about me name?*'

Took us nearly half an hour before he was able to tell me that the signs I'd used before meant 'good dog'. Which really was kind of funny, considering who I'd stolen my name from in the first place.

The boy's name turned out to mean 'Bluebird' – which he was able to make me understand because his soiled and ragged tunic had once been blue, and it's not hard to communicate the idea of a bird. There's a particular species of finch, with indigo feathers, called a 'binta'. Scholars study it because it sings only when there are no other creatures about, when it feels completely safe.

So I used the sign he'd shown me, but decided to call him Binta to myself, since it suited him, and because I hoped that maybe, if

I could get him someplace secure, it might turn out that he wasn't mute after all, but just waiting for the right time to talk.

'Where is your mother?' I asked.

I was discovering that there were tiny variations in the gestures allowed for communicating ideas such as 'is' instead of 'was' or 'will be'.

Binta replied with, 'She has gone to . . .'

I didn't recognise the next gesture, which took a while to sort out as meaning 'the embrace of the gods'.

'Where is your father?' I tried next.

Binta got to his feet and walked past me. I followed him over to the dead man. He pointed to the corpse and signed, 'You killed him.'

3

Language Lessons

Quadlopo kept up a slow but steady pace as the miles rolled beneath his hoofs. We'd buried the bodies as best we could beneath the sand, but lacking a shovel it was hard work and I wasn't sure how much time I could afford to waste. On the other hand, in case whatever disease, curse or spell had driven the man and woman mad was contagious, they were probably best not left out in the sun for somebody else to stumble across. Despite how close the pair of them had gotten to me, I wasn't getting any insane urges, and the boy didn't seem worried about the prospect of me turning into a slavering bloody-tongued lunatic. Maybe the infection spread through some other means than physical contact?

I needed to get the boy somewhere safe. Somewhere with a healer or wise woman who could watch over Binta to make sure he didn't show any signs of the unnatural madness. Somewhere I could leave him and not spend the rest of my life wondering whether I'd condemned him to the sort of childhood that had left me as screwed up as I was.

The moon being bright that night, and neither of us wanting to spend longer in that now-cursed patch of desert than was absolutely necessary, we set off north towards a village whose name, Binta insisted, was simply 'the village'.

From the boy's disjointed recollections – and my evolving understanding of his silent language – he'd spent four days fleeing his father and the woman, who was apparently his father's mistress.

'*Mistress is not the word we use at the monastery*,' he corrected me when I'd asked what business a monk had taking a lover. '*Mistress Groundhog –*' that probably wasn't her name, but it was as close as I could figure from the signs Binta used when referring to her – '*was my father's spiritual companion. She lived with him and helped him translate the sacred books in the monastery library.*'

The boy sat facing me on the front of the saddle, this being the only way we could talk to each other as we rode. I'd noticed that he wasn't prone to touching, preferring to keep a little distance between us at all times, so I did my best to respect that. Quadlopo didn't need much guidance to follow the northern road, so we passed the hours in conversation, my fingers getting sore and my brain exhausted from trying to pick up more and more of the endless signs and their countless variations.

'*You learn the quiet voice very quickly*,' he informed me after I'd managed to ask a question using multiple verb tenses.

I was caught off guard by his praise. It occurred to me to wonder if Durral and Enna would be proud of my arta loquit, but that line of thinking would lead me down paths I wasn't ready to travel.

'*Thank you*,' I signed to Binta. '*Now, can you tell m—*'

It is surprisingly easy to cut someone off in a gestural language.

'*Are you a scholar of languages?*' he asked.

'*No. But my teachers believe that learning to speak as others do is necessary for one who travels much.*'

'*You study travelling? Are you a merchant? A soldier? A priest?*'

I'd noticed he'd rattle off lists of things when we were trying to find a word to describe something new. If I didn't stop him, he could go on for ages.

'None of those,' I signed. 'Something without a word you know.'
Binta frowned. 'Explain.'

That was a tough one. How was I supposed to describe the Argosi?

'I study to become one who can travel far and understand much. One who can protect themselves and others if necessary, but make peace when possible. One who—'

He shook his head. 'You make no sense. Give me a word for what you are.'

That was another thing about the way his mind worked: whenever I was trying to explain something to him, he first wanted a specific sign to anchor whatever followed. If there wasn't a word for the concept I was describing, he demanded I make one up using as many signs as were necessary.

Good luck with this one, kid, I thought.

'I am trying to be a . . . gambler-mapmaker-warrior-diplomat.'

He chewed on that a while. His equivalent of mumbling was the twitching of his fingers into partial bits and pieces of words, never quite finishing one before starting the next. Finally he looked up at me wide-eyed, first snapping his fingers – which I'd learned was both for attracting attention and to express surprise. 'You are a . . .'

He rattled off four sentences so quickly I couldn't follow them and had to ask him to repeat them slowly. When that was still too fast, I had to instruct him to tell me, 'As you would a very young child.'

He signed them out at a plodding, frustrated pace.

'You are a walker-of-water, follower-of-wind, knife-of-lightning, wall-of-stone.'

My amazement nearly had me falling out of the saddle. What Binta had just signed was remarkably close to the four Ways of the Argosi: water, wind, thunder and stone.

'You know of us?'

'Yes. My father was studying an old book that described the teachings of such people before he . . . changed.'

That made no sense. First of all, the Argosi ways aren't written down anywhere, so far as Durral and Enna had ever told me. There wasn't any one method to teach the arts, and so each *maetri* had to find the right way to pass their knowledge along to their *teysan*. More importantly, how could any such book have a connection to whatever had driven the boy's father insane?

'Binta, what is this book your fath—'

'Mouth speak the name of what you are,' he said, holding up his index and middle finger to my lips. He did this sometimes, wanting me to sound a word out loud with his fingers pressed to my lips so he could feel the shape and the vibrations of it.

'Ar-go-see.'

'Again,' he commanded. 'More angry.'

'More angry' was his way of saying louder, I guess because he associated greater volume with people being emotional.

'AR-GO-SEE,' I said, loud enough that Quadlopo gave a concerned whinny.

I patted the horse's neck to reassure him. He responded with a snort to tell me he'd prefer it if I not shout at him, thank you very much.

Binta made a series of short humming sounds that sounded nothing like the word 'Argosi', but which he seemed quite satisfied with. He repeated the three-syllable hum. '*I like this word. It feels like what it describes.*'

'I'm glad you like it. Now, I need you to tell me abou—'

'What are the skills you learn from your teachers?' he asked. 'How to fight as you did when you killed my father and his mistress?'

30

'That was not . . . Yes. One of the skills is . . .' I searched for a way to describe arta eres and finally settled on, 'fight-dancing.'

'So you are a warrior.'

'No. Fight-dancing is only a small part of what we learn. There are seven skills for an . . .' I made a mangled version of his complicated sign pattern for Argosi.

'Tell me these seven skills.'

Another distraction. Until now I'd been treading carefully with him. I knew from personal experience that the appearance of calm, of disinterest in traumatic events, could be a mask that was dangerous to remove. But I needed to know what had happened at the monastery and so far Binta had given me nothing but vague deflections.

'I will speak to you of one of the seven skills,' I told him. 'This one is called . . . hearing-what-is-not-said-and-seeing-what-is-not-there.'

Okay, I admit that's not the most precise description of arta precis, but I was doing the best I could in an unfamiliar language.

'Tell me,' he said.

'With this skill, we learn that sometimes when someone appears very interested in you it is not quite true.'

He pursed his lips. 'You mean such a person is a liar.'

'Not a liar. Sometimes they ask you questions to avoid answering their own.'

I'd probably muddled some of that – I wasn't sure whether 'avoid' was different to 'flee' or 'shun'. Still, he got my meaning.

'My name is Binta,' he said, though of course he used the signs for 'bluebird'. I'd gotten into the habit of translating his signs and gestures into sentences in my head. 'I am nine years old.'

'I don't understand.'

He made the short, sharp gesture that meant both 'cut' and 'be quiet'. I nodded to convey my acquiescence.

31

After glaring at me for a few seconds longer, he continued. *'Four days and many miles I have been brave. I do this by staying here. Not there.'*

'There?'

'The time before. To what happened. If I live here, now, in the sand, under the moon, thinking only of the next step, I can be brave. If in my mind I go back to the time before, I will not be brave any more. Do you understand?'

More than you can imagine, kid, I thought.

I nodded.

'If I am not brave, I cannot survive,' he went on.

For a few seconds he hesitated, his fingers approaching several different shapes but abandoning each one. Finally I took his twitching fingers in mine, and with my free hand signed, *'I will be brave for you until you are ready to be brave for yourself again.'*

He looked up at me a good long while, which was unusual for him. Mostly it was his habit to focus on what was going on around us or on my hands to see what I was signing. But now he held my gaze as if he were trying to see what my eyes might be telling him.

At last he broke, like a dam that had held back a river too long. The tears rushed out with a wailing that was unnatural to my ears and yet somehow entirely familiar, telling of pain and terror with an eloquence that no language could ever match.

I was careful about touching him as I'd noticed his aversion, but now I lifted his chin with my thumb and forefinger so he'd see what I was about to say.

'May I hold you?'

Still weeping, still wailing, his hand shook as he signed, *'If I let you hold me, will you laugh?'*

I was confused by that. *'I will not laugh at you, Binta.'*

32

He shook his head, then signed again. *'I want you to laugh. Please. Hold me and laugh so I can feel that and not what I feel now.'*

I still wasn't sure what to make of his request, but one thing I'd learned about arta loquit is that every one of us carries our own language inside us, deeper than words, and sometimes we must learn to speak the other's tongue.

So I wrapped Binta in my arms and held him close as I sent my own thoughts whirling back to Durral and Enna and the home they'd given me these past eighteen months. As Quadlopo kept up his steady, reassuring clomping across the golden sand, I made my mind walk through all those moments of joy and laughter, remembering not to bypass the last one, when it all fell apart. I didn't just laugh – I guffawed. Hard and loud as I could, weathering the horse's periodic irritated snorts as I let the rumbling in my chest rattle Binta's own. I did that for a good long while until at last the boy had settled and pushed away from me so I could see his hands, and he could tell me his tale.

After that? I was the one wishing there was someone who could hold me and laugh away my fears.

4

Binta's Tale

My name is Binta. I am nine years old. I am small for my age. I was born at the monastery of Garden-Without-Flowers—

Yes, that is the name. Do not interrupt.

The monks at Garden-Without-Flowers do not utter words with their mouths because they believe all words are sacred seeds that can grow in dangerous ways if they are not tended carefully.

No, it is not like the magic of the silk-robe people.

And stop interrupting.

My father was a very important monk. He kept the library of special books that can only be read by those who know how to be silent. Many at the monastery did not speak with their mouths, but that is not the same as being silent.

Years ago, he met a woman in the village near the monastery and they had sex . . .

Why are you laughing? No, the sign is *not* funny. It is just a sign.

They had sex many times and eventually I was born. At the monastery of the Garden-Without-Flowers there is no law against having sex because sex—

Stop laughing!

In union they find a sacred wisdom that does not exist in books and cannot be discovered alone. This is what my father told me.

My mother died when I was very young. I do not know what happened to her. My father could not speak of her without crying, and so he did not speak of my mother with me. Mistress Groundhog loved me and promised that when I turned ten she would tell me. But I am only nine and you broke Mistress Groundhog's neck, so now I will never know.

You are making a face. Why?

Then stop making faces. It is very distracting, and if what I have told you so far causes you to make this face, then I do not think you are able to hear the rest of my story.

Fine. But I warned you.

When I was very young, I could make sounds with my mouth as you do. I could hear the sounds others made. But as I got older the sounds became quieter, and now all I hear is . . . like this – when cloth is rubbed against cloth. Do you hear that? That is what I hear all the time.

Again you are making a face. It is not so bad. I like this sound. It is peaceful. And I was lucky too, because at the monastery they use the silent voice always. My signs are the best of everyone who lives there . . . of everyone who once lived there.

What? Oh, how many?

There were thirty-seven until my father and Mistress Groundhog . . .

One week ago a visitor came to the monastery. She spoke with many monks there, and knew the silent voice. Not perfectly, but as well as you do, Good Dog.

What? You told me Good Dog is your name.

No, I will not learn a new sign for you. Good Dog is the name you signed to me, so Good Dog is what I will sign to you.

I did not see much of the visitor, but I know she asked many questions about our books. That is not unusual. Scholars come from many countries asking to see our books. My father does not allow this. However this woman, because she had learned the silent tongue, was allowed to see some of the books.

Mistress Groundhog said this was okay because the visitor did not ask to see the most sacred books. She saw mostly books of songs and poems. Now I wonder why such books were in our library at all. The library at the monastery of Garden-Without-Flowers is very important, and only important books are kept there.

The morning after the visitor had left, there was a commotion at the monastery. The visitor had stolen two of our books. Again, these were not the sacred books, but a visitor should not steal from someone else's library. Many of the monks were very upset, but Father said it was not so bad. The visitor had left several pages of notes that he said contained many interesting things.

He went to the scriptorium that same day to make a proper copy of the visitor's notes because she had poor handwriting and at the Garden-Without-Flowers we do things properly.

What? No, my father did not describe to me what was in the visitor's notes. I am nine. Why would he tell me?

Father stayed up late that night working. Mistress Groundhog said it was because the writing was in many different languages and did not all make sense. She put me to bed and went back to help him because she is very good at looking up words and my father can be sloppy sometimes.

When the sun woke me, he had not returned from the scriptorium. My father always has breakfast with me. Breakfast is important and you must always smile at the person you are eating with. I went to the kitchens and asked for bread and eggs and ham

36

and jam because these are things my father likes. I took them to the big stone house that contains the scriptorium and other important places.

At first I did not know what was happening. There was much rumbling on the floor. Some of the monks were angry because my father was mouth-talking, and no one is supposed to do that at the monastery. But Father would not stop, and soon he began to . . . he made words-with-music.

No, wait, I have seen the word somewhere. Singing. Yes. He made singing. I could not see-it-with-my-ears, of course, but the other monks were signing that his words were upsetting them very much. Some of them made angry mouth sounds and their faces were the faces of dogs, showing teeth. Some tried to put their fingers in their ears, but then they . . . they clawed at the insides of their ears until they bled.

I dropped the tray with the bread and eggs and ham and jam. I made a very bad mess. The plates and bowls and glasses smashed against the floor.

My father kept on singing. Then Mistress Groundhog sang too. Then the other monks smiled and began to sing. Everyone but me was singing. I hid in a cupboard, but they kept singing. All day. All night. They began to cough, I think because they sang too long. And when they could no longer sing . . .

It was my father who stopped singing first, even though his mouth kept moving the same way, but I could see that he couldn't make the words come out because he had chewed off his own tongue, and blood was spilling from inside his mouth. This made him very angry, and he took a brass candlestick and used it to break apart the head of the monk closest to him. He broke apart the heads of other monks too, even as they sang. When he was about to break the head of Mistress Groundhog, I saw that she also could no longer make words with her mouth, and blood was coming out from where her tongue had been.

But something was coming out of their mouths. Not a word like they spoke before, but something.

They didn't try to hurt each other any more, but instead they hurt the rest of the monks, all of them, one by one. The monks tried to flee, but my father and Mistress Groundhog were moving very fast. When there were no more monks left, my father turned, and he saw me because the cupboard door had opened. He . . . My father did not love me any more. Mistress Groundhog did not love me any more. They tried to make mouth-words at me, as if they had forgotten that I do not see-with-my-ears. They became angry, like they were with you when they saw you in the desert.

My father had never been angry with me before. Not even when I was slow at learning my lessons. Not even when I was clumsy and dropped things. But now he looked at me and he . . .

No. Do not hold me again yet. I want to finish.

In the passage outside the monastery kitchens there is a narrow chute that leads down to the cellar, where a stream passes underneath. This is where the monks clean their clothes. I ran and slid down the chute. My father and Mistress Groundhog tried to follow, but they were too big to fit inside. When I had slid down to the bottom, I ran along the tiny stream to the hole that leads outside.

I ran a long way, until I was tired and couldn't run any more. When I woke up I was lost and confused. I had run in the wrong direction. I should've gone to the village for help, but I had run towards the desert.

No, I was not being brave. I was not trying to protect the people in the village from my father. I was just confused.

I looked around and around for someone to help me, and then I saw two people and waved to them. I was worried that they might not know the silent voice, and so I would have trouble making them understand me. But I should not have worried about that, because the two people coming were Father and Mistress Groundhog.

They nearly got me that time.

How did I escape?

I don't know. My father got very close to me. He was so fast. I made a sound with my mouth without meaning to, and he . . . the sound I made hurt him, and hurt Mistress Groundhog. I ran away again, and kept running.

What?

How would *I* know what sound I made? Did you forget the part where I told you I can't see-with-my-ears? Yes, I know the word is 'hear'. I just forgot, okay?

No. Stop telling me it's important that I remember the sound I made. It's not important that I remember. My father is dead. Mistress Groundhog is dead. The monks are dead.

I have told you my story.

I want to go to the village now, where you will find someone nice for me. Someone who will give me food and a place to sleep. I will work as hard as I can and never make trouble. You will tell them my story so that I never have to tell it again.

So that I can forget.

Arta Tuco

The teysan witnesses the skilful way their maetri navigates the world and mistakes this for knowledge of its workings. But the world is always changing, and a true Argosi cannot rely on maps drawn by another's hand; instead we must venture into every new situation as if it were an undiscovered country and become mapmakers ourselves.

5

The Village

Binta's tale had left me anticipating a hundred horrors lurking in wait around every corner. Fortunately there aren't a whole lot of corners in the desert. Mostly it's just long stretches of sand and scrub, with mountains in the distance that never seem to get closer and the occasional town or hamlet hardly worth the name. Tinto Rhea – or, as the boy had referred to it, 'the village' – was one such place.

'You sure it's safe here?' I asked.

Binta stared at me and tapped his ear.

'*Apology*,' I signed.

Over the past two days of riding, with nothing to do but twiddle our fingers at each other, I'd gotten so used to his language that I'd sometimes forget he couldn't hear me if I spoke aloud. I wondered why he'd never learned to read lips, but when I'd pressed him on the subject, he'd shrugged and informed me that nobody at the monastery of the Garden-Without-Flowers spoke with mouth sounds, so there was no point.

That would have to change if he was going to make a life for himself among regular folk. Assuming there were any regular folk left in Tinto Rhea.

'*I need to go ahead to make sure the village is safe,*' I signed to him. '*Will you stay here and guard the horse? He gets scared when he's by himself.*'

45

I guess Binta assumed I was patronising him because his reply was a rather sharp upwards gesture with two fingers that he hadn't taught me, but which required no translation.

Dusk had settled over the azurite sands that gave everything in these parts a glittering blue sheen. We were about half a mile from the village. Far enough that I could get Binta and the horse settled in without anyone likely to spot us. Close enough that I could sprint back, grab the boy and mount Quadlopo to make our getaway if things turned ugly. At this point, I was having trouble believing in any outcome that *didn't* turn ugly.

From what I'd been able to glean from our conversations, the monastery itself was about two miles east of the village. Since his father and Mistress Groundhog had murdered all the other monks and then stayed on his trail until I'd come upon him, there was no particular reason to assume the villagers had been infected. But the image of that tall, slender man and the shorter, broader woman, their bodies scarlet with the blood of their victims, their jaws gnashing as their throats hissed out words that their severed tongues could no longer form . . . Let's just say I was in a cautious mood.

I removed my smallsword from the mapmaker's case I kept slung across my back and set about getting it ready for the mission ahead.

Binta tapped me on the arm to get my attention.

'*What is that?*' he asked, then pointed at the little jar I'd unstoppered before shaking out a tablespoon's worth of black goop onto a cloth.

I rubbed the oily paste along the length of my blade. The concoction was made from vandal's root, flour and the sticky resin you get from boiling grey cactus. Combine them in the right quantities and you get a substance thieves call 'bladeblack', which, as a coating on a shiny piece of steel, does exactly what you'd expect.

'*This will keep my sword from being seen,*' I explained when I'd finished the first coat.

He shot me a dubious look. '*If the villagers have turned, a sword will not be helpful.*'

He had a point, but for a young woman travelling alone into a new town, there are more than just monsters to worry about. I thought it best not to bring that up though. I let the second coat dry while I tested the edge and balance on each of my six throwing cards.

'*What are those?*' Binta asked.

As with so many other conversations I'd been having with the boy, this one required me to come up with a term that would make sense to him. Something as simplistic as 'weapon' or even 'throwing cards' would only annoy him. He liked names that were evocative of something beyond their basic function.

Durral jokingly referred to them as 'love letters' because they were meant to convey a message, but I didn't think Binta would appreciate the humour. Enna just called them 'sharps', but again, with something so simple, the boy would assume I was patronising him.

I fanned the six cards out in my hand, letting the fading light catch them. I loved their smoothness, the way you had to hold them just right or else they'd slip from your fingers. There was nothing easy about throwing these cards, and there were plenty of bigger and more deadly projectile weapons out there, but when you released one just right – the perfect snap of your fingers, flick of the wrist and extension from the elbow – you could really make an impression on folks.

'*You ever seen a squirrel cat?*' I asked the boy.

He shook his head, then jerked one finger up to his lips to stop me from explaining. This wasn't uncommon with him: he'd know a thing by a different term than I did, but would then put the characteristics of something that was both 'squirrel' and 'cat' together to work out that it might refer to something else.

'A *tree-diving-biting-growl-thief?* he signed.

I chuckled. Not the worst description of a squirrel cat.

'*Yes,*' I signed back, then held up one of the cards. There was a decent breeze coming from the west, so I tossed it up in that direction on an upward angle, like Durral used to do when he was showing off. The card soared, whirling for a couple of seconds before it got picked up by the opposing wind and came back down almost as fast. I caught it neatly between my thumb and forefinger. Durral would've been proud, if he weren't too busy wringing my neck.

'*That does not look dangerous to me,*' Binta said, then reached out to trace the edge of the card only to pull back and suck on his now-bleeding fingertip. '*That hurt!*' he signed with his other hand.

'*Squirrel cats have sharp bites,*' I signed back as I slid the card in with the others. '*And they travel in packs.*'

I tested the flat of my smallsword with my own finger to make sure the bladeblack was dry, then slid the weapon back into the mapmaker's case.

'*What about your face and hands?*' Binta asked. '*They are easy to see in the dark too.*'

I almost laughed. That was the first question I'd asked the delinquents in the Black Galleon gang back when they'd shown me how to use bladeblack.

'*If someone sees me with my face covered that way, they'll believe I came to their village with ill intent.*'

Before he could pepper me with more questions, I slung the mapmaker's case across my back and put my throwing cards into the leather-lined pocket of my coat. I gave the sullen Quadlopo a quick pat on the neck to reassure him I'd return soon, then set off at a jog towards the village.

I spent those next precious minutes preparing myself for what I might encounter there, focusing my *arta tuco* – the Argosi talent for strategy and subtlety.

'*The wise traveller always walks into a room with a plan to get out,*' Durral used to say. '*An Argosi never walks into a room without a dozen.*'

'*And how do you know which of those plans to execute when the time comes, Pappy?*'

'*Don't matter. First thing you learn wanderin' the long roads, kid. Plans are like prayers – good for the soul, but nothing to count on.*'

This was typical of my foster father: bestowing confounding and contradictory axioms on me, expecting me to work out for myself what they meant. Enna, my foster mother, had a different approach to teaching the Argosi ways, and after Durral had gone to bed she explained the paradox.

'*The purpose of arta tuco is to tune the mind so that it perceives* possibilities *rather than* probabilities. *To shift from* expectation *to* anticipation.'

Yeah, she wasn't much more helpful than Durral when it came down to it.

Eventually, though, I'd come to understand that the purpose of constantly devising plans was so that it became so instinctive that every time you walked into a situation you'd instantly work out multiple schemes to distract opponents or disable traps. After enough practice – and I mean a *lot* of practice – your thoughts speed up from a slow walk to a fast gallop. By the time you see what's waiting for you in that theoretical room Durral had talked about, your brain would already be coming up with the means to escape.

My arta tuco was never as good as his of course, and even he couldn't keep up with Enna. But there were times when I slid into that way of thinking like it was . . . like I was seeing everything around me in a completely new way. A tree wasn't a tree any more: it was a ladder that could be climbed; a barrier that could deflect a killing blow; a rough surface that could wear through rope if you rubbed against it just right. Sometimes it was as if the physical world disappeared and in its place were thousands upon thousands of tools and tricks, traps and evasions, all just waiting to be turned to my use.

Of all the Argosi talents, however, arta tuco is the most dangerous. There's a coldness to that way of thinking. People and animals start to look like nothing more than devices, and notions like dignity and decency can disappear altogether. Like with arta eres, the talent of defence, when you can become so obsessed with how best to wield a blade that you forget why you drew it in the first place.

I'm sorry, Mamma. I never meant—

No.

Had Enna been there, she would've reminded me that, to an Argosi, guilt, grief and shame are three names for the same poison. You either make restitution or you find some other way to live with yourself. There was no restitution I could make, so I had to keep moving, running before my foster father caught up with me and things went bad for both of us.

I couldn't leave Binta to fend for himself in the desert, so that meant I had to find him a home. Tinto Rhea was the only place outside the monastery he knew, so that was my best shot.

The village was quiet, at least from outside the sixteen-foot walls. There must've been a castle or fortress here centuries ago for which these fortifications had been built. I climbed up and began casing

50

the perimeter, keeping my eyes, ears and nose alert for anything happening below that would signal trouble. But there was nothing. It's not that the village was dead quiet, but that it was filled with the sounds you'd expect to hear after dark: people cooking in their homes, clanging pots and talking over each other. I smelled smoke coming out of a few chimneys and saw one or two men and women walking broken cobblestone paths.

No blood. No mayhem.

You can tell a lot about a place by how people go about their lives when they don't know anyone's watching. Tinto Rhea was as nice a village as I'd ever seen in the Seven Sands. Was it the perfect place to leave a deaf and mute young boy who'd lost everything he knew in an act of unimaginable savagery? I couldn't say for sure. But it was a damned sight better than the alternative.

I made my way around the wall till I returned to the front gates, where I slid back down to the ground. Villages out here in the borderlands place a bell outside that travellers are meant to ring before coming inside. I tugged on the rope three times, good and loud, to announce my arrival. Even the bell sounded friendly.

Okay, I thought, listening for the sounds of people approaching the gates to let me in. *Let's find out what's wrong with this place.*

6

Tinto Rhea

If there was a place with kinder, more decent folk than the ones that came to greet me at the gates of Tinto Rhea, I'd never been there in all my travels. In the half-hour I spent there before heading back to retrieve Binta, I was treated with respect, courtesy and generosity by everyone I met.

Now, I know what you're thinking: there's got to be a trick here, right? Some kind of desert scam played on gullible travellers who get invited for dinner only to find themselves in the stewpot. But while friendliness is easy enough to fake, it's much harder for people to pretend at grieving.

'We got word two days ago,' the burly mayor informed me.

Orphanus was an older man, maybe in his early sixties, but his shoulders still showed the vigour that came from a life of sustained labour without excessive suffering or injury. If his belly was starting to push at his trouser belt, well, he wore the weight like he'd earned it.

He shook his head and chewed on his lip a lot. 'Those monks never hurt a soul. Whole village has been talking about an expedition to the monastery to give the dead a decent burial. Problem is, without knowing what happened to them, well . . .' He gestured to some of the folks who'd abandoned their suppers to come see what the fuss was about. 'A place like this, we depend on each other every day. Can't afford to risk my people if there could be danger out there.'

'How well did you know the monk who ran the scriptorium?'

'Khatam? Better than most of them, I reckon. He used to come round once in a while with his ... Oh, spirits of earth and air, that poor boy.'

'He had a son?' I asked. 'What happened to him?'

I wasn't yet ready to reveal that I had Binta camped out barely half a mile away.

Orphanus wiped at the corner of his eye with the hairy knuckle of his forefinger. 'Strange little thing. Never spoke a word except in that monk's fingertongue they use up at the monastery. Khatam said he wasn't deaf nor mute, just ... something about his head, I guess. Stopped working after his mamma died.'

He's not deaf?

I would've pressed him for more, but I still wasn't about to show my hand.

'Was Khatam ever violent?' I asked. 'Maybe he drank some?'

Orphanus shot me a look that suggested I'd given offence, but he settled himself with a sigh. 'Guess you've never been to the monastery then,' he said. 'Never met gentler people in my whole life. No, Khatam wasn't given to violence, no more than any of them. He liked his books, and loved his boy, and that's all there was to him.'

'And his companion? Mistress ... Groundhog?'

Orphanus stared at me wide-eyed for a second, then broke out laughing. 'Padra? You're talking about Padra?' He wiped at his eye a second time. 'Guess she did kinda look a little like a—'

He broke off as we both realised how I'd screwed up. Who would've come up with a silly name for the woman Khatam lived with other than his son?

53

The mayor reached out to seize me by the collar. I drove my elbow up into the underside of his wrist. There's a nerve cluster you can strike there that won't cause any lasting damage but makes someone think twice about grabbing you. By the time he was ready for a second try with his other hand I'd backed away three steps and uncapped my mapmaker's case.

'I didn't come to make trouble,' I said.

There were about a dozen people with him, none of them carrying a crossbow or anything that could hit me from a distance. I'd kept track of everyone who'd stepped out into the street since I'd come through the gates, and none had gotten behind me. Theoretically someone could've passed through the outer wall a different way and snuck up to the gates, but I was keeping track of everybody's eyeballs and no one was looking past me. If it came to a fight, I'd need to stab Orphanus or whoever came first with my smallsword, throw a couple of sharps at the rest to make them wary, and then run like hell.

So now we find out who we all are, I thought, and waited to hear what Orphanus would say next.

'We have money,' he said.

Okay, that's not what I expected.

I kept my hand on the hilt of the sword over my shoulder but didn't draw it yet.

'Money?'

'For Bluebird. The little boy. We don't have much, but if you've come to ransom him, we'll give you what we can. If you aim to pawn him off into forced labour or to some bawdy house up north though, I'll hunt you down myself.'

'I didn't . . . I'm not some child-seller!'

Orphanus gave me a slightly dubious look. 'When a stranger comes to your gates asking about a massacre and hiding that she's keeping the son of a friend of our village, well, you haven't exactly given us reason to trust you.'

'I needed to know if I could trust *you* first,' I said, though I was aware of the irony. 'I didn't mean to cause offence.'

Orphanus put up his hands. 'Then maybe we should start over.'

A young woman a couple of years older than me with curly chestnut hair, who looked enough like the mayor that I assumed she was his daughter, came to his side. 'Is he all right? Bluebird . . . I used to look after him sometimes when Khatam brought him to town.'

I let go of the hilt of the sword and let it slide back into the mapmaker's case so I wouldn't look like I was one wrong move away from skewering somebody. 'He's had some rough days and nights, but he's not physically hurt.'

The young woman's relief only lasted a second before trepidation washed over her features again. 'Did he . . . ? Was he there when it happened?'

I nodded.

Orphanus and several of his folk muttered near-silent prayers. I don't know why, but that bothered me. I've never been one for religion, and it sure hadn't helped the monks.

'Prayers aren't going to do him any good,' I said, with more ire than I should've. Guess I was more on edge than I'd pretended. 'He needs a home now, and people who will look after him. Teach him to read lips and hold him through the night once all the horror he ran away from catches up to him. Keep caring for him even when he acts up – and he *will* act up. He'll be bitter and belligerent and even cruel to the people who take care of him, because that's what you do when you're broken. You shout when you shouldn't and say horrible, horrible things, and sometimes you even—'

Get ahold of yourself, Ferius! Where the hell's your arta forteize?

Arta forteize is the Argosi talent for resilience. A wanderer who travels from one perilous situation to another needs to be able to overcome pain and suffering whether physical, mental or emotional. I wasn't too good at arta forteize.

Orphanus's daughter, whose name I would learn later that night was Lyrida, said something strange then. The kind of thing I wouldn't have expected from anyone who wasn't Enna Brown. Something that skipped by a thousand other words to get to the right ones.

'It's good that he found someone who understands him,' she said.

There was quiet in the village then, and Orphanus put an arm around his daughter before he spoke to me next.

'What worth an oath can bring, I'll offer in my name and the names of everyone in this village. The boy isn't our kin, but we're as close to kin as he's got. He's welcome to stay here for as long as he wants, and we'll give him such care as we can. You can stay as long as you need too – to make sure Bluebird's happy with us.' He hesitated a moment before adding, 'You can stay longer than that even.'

In my seventeen years I've met a thousand liars. Distrust is as much a part of me as the red curls of my hair or the scars on my skin. Even before I'd trained in the ways of the Argosi, I'd learned through experience to spot deception in every smile or squint someone cared to offer me. This man wasn't lying. The people with him weren't lying. They genuinely wanted to give Binta a home, not because it suited their purposes but because they needed to find some act of goodness with which to counter the senseless savagery suffered by the monks they'd known as neighbours and friends.

'I'll go get Binta . . . I mean, Bluebird,' I said.

'His name is Binta?' Lyrida asked.

'No, that's just . . . That's just what I call him, is all.'

'A boy ought to have a proper name,' Orphanus said. 'Binta is a good one.'

I turned and headed back out the gates to get the boy and bring him to the best home I could have hoped to find him. The tightness I'd been carrying in my chest since the moment his life had become my responsibility eased as I saw my own road open up, just a little.

It took me fifteen minutes to walk back that half a mile along the sandy road. Three more to tell Binta what I'd found and make sure he wanted to come. Just five to return to Tinto Rhea on Quadlopo's back. Seemed like the entire village was waiting there for him. My relief at how happy he was to see them, and how happy they were to see him, kept me from realising then that there was a piece missing to all of this.

'Got word two days ago.'

That was what Orphanus had said to me after I'd mentioned the massacre at the monastery. No malice in his expression. No subterfuge in his words.

Any Argosi worth their salt – heck, any half-witted town constable – would've asked the simple, obvious question.

The deadliest tricks? The ones you can't see coming no matter how much arta precis you *think* you have?

They're the ones nobody's playing on you.

7

The Question

I didn't drink that night, not even the ritual sip of liquor that Binta sampled as part of the celebration the villagers held for him. I smiled when people smiled at me, shared stories and anecdotes when asked, and even danced with a couple of the local fellas. Not once, though, did I stop looking for signs of deception. I guess that's why I was so taken by surprise when it finally appeared.

Guess they were surprised too.

'Life is hard in the Seven Sands,' Orphanus began, taking to the hall's little wooden dais as the evening's festivities were beginning to die down. 'Nobody knows that better than the seventy-three souls who live in this town.' He held up a finger and corrected himself. 'Seventy-*four* souls.'

There were a few cheers around the hall and the people sitting on either side of Binta and me reached over to touch him on the shoulder. He looked up, bleary-eyed, and smiled at them as if he understood, then gestured to me.

'*What is he saying?*' he signed.

'*He says that you're a terribly ugly boy and you smell worse than the skunks that sometimes come to steal their cabbages, but if you promise not to make trouble for them you can live with the pigs.*'

58

Binta offered up his now-customary two-fingered salute before laying his head back down on the table and snoring quietly.

Lyrida, sitting next to me, chuckled.

'What were you saying about sleeping with pigs?'

'You know the fingertongue?' I asked, surprised.

'A little. Khatam taught me a bit each time he brought Bluebird . . . *Binta* to the village. I can't speak it nearly as well as you, though. How long have you been studying the silent voice?'

The first lesson Enna had taught me in arta loquit is that you have to listen to *all* of what a person's saying to you. Lyrida's casual tone hid beneath it a lilting fragility, as if my answer might have more meaning to her than her question suggested.

It's important to her that she's tried hard to learn Binta's language, I realised then, and found the chestnut-haired young woman's subtle nervousness sweetly endearing.

Enna's second lesson in arta loquit was to always know why you're about to say something. Is it simply to impart information? To try to learn something? Or are you doing it to make yourself sound important? What's the value of what you're saying, and how will it affect your relationship to the person asking?

'I've been studying it a while now,' I said. 'Feels like forever.'

She smiled, and seemed reassured by my answer. 'It's hard, isn't it? I keep thinking I must be thick to have so much trouble getting all those finger twitches right.'

I groaned aloud. 'Ugh, I know. And Binta's so *fast*! I can barely keep up with him.'

Lyrida laughed. It was a warm laugh that drew my attention to her eyes, which were green, and then to her lips, which were . . .

'What are you doing, Good Dog?' Binta asked with a few subtle twirls of his fingers. His head was still down, but his sleepy eyelids were open a crack.

Lyrida's own eyes were focused on my face, so I was able to respond to Binta surreptitiously.

'Nothing. Go back to sleep or I'll feed you to the pigs myself.'

'Are you staying the night?' Lyrida asked. Her voice was different this time, maybe a fraction deeper, and there was just a tiny bit more breath in her words.

The two of us hadn't danced together, but when we'd been out on the floor as Orphanus and a couple of the old folks had played country jigs on battered instruments, we'd brushed against each other more than once. Now I saw her hand was on the table, closer to mine than it had been before, and the way she'd shifted her chair . . . her knee was barely an inch away.

And how do you feel about that, Good Dog? I imagined Binta asking, though now he really was asleep.

I'd never . . . been with anyone. Most of my life I'd avoided even touching people on account of the Jan'Tep spells embedded into the now-fading sigils tattooed around my neck that made people hate me. By the time the effects of those spells had died down, I was living with Durral and Enna – and that lady is a hugger, I tell you. So that had been enough for me, for a while. Now though?

I reached across the table to a trencher filled with a kind of fried potato they sliced up and served with a spectacularly spicy sauce. When I was done, my knee was touching Lyrida's. She didn't move away, and now, by some miracle I hadn't noticed despite all my arta precis, her fingers and mine were intertwined.

'Are you all right?' she asked quietly.

'I'm fine. Why do you ask?'

That smile of hers was back, but it was different now. More . . . intimate. 'You're breathing quite rapidly, Ferius.'

I reached for my *arta valar* – what Durral calls 'daring' but which I'd come to realise was pretty much identical to swagger. Unfortunately it failed me utterly.

'The sauce on the potatoes is really hot,' I said.

My embarrassment having become painfully obvious, Lyrida started taking her hand away. I held on.

Sometimes you don't realise how lonely you've been until, for even one second, you don't feel lonely any more.

'I'd like to stay the night,' I said.

She nodded, and held my gaze, and just like that, plans were made that didn't require any discussion or debate. No second guessing or awkward confirmations.

I'd never been with anyone, boy or girl. Never kissed, never touched in that way that—

It would've been grand, I think.

Orphanus was working his way up to a crescendo in his speech. Lyrida and I turned to listen, silently acknowledging to each other that at least a little discretion was called for.

'So now we can give some of ourselves to this boy, to Binta, and in every act of love we show him fight back against the terrible darkness that took his father and the good brothers and sisters of the Silent Garden monastery.' He reached into his pocket and took out a crumpled piece of parchment. 'The traveller gave me this before she left. A poem. A promise of better times to come. I don't know all the words, of course. Reckon there's seven different languages in this poem, but she wrote it all down in syllables so I could share them with all of you.'

'The traveller?' I asked Lyrida.

She tried to shush me, but I grabbed her arm and squeezed it hard. 'Who is your father talking about?'

Lyrida winced, then answered. 'The traveller. The woman who came to Tinto Rhea to warn us about what had happened at the monastery.'

And there it was: the question I hadn't asked.

'We got word two days ago,' Orphanus had told me.

'Got word from who? Who told you about the monastery?' I'd failed to ask.

Orphanus was reading out his poem, and on the first line he was awkward, stilted, like you might expect of someone reading a language they don't speak. But by the second the syllables came swift and sure, so effortless it was like they were being drawn out of him by an unseen hand. By the third line, the others in the room were repeating the first, trailing after his every utterance like ducks following their mother. And then Lyrida was saying them, and I heard those same beautiful, transcendent and unknowable words slipping from my own mouth, pulling me along with them into the abyss I already saw appearing in Lyrida's eyes as she stared back at me with a hunger that bore no resemblance to the gentle ache we'd both felt moments ago.

And then a shriek, so loud it deafened me in my left ear – the side where Binta had been sleeping. I turned, and saw he was standing on the bench, his mouth wide open as the boy who couldn't speak screamed and screamed and screamed.

8

Two Arrows

'Hey, kid.'

'Yeah, Pappy?'

'Two arrows. One's flyin' twice as fast as the other. Which arrow hits the target first?

'Pappy?'

'Yeah, kid?'

'Did you really wake me up in the middle of the night to ask me whether a fast arrow is faster than a slow arrow?'

'Answer the question, Ferius Parfax. It'll save your life one day.'

The first time I'd met Durral Brown and witnessed the incredible, almost magical – only he'd never stoop to something so pitiful as magic – things he could do, all I wanted was to be like him. Durral could walk into any room and instantly find a dozen ways out that would surprise even the architect who first built it. He could face down murderers and military generals with a smile that warned them any fight they hoped to start with him had already been lost.

'Tricks, kid. Nothin' but schemes and scams unless you know how to walk a path.'

Hence that question – or any of a hundred others like it – that he'd periodically taunt me with, trying to make me understand the true way of the Argosi.

See, the most important skill an Argosi wanderer must develop within themselves isn't found in the fighting techniques of arta eres nor the strategic ingenuity of arta tuco. It's not in the daring of arta valar nor the persuasive charm we call *arta siva*. You won't find the crucial ability within the eloquence of arta loquit, the resilience of arta forteize, or even the perceptive abilities hidden within arta precis that had taken me so long just to begin to understand.

Those are merely tools.

Which arrow hits the target first? The one that's aimed in the right direction, of course.

The innumerable techniques contained within the seven talents all depend on knowing which of the four ways to follow. Water. Wind. Thunder. Stone. How we navigate these cardinal directions at every single moment of our lives determines whether we live to a ripe old age or die in a ditch; help those we care about or bring them suffering; serve our highest aspirations or become enslaved by our cruellest desires.

Sounds difficult, right?

I haven't even gotten to the hard part.

Because a true Argosi? Someone like Durral or Enna – someone I so badly wanted to be but kept failing at becoming? Trapped in the middle of a crowded hall filled with men and women driven mad by nothing more than a bunch of verses scrawled on a scrap of paper, with a screaming child who'd already witnessed more horror than any soul ought to suffer, and now knew more was coming . . . when there's no way to escape and all that's left is to fall under the tide of madness and bloodshed?

That's when an Argosi must wield all seven talents, travel all four ways, of water, wind, thunder and stone, all at once.

'Pappy, what you're talking about . . . That's impossible. Nobody can do that.'

'Sure you can, kid. You know why?'

'Why?'

Durral had patted me on the head and ruffled my hair – even though I was sixteen and far too old for such nonsense – and left the room, saying, 'Because otherwise you'll end up dead, that's why.'

I'd called out to him. 'But, Pappy, how am I supposed to wield all seven talents and walk all four ways at the same time?'

He'd stopped and turned, not much more than a shadow in the doorway. 'That's up to you, kid.' Then he gave me one of those smiles that I knew was there even though I couldn't see it in the darkness. 'Me personally? I always like to start with a little arta valar.'

Maybe that's why, with madness erupting all around me and doom coming fast on its heels, with my ears ringing from Binta's screams, I stood up from the chair, scooped him up in my arms and, though the terror in his eyes had spilled into every part of my body, I grinned and got one hand free so I could sign to him, 'Smile, kid. I got this.'

9

The Dance of Thunder

I begin with arta tuco.

The screams disappear, as do the growls and snarls and the grasping hands reaching for me. There is no hall with its walls to keep us in, no floor slick with spilled drinks and the sweat of revels and already the blood from tongues being bitten off.

I shed all my questions like dead skin because right now they're no use to me. Does the infection make them chew off their own tongues or is that some last, desperate, human struggle to keep themselves from spreading the plague to others? Makes no difference. Right now they're more interested in ripping me apart. How can a few sentences – a poem written in several languages these people don't even speak – be driving them insane? Doesn't matter. They aren't people any more. They're fingernails that can cut skin, teeth that can tear flesh. Did Binta's screaming in my ear protect me from the madness infecting the others until they'd bitten off their tongues and couldn't form the words any more? And is there some connection between the boy's inability to use spoken language and his immunity to this strange plague?

Questions for another time, for when we get out of here.

If we get out of here.

When I look up, the hall has disintegrated into its constituent parts. Forty feet wide, just under two hundred feet long. The floor isn't a floor any more because the tables and chairs strewn throughout have made it into a landscape filled with places to climb and jump. Barriers waiting to serve our needs. Weapons, if things get bad.

I hoist Binta over my shoulder. His weight is a burden that—

No, there are no burdens in arta tuco, only tools.

I can't quite envision right now how a screaming kid is a tool, but I'll work that out later. His weight on my shoulder is affecting my balance so I adjust the way I move as I begin running for the door. There are three young men blocking us there, but I ignore them for now. I've got plenty more to deal with.

First a man and a woman, late sixties, I'd guess, though they come at us with a ragged speed that suggests they've forgotten all about being old. With hands curled into claws they reach for Binta. I follow the Way of Water, ducking under their arms without losing pace, taking nothing from them, leaving nothing behind.

I can hear the sounds of sandals and boot heels thudding on the floor. It's like they've all been caught up in a mad whirling dance. I follow the Way of Wind, using the sound to inform me how many are close behind, and which way to turn to make them run into each other.

The infected don't seem interested in attacking one another. Maybe the rattling hiss spurting from bloody mouths through broken teeth is like its own language that unites them. I doubt it's a sound I could reproduce though, and I don't intend to smash my own teeth and bite off my tongue to find out.

The path before us closes as more of the villagers cut off our escape. I choose another direction, seeming to circle back only to jump onto a chair, then up to a nearby table. As the villagers begin to surround us, I leap with Binta still over my shoulder onto the next table. There's a screech as the maddened men and women keep shoving the first table, trying to get to us. I need to come down – get back on a path to the door – but it's no good. There are too many of them, and they're getting too close. It's time for the Way of Thunder.

Drawing on my arta eres, I begin a dance with many partners. My smallsword is inside the mapmaker's case strapped to my back, but the cost of uncapping the case and drawing the weapon is more time than I can afford – especially with Binta overtop my shoulder. The throwing cards would be faster, but futile against an enemy who doesn't feel pain. Instead, my free hand grabs what would have been a tin beer stein but in my hands is a weapon with a handle for a sure grip and a hard curved surface perfect for breaking small bones.

A kindly-faced woman who first offered me those spiced potatoes I now oddly find myself craving. I shatter her nose, driving the stein upwards to spread the spatter of blood into her eyes.

A young man, broad in the shoulder and slim in the waist, who danced with me earlier. He had a nice smile. I break his front teeth with the reinforced base of the tin vessel.

With my left foot I kick one of the chairs out to send it into the legs of two others coming our way. A hand grabs hold of my right shoulder and I drop the stein and cover my attacker's hand with my own, holding it tight in place as I drop down low until I hear the crack of finger bones.

As I lurch forward out of the grasping hands of two others, I see a knife on the ground and swoop low to snatch it up. My slashes don't slow anyone down, but the bleeding cuts on their palms make it harder for them to get a grip on me, which buys me another three seconds and ten feet towards the door.

And all the while, my ears are filled with the hissing of our pursuers as their throats fight to spread a madness I now know comes from a scrap of paper, given to them by the mystery woman who'd turned up at the Monastery of the Silent Garden seeking words from old books that could drive the world insane.

That's the Way of Wind, I can almost imagine Durral warning me. *Leave it for later*.

I'm just about to make that most foolish of mistakes – looking into the future and imagining we've already escaped – when Orphanus blocks my path forward. That big belly of his is coming to trap me between him and his folk so they can bring me down like a pack of wolves surrounding a cornered deer. I could stab him, but the blade isn't long enough to get through his abdomen to something instantly fatal. As he reaches for us, my arta precis tells me he wants Binta even more than he wants me.

I toss the boy to him.

Sorry, kid. But in a fight, arta tuco turns everything into a weapon.

While Orphanus is catching Binta, I slip behind him and drive the knife deep into the back of his neck. His arms and legs start to twitch, and his body begins that last, shivering dance that will send him to his grave. I grab him by the fringe of greying brown hair on the back of his head and yank him backwards. As he tumbles, his arms lose their grip on the boy. I pick Binta up and smoothly turn to run for the exit.

But the Way of Thunder is about to fail me.

Though we're just a few feet from the doorway, I can hear the villagers are too close behind us. With Binta in my arms, I can't run fast enough. Quadlopo is forty yards away inside a barn, still saddled just in case. It would only take a few seconds to reach him, mount up and gallop away. But those are seconds Binta and I don't have.

I will have to follow the Way of Stone.

I drop Binta and push him out the open door. He turns, seeing only the angry, almost violent twitch of my fingers that command him, 'Go. Horse. Run.'

I pivot on my heel to face the kind men and women of Tinto Rhea who will now tear me apart, but with all my skill and every part of my body, I will walk the Way of Stone for these last seconds of life, and hold them off as Binta flees.

As the grinning, snarling mass comes for me, I allow myself one single moment to imagine a future I'll never see. Binta's a smart boy. He'll run to Quadlopo and climb into the saddle. He'll come back, but he'll see there's no hope and turn and run. Quadlopo's a good horse. He'll take them both back to Durral and Enna. They'll pick up his language – even if it might take them a little longer than it took me – and know what to do.

They'll give him a home.

Maybe even teach him the Argosi ways.

Not a bad thought to die on, I think, as the first hands grab for me. I almost laugh when I look up to see Lyrida there, and I think to myself that it looks like we're going to have that dance after all.

10

The Price of Eleven Seconds

Time is an essential aspect of all the Argosi talents. Arta loquit teaches us to recognise the distinctly different meanings between long pauses and short ones in a conversation. An Argosi's ability to perceive that which is hidden using arta precis depends entirely on how many hours, minutes or fractions of a second you can afford to spend on it. All the dancing ways Durral had taught me in arta eres relied on developing my sense of timing. As for arta forteize, the talent for resilience – for enduring that which others cannot?

Time becomes everything.

By my reckoning, Binta needed an eleven-second head start to run to the barn and untether Quadlopo so the two of them could escape.

Eleven seconds is a long time when you're holding off death's embrace. But I swore to myself I'd hold the line, there in that doorway in the hall of that damned village, and walk the Way of Stone until I'd given Binta those eleven seconds.

Lyrida's left hand reaches out for me. Instead of trying to brush it aside, I bring my left elbow up high and then drive it down into her palm. She might not care about the pain, but striking the nerves numbs her hand and prevents her from getting a grip on me.

That buys me one second. I need ten more.

Two other villagers catch up with Lyrida at the front of the pack. The first throws himself at me, which is lucky because all I have to do now is slip a few inches to my left and he falls off balance, hitting the ground face first. I drive my heel into his skull and hope that somewhere in the next nine seconds I'll forget the hideous cracking sound his jaw makes as it shatters against the floor.

Nine seconds.

The next one . . . spirits of all things merciful and bad, he's just a boy, maybe eleven years old. He's trying to bite at me like a snarling dog. I bring up my knee, grab the back of his head and smash his teeth in, breaking his upper palate. He reels back, which is too bad because two kindly-looking folks with murder in their eyes who look like they might be his parents take his place.

I need eight more seconds.

Earlier than I'd planned, I take a step back, putting me just outside the hall so that the doorway now prevents more than two of them from attacking me at once. Problem is, the next time I give ground it will open up a gap that will let the others rush out to surround me.

The mother comes at me first. I duck down low, dig my shoulder into her belly and then rise up to throw her over my back. I know she's going to get right back on her feet and come at me from behind, but that's okay. That's part of the plan.

Seven seconds. I need just seven more seconds.

The father gets a punch to the throat that turns his endless hissing into gasps. As someone drags him away from the doorway to make room, Lyrida grabs my arm. Her grip is stronger than I'd hoped, but she's not much bigger than me and my knees are bent, which gives me surer footing. I yank her back as I turn, sending

72

her into the woman who was about to grapple me from behind as predicted. I guess the sudden closeness confuses the two of them, because they wind up in a hideous dance, biting at each other's necks as their fingernails search for soft flesh to tear.

Five seconds.

The madness infecting this place only seems to get worse. At first they were all after me, but now Lyrida's ripping the throat out of some woman that might've been her best friend for all I know, and the others have so crowded the doorway that it's become a mass of arms and faces all trying to get to me at once.

Their rage has given me two precious seconds. I spend them taking in a breath and reaching back to uncap the mapmaker's case. As I draw the sword though, the strongest ones break free of the mass of bodies, and I know now that I can't hold them back any more.

Three seconds. All Binta needs is three more seconds.

It's Lyrida that gets to me first, ramming a bigger man aside with a strength that makes me wonder if that brief connection we'd had, the attraction between us, has been translated into a more burning hatred than the petty physics of muscle and bone can contain. I try to stab her with the smallsword, but drawing it was a mistake. I can't hold the distance needed between us. She gets both her hands on me, one on each side of my face, squeezing so tight I think maybe she'll crush my skull before her teeth get to my neck. I drop the smallsword and push back at her with everything I have left even as I feel her bearing down on me. Her lips part, and it's almost as if she wants to kiss me, only the hissing sound from deep inside her chest tells me otherwise. Her mouth gets wider and wider, like she's going to swallow me whole. I look inside that abyss, and suddenly find myself staring at the iron tip of an arrowhead.

Before I even know what's happening, I hear the *thwhip* of a second arrow that takes out the man Lyrida had pushed aside. She's still trying to bite me, but the strength has gone from her limbs. I pivot my hips and yank her head down to send her to the ground.

Like an idiot, I turn to see who's firing the arrows into the mob, piling up bodies outside the doorway that become a barrier to the others. My saviour's face is hidden from me by gauzy beige linen wrapped all around her head, her torso and arms, as if her clothing is all made from a single bolt of fabric held in place by straps of brown leather. She's wielding a recurve bow about four feet long, not unlike the ones Zhuban warriors use on horseback.

'I'd get down on the ground if I were you,' she says to me in a lilting voice. I can't place the accent, which is almost as unnerving to me as the fact that she sounds as calm as if we were discussing the weather.

'You haven't got enough arrows for them all,' I inform her. To get some distance from the hall I dart between two burly men who look so alike they have to be brothers.

The masked woman sends them to their deaths with a pair of arrows as she walks casually towards me. She drops the bow, grabs me by the back of the hand and pulls me to the ground just as an eruption louder than any thunder deafens me and I feel a burning heat raze across my back as the hall explodes into flames.

'Stay down,' she instructs me.

When I look up, I see a few of the villagers running around, blinded by smoke, their blazing clothes turning them into torches that light up the night. There's another crack, different this time, as the roof of the hall collapses.

Through the gauzy fabric of her linen garb, I make out a quizzical expression on the face of this woman who has just saved my life

74

and consigned all these others to death. 'I was perhaps too generous in the amount of explosive I used.'

As the hissing of the infected and the crackling of the flames becomes a symphony of chaos all around us, I lie there on the ground, on my belly, staring up at this strange woman who seems to barely notice the destruction she's caused.

When she looks back at me, it's like I'm this pitiful, lost waif she's just found in the forest. 'Do not worry,' she says. 'You are safe now.'

The tremendous relief welling up inside me, and the boundless gratitude I owe her, is stifled somewhat by just how arrogant she sounds.

'Who are you?' I ask.

She pulls down the fabric covering the lower half of her face, revealing skin darker than mine. The smoothness of her features suggests she can't be much older than me.

'You may call me the Path of Thorns and Roses,' she tells me. 'I am an Argosi.'

11

The Pyre

When at last my body agreed to work again, and my mind – foolishly perhaps – decided it was ready to witness the rampant destruction that had been unleashed upon the once quiet village of Tinto Rhea, I rose clumsily to my feet.

'We should put out the fire,' I mumbled, gazing at the burning hall that was now a funeral pyre for the dozens of families who'd once lived, laboured and loved in this now cursed place.

The woman who'd called herself the Path of Thorns and Roses came to stand beside me. She tugged some of the linen fabric wrapped around her neck up to cover her mouth and nose, protecting her lungs from the smoke that had already set me to coughing.

'Why would we attempt something so foolish?' she asked.

My hand floated upward, like an ember, and my finger pointed feebly at the roof of the hall. Flames were already threatening to leap across to the thatched roofs of nearby cottages. 'The fire will spread. The whole village will burn to the ground.'

'This village is dead,' came her blunt reply. 'Every man, woman and child who lived here perished within those walls.'

I considered that for a moment. Could it really have been all of them? Every single soul in Tinto Rhea? I'd seen no babies or toddlers inside the hall, but this was a tiny village after all. Lyrida had mentioned something about parents of newborns going north to the larger settlements of the Seven Sands, away from the harshness of the desert, returning when their children turned seven and could better endure this life.

'There could still be others,' I insisted, though my feeble objection sounded listless, almost sleepy to my ears. 'They might have stayed home and—'

'I checked every home in the village before I set the explosives. There is no one left.'

Smoke streamed out of the ruins of the hall, aggravating my cough until I could barely breathe at all. The Path of Thorns and Roses grabbed me by the back of my collar and hauled me a few yards away from the fire like a recalcitrant mule.

'You appear to be in some sort of shock induced by the trauma of witnessing the deaths of these people with whom you so quickly formed an emotional bond,' she informed me. 'It would be helpful if you would snap out of it now.'

I wanted to shout at her, but all I could summon was a piteous groan. 'We just massacred an entire village.'

Why was I so sluggish? I was exhausted from the fight, sure, and the agonising concentration that had been required to keep my mind in arta tuco for all that time. I had cuts on my hands and cheeks. Someone had bitten my shoulder. Twice. Bruises I would have aplenty by morning. Yet the real wounds were deeper, and made worse because I couldn't seem to give them voice.

The Path of Thorns and Roses began pulling her arrows out of the dead bodies strewn about the grounds outside the hall. She examined each one carefully before wiping it off with a cloth and placing it back in the leather quiver belted to her hip. She barely spared me a glance.

'I admit to being confused,' she said. 'I watched you from the rafters as you fought through the screamers. You appeared to be utilising an elementary form of arta eres – though with rather too much fluttering about, I should say. Nonetheless, I assumed you were an Argosi like me.'

'I *am* an Argosi,' I said. 'Just not like you.'

The Path of Thorns and Roses looked up from her grizzly work. 'Tell me your name.'

'Ferius Parfax.'

'That is not an Argosi name. What is your path?'

'What? I don't have one.'

'Then you are not Argosi.'

'Go to hell.'

She slid the final arrow back in her quiver and strode over to me with such directness that I flinched, thinking she was about to attack me. Then I realised she probably always walked that way – as if her every step was filled with grand and glorious purpose.

'Raise one of the dead,' she commanded.

'What?'

She pointed to the corpse of a middle-aged man on the ground.

'With your guilt. Bring him back to life. Have you not learned to channel guilt, grief and shame into the power of resurrection?'

I gaped at her. 'You can . . . ? Is that possible?'

A sting bloomed on my cheek before I even realised she'd slapped me across the face. 'Of course not, you idiot. Now stop being a child.'

Mere minutes ago my mind and body had been fully immersed in the dance of arta eres. Her slap caused me to slip back there. I drove my right fist at her jaw, already knowing it would never connect. She'd simply duck beneath and follow up with a palm

78

strike to my chest to drive me back and give her the extra foot of distance needed for a proper counter-attack. But my punch had been a feint. As she went to shove me, I dropped down low, pivoting on my heels and letting her hands pass overhead. I grabbed her right forearm and twisted as I stood back up, pushing my hip out behind me and throwing her over my shoulder.

Durral didn't approve of such blunt martial forms. He wanted everything to be a dance, arguing some nonsense or other about how no matter how effective the technique might be, an Argosi who fights like a soldier has already given up the most important ground. Maybe he was right, because while my throw had been perfect, somehow my opponent used the momentum I'd given her to somersault through the air, landing gracefully back down with my wrist trapped in a joint lock.

'Does it hurt?' she asked, her casual tone belying the vicious twist she gave.

In quick succession, I attempted three different manoeuvres out of the wrist lock. Each one worked, yet every time she simply adjusted her grip and got me into a different and more complex lock. She bent my fingers back until I had to bite my tongue to keep from screaming.

'Does pain not grant you supernatural powers, Ferius Parfax? Does your noble suffering not imbue such mighty righteousness into your limbs that I should be unable to harm you?'

She spun me around so that she was now behind me, with my arm twisted painfully into the small of my back and her forearm around my neck as she forced me to face the still-burning fire.

'Or is your discomfort as useless as your guilt, no more able to free you from my grip than your grief can raise the dead? The people of this village are no more. Blame me. Blame yourself, if it pleases you. But do not doubt that every one of them died the moment their witless mayor uttered the Scarlet Verses aloud. Shame and regret cannot bend the road of time back upon itself.'

I spoke through gritted teeth. 'So you don't care at all about those you killed?'

She twisted my arm harder. 'Not one bit. Not so much as a tear will I shed for them. An Argosi does not grieve, for grief is wasted love. There are hundreds of villages littered about the Seven Sands. You wish to weep? Weep for those who will die if this plague spreads. And it *will* spread, Ferius Parfax.'

She gave me a shake that caused my already stretched ligaments to scream.

'I have seen the destruction at the Monastery of the Silent Garden,' she informed me. 'The distance between the dead suggested it took several repetitions of the verses to spread from person to person. Yet here in Tinto Rhea, a single recitation took all those who heard it save you and the boy. From this we can only conclude that the one who brought the plague here has been refining the verses.'

'How did you resist being infected then?' I asked, what should've been the obvious suspicion coming to me at a most inopportune moment. 'Binta doesn't understand spoken language, and he was screaming in my ears when the mayor began reading out the verses. But you must've been nearby, so why weren't you infected?'

She gave a soft snort in my ear as if the answer was so obvious that my question revealed just how bad I was at all this.

'I used candle wax in my ears to deafen myself, obviously. Had you an ounce of arta tuco, you would've done the same before you came here.'

'Let me go,' I grunted, still trying to find some way out of her endless joint locks. I couldn't though. When it came to arta eres, I was utterly outclassed.

My inability to escape seemed to annoy the Path of Thorns and Roses even more than my ignorance – not that that stopped her from making it apparent to me.

'Amateur. Listen to me now: the only thing that stops the plague spreading outside these villages is that the infected bite off their tongue and shatter their own teeth. We must assume this is a flaw in the means by which the disease is transmitted and not by design. What happens when she who brought it to these people you seem so intent on wasting your time weeping over perfects the verses so that the next victims can spread it to every region of the Seven Sands and beyond? *That* is what we face, Ferius Parfax.'

At last she released me, shoving me away from her and sending me stumbling towards the still-burning hall.

'So either summon up all your tears to make an ocean of the desert, or choose the path true compassion demands and help me find a way to put an end to the Red Scream.'

'The Red Scream?' I asked, retreating from the flames.

She took my question as surrender and her anger seemed to dissipate.

'That is the name I have given to this plague. I believe the madness is like ... like an endless shriek rising up out of the victims. These words used to spread it, these Scarlet Verses as I call them, they trigger something inside the mind that destroys the victim's humanity.'

Seeing my smallsword lying on the ground a few feet away, I went to retrieve it. 'You seem to know a lot about this disease. Who is this woman they call "the traveller" who brought it here? How did she create the Red Scream in the first place? Why would she—'

'I have few answers, Ferius Parfax. Only what little I learned from the bodies that lay rotting at the Monastery of the Silent

Garden, what you and I have witnessed in this village, and . . . this.'

I slid the smallsword back into its case and turned to find her holding something, a playing card. As I approached, I noted there was no suit, only a beautifully painted design of a shadowy figure walking a winding path, old tomes left strewn on the ground behind her. The flames flickering behind me made the figure almost seem alive. Underneath the image was written, 'The Seeker of Verses'.

The only other card I'd seen like that had been painted by Durral Brown, and the picture had been of me. Well, a me that was a little older and who bore a proper Argosi smile on her face. I still kept that card with me always, still dreamed of one day becoming that woman. So far it wasn't working out too good.

'Someone gave you a discordance card?' I asked.

Enna had been the one to teach me how the Argosi decks worked. The most common one contained a suit for each civilisation on the continent. These were called the concordances, and represented the hierarchies and workings of the societies they depicted. But when an Argosi came upon something unexpected – something that could alter the course of history – they painted a discordance card. These designs were more symbolic than realistic, capturing those elements the Argosi believed were relevant to the discordance's nature. When that Argosi reached the limit of their own ability to pursue the matter, they would give the card over to another, in hopes a different path would yield greater understanding.

Seeing the way my gaze moved slowly and methodically across each element of the card, the Path of Thorns and Roses said, 'Good. You are not entirely unlearned in our ways.'

I looked up at her, taking in her features as closely as I had the details on the card. The winding fabric around her face had slid down again, revealing the wide mouth and high cheekbones, the dark eyes that were ever so slightly angled upward at the outer corners. She could've been Berabesq, I supposed, or maybe even Gitabrian, yet neither ancestry seemed to capture wherever she came from.

'Are you done admiring me?' she asked, not a trace of self-consciousness in her tone.

The seventh talent of the Argosi is arta siva, which is the art of persuasion, or, as Durral likes to call it, 'charm'.

Your arta siva sucks, Path of Thorns and Roses.

The Argosi don't believe in divination. Cards like the one she was holding were for understanding the present, not looking into the future. Yet I was pretty confident predicting that I wasn't going to like being around this girl one bit. I couldn't imagine what Binta would—

Binta!

'Seventeen hells and a devil's thumbscrew,' I swore, taking off at a run towards the barn. I'd sent Binta away, and while I'd stood here arguing with this arrogant, heartless Argosi, he could've gone miles by now. If someone else found him before I did . . .

'Where are you going?' the Path of Thorns and Roses called out.

'The boy who saved me from being infected by those verses!' I shouted back, still running for the barn. 'I sent him to flee on horseback. I've got to follow his tracks before the desert winds wipe them away!'

12

Bad Words

Before I could reach the barn, the Path of Thorns and Roses caught up with me. I hadn't even heard her following me.

'You needn't worry, Ferius Parfax. I dealt with the boy before I set off the explosives.'

Dealt with him? Oh, no. Please, no. Don't let this cold-blooded lunatic have—

As I arrived at the old timber and stone building, I could hear the soft pounding of a young boy's fist on the other side of the doors, which I now saw were barred with a heavy oak plank. I was just about to lift it when a much louder crack to my right preceded the iron-shod hoofs of a big, angry horse smashing through the stable wall. Shards of wood, stone and crumbling mortar exploded out at us. Apparently Quadlopo wasn't done though, because he bludgeoned two more sections of the outer wall until there was enough room for him to wander out and give me a baleful look.

'Wasn't me who locked you in there,' I said.

Quadlopo seemed dubious about the degree to which such testimony exonerated me in the matter of his unlawful confinement.

Binta ran through the gap behind him, wide-eyed and weeping. When he saw me standing there he raced for me, arms and legs pumping for those few steps even as his fingers twitched 'Good Dog' over and over.

I grabbed him up into a hug and held him tight. His whole body shook as he sobbed in silence.

'As I told you,' the Path of Thorns and Roses said behind me. 'I took care of the child for you.'

I am going to redouble my efforts to learn the Argosi ways, I promised myself. *I am going to master arta eres as no one has mastered it before. All so I can one day beat the crap out of you, lady.*

I gently put Binta back down and knelt to face him.

'Are you hurt?' I signed.

'*I am unharmed. Who is that awful bitch?*'

Almost reflexively, I signed back, '*That is a bad word.*' Master Phinus, my old Daroman comportment instructor in the ways in which proper young boys and girls should behave, would've been proud.

'*She is a bad woman,*' Binta replied unapologetically.

When I turned back, the Path of Thorns and Roses was watching us. Though I could see she didn't know the monkish silent voice, still I could tell she was starting to work out the gestures Binta and I made, inferring from the context and our expressions what they might mean.

We don't look more than a year or so apart. How can she be so much better at all this than me?

Binta tapped me on the arm and informed me it was rude not to introduce him to our unpleasant rescuer.

Trying to come up with the exact signs to explain that her name was 'The Path of Thorns and Roses' proved remarkably difficult. After three tries, Binta shook his head and signed, '*Rose. She is Rose.*'

I tried to correct him, but I suppose the boy had decided the subject was closed.

'What did he say?' the Path of Thorns and Roses asked.

'He signed your name.'

'It seems . . . short,' the Argosi said, and repeated the sign herself, graceful fingers already mastering the shapes. She seemed disappointed by its simplicity.

'It means Rose,' I explained, then, seeing the irritation on her face, decided to do one better. 'Actually, it means "Rosie". Binta says your name will be Rosie from now on.'

I left Rosie to her discomfort and entered the barn through the ruined wall to retrieve Quadlopo's saddle, which he'd somehow wriggled out of during his escape. After undertaking the unnecessarily difficult steps of saddling a horse who wanted to make sure I knew just how displeased he was with me, I turned to find the Argosi and Binta staring at each other as if locked in some sort of contest of wills.

'The boy is unusually defective,' she said, apparently unaware at how horrible that sounded. 'He does not appear to read lips, which any deaf child ought to have learned. And while he does not react to sound, still I see signs that some part of his mind does, in fact, notice noises around him. Furthermore, when the mayor began reading the Scarlet Verses inside the hall, he screamed, which suggests he ought to be capable of at least rudimentary speech. Yet he makes no effort to use words. From this we may deduce that his peculiar behaviours around language are the result of conditioning, which means his father at the monastery trained him to be this way.'

'You got all that out of a minute of glaring at him?'

She responded with a light, almost musical snort. 'I "got" far more than that, Ferius Parfax.'

'Enlighten me.'

She pointed at Binta. 'The child appears to be immune from the Red Scream, which explains why he was the only survivor of the massacre at the Monastery of the Silent Garden. Furthermore, given you were closer to the dais where the mayor recited the Scarlet Verses than many of the villagers, it is clear that the boy's own scream so close was able to protect you from the effects. Thus an avenue of inquiry opens to us, as well as a source of substantial concern.'

I helped Binta up and settled him on Quadlopo's saddle. 'What concern?'

'The Traveller, whoever she is, enacts a sophisticated plan towards a purpose that we do not yet know. To have discovered the means to concoct a plague that infects the human mind using only a sequence of syllables indicates our enemy possesses an unparalleled intellect. That she has done all this without anyone yet uncovering her scheme demonstrates significant cunning. We cannot, therefore, be in doubt that either this woman is already aware, or will soon become so, of the boy's immunity. The Traveller *will* come for him.' She glanced back at me. 'You and I will have to keep the boy alive until we can find a way to replicate his resistance to the Scarlet Verses.'

'And how do we do that? We don't know anything about this "Traveller" woman, nor are either of us experts in whatever science or magic we'll need to counter this plague. Besides, where are we supposed to take Binta?'

The Path of Thorns and Roses tightened the leather straps that kept her billowing linen sleeves in place around her shoulders and forearms. 'As the first evidence we have of the plague is from the Monastery of the Silent Garden, the inevitable conclusion is that the final pieces the Traveller needed to construct her plague were found there.'

'Sure, but if all the monks are now dead, how does that do us any good? You think she left some of the relevant books behind?'

The Argosi gave me a look that wasn't so much withering as curious whether I'd prove to be any use at all or whether she'd have to save the world all by herself. 'Obviously not. However I said she found the *final components* of her seven deadly verses at the monastery, not *all* the elements. The Silent Garden was unlikely to have been the first stop on her journey, and thus if we extrapolate her intentions to other places where forbidden texts are held, we may well find someone alive who has met the Traveller, and through them gain insight as to her purpose and destination.'

'Or just follow the trail of dead bodies,' I muttered.

Binta, sensing he was the subject of discussion, asked, '*What does the unpleasant woman say?*'

I considered my reply, still trying to piece together in my thoughts all that the Path of Thorns and Roses had deduced so swiftly.

'*She says that she and I will protect you,*' I said at last, which had the virtue of being true, if incomplete.

'*I do not like her. She has a smug face.*'

I chuckled, and signed, '*On that, little one, we agree.*'

The Argosi started heading back up the path into the village. When we didn't follow she stopped and turned. 'Well, are you going to help or not? I thought you were so filled with compassion for the souls of this poor village that your heart would fairly burst if you didn't exert yourself in their cause.'

'You said everyone here was dead!'

'I said the villagers were dead. There are still animals here. Livestock in pens, dogs chained in their kennels. Do you not hear their barks and braying? Or are their lives unworthy of our efforts?'

She continued her march up the path.

'*What's wrong?*' Binta asked, staring down at me from Quadlopo's saddle. '*You are twisting your face in confusing ways.*'

I gave a tug on Quadlopo's reins to follow the Argosi so we could set about freeing the easily forgotten innocent denizens of this cursed place.

'This is the face I make when I feel foolish.'

As we began what would be a task of many hours to release all the various goats, sheepdogs and other animals from their captivity, the enigmatic young woman who, despite pursuing the Argosi ways as I did, and was utterly unlike me in every conceivable way, stopped and turned to me as if she'd arrived at some momentous conclusion.

'What is it?' I asked.

She tugged down the linen coverings on her face, full lips pressed into a thin line, brows furrowed and cheeks flustered as if she'd just experienced embarrassment for the first time in her life.

'I have decided that I do not enjoy this name "Rosie",' she informed us. 'From now on you will refer to me as "The Path of Thorns and Roses", and teach the child to do the same.'

I gave her a wink before leading Quadlopo with Binta on his back up the path towards the first of the fenced cottages.

'Anything you say, Rosie.'

Arta Precis

To uncover that which another hides is the weakest form of arta precis. Far more valuable is the talent for perceiving those secrets the bearer does not realise they possess.

13

Teachings

I used to badger Durral and Enna for details on the inner workings of the Argosi talents. What use is it to study defence – arta eres – for example, if your teachers never show you the specific movements? Instead, my education consisted of vague principles and scraps of frontier philosophy that sounded clever but made no sense. Worse, when I tried to translate my hazy speculations as to what those concepts actually meant into practice, I could never get my teachers to evaluate my performance. I could dance about the room all day long, attempting to transform such axioms as 'the warrior uses the enemy's strength against them, the Argosi merely helps them along' into something usable in a fight, but for all I knew I was just dancing.

'*Keep it up, kid,*' Durral would say.

'*But am I doing it right?*' I'd ask.

Enna, to whom I usually looked for practical guidance, would reply, '*You're doing it your way, Ferius. The only way you can.*'

Maddening.

In those first days and weeks on the road with the Path of Thorns and Roses, however, I learned that there are worse things than ambiguously supportive teachers.

'You're doing it wrong again.'

I continued my flowing, almost wistful turns on the precariously icy rocky ground. This high up in the Syphitian range that ran north–south in the upper reaches of the Seven Sands, the morning mists wound around your feet, making it seem as if you were walking on clouds. The experience of dancing upon such unusual terrain was magical, almost dreamlike. Unless, of course, someone was criticising you the entire time.

'I didn't ask your opinion,' I reminded her.

'Nevertheless.'

Nevertheless was the opening of a speech I had memorised by this point. It goes like this: *Nevertheless, we are companions on a journey whose outcome is of greater importance than either of our lives. As such, it is incumbent upon both of us to ensure we are able to fulfil our responsibilities to this mission to the full extent of our abilities. Therefore your skills in combat, however limited by your innately poor coordination and almost non-existent concentration, may be critical in our endeavours. Our safety depends on each other. For me to ignore your obvious failings in arta eres would be worse than neglect on my part. It would constitute the knowing sabotage of our quest.*

I stopped and let the swirling mist around my legs settle.

'Prove it,' I said.

Rosie, garbed as always in lengths of gauzy beige linen, folded her arms across her chest. 'The conclusion will be the same today as it was yesterday, resulting in you complaining of your bruises as we make our ascent to the convent.'

She had a point. Twelve days it had taken us to get this far, and, with any luck, by tonight we'd finish our climb to the unpleasantly named Convent of Scarlet Words. If anyone possessed knowledge of how a sequence of mere syllables could trigger madness, it would be the Red Nuns. So really, I should just suck up my irritation and keep quiet.

'Prove it,' I said again, then added, 'Rosie.'

I closed my eyes and listened as the Path of Thorns and Roses approached. Up here in the mountain ranges, sounds echoed in confusing ways and the soft pad of footsteps could seem to have their source both in front and behind at the same time. But I'd been paying attention, learning to discern the subtle differences in the reverberations, and today – *today* – I was finally going to knock her down.

I ducked the first blow, then slammed my forearms together in front of me to block what I knew would be a knee strike. Rosie tended to use the same sequence of moves on me every time – not because she was predictable, but because she enjoyed showing me that no amount of preparation on my part would save me from getting dropped on my arse.

'Slow,' she said, grabbing both my wrists and rolling backwards, tossing me over her.

Most days, this was when I'd end up on my butt. Today, however, I went with the throw, adding my momentum to her pull and flipping myself over in a somersault.

'Graceless,' she added, somehow back on her feet before I'd even landed. 'But not entirely ineffective.'

As was her tendency, she came at me with a flurry of blows. Punches. Elbow strikes. Slaps to the side of the head that could knock you halfway unconscious and backhands that would finish the job. Bizarre attacks like the 'Falcon's Beak', where she'd press her fingers together into a tiny striking area that would leave little round bruises that hurt like seven hungry devils feasting on your flesh.

'Dodge. Slip. Evade. Counter.' She offered up each of these instructions with perfect timing. All I had to do was follow her commands and I'd be fine.

But, as Durral Brown would have said, '*I ain't built that way, sister.*'

Instead I danced with her, allowing each attack to come to me, whirling and swaying, staying just out of reach of the worst of her blows even as I always made sure some part of my body, whether an arm or leg or even a shoulder, touched Rosie. My technique infuriated her, which was good, but it never worked for long, which resulted in . . . discomfort.

One of her jabs struck a nerve cluster just under my right breast. I let out a scream, and the next thing I knew I was being flipped in the air.

'*How come you won't teach me to fight like you do, Pappy?*'

'*Because you're not me. Your body isn't mine. It's not Enna's. It's not anybody's but yours. So you gotta learn to fight your way, kid.*'

'*How long will that take?*'

Durral replied with my least favourite answer of all time: '*Long as it takes.*'

Somewhere around the hundredth time I'd asked him that question, maybe because I'd done better that day than I ever had before, he'd added, '*But when you do find your arta eres, well, kid, that will be a sight to see. A. Sight. To. See.*'

All the air fled my lungs as Rosie slammed me to the ground.

'You have no discipline,' she said, aiming a punch an inch above my mouth that would've left me with a broken nose had I not batted it away just in time. 'How have you survived this long?'

'I've outlasted murderers and mages,' I informed her. 'Spells and beatings and things even worse. You want to know how?'

'Luck, I would assume,' she said, the first hint of a sneer on her lips. 'Or perhaps begging for mercy?'

Enna once told me that an Argosi seeks to develop adaptability rather than mastery, resilience rather than strength. I'd asked her why I couldn't have both.

'The duellist who hones her blade too sharp weakens the weapon in ways she cannot see. An Argosi recognises where the steel is strong and where it is fragile.'

Rosie's speed and timing were a wonder to behold, but I'd noticed that moments of unexpected intimacy, like if she saw Binta hugging me or I laughed in appreciation of something she said, would make her stiffen up. I used to be the same, but Enna had cured me of that. I guessed nobody had done the same for Rosie.

'Mostly I've survived on my charm,' I said. Then I caught her eyes and smiled at her like we'd been dancing under the stars at the end of a warm starlit night rather than fighting on this cold and merciless clifftop. 'That, and I'm a hell of a kisser.'

As the closest I'd ever come to kissing anybody had been with Lyrida, the girl who'd tried to rip my face off back in Tinto Rhea, my boast was all swagger of course. But I'll put my arta valar up against just about anybody's other than Durral's.

Rosie's arta precis must've warned her I was setting her up, but between two opponents like us, every fraction of a second counts. She couldn't stop her shoulders from tensing. I held her gaze, distracting her as I swung my left leg up and over her shoulder, catching her neck between my heel and calf. I pivoted onto my right side, hauling her down to the ground as I rolled myself on top of her.

I had my right fist cocked and ready. After twelve days of being denigrated and humiliated, I was going to punch the almighty Path of Thorns and Roses right in the nose. Not hard, just enough to show her I wasn't some errant child to be—

Now that was strange. A second before, I'd been above her with victory at hand. Now I seemed to be flat on my stomach, winded once again as the skin of my cheek scraped painfully against the rocky grey shale. Rosie was sitting astride my back like I was some pony she was riding.

'You had the advantage,' she said, her tone flat and lifeless. 'Your finishing strike was too slow because you held back.'

I tried squirming out from under her, but couldn't get away. 'Maybe the reason I didn't punch your lights out is because I don't consider it proper etiquette to injure my travelling companions! Get off me, Rosie!'

She slapped the back of my head – not too hard – just enough to show me that as far as she was concerned, I *was* an errant child. Now I was going to get a badly needed lesson.

'Is this what you will do when next we encounter victims of the Red Scream and the infected swarm over us?'

I tried to spin myself around so I could use my arms and legs to fight back, but her thighs were gripping my sides too tightly, trapping me on my stomach.

'I mean it, Rosie. Let me go.'

She slapped the back of my head again.

'You are Mahdek, are you not? I wonder, do the Jan'Tep mages take pity on you when you beg them to stop?' Another slap. 'Do their spells fail when you wink at them like a strumpet in a cheap saloon?' Another, and another after that. 'Do the war covens cower at the flash of your smile?'

I pushed against the ground with all the strength in my arms. A stupid waste of effort. Rosie was stronger than me and she had me pinned. Worse, she was messing with me now, playing the reverse of the tactic I'd used moments before. The crack about the Jan'Tep was meant to fluster me. It worked.

I'd taken to keeping one of Durral's throwing cards in the leather cuff of my right coat sleeve. I shook my arm, flinging the card into my waiting hand.

'Get the hell off me now, Rosie, or I swear I'll—'

Her fist slammed against the back of my hand, shaking my grip on the card loose and drawing a groan from between my gritted teeth.

'A gambler's weapon,' she said dismissively. 'A plaything meant to impress or unnerve, not kill.'

Had it not been for the shadow cast by the morning sun, I wouldn't have seen the four-bladed weapon coming down for my hand. I jerked my arm away just as the curved front blade buried itself in the frozen ground.

I'd seen Rosie use the unusual steel contraption strapped to her back to cut away foliage and to skin the hares we'd caught for food before we'd started up the mountain. It was an ungainly beast to look at. None of its four blades was the same shape or curvature. Three of them had leather wrappings a few inches above the sharpened ends that served as handles, depending on whether she was using it as a machete or a knife or an axe. Only now did my arta tuco reveal to me the many ways it could be used to inflict violence on another human being.

'The double-crescent is an ugly weapon,' she said, pressing her palm into the back of my head, shoving my chin into the frozen shale. 'I can cut off a man's hand with it if the situation requires, bind a spear between its blades. The double-crescent is not half so pretty or elegant as your cards when it flies . . .' She gripped my hair and yanked my head up even as she tugged the strange four-bladed weapon from the ground and with a single smooth motion sent it spinning into the trunk of a nearby tree. The snow shook away from the branches as if fleeing the scene of a crime. 'But its bite is never forgotten.'

'Glad we agree on something,' I said, fighting the fear rising up inside me with arta valar, searching for the calm I'd need to find a way to escape her grip. 'My cards are definitely prettier.'

101

She jammed my face into the ground again as she leaned in close to whisper in my ear.

'Will you defeat the Traveller with your jokes and sly looks, Ferius Parfax? She has created a plague from mere words. Whatever paltry skills you and I possess, only a fool would fail to see we are outmatched. Without time to find other Argosi, our only chance lies in the Way of Thunder. We must hope for a single moment when we can take her unawares and strike without hesitation, without mercy. Yet every time you and I fight, no matter how many opportunities I give you, you hesitate at the crucial moment. Why?'

'Human decency. I can see why it would confound you.'

Rosie laughed then – an unusual sound for her. I didn't find it pleasant at all.

'Your arta loquit betrays you, sister. "Human decency"? You fail to hide the irony in your voice when you use those words. The shame. What did you do, Ferius? You hurt someone, didn't you? Someone you cared about.'

'You don't know what you're talking about, you heartless bi—'

'Arta precis,' she said, like she was standing in front of a classroom lecturing to a class of dim-witted students instead of sitting on my back. 'To perceive that which others keep hidden. Your refusal to take advantage of the superior techniques I offer you, this blind obsession with following a set of obviously flawed teachings . . . was it your maetri you hurt, Ferius? Is this some misguided redemption you seek by insisting on repeating their mistakes?'

It took every ounce of self-control I could muster to slow my breathing, to say what I said next with the same callous disdain as everything that came out of Rosie's mouth.

'Listen to my voice, Path of Thorns and Roses,' I said slowly. 'What does your arta loquit tell you about what is going to happen if you take one more step down this road? Because you know what mine is telling me? It's telling me you're as much a liar as me, and all this so-called "teaching" is really about is hiding your fear.'

Slowly, almost dismissively, the weight on my back became lighter until she was off me. I turned and looked up to see her standing over me.

'Fool,' she said. 'I try to show you the proper Argosi ways as my maetri taught me, and you spit on my gift. You want to know what I fear? I fear a continent overrun with those infected by the Red Scream because the girl I counted on to watch my back proved sentimental and weak.'

I rose to my feet and dusted myself off.

'Yeah, nice dancin' with you too, Rosie.'

I'd barely said the words out loud, but I guess she heard them, because she spun around and grabbed me by the front of my shirt, shaking me so hard I thought she might actually throw me off the cliff.

'We did not *dance*, Ferius Parfax. This is not a game. I have come to this place because this is where my path takes me. Because I have sworn to find the Traveller and kill her before she can spread the Red Scream any further. I allow you to accompany me because, even with your pathetic understanding of the Argosi ways, only a fool believes she is better off alone when facing unknown adversaries. But I am not your friend. I am not your lover. Do not ever suggest that you and I could be more than reluctant travelling companions.'

She strode off. Even that she did with the graceful contempt of a cat off to pursue more suitable prey. I turned to find Binta standing there outside our tent, staring at me. I didn't have to guess how much he'd seen.

'*Now can I call her a bitch?*' he signed.

I stood there a moment, breathing in slow and deep as the various pains Rosie had inflicted on me competed to see which could draw tears first.

'No,' I signed back at last. '*She wasn't trying to be cruel. This is something else.*'

'*What, then?*'

I had no answer to give Binta, so I went and hugged him instead, pretending to reassure him when it was me who was in need. I'm not a praying person by nature, but I sure was hoping the Red Nuns at the Convent of Scarlet Words would know something that could help us put an end to the Traveller's plague. Rosie was hiding something from me, and whatever it was, I wasn't sure how long the two of us could be around each other before something real bad happened.

14

Footsteps

The clomp and clack of horse hoofs accompanied us along the rocky trail. Binta sat atop Quadlopo's back. I led the big, irascible horse on foot since the loose shale and narrow passes made riding risky for both beast and rider. Back in Tinto Rhea, Rosie had adopted from one of the stables a stallion who, by coincidence or destiny, shared her cheerful disposition. Biter (not the name she'd given him, but the only one the mean-spirited monster deserved) periodically came up to nip at my shoulder any time our pace slowed or my boots slipped on the stony shards. I was convinced he did this to relieve Rosie of the burden of pointing out my ineptitude. A more supportive animal than Quadlopo might've turned to snap at Biter or whinny a few threats here or there, but he – perhaps wisely – decided to remain neutral in the ongoing conflict.

'*I can see the convent ahead,*' Binta signed.

He did this without bothering to look down to see if I was watching. The child had an uncanny knack for sensing whether someone was paying attention to him. That, or else he nattered at me all the time and I only occasionally noticed.

I tapped him on the thigh so he'd watch as I signed my question. '*What do you see?*'

My fluency in the silent voice had grown steadily over these past two weeks, but I wasn't expecting much in response; it wasn't a language particularly well suited to elaborate descriptions.

'Big,' he replied. '*Stone walls rise and fall as they follow the shape of the ridge. Like someone poured molten rock onto the mountain side and it cooled into a misshapen fortress.*'

'Can you see any people?'

'*No, but there's a tiny stone square building in the wall.*'

A gatehouse. I relayed Binta's observations to Rosie, whose short 'Obviously' suggested she'd already worked out the design and form of the convent entirely through inferences from its natural surroundings.

I'd noted a souring of her mood the closer we got to our destination. It wasn't that there were any overt changes in her aloof demeanour, and since she had me walk in front of her, I wasn't in a position to note any alterations in her expressions of bland disdain which were, blessedly, covered up by her wrappings. So really I had no reason to suspect anything untoward. However, while Durral Brown had often been a frustrating teacher in the ways of the Argosi, he'd taught me one thing about arta loquit that was proving unexpectedly useful in my travels.

'*Close your eyes and tell me what you hear,*' he'd said once.

We'd been sitting outside a chic – and unbearably expensive – coffee house in a little Gitabrian border town called Escusha.

'*Listen to what?*' I'd asked.

'*To the people walking by. Tell me about them.*'

This being a lesson in arta loquit, I'd been momentarily delighted that his instructions actually made sense: he wanted me to pick up as much as I could from the brief snatches of the conversations of Gitabrian passers-by and report back to him what I'd learned about my subjects.

What had possessed me to imagine Durral Brown could ask a question that *wasn't* as circuitous as a snake tying itself in knots as it tries to eat its own tail?

'*Don't need you translatin' their words for me,*' he'd scolded me after my first attempts to interpret their lilting, musical language had proved unsatisfactory.

Right, I'd thought. *Too obvious.*

So I'd tried again, this time focusing only on the tonal qualities of their voices and what those might imply about their conversations.

'*Don't care about their tone, neither. You forget that Gitabrian verbs use tonal shifts to indicate tense? Can't tell nothing from 'em.*'

On we went like this, with my third, fourth and fifth tries all failing to fulfil the obscure purpose of the exercise. Finally I demanded to know what – *precisely* – I was supposed to be listening for.

'*Footsteps, kid. Let the soles of their feet sing to you.*'

Oh, right. *Footsteps.* How could I have missed that?

So what can you learn from listening to the subtle variations in how a person walks? A great deal, it turns out.

'*A nervous or guilty person,*' Durral expounded, '*spends a long time setting each foot, like they're not sure they can trust the ground. That's cos they don't actually want to get where they're going.*'

'How can you be su—'

But he was on a roll. '*Placin' more weight on the foot that's on the same side as the person they're walkin' with means they want to be closer to them. The reverse is true if they put the weight on the opposite foot.*'

'What if they just have a limp?'

That had gotten me a raised eyebrow and a dismissive snort. '*A limp and a lean don't sound nothin' alike.*' Before I could object, he reached over and pinched my ear. '*Listen to what folks are sayin'*'

107

with their heels, kid. They'll tell you things they wouldn't tell their own mother.'

Durral claimed you could pick up hundreds of different cues just from a person's footsteps. He'd gone on to insist that you could never even begin to master arta loquit – the Argosi talent for eloquence – until you knew these signals.

Like a lot of his teachings, I'd been suspicious of how serious he was. He had a habit of earnestly describing some bizarre Argosi trick, only to smirk when I asked him to demonstrate it.

'I'll show you when I figure it out myself, kid.'

I think there was a bit of the card sharp in Durral's nature that even his Argosi path couldn't stop him returning to. At heart he was a frontier con man who always had to push his stories and lessons right to the edge of plausibility just to see if he could make you believe in a world more wondrous than the one in which we lived.

I loved him for that.

'Why are you sad?' Binta asked as I was leading Quadlopo around a patch of particularly treacherous shale that caused his iron-shod hoofs to scrabble as he fought for purchase on the uneven ground.

'I'm not sad,' I replied.

'You were sad just then,' he insisted. *'Sad and scared. Why are you scared?'*

'I was worried about Quadlopo falling off the side of the mountain.'

Lying with your fingers isn't any harder than doing it with your lips. Lying with your feet though? That, as Durral had taught me, is much harder.

The longer we'd been walking up this ridge, the closer we got to the convent, the more I heard the variations in Rosie's footsteps. She was grinding her boot heels into the shale, delaying each step just a fraction longer than necessary.

108

That's how I knew something was wrong, and that there was something about the Convent of Scarlet Words that troubled the taciturn, arrogant Argosi far more than she was prepared to let on.

When the gatehouse came in view about a hundred yards ahead, I pulled on Quadlopo's reins to get him to stop. Before Biter could convey his customary annoyance, I spun on my heels and showed him my teeth.

'You even think about taking a nip out of my hide, you lousy, foul-tempered old nag, and I'll take a bigger one out of yours.'

Rosie arched an eyebrow – which almost always preceded an extended commentary on the necessity for an Argosi to always be in control of their emotions.

I didn't give her the chance.

'Talk,' I said.

She stared back at me impassively. I think she prided herself on never using words when a dirty look would suffice.

'Talk, Rosie, or we ain't going another step.'

'Talk about what?'

No angry retort, no shift in tone, yet already she'd confirmed three of my suspicions. First, I wasn't just tagging along with her; she *needed* me here. Otherwise my threat not to continue would've resulted in her walking right by me and leaving me there. Second, she hadn't tried to change the topic, which meant not only had she known this conversation was coming, but in fact there was something I needed to know before we reached the convent. Third, she'd waited this long because she'd been dreading having this conversation.

'Take off your head wrappings, Rosie.'

'Why?'

'Because this being the most words we've exchanged in days, I'd like to see your face.'

109

Instead of just tugging down part of the gauzy covering, she unwound it all until it lay across her shoulders like a long scarf. Usually I only saw her face in brief glimpses: the dispassionate line of her mouth, the wide set of her jaw, the almost black eyes that never revealed anything. Only occasionally had I caught a flash of her hair, which was the darkest, purest brown I'd ever seen. Now that it was entirely uncovered, those thick curls draping either side of the smooth lines of her face, I was quite convinced that the Path of Thorns and Roses was the most beautiful person I'd ever met.

Too bad she had the personality of a poison-quilled porcupine.

'You've been here before,' I said, and made sure she knew it wasn't a question.

'I have.'

She gave me nothing in that reply. No hesitation that might suggest ambiguity about precisely *when* she'd been here, no fluctuations in tone to hint at the nature of her experiences. She hadn't even replied tersely to indicate a resistance to further inquiries on my part. This is the problem with people who learn arta loquit: they know how to be miserly with their words.

Rosie was goading me into demanding proper answers, and in so doing was betting I'd reveal my own speculations about what was going on here. But every once in a while, Durral's twisting, almost slippery, tactics could be remarkably useful.

'*Abide a while,*' I signed to Binta.

'*What are the two of you doing?*' he asked.

'*Nothing. It's all right. Rosie needs a little time. She has bad memories of this place to which we travel. We must be patient, you and I.*'

Rosie snapped at that. 'I have no need of "time",' she said angrily. 'Nor are my memories relevant to the matter at hand, which, in case you have forgotten, involves getting information about the source of a plague which could spread across the entire continent while we waste time with you wanting to get in touch with my "feelings".'

'Why is she so upset?' Binta asked.

I could've kissed that kid.

'Do not discuss me as if I am not here,' Rosie signed testily.

I put my hands up in surrender. 'No need to scare the boy, Rosie. He's just wondering the same thing I am.'

'Which is?'

'Why, given you seem to think it's so important that we beg entry into the convent so we can consult with the Red Nuns, are you not planning on coming with us?'

Okay, sure, that was a *bit* of a shot in the dark. But the way Rosie had insisted on bringing us here and yet been unwilling to discuss any details about the place, the way her own pace kept dragging the closer we got, and, above all, the way she constantly – *constantly* – criticised my Argosi talents, all suggested I was headed into a situation for which Rosie worried I wasn't prepared. So why wasn't she just telling me to stay behind so she could go inside and find out what we needed to know?

'The nuns will not allow me inside,' she said at last.

A hundred questions came to mind. 'Why?' being the obvious one. The barely hidden anguish in Rosie's eyes told me it would be the wrong one to ask. Whatever secrets she was keeping from me, I wouldn't be able to pry them out of her like jamming a flat piece of steel into a locked door. Besides, Durral always said that sometimes the best way to break into a place is just wait outside until somebody invites you in. Maybe if I gave her time, Rosie would open the door a little.

'Okay,' I said. 'Two things. First, tell me what you want me to do at the convent, and second, I need to know that Binta won't be in danger.'

111

Rosie seemed as surprised as she was relieved. 'I . . . You must inquire within about the possible origins of this plague that spreads through language. Do not call it the Red Scream in the presence of the nuns, nor refer to the Scarlet Verses, lest they take offence that those names suggest a connection to their own order.'

'A connection I assume you're pretty sure exists.'

'The Monastery of the Silent Garden and the Convent of Scarlet Words both study the esoteric aspects of language. This is not magic, you understand, but scholarship into the underlying potency of words themselves. Theirs is a form of research so foreign to normal ways of thinking that their highest scholars forsake what you and I would think of as normal speech so as to not limit their ability to interpret the ancient texts in their keeping.'

'You mean that just using words themselves renders them . . .'

'Inert,' she finished for me. 'To utter a word out loud risks binding that combination of syllables to a singular meaning. What they study is how combinations of words may be formed to construct meanings so potent as to alter the minds of those who hear them.'

Combinations which might, theoretically, turn the listener insane.

'And you think this "Traveller" came here?' I asked.

Rosie nodded. 'The monks of the Silent Garden specialised in the deeper aspects of tone, pronunciation and emphasis. But the Red Nuns have a far wider knowledge of the specific origins and cognitive effects of individual words. I believe at least some of the Scarlet Verses had to have come from here.'

None of that sounded reassuring to me. I glanced up at Binta, sitting on Quadlopo's saddle. He looked for all the world like a regular, tousled-haired nine-year-old boy out for a pleasant ride in the mountains on his favourite horse.

'Maybe it's best if I enter the convent on my own,' I said.

Rosie put a hand on my arm, a gesture that should have been perfectly normal and yet nearly resulted in my slugging her. If she noticed, she managed not to show it.

'The nuns will not allow a stranger inside. Not unless one brings some ancient text they do not themselves possess, or have something else of interest to them.'

Rosie's eyes flashed briefly at Binta. I instantly understood what she'd been keeping from me.

'You expect me to use a traumatised child as a bribe to get in?'

For once the Path of Thorns and Roses had the decency to look uncomfortable. 'It's the only way. The Red Nuns will be . . . intrigued by the boy. In exchange for the opportunity to examine him, even for a short while, they may be open to revealing to you what they know about the Traveller and the Scarlet Verses.'

Okay, so my job is to trade on an emotionally fragile young boy's psyche for a few answers from a gang of possibly crazy nuns and then get Binta out of there before they imprison him and murder me. Simple.

'You never answered my second question,' I said.

'The nuns won't harm the boy,' Rosie insisted. 'They will consider him to be . . . special. Unique. To interfere with his development in any way would risk tampering with his nature. Instead, they will seek to convince you to leave him in their care.'

'And how do you suppose they'll take my refusal?'

I untied my mapmaker's case from Quadlopo's saddle and strapped it across my back. For the first time since I'd met her, Rosie looked genuinely concerned for me. She came closer, and her expression, her movements, even her tone of voice, suggested I was in more trouble than I understood.

113

'The nuns won't attempt to harm you physically,' she said. 'They may, however . . .'

She was wrestling with how to phrase her next words, which implied she was concerned with how I might interpret them.

If the Path of Thorns and Roses is trying not to piss me off, I'm going to be extremely nervous.

'Rosie?' I asked. 'What's going on?'

'How is your arta siva?'

The question took me aback. Of all the Argosi talents, I suspected it was the one she cared about the least. 'Reckon my charm is about as good as yours,' I replied.

She nodded as if my answer confirmed her fears. 'Persuasion is one of the most difficult of the seven talents to master. Do you know where the Argosi who first came to this continent acquired their knowledge of arta siva?'

I'd never even thought about it. I'd always just assumed the Argosi had developed the seven talents on their own, refining and passing them down through the generations, maetri to teysan.

In retrospect, that was a naive view.

'Ferius, some of the women in that convent could convince you to slit your own throat, or to give up our mission entirely and devote the rest of your life to becoming their servant. What you and I call arta siva and dismiss as simple persuasion, they have turned into a science that can mesmerise a person with a single sentence.'

That sounded dubious, even to me. But hadn't Durral implied such possibilities with all his talk of how the most powerful forms of magic ever devised were those simple, human things we all took for granted? Music. Dance. Rhetoric. Had the first Argosi come up into these mountains and adapted some portion of the nuns' arcane knowledge into arta siva?

114

A thought occurred to me then.

'Rosie, given most folk probably have never heard of the Convent of Scarlet Words, I'd have to assume the nuns prefer their secrets are kept inside their walls.'

'You would be correct.'

'So if those early Argosi took – stole, I guess you'd have to say, if you were looking at it from the nuns' perspective – some of their techniques . . .'

Rosie put a hand on my shoulder, a comradely gesture that only made me more terrified at the thought of what I was walking into. This time I was so unnerved I didn't even react, just froze there like a frightened deer.

'Beware the Red Nuns,' she said. 'They may seem quaint at first, even humorous, yet they are reclusive, studious and secretive. They care nothing about the outside world and are dispassionate about the lives of those beyond their walls, with one exception: they despise the Argosi beyond all words. And they know a great many words, Ferius.'

I looked up again at Binta, wondering how much of this I ought to reveal to him. Having spent most of my own life dealing with people keeping things from me, I decided to tell him all of it.

Any normal kid would've used this as an excuse to refuse to go. Yet even when I repeated myself, trying to make him understand the danger, Binta didn't raise the possibility of abandoning our quest. His fingers merely formed the signs for two simple place names.

'The Monastery. The Village.'

I squeezed his hand and began leading Quadlopo up the path to the gatehouse. Behind me I could hear the heels of Rosie's boots grinding in the loose shale, and smiled as I thought about

Durral's lessons in the hidden words uttered by a person's footsteps.

All my arta loquit couldn't tell me if Rosie's apparent concern would be enough to make her come and get us if things went bad inside the convent.

15

The Gatehouse

The nun who occupied the gatehouse was a cheerful woman of middle years whose wide, amiable smile was contradicted by the crossbow she kept trained on me.

'Trundle along now, dearest,' she instructed me once we'd established that I spoke what the nun pleasantly referred to as a 'darlingly inept' Daroman dialect. 'You're not that pretty to begin with, and a crossbow bolt through the eye socket is unlikely to improve matters.'

The gatehouse was actually a windowed room built atop the massive stone arch that separated the convent from the outside world with a heavy iron gate. From her window at the top of the arch, the nun had both an excellent view of anyone approaching and a convenient spot from which to rain steel-tipped bolts down on them.

'Sister,' I began for the third time, 'as I keep trying to tell you, my name is Ferius Parfax, and I come to you on a mission of vital . . .'

The nun kept smiling even as she made it plain her index finger was tightening on the trigger, so I stopped talking.

'*What are you doing?*' Binta signed.

'*Abide,*' I signed back.

This was getting us nowhere. From what Rosie had said, the Red Nuns would expect me to show humility and submission before them. I'd done my best throughout my initial exchanges, and thus far politeness had won me only insults and threats. Was further bowing and scraping really going to earn my entrance? No doubt every pilgrim who made the journey up the mountain in search of arcane knowledge offered similarly passionate entreaties. In fact, wasn't it entirely likely that the Traveller had used them to worm herself inside these walls?

The Way of Water is the way of peace – of seeking to create and maintain balance between two people or nations. It's not begging. Attempting to use my arta loquit to convey the severity of the situation wasn't working. Time for a little arta valar.

I took two steps away from Quadlopo and Binta, and a third that brought me closer to the gatehouse.

'Oh, goody,' said the nun, adjusting the angle of her crossbow a fraction while using her free hand to place a quiver of bolts onto the stone shelf of her window. 'It's been ages since I've had any real target practice. Shall I begin with those unpleasantly green eyes of yours or that liar's mouth? Then when you turn tail and run, I can shoot off one of your flat, unwomanly buttocks.'

I'd never had someone disparage my buttocks before. Certainly not while threatening to shoot one of them off. I took another step closer to the gate and gave her a taste of her own medicine.

'Listen, you mule-faced canker sore. You already know why I'm here, so drop the act. You and your fellow senile old biddies got suckered by a lunatic into giving out secrets that have already put dozens, maybe hundreds, of innocent people into the ground.' I paused long enough to contemplate and discard one of Rosie's other warnings. 'Soon the entire continent's going to be ablaze with the *Red Scream* if somebody doesn't do something about it.'

I let myself get another half-step closer and made a show of leaning forward to peer across the distance between us. 'Now, since by the looks of you it's been a while since you've gotten off your arse long enough to wipe the drool off that rusted sheep-shooter – which, by the way, I can see from here has a sighting line that's off by a good eight degrees – somebody else is going to have to clean up your mess.'

The nun's crooked smile stayed where it was, but her eyes had narrowed. That didn't worry me though, because along the way she'd glanced at the angle of her bolt, which meant she wasn't sure I was lying about it, and that alone would put her aim off.

'And you, my dull-witted, future threepenny, back-alley hand-jobber, think you're the girl who can rectify the situation for us?'

Well, clearly they know something about the Red Scream and that some part of it at least came from here.

'I'm all you've got, lady.'

To my surprise, the nun's smirk grew into a grin. She set the crossbow aside and began turning some sort of crank from within her room at the top of the arch.

'Well then, best we get you inside to see the Mothers Superior.'

With a groan, the heavy iron gate began to rise to offer us passage beneath.

'Did you just say *Mothers* Superior?' I asked. 'There's more than one?'

Rosie hadn't mentioned anything about mothers, superior or otherwise. Now I was wondering what other surprises were waiting for us.

The nun laughed. It was a pleasant laugh that promised unpleasant discoveries to come. 'Oh, you'll see when you get inside, my delightful little arse-faced strumpet. A few words out of your filthy mouth and the Mothers will be most eager to make your acquaintance.'

As I led Quadlopo beneath the arch, Binta waved up at the nun in the gatehouse.

'*She's nice,*' the boy signed to me with his other hand. '*I like her.*'

The nun waved back, and said aloud, 'What a fine little boy you are, sweet one. The Red Nuns are going to eat you alive.'

16

The Confessorium

A second nun – this one a girl who looked younger than me yet shared the gatehouse keeper's propensity for verbalising her opinions regarding my appearance, demeanour and presumed sexual history – led me into the stone-walled compound. Her sleeveless crimson habit revealed supple shoulders and arms covered in a latticework of silver chains that ended in rings around each of her fingers and thumbs. The tresses that slipped out beneath the sister's hood – of an even purer red than mine – lent the ensemble an oddly militaristic appearance.

The Convent of Scarlet Words would've made a fine fortress, and as Binta had opined when he'd first seen it from a distance, the sloping walls followed the undulations of the mountaintop as if poured from a giant cauldron of molten stone. On closer inspection, however, the walls were of the typical cut-block construction you can find in any number of citadels across the continent. The calibre of work, however, suggested decades of patient, masterful labour, and a place designed as much for warfare as scholarship.

'You will enter the *confessorium* with the boy and await the Mothers Superior,' the young nun informed me, pointing to the arched entrance to a small domed building at the centre of the convent grounds. 'Touch anything inside, and you'll find yourself taking a much shorter and quicker route down the mountain than the one that brought you here. Walk outside those doors before you're given leave, and my sisters and I will break both your legs and drag you back inside until the Mothers Superior tell us they are done with you.' She looked up at Binta, who was still sitting on Quadlopo's back, staring around in awe at the courtyard. 'Is the child listening to me?'

'He doesn't hear,' I said, keeping my cool.

The young nun walked over and pinched Binta's leg. The boy's head swivelled round.

'That hurt!' he signed. *'Why did you—'*

'You will do as the ugly bitch does, understand?' the nun signed back.

I was impressed both with how quickly she'd determined that Binta used the Silent Garden's particular variant of a gesture-based language, given there had to be many across the continent, and how fluent she was in its usage.

Binta looked at me, confused and rubbing the sore spot on his thigh. *'Why does the pretty one hurt me, Good Dog? Did I do something wrong?'*

'It's not your fault. She's having a bad day. Her jaw is very sore.'

The nun turned. 'What are you talking abou—'

Now, Durral would want me to mention here that violence is not the Argosi way. Enna, on the other hand, would argue that there are, in fact, *four* Argosi ways – Water, Wind, Thunder and Stone – and each has its time and its place. Durral, despite his remarkable skills at arta eres, would've then pointed out that the world is mostly covered in water, not thunder, and *that* should guide a young teysan's choices. Enna would smile and nod, give him a big kiss on the lips and say how insightful he was. Later, she'd casually mention to me that big, strapping men can afford to ignore petty acts of violence done against them because the instigators rarely assume that gives them license to commit worse ones later. Now, Durral is wise to Enna's opinions on these matters and would therefore not have allowed me to go to bed that night without reminding me that with four ways and seven talents, an Argosi ought to be able to find the one path that allows them to preserve their own safety without resorting to bumbling fisticuffs with every ill-tempered bumpkin they come across.

As for me? I slugged the nun so hard she spun in a circle like I'd twirled her at the local festival dance.

She came up quickly, fists ready for a fight. I was suitably impressed, and punched her a second time in the exact same spot.

'Don't open your mouth,' I warned her as she glared up at me from the ground. 'You want me to follow your rules? Fine. I got business in these walls, and I aim to get it done. If that means putting up with your insults, well, sister, I've heard worse. But you lay hands on the boy without his consent again and I'll take you, your Mothers Superior and every other nasty piece of work infesting this mountaintop and teach you all the Way of Thunder. Got it?'

The nun spat on the ground. 'Argosi.'

'Damn straight,' I said, and lifted Binta off Quadlopo's saddle to set him on the ground.

I took his hand as the two of us walked towards the confessorium. As we neared the narrow, domed building, Binta and I both looked up and noted the faces carved into the stone above each of the seven arched doorways. Some of the faces were scowling, others snarling, still others laughing madly.

'*What is this place?*' Binta asked.

123

I couldn't imagine what the sign for confessorium might be, so I replied simply, 'A *place one makes confessions.*'

'*What are we to confess?*'

I pushed open the nearest door and led him inside.

'*Right now? I confess I don't much like these nuns.*'

17

The Mothers Superior

There were seven of them in all. Seven Mothers Superior garbed in sleeveless crimson habits with latticework of silver chains along their arms like those worn by the young nun outside. Heavy black cloaks covered their shoulders, trailing after them as they stepped inside the confessorium through seven different doors. Beneath their black hoods, I glimpsed strands of hair the same arresting shade of scarlet as that of the nun who had led me here. None of them appeared related, however, so I assumed they dyed it as part of some spiritual rite required by their order.

Four were old, which was unsurprising for the leaders of a convent, though two others looked to be in their thirties or forties and one couldn't have been more than twenty. This too seemed reasonable enough; you couldn't expect all the matriarchs to be septuagenarians. What *was* rather unusual – to my perhaps limited education in the affairs of religious hierarchies – was that two of the Mothers Superior appeared to be men.

'Does our presence offend you?' the younger of the two asked as he took his place in the circle that now surrounded me. His tone suggested he was less concerned with any prejudice on my part and more curious about what it said about me. 'We are mothers because each of us gives birth to our art, not because of what dangles between our legs.'

Binta, unhelpfully, signed, *'Why is that man dressed like a nun?'*

'Forgive me,' I said. 'We simply hadn't expected a Mother Superior to be a . . .'

The other fellow, beak-nosed, face wrinkled like wet leather left out in the sun too long, snapped his fingers to get my attention. He stared at me for a moment, then began rattling off words in such quick succession I had trouble distinguishing one from the other.

'Mother. Mom. Mammy. Matricide. Womb. Old Lady. Nurturer. Punisher. Foster mother. Procrea— Ah, there. Yes, you all see?'

The Mother Superiors on either side of the old man nodded. *'Foster mother.'*

The younger man snapped his fingers now, causing me to swivel my head in his direction. 'Tell us, orphan girl, was the womb of the woman who adopted you determinative of her role as your foster mother?'

'Are you even sure she *had* a womb?' one of the female Mothers asked with the customary snideness they all seemed to share. 'Were you careful to check her uterus for qualities suitable to providing you with a supportive home?'

'How did you know I had a foster moth—' I turned back to the older man. 'Those words you spoke to me. You were watching my face, looking for subtle cues in my spontaneous reaction to each one to determine my—'

'Behold,' another of the women, her features hidden beneath her hood save for her angular jaw and piercing blue eyes. 'The teysan purports to explain our own arts to us. What is it the Argosi call it? Arta loquit?'

'Eloquence,' the youngest of the women said dismissively. She had high cheekbones at odds with her small, almost sunken eyes. She reminded me of one of those tiny serpents you find in the copper desert region of the Seven Sands – the sort of snake that even much bigger snakes know to avoid.

'Such an infantile diminution of the stolen secrets of finer minds,' she said. 'Better that the Argosi had been wiped out centuries ago than allowed to fester as they do.'

Go on and keep spitting your venom at me, sister, I thought. *See what it gets you.*

The old man gave a sudden grunt. 'Did you see that, Mother Gossip? She didn't appreciate that observation at all, did she?'

'Indeed, Mother Sigh,' said the young woman. 'From this simple slight a crevice appears in her shell, so easily cracked.'

'Mothers Superior,' I began, as respectfully as my rebellious tongue would allow, 'I didn't come here to—'

The old man, 'Mother Sigh', took a creaking step towards me and snapped his wrinkled fingers in my face before again peppering me with a string of words.

'Father. Daddy. Dad. Dada. Papa. Pappy. Ah, there. *Pappy.* Interesting.'

Thus far the venerable nuns of the Convent of Scarlet Words hadn't given me much reason to enjoy their company. I had to hold my temper or risk getting into a scrap with the lot of them, which wouldn't get me anywhere closer to understanding the Red Scream.

'If there is something you wish to ask me,' I said through gritted teeth, 'then ask, and I will answer.'

The hooded woman with the blue eyes seemed unimpressed with my openness. 'Why would we bother to *ask* you anything? You'd only lie – to yourself if not to us. More effective by far to wrest the truth from you by our own means.'

A third snap of the fingers. This time it came from the youngest woman, Mother Gossip; the one who hissed when she spoke to me.

'Teacher. Tutor. Maetri. Lover. Abuser. Scholar. Saviour . . .'

'There it is,' observed a heavyset woman on my right who'd been silent until now. 'She saw him as her saviour. How typical.'

'But what did he save, I wonder, Mother Rumour?' The young one – the snake – began circling me, pairing each step with a snap of her fingers and another word. 'Mind. Sanity. Body. Dignity. Soul. Purpose.' She stopped, and her tiny eyes widened. 'Oh, my. Did you all see that? A saviour of not merely one part of her being but *all* parts? Quite the fellow this "Pappy" must've been.'

Nods and mumbles of agreement followed her as she stepped back into her position in the circle.

Binta tugged at my sleeve. *'Good Dog, what are they doing?'*

I began to answer, but my fingers were trembling, garbling the signs. My breathing was too fast, trying to keep pace with the pounding of my heart. I felt dizzy. The nuns were doing more than just pelting me with words to snatch pieces of my history from my reactions. They were tampering with my emotions somehow. Opening me up like an old book, reading in my expressions things that I didn't want read.

Arta valar, I told myself. *Enna said that the purpose of daring is to free the spirit from the burden of being and allow the Argosi to become their deeds rather than their thoughts.*

My past didn't matter. My future didn't exist. I was here to acquire information about the Scarlet Verses and the Traveller. If the clucking of these unpleasant red hens allowed them to glean some insight into my upbringing, well, Durral always did advocate for the Way of Water. Give them what they want and move on.

But I didn't have to kiss their feet while I was doing it.

'They're showing off,' I informed Binta, my fingers calmer now. *'Lonely old women and men need to feel important sometimes. Let us allow them this small gift to feed their starving hearts.'*

One of the Mothers Superior, the oldest person in that seven-sided room, smiled, revealing a mouth of missing teeth and a tongue that licked her lips even as she signed at Binta in the silent voice.

'The one you call Good Dog comes here seeking truth yet holds secrets of her own. Such a one is not deserving of your trust. Let us see what she hides inside herself.'

The six others began signing as well, all at once, fingers twirling in a cacophony of silent speech.

'Mother Chatter is right,' the young man who'd first spoken signed. *'Let us know more of this wanderer who came begging wisdom from us yet threatened one of our sisters and struck another.'*

'Indeed, Mother Murmur,' agreed one of the others, whose age I couldn't determine because whenever she spoke I found myself looking away. *'Violent desires lurk deep inside her, chained only by shame. Let us loosen the shackles and see from whence this shame comes.'*

'Yes,' concurred the others. They were all signing on top of each other now.

'Let us see.'

'Let us hear.'

'Make her dance for us, Mother Murmur.'

The younger of the two men took this as his cue. He stepped forward and started snapping his fingers at me yet again. Pretty soon I was going to have to break some finger bones.

'You plannin' on recitin' the dictionary at me all day to count the number of times I blink, or can we get down to business?' I asked.

'"*Plannin*'",' the young one, Mother Gossip, mimicked. 'Did you hear that, Mother Drawl?'

'An emulation,' agreed a pleasant-faced woman standing to her left who, ironically, spoke without any discernible drawl or accent herself. 'We may presume this is associated with the one she calls "Pappy".'

'*Business*,' the old man, Mother Sigh, added. 'A deflection towards the impersonal. There is much the teysan hides. Proceed, Mother Murmur.'

The man came closer, and it seemed to me that I could taste his breath when he spoke to me. 'You will tell us of the circumstances that brought you here. Nothing will be held back. Every rudimentary thought, every word, every childish sob you will perform just as it happened. This you will do, and only once it is done will we decide whether to answer your questions or dispose of you off the side of the mountain for your impertinence in violating this sanctuary with your lies and your violence.'

My temper was going to get the best of me if these people didn't stop messing with me. Only Binta's presence and my nagging awareness that Rosie was counting on us to acquire information about the Scarlet Verses kept my tongue civil.

'Yes, Mothers Superior. That's what I've been trying to do since I got here. Now, I first became aware of the plague when—'

'No,' Mother Murmur said, cutting me off with another snap of his fingers. 'That is not *your* violence. Yours is personal. Intimate. It drives you, compels your every decision. We must witness the nature of your shame before we reveal our own.'

'I . . . I don't know what you're talking about. I'm here because of the Red Scream, not some—'

'She will be difficult, this one.' Mother Murmur turned to his colleagues. 'Beneath her feeble mutterings you can see the turnings of her thoughts. They twist and twirl even more than those of other Argosi.'

'She is broken,' said the young snake, Mother Gossip.

130

I was starting to wonder what I'd done to piss her off. Usually it takes people more than a few minutes to summon up this much dislike towards me.

'Not quite broken,' said the eldest, toothless one, Mother Chatter. 'Rather say that she is *bent*. Now, a tool must be bent to find its proper shape, or it can be bent too far, shattering it entirely and rendering it useful only when melted down into its raw materials. Let us see which way this one bends.'

Something strange happened then. They all began snapping their fingers and shouting at me at the same time. Words. More words. So fast I couldn't tell who was saying what, yet somehow my mind was picking each one out, responding to it. I tried reaching for one of my throwing cards, but my hands were shaking so badly I cut the skin of my own fingers. The nuns' chatter battered about inside my mind, a storm that blew away the dust of my own thoughts, leaving behind an emptiness that began to fill with something else. Something I didn't want inside me.

A compulsion overtook me, stripping away defences I hadn't known I had – those simple, fundamental barriers we place between ourselves and those memories we can't endure.

The Mothers tore those protections away from me, and soon I heard an eighth voice echoing around the seven walls of the confessorium.

My own.

I began to talk, and in that talking not only recounted the tale they demanded from me, but relived every awful second of it.

'No, *please*,' I found my fingers signing. They were the only parts of me still under my control. '*Don't make me do this!*'

But it was too late.

In that damnable little domed building, surrounded by seven strangers, I told the story of how I had lost any right I would ever have to call myself an Argosi.

I told the story of what I did to Enna.

18

Enna

I don't know much about the conflicts of great nations or the wars waged by opposing armies, but I do know this: there is no battle so fierce as that between mother and daughter.

'Oh, Ferius . . . What have you done?'

I'm awake as she comes to the door of my bedroom. I'm curled up in my bedding, head perfectly nestled into my pillow. The fire from the hearth downstairs sends its delicious warmth up through the ceiling, past the upper-storey floorboards and into my mattress and sheets before soothing the bruises on my naked skin. The ointments I stole from Enna's cupboard ease the burns on my back and the cuts – hastily stitched in my own slapdash style – on my left shoulder and right forearm. The aches and pains crowded into the bed with me don't hurt though. I'm proud of them. It's that pride that will fuel the coming strife between Enna and myself. My smart mouth provides the spark.

'I taught him a lesson.'

She's standing in the doorway, a shadow lit from behind by the oil lantern hanging in the hallway. It's only when she steps inside that I can see her properly, and for a second my smug self-satisfaction wavers.

'You taught him a lesson?' she echoes, but I already know she's not expecting an answer.

Enna has that type of beauty that Durral refers to with dubious romanticism as being, 'like a forest'.

'Ain't the individual trees that make a wood lovely, kid. It's how they all fit together.'

He liked to say that he could spend every day of the rest of his life wandering through that forest and never see all its hidden wonders – though he was damned well going to try.

Looking at Enna is different for me. I guess there's always a tension between foster mother and daughter. How can that sacred bond, formed when a child emerges from the womb, still tethered body and soul to its mother, ever truly exist between two people who were strangers? There's always that uncertainty – that suspicion – that if you look deep enough into your foster mother's eyes, past all their dutiful affection, you'll hit a wall that reminds you they could never love you as much as they would their own flesh and blood.

So when *I* say that Enna's beauty is like a forest, I'm not talking about what Durral sees in her. I mean that in those eighteen months since he'd brought me into their home, plunked me in front of her and said he wanted them to adopt me, every time I'd scoured her gaze for some boundary or border that signified a limit to her love for me – every time – I found myself deep inside an endless forest waiting to embrace me and hold me lovingly for all of my days.

Until today.

'You nearly killed that boy,' she says.

'He's not a boy,' I correct her, still snuggled under my covers, unwilling to acknowledge the seriousness of what I've done – or what I fear so badly is coming. 'He's a Jan'Tep mage. Older than me.'

Dak'alid of the House of Dak – what's left of him, anyway – is eighteen years old. That puts him at two years past his mage trials. Old enough to call himself a war mage. Old enough to know better.

Like other Jan'Tep who form hunter covens to track down stray Mahdek refugees around the borderlands, he goes by an alias so that any failures or embarrassments won't be traced back to his family. He calls himself Silk Wolf. He was kind enough to give me his true name after I beat it out of him.

Silk Wolf and two other young mages, who went by Iron Serpent and Ember Frog (you knew that guy was the least powerful of the group to get stuck with that lousy name) had decided that their clan prince's decree some eighteen months ago, forbidding the tormenting of those few remaining Mahdek still trying to make a life for themselves in the Seven Sands, was more of a suggestion than a law. Besides, hunting Mahdek was a rite of passage for young mages – proof they had the calibre of magic and determination necessary to protect the Jan'Tep nation.

The pickings were slim, of course. There aren't a lot of my people left. Weeks of trekking through the desert, dozens of tracking spells, and all they'd gotten for their troubles was one old coot, the last of his clan, who'd had the misfortune to set up shop as an apothecary in a village sorely in need of one.

Our trio of brave mages must've been disappointed, because they made the old man run a long while. Alone in the desert, knees and lungs failing him, dying the slow death of those who've seen that the quick ones ain't so quick when they're coming at the end of an ember spell, he somehow made it all the way to the next village. The fine folk who lived there stood around and watched in suitable horror as the three young mages punished him for crimes that – if they'd ever happened at all – had been committed by his ancestors three hundred years ago during a long-forgotten war.

But hey, when you're burning a filthy Mahdek demon-worshipper alive, who needs evidence or a trial, right?

After it was done, Silk Wolf, Iron Serpent and Ember Frog spent the next three weeks getting drunk, prancing about in small towns giving speeches about the moral supremacy of the Jan'Tep people. And, of course, hunting for more Mahdek. They were about to return home when they got word of a lost Mahdek girl – red-haired the way the worst of them always were – wandering around the desert. Alone. Weak. Frightened.

'You tricked those boys,' Enna says to me.

There's a plaintive note in her voice. She wants me to see reason – to see the world through her eyes. Durral's eyes. Enna wants me to follow the Path of the Rambling Thistle, as they do.

'No one forced them to attack me.'

'You set an ambush for them,' she says. 'It's not the first time you've done this either. You abuse the skills Durral and I teach you, turn the talents meant to help you find your path into weapons so you can get a little taste of revenge against the Jan'Tep for all the hurt they've done you.'

I'm starting to taste copper on my tongue, like I do before a fight. I try to remind myself that Enna's the wisest person I've ever met, and that she has no idea how self-righteous she sounds right now.

'Maybe this is *my* path, Enna. Have you ever considered that? Three hundred years the Jan'Tep have been hunting my people.'

I pull down the blankets, revealing the tattooed sigils around my neck, imprinted there by two mages who used me for experiments so foul even their own clan prince decreed they were a crime.

'Those markings are fading, Ferius,' she says, practically pleading with me. 'Every day they fade a little more, but you keep etching them onto your own heart with all this hate you're holding on to. The mage who did this to you is dead.'

'Shadow Falcon isn't.'

'He's never touched you since. He abides by the deal Durral made with that Jan'Tep clan prince. When you came to live with us, Ferius, you told me you'd let go of your hate for that boy, that "Shadow Falcon" as he called himself.'

I scratch at one of the sigils around my neck. They didn't itch or burn any more, but sometimes I scratched at them just the same.

'Well, turns out the hate came back.'

'Oh, Ferius,' she says, and there's more sadness in the way she says my name than I've ever heard in her. 'Can't you see the prison you're building for yourself? Whoever this Shadow Falcon is, he's probably off making a new life for himself. Maybe he's found himself a wife. They marry young, those Jan'Tep. By now he may even have a child he loves so much he—'

'Don't,' I warn her. The word comes out in a growl, like I was turning into some rabid dog foaming at the mouth. 'Don't make out like Shadow Falcon was just some confused teenager who got led astray by a cabal of mages!' I slam my fist on the bedspread, a gesture both unsatisfying and embarrassing. It only makes my anger worse. 'He nearly destroyed my life! If he has a wife, then she's my enemy too! If they have a kid, then guess what, Enna? That kid is gonna be—'

'What, Ferius? Your enemy? Some little boy or girl who's never met you?' She starts laughing, a warm, welcoming sound that beckoned you to join in.

'What the hell are you laughing at?' I demand.

She shakes her head. 'Just got this funny image in my head. You, stomping into some Jan'Tep oasis, out for blood, seeing some dumb kid standing there, shaking like a leaf, probably facing off against some other dumb kid because those people make their own children fight each other with spells to prove they're worthy of calling themselves mages. Maybe Shadow Falcon's kid gets hurt. Needs help real bad. You know what my arta tuco tells me you're going to do then, Ferius Parfax?'

'Stop it!' I shout, slamming my palms against my ears because I can't bear to hear another word. I love Enna and Durral. I admire everything about the Argosi. I want to be one so bad it's like a song inside me I know I'm meant to sing if I can just find the words. But she's pushing me too far, too fast. I'm not ready to be like her yet. I'm not ready to forgive.

'Ferius,' she says, 'letting go of hate is only the first price we pay to become Argosi. There's a lot more that come after. If you can't take that first step—'

'They killed an old man!' I scream at her. 'Hurled fire and lightning at him from their hands until there was nothing left of him! No proof of the crime they'd committed!'

'So you broke the bones in their hands. You broke them in a way that'll never heal right.'

I know I shouldn't do it, but I can't stop myself. I grin at my foster mother, who I adore and look up to more than anyone in the world, even Durral, and who I know would be repelled by the feral joy on my face if he were here. I make it worse by speaking in a mockery of the way he does. 'Can't cast no spells if you ain't got no fingers.'

Enna turns and starts to walk out of the room. For a moment, I'm relieved. I know I've said things I shouldn't. I know, even now, that the fear and pain and despair I put in the eyes of those three boys is going to haunt me in a way that their killing of the old Mahdek man will never haunt them. Right now, though, I need to let myself revel in that memory. I need to gloat. I need to hate.

Tomorrow.

Tomorrow I'll let the guilt in, and listen to Enna tell me that the Way of the Argosi is the Way of Water, and no path worth walking ever leads to revenge.

Tomorrow I might even believe it.

'Get up,' she says.

You can't know what it's like to hear Enna speak unless you can imagine words that soothe and warm and comfort with every syllable. Now her voice is so cold it steals all the heat from my bed. It's so cold that when I try to open my mouth to refuse, I can't find the breath. It's so cold that even though I'm determined to just lie there, I find myself pushing the covers aside and rising to my feet, hoping that when she sees me standing there, naked, bruised and miserable, she'll relent. But she's not looking at me. She's already heading out of the room and down the stairs.

'Bring your sword,' she says.

19

The Lesson

'No more,' I gesture with my fingers to the Mothers Superior. *'Don't make me relive this, please!'*

They aren't listening, just talking. Words I know, words I don't. They mutter and mumble and whisper at me, snapping their fingers – always snapping their fingers to draw me into their babble. Every word is another lead weight on the chain hanging heavy around my neck, pulling me down, all the way down, into the memories of what came next.

'Please,' I sign to the Mothers again. It's the only one my fingers can still make.

'Please.'

'Please.'

'Please, Mamma, come back inside!'

My travelling shirt and trousers cling to me uncomfortably. They're caked in dust and grime from the road and stained with the blood of the three mages I fought. All I want to do is be rid of them, to go back to bed and pretend for one more night that I'm Enna's daughter.

Enna's not listening though. She's out in the back garden, one of her rapiers in hand. It's not the blunted practice one she uses to teach me fencing. This isn't like her. Enna's wise, calm, controlled. She's not as much a pacifist as Durral, but still she believes with all her heart in the Path of the Rambling Thistle – that one can seek the truth and protect the innocent without succumbing to violence and cruelty.

'Get out here,' she says.

'I won't fight you,' I tell her, walking down the steps so that she can see my face lit by moonlight. See that I'm sorry, that I'm ready to listen.

She takes three steps back, leaving me the smoother ground of the garden. 'Get your blade up.'

'I won't fight you, Mamma,' I say again. 'I could never hurt you.'

'Of course you can. You hurt those boys, didn't you?'

'That was different! They were killers! Monsters!'

She's so still it's like she's not even there. A silhouette you think you see in front of you that turns out to be a shadow cast by a tree.

'There's no such thing as monsters, Ferius. Now get your blade up.'

Why is she doing this? She's never been this way with me before. It's like I'm some stranger who wandered into her garden.

I try to find my own calm, to fill myself so full of peace that it seeps out my mouth and spreads into the garden to bridge the gap between Enna and me.

'I told you, I won't hurt you,' I tell her.

'Really?' she asks.

'Yes, really!'

'Are you sure?'

'Of course I'm sure! Mamma, I could nev—'

'Then why did you bring your sword?'

All of a sudden I'm staring at the smallsword in my hand. She told me to bring it. *Ordered* me to bring it. But why did I? Why

141

didn't I just leave the sword in the old leather mapmaker's case in my room, come out here and beg her forgiveness and promise to never again abuse the Argosi talents even though in my heart I still believe I had the right to do what I did to those mages.

'You brought the sword because you can't help yourself,' she says.

I'm still looking down at the weapon. It's like it belongs to somebody else and I just picked it up off the street. I want to throw it away, but the hilt feels so good in my hand that all I can do is squeeze it tighter.

'They murdered that old man,' I say.

'That they did.'

'I didn't force them to attack me. I just let them come. They would've killed me if they could. I had the right to kill them in return.'

'That you did.'

'Then why are you doing this?' I ask, trying to find her eyes in the moonlight. All I see in the darkness are two tiny black holes where her love for me has always been, ever since the first day I walked into her home. 'I had to stop them! I had to—'

'What would've happened if you hadn't?' she asks.

'They would've gotten away with it! They would've gone back to their city and boasted to their friends about how they bravely faced a Mahdek demon-worshipper and rid the world of one more of their people's ancient enemies.'

'And then what?'

'What do you mean?'

'Use your arta tuco, Ferius. What would've happened next?'

I want to scream at her that I don't know, or invent some theory that more young Jan'Tep mages would've taken up the cause and gone out raining more misery and ember spells on the world. It's plausible, isn't it?

142

Arta tuco.

The Argosi talent for strategy. Its most basic use is finding paths out of seemingly inescapable scenarios, but it's also the means by which you figure out how a situation will unfold if left alone.

I can't tell her I don't know, because I *do* know exactly what would've happened next. The clan prince of Oatas Jan'Dal had made it his decree that there could be no more attacks upon the Mahdek. Those three idiots would've bragged all over town about their exploits. The clan prince couldn't allow such a violation of his commandments. He would've rounded them up, held a trial. The three would've been counter-banded, taking away their ability to use magic, and exiled. Their houses would've been forced to make restitution. Since the old man likely had no family, the heads of some very important Jan'Tep houses would've had to go out and make that restitution to his clan, or his tribe, or failing that, to any Mahdek they could find, knowing that failing to do so would result in their own exile.

'What will happen now, Ferius?'

I don't answer, because I don't want to have to say it out loud. Those three will run back to their city. They won't admit to having killed the old man. Instead they'll tell the story of how an Argosi ambushed them and shattered the bones in their fingers. The clan prince's enemies will use this as proof that his policies of peaceful co-existence are doing exactly what the Jan'Tep fear most: demonstrating weakness to their enemies, both real and imagined. Word will get out to other Jan'Tep cities, and resentment will spread. Silk Wolf, Iron Serpent and Ember Frog will become martyrs in a cause that stretches back three hundred years and, thanks to me, might go on for three hundred more.

I can see it all so clearly now, just like some part of me must've seen it even before I'd gone after those three boys.

Durral always says that the problem with becoming an Argosi is that once you learn to see the world as it truly is, you no longer have the excuse of being blind.

I have made the lives of my people worse than they already were. I have allowed my desperate, burning desire for violence against those who hurt me in the past to make the world a meaner place than it was – than it would've been even if those three mages had gotten away with their crime entirely. I should be ashamed. I *am* ashamed.

But I'm also proud of having hurt those boys.

And I can't seem to make that pride go away.

'Durral is out there now,' Enna says, gesturing off to the west, 'finding those three mages. Do you know what he's doing?'

'Don't,' I warn her.

She knows me too well, I realise now. Knows me better than I know myself. She ought to know better than to keep talking.

'He's following the Way of Water. He's going to apologise to those Jan'Tep boys. Heal their wounds as best he can. Beg them for forgiveness. Offer them money. It won't work, of course. So tomorrow, Durral Brown, who tries so hard to live a peaceful life yet despises bullies and tyrants so much he spends his whole time struggling to rid himself of that hatred, is going to have to set out for their city, and bow and scrape before their clan prince and their families, making more promises. More deals. Hoping that if he can make the Argosi look small and subservient, the Jan'Tep will feel big and powerful.'

'He shouldn't do that,' I say, and now it's my voice that's gone colder than the night air. 'He's got no right to make amends with my enemies. Just like *you've* got no right to carp at me for doing what the Argosi should've been doing all along.'

'Get your point up, *teysan*.'

144

She hardly ever uses that word. I see her blade glistening in the dim light like an accusing finger. I slap it away with my smallsword.

'Leave me alone, Enna.'

Her blade is right back where it was a second ago. Now I'm not even sure if I hit it.

'You need to see.'

'See what?'

I keep expecting her to attack me, but she doesn't. At least, not with her sword. Her words, though – those are sharp as razors.

'The lesson Durral's too afraid to teach you.'

I don't know what it is that sets me off. Why those words and not any of the others? What's so terrifying to me about what she's just said that makes me go after her, the tip of my sword darting through the night air so fast neither of us can see it and we're both thrusting and parrying on instinct rather than skill? I nearly drop my weapon when her tip pierces the skin on the back of my hand. I barely feel it.

'What's this grand lesson then?' I ask, cutting and slashing and lunging at her over and over. I should be awkward, clumsy on account of my anger, but I'm not. My every attack is precise. Flawless. Deadly. 'Come on, Enna. Teach me. Teach me about the Way of Water, and the deals I should be making with those who massacred my clan and tortured me over and over and over! Teach me about the Way of Wind, and how I should ignore it whenever I hear that there are more Jan'Tep mages out there hunting for people like me! Teach me about the Way of Thunder, and how I should never use it unless you and Durral tell me to! Teach me about the Way of Stone, so that I can take the pommel of my sword and smash it to pieces!'

My slashes become wild. Savage. Reckless. My technique is gone. There's no dancing here, no arta eres. I'm just a blundering child swinging a sword that feels so light she can't even tell that . . .

145

That . . .

I finally stop and look down at my hand, wondering why I can't feel the weight of the weapon any more. The answer is that I'm not holding it. My hand is empty.

When I look up, Enna's silhouette is still there, the shadow of a woman standing before me, only the shape is wrong somehow. Something's sticking out of her chest.

It's the hilt of my smallsword.

As if she has been waiting for me all this time, holding herself upright until at last the madness had left me, she says, 'Here endeth the lesson,' and collapses to her knees.

I run to her. She's got her hands wrapped around the blade of my smallsword and starts pulling it out.

'Mamma, don't!'

'Got to . . . get it out,' she says.

There's blood. So much blood. Why can I see the blood so clearly when I can't see anything else in this darkness?

As the blade finally comes all the way out, and the smallsword drops to the grassy ground, she falls into my arms.

'Mamma? Mamma, please! Don't—'

She reaches into the pocket of her trousers, pulls out a vial of *oleus regia* and hands it to me. I've never seen this much of it before. The ointment is one of the most powerful healing agents there is, but even as I slather it all over the wound, I'm doubtful it can save her.

'Meant to use it on you,' she says, wheezing. My sword punctured one of her lungs. 'In case you got scraped up in the fight.' Her laugh is both brittle and wet.

'I'm sorry, Mamma. I didn't mean—'

'My own fault,' she says. 'Thought I could . . . let you see what's inside you without . . . forgot you're so fast, my girl. So very fast.

146

People think that's good, but it's not. What is it Durral always says? *"The hand is quicker than the eye but should never be faster than the heart?"'*

I tear the sleeve from my shirt and start bandaging her with it. 'Mamma, stop talking. I've got to get you inside and—'

'No. Ferius, you've got to run.'

'What? No! I'll stay and—'

'Durral's going to be back soon from gathering supplies for his trip to the Jan'Tep territories. When he sees me . . . Ferius, he's not . . . he won't understand. He'll kill you.'

'Good,' I say, sobbing over her. 'It's what I deserve!'

She shakes her head, coughing up blood. 'You don't understand. Durral . . . he was never really meant to walk the Path of the Rambling Thistle. That's *my* path. He just . . . it was the only way we could be together. Do you understand? That's why he tries so hard all the time. It's why he never . . . Ferius, if he hurts you, he steps off the path forever. We won't be able to be together again.' She starts crying, and it's not from the pain or even the fear of dying. 'I don't want to live without him. I don't want to die knowing he'll be lost.' She grabs my arm and squeezes. 'Please, Ferius. I love him. Don't let him find you. Don't make me lose him.'

'Mamma . . .'

Even now she gives of herself to me. Against all the pain and anguish she must be feeling, she pulls an Argosi smile to her lips. 'I'm a tough bird, my love. We'll see each other again, I promise. But right now, darling, you've got to run. Run, and keep running.'

I'm so full of tears that won't come out, I'm drowning in them. Some small part of me wakes up though, and remembers that the first thing Enna tried to teach me is that an Argosi doesn't allow guilt, shame and grief to steer them off their path.

Even if they don't yet know what their path is.

I smear the rest of the oleus regia on her chest more carefully now. I run inside the house and get bandages and wrap the wound the way she taught me. I wrap her up in blankets, put a pillow under her head. It's too dangerous to move her. When I'm certain I've done everything for her that can be done, I go back inside and grab my things. I get Quadlopo from the barn and saddle him up. I take my smallsword with me, because to do otherwise would be to pretend it's not part of me. I kiss my mother on the forehead, tell myself that my lips felt the warmth of her skin.

And I run, pursued by the chilling voice inside my head that reminds me that even an Argosi like Enna hardly ever survives a wound like the one I gave her.

20

The Silence

My senses returned to me one by one. The taste of salty tears on my lips. The ache in my knees where I'd fallen to the confess-orium's stone floor. The smell of the seven nuns surrounding me. Lilac. Garlic. Sweat. I opened my eyes and saw the old man, Mother Sigh, being held up by the youngest woman in the room, Mother Gossip, on his left, and by the oldest, Mother Chatter, at his right. At first I thought the confessorium had descended into silence, but then my hearing returned and I listened to the sound of my own sobbing.

The Mothers Superior all looked weary, perhaps as exhausted from their exertions as I was from being the victim of them.

Binta was kneeling next to me, rubbing a hand awkwardly up and down my arm. With his other, he signed, *'Good Dog. You are Good Dog. You are here with me and nowhere else.'*

'I am Good Dog,' I assured him. *'I am here with you.'*

With the boy's help I rose to my feet. Tears were still streaming down my cheeks. My guts churned from too much misery and shame. I swallowed it all and faced the Mothers Superior of the Convent of Scarlet Words.

'Your turn,' I said.

The youthful and waspish Mother Gossip elected to speak first. The curl of her lip and narrowing of her eyes told me she was about to launch into another snide comment about primitive Argosi daring to make demands of their betters. I held up a finger to silence her. If I was to honour Enna and Durral's teachings I should probably limit the number of nuns I punched in the face on any given day. So I turned to Mother Drawl. She'd spoken the least of any of them, and therefore the sight of her didn't cause my fist to clench quite so tightly.

'You,' I said.

Outrage played across the expressions of her colleagues, but she merely chuckled. A low sound, deep, as if it began in her belly and didn't need to reach her mouth to be heard. I found it unexpectedly comforting.

'You have confessed your crime to us, Ferius Parfax. And yes, it is only fitting that we confess ours to you in return.' She spread her hands, palms out. An unusually submissive gesture for these people. 'Where would you like us to begin?'

There were a thousand questions I wanted to ask her. How had they reduced me to a blubbering mess with only a few words? Was the Red Scream some kind of variant of what they'd done to me? Were these reclusive nuns the true originators of the Argosi talent of arta siva? What other secret skills were hidden in this convent in the mountains?

The memory of those kind and decent folk back in Tinto Rhea, eyes filled with hate, hands curled like claws grabbing for us, wide-open mouths pooled with blood from their chewed-off tongues hissing their madness at me, reminded me why I was here.

'The Scarlet Verses,' I said, ignoring Rosie's warning not to call them that in front of the nuns. I didn't much care about their feelings at this point. 'These combinations of words that drive people insane. The Traveller got them from you, didn't she?'

Mother Drawl folded her hands over the thick scarlet fabric covering her ample belly. The gesture struck me as almost penitent. 'We believe so.'

'She came to us many months ago,' said Mother Chatter, tongue running along her gums as if searching for her missing teeth. I wondered if the vagueness of her statement was due to failing memory or caution about how much to reveal to me. 'Young. Quiet. Pretty, as I recall.'

Young. Quiet. Pretty.

'I don't suppose I could trouble you for something more specific?' I asked.

'We hardly pay attention to trivialities,' Mother Gossip said, apparently deciding her smart mouth was a necessary addition to the conversation.

'Is that so?'

She took my question poorly. 'We are explorers of the realm of thought, Argosi. Scholars of a discipline so foreign to simple minds such as yours that to give it a name would serve only to obscure its true meaning. We are guardians of arts so potent they would cause a Jan'Tep lord magus to abandon their magic as futile and childlike.'

Spoken like someone who's never had a blast of ember magic singe their eyebrows.

'Fine, then how about you scribble down the words I need to cure those afflicted by the Red Scream and I'll be on my way so you can get back to your oh-so-important studies? Or if a mere Argosi like me isn't up to the job, one of you saddle up and come with me.'

'We cannot,' Mother Murmur said. Even beneath his scarlet robes he looked more warrior than nun. From the look in his eyes

I guessed he was neither accustomed to nor fond of feeling helpless. 'We don't know how the verses work.'

'What do you mean, you don't know how? Ten minutes ago you were messing with my head, making me—'

'That was different,' Mother Chatter said.

'Different how?'

The old woman came closer to me, stopping just inches away. Her breath smelled of mint leaves chewed to cover the stench of rot and the slow succumbing of the body's internal organs to death soon to come. 'May I demonstrate?' she asked.

'*Now* you decide to ask my permission?'

'Before we did not know you, child. Our relations with the Argosi are –' she glanced back at Mother Gossip – 'occasionally somewhat fraught.'

I caught the younger nun's scowl, and though I had no evidence, I would've bet all the coins in my pocket that she was at least part of the reason why Rosie was insistent that she wasn't welcome back to this place.

When this is done, Rosie, you and me are having a talk about which secrets you're allowed to keep and which ones I need to know.

Mother Chatter's frail, unsteady hand rested on my arm. 'Please, Ferius Parfax. Allow me to demonstrate the way our abilities work. It will make it easier for you to perceive our limitations.'

The fact that she was so insistent on getting my consent told me I wasn't going to like this one bit. But she was right; I needed to understand more about how simple words could have such power over me.

'Go ahead,' I said at last.

The nun stood there a moment, the wisps of thin, sparse red hair sticking out of her black hood fluttering as she took in a slow, deep breath. Her eyes rose to meet mine and she snapped her fingers seven times, pairing each snap with a word.

'Bed. Bruise. Shame. Ointment. Soothing. Tomorrow. Tomorrow.'

That was the last thing I heard before I passed out.

21

The Loquatium

When next I opened my eyes I was staring up at a beautifully painted ceiling, its vivid colours depicting songbirds fluttering among the clouds. Out of their mouths emerged fantastical realms. Castles, forests, oceans and even the stars themselves.

Singing the world into being, I thought, which was rather poetic, for me.

I was lying on the floor, which was cold and hard, but there was a pillow under my head. I found the contrast confusing. First thing I did was check for any kind of shackles or restraints around my wrists or ankles. There were none. That would be convenient for when I punched that kindly old nun in the nose.

'She's awake,' came Mother Drawl's contralto voice.

Seven hooded faces were arrayed across my field of vision. Mothers Gossip, Chatter, Sigh, Drawl, Murmur, Rumour, and—

'*Good Dog,*' Binta signed, pushing between two of the nuns to stand over me, '*are you okay? You fell asleep!*'

Poor kid, I thought. *He's got no idea what's going on here. First he sees me rant and rage, then sob uncontrollably, and then I pass out right in front of him. Probably thinks I've lost it entirely.*

I sat up, fought against the dizziness and took in my surroundings. This place had a similar shape to the confessorium, but was vastly larger, and where the seventh wall would have been, the room stretched out into a long rectangular area, as if the building was shaped like a giant key. There were desks at the far end, and I could just make out small figures seated at them.

I rose unsteadily to my feet and glanced at the other walls, each of which was lined with oak shelves filled with books and rolled-up pieces of parchment tied with ribbons.

'Is this some sort of scriptorium?' I asked.

'Not exactly,' Mother Drawl replied, putting a hand on my shoulder to steady me. 'We call this the *loquatium*.'

'Never heard of it,' I said.

'Because you aren't meant to, Argosi.'

Seriously, sister, I thought wearily, turning to meet Mother Gossip's glare, *just how bad are you looking for a scrap?*

'It was decided,' Mother Drawl said, and I got the impression there'd been considerable debate prior to my awakening, 'that we could best convey the knowledge you seek inside these walls.'

'How long was I out?' I signed to Binta.

'Almost an hour,' he replied. *'The nuns made many angry faces at each other.'*

Well, that was something, at least.

I turned to Mother Chatter.

'You knocked me out,' I accused the frail old woman.

'I uttered seven words. Your mind put you to sleep.'

'But . . . how is that possible? Anyone shouts those seven words and whoever they're talking to faints?'

'There is a great deal more to it than shouting, my dear,' she said, pausing as her tongue ran across those old gums of hers again. 'Tone. Diction. Fluctuations of volume. All of these, in combination, yes, with those specific words, become a kind of formula. A potion for the mind. *Your* mind.'

'Bed. Bruise. Shame. Ointment . . .' I recited. 'Those were all words I used in the story you made me tell.'

The old woman nodded. 'They hold special meaning to you now, Ferius Parfax, and uttered in that precise combination, with the exact tonal modes I used, will cause you to want to sleep.'

Before I could press her further, she stepped back as if she were having trouble staying on her feet. Mother Murmur offered her his arm and took over the explanations. 'This is the way of language. It is only loosely true to say that any of us "share" a tongue. While you and I might both see a feline and call it a "cat", there are layers upon layers of meanings within that word that will be different for you than for me.'

That all made a certain kind of sense. The first lesson of arta loquit is the recognition that if beauty is in the eye of the beholder, then eloquence is in the ear of the listener. In making me recount one of the most traumatic events of my life, the nuns had harvested from my story the words needed to control me.

No wonder Rosie didn't want to come back to this place.

Something else was bothering me though.

'The Scarlet Verses,' I said. 'The Traveller wrote them down for one of the villagers to read aloud. Told him it was a poem to commemorate the dead. He didn't even know what most of the words meant. How could they have worked on the entire village unless . . .' I looked up to see the furtive glances being shared by the Mothers Superior. 'Some words, some combinations of syllables, work on everyone, don't they?'

It was Mother Sigh, the old man, who replied. 'It is the highest form of our art. The one to which we all aspire.'

'How does it—'

156

'Come,' Mother Chatter said, taking my arm as if she was my gran. With her free hand she reached down to take hold of Binta's, and led us along the arched hallway towards the desks at the far end. The rest of the Mothers Superior followed.

The figures I'd spotted before were actually a group of a dozen children, some as young as Binta, the others a few years older. All were girls save one.

'It is rare we find the talent in boys,' Mother Chatter explained to me. 'They lack –' she got one of those weird old-lady smiles on her face you're supposed to nod at to agree how wise they are – 'subtlety.'

The children all stood to attention when we arrived, like little soldiers waiting for inspection. Mother Gossip went to take her place before them. Evidently she was the general. She glanced back at Mother Chatter with an expression that said quite clearly that this was a bad idea.

'Go on now,' Mother Chatter told her. 'If one of them has the skill.'

Mother Gossip aimed a finger at the children, sliding past each one in turn until she stopped at a girl who was perhaps seven years old.

'You,' she said. 'The ninth fundament and the second. Third derivation with the flutter.'

'Daroman, Mother?' she asked.

Mother Gossip nodded.

All the other children immediately put their hands up to cover their ears. Mother Gossip turned the glare I was becoming all too familiar with on them, and they reluctantly dropped their hands to their sides.

The young girl she'd selected took in a deep breath, and sang two notes. Syllables, I thought, though I couldn't say what they

157

were because by then I was overcome by the scent of lilacs – so powerful it made me sick to my stomach. I could see the Mothers Superior were similarly afflicted, as were the children. The lone boy turned and puked on the floor.

Seconds later, the smell of lilac disappeared.

Mother Gossip gave the girl an approving nod. The girls sat back down to their studies and the boy went off, presumably in search of a rag to clean up his vomit.

'What happened?' Binta signed to me.

'You *didn't smell flowers?'* I asked.

'I didn't smell anything. You made a funny face though.'

'This is the highest form of our art,' Mother Chatter explained to me. 'To discover those elements of language that exist beneath the layer of human cognition and operate instead on the most primitive aspects of our minds. We call these the *fundaments.'*

'They can affect many people,' Mother Murmur said, a slight groan in his deep baritone revealing he hadn't been fond of the sickly scent of lilacs either. 'Most require the shared knowledge of a tongue, such as Gitabrian or Berabesq, and thus must be tuned to the peculiarities of those languages.'

Which explains why the girl asked Mother Gossip about performing her test in Daroman.

'The syllables are only the beginning,' the young nun said, turning to the rest of us. 'All the elements of the voice must be calibrated perfectly to achieve the effect.'

'Except the ones that are driving innocent people mad,' I pointed out.

Mother Chatter looked stricken. 'An accomplishment beyond anything I have witnessed in all my years, beyond anything we imagined possible. A dark and terrible achievement. We think the Traveller found patterns which—'

158

'You *think?*' I demanded, my voice booming unnaturally in the massive stone chamber. 'You claim these "fundaments" are the most potent, deadly aspect of your arts, and some woman walks up the mountain to your convent and you just hand them over to—'

Mother Gossip stepped forward and snapped her fingers repeatedly in my face. 'Flawless. Water. Blade. Blood. Enna. Enna. Enna.'

I doubled over, overcome by such wrenching pain I couldn't breathe.

'Mother Gossip, that is enough,' I heard Mother Chatter say.

'Do not interfere, sister,' the young nun said. 'The Argosi will learn her place.'

She repeated the words again, and the agony grew inside me, like someone digging their hand into my belly and squeezing my intestines. I tried to reach over my shoulder for the smallsword inside my mapmaker's case, but I couldn't raise my hand above my waist. Despite my efforts not to, I started moaning from the pain.

'*Good Dog!*' Binta signed at me. '*Good Dog, what's wrong?*'

I tried to answer, but my hands wouldn't work. Suddenly Binta turned to Mother Gossip, and I heard a scream so piercing I thought the stone ceiling was going to come crashing down on all of us.

But the pain was gone.

'Impossible,' the young nun said.

I let her get that much out before I slammed my right fist into her temple. I picked my target carefully, and Mother Gossip went down hard. Out of respect for my foster parents' teachings, I caught her before she hit the floor, and lay her down gently.

159

Binta looked up at me. *'Is she a . . . that word I'm not supposed to use?'*

'Definitely,' I replied.

'The boy,' Mother Chatter began, her frail voice quavering in awe. 'Where does he come from?'

'None of your business,' I replied.

'His scream,' Mother Murmur said. 'There is a unique pattern within it . . . It is a kind of language of its own.'

'He must stay with us,' Mother Sigh declared with that certainty that only old men can express with quite so much vigour. 'He will join the convent, and we will study him.'

I tapped Binta on the shoulder. *'You want to live here, kid, with the nuns?'*

He looked up at me with a curl in his lip. *'Are you making a joke, Good Dog? Because it isn't funny.'*

'We were not asking the boy's permission,' the old man informed me. 'Nor yours, Argosi.'

I reached back over my shoulder and uncapped the mapmaker's case. With my free hand I signed to Binta. *'I might need you to scream again in a moment.'*

Had Durral been there – well, if he'd been there but not choking the life out of me – he would've given me that special chuckle of his that somehow evoked disappointment more than mirth.

'What are we doin' here, kid?'

'Trying to get to the truth, Pappy. And trying to protect the boy.'

'That so? Cos it looks more like you're searchin' for an excuse to get back at these lovely ladies for havin' hurt your feelings.'

He would've been right too. I needed to get my head straight. Fighting my way out of here with Binta wasn't likely to have a happy ending. Besides, I already knew how this had to end. I'd known it since the moment Mother Chatter had said three simple words. Not even magic ones.

I walked over to the old woman. '"Tomorrow",' I said. 'You used that word twice on me when you put me out.'

A faint smile came to her lips. The smile of someone for whom something complex to you is obvious to them. 'Indeed, for in your mind the word "tomorrow" contains two completely distinct sets of meanings. One relates to time in its strictest sense, and the other to a desire to abandon the present.'

Tomorrow, I said to myself silently, letting the word slither around my head. *The day after today, but also a future to which the problems of today can be put off.*

Even thinking of that meaning of the word made me, in some barely discernible way, want to curl up on a soft bed and go to sleep, hoping to awaken to a lessening of all the complications in my life.

Very carefully, and with as much precision as I could manage, I reproduced the combination of syllables that Mother Chatter had uttered to me. 'Bed. Bruise. Shame. Ointment. Soothing. Tomorrow. Tomorrow.'

I felt my eyelids begin to flutter and the muscles in my legs relax. I had to jerk myself awake to remain standing.

'Not bad,' Mother Chatter said, favouring me with an unsightly view of her rotting gums. 'You muddled several of the vowel pairings and your tonal shifts were amateurish at best, but I've witnessed many neophytes to our order do worse.'

Good to know I've got a future as an incredibly annoying nun if I get tired of failing as an Argosi. More importantly, however, I'd gotten what I needed out of her.

'What is the purpose of this demonstration?' asked the blue-eyed nun. 'You wish to live here, with the boy? Your influence would not be—'

I turned away from her, gazing up at the massive, seemingly impenetrable stone walls that had been so easily breached. 'I don't want to live here any more than he does, Mother Superior. I just needed to show you how she did it.'

'How who did what?' Mother Chatter asked.

'The Traveller,' I replied. 'That's how she got to you. She came here as a neophyte. Impressed you with her natural aptitude. Not too much though, just enough that, combined with some judicious bowing and scraping, you gave her admission to the convent.'

'She was an indifferent student at best,' Mother Gossip said, rising unsteadily to her feet with the help of two of the children.

I hear the tension in your voice, sister. You've figured it out too.

It was reassuring somehow to know that my lessons in arta loquit weren't wasted even here among these grand geniuses of the mind.

I let my gaze drift across the faces of the Mothers Superior, wondering which ones had let slip fragments of their secrets to her. Small, insignificant details of the higher forms of their arts. Unaware that the Traveller was piecing together everything she needed to construct the Scarlet Verses.

I returned to Mother Chatter. 'Young. Quiet. Pretty. That's how you described the Traveller, isn't it?'

'Yes,' she agreed, doing a reasonable job of not betraying her unease.

I turned to the others. 'Would the rest of you agree with that description?'

One by one they nodded in turn.

Young. Quiet. Pretty.

Nobody added anything. No details of her height, build, hair, skin colour, or whether she had one arm and a limp. No reference to whether she was Daroman, Berabesq, Gitabrian, Jan'Tep, Mahdek, or Zhuban. No mention of anything but that she was young, quiet and pretty.

I waved to the children sitting at their desks. 'Do any of you remember a woman who came here for a while and then left not long ago?'

'Do not address my students,' Mother Gossip warned.

I ignored her. Time to reveal my magic trick. Well, not *mine*, precisely.

'Describe her,' I ordered the children.

'I told you, do not—'

'Young. Quiet. Pretty,' said the first girl.

'Young. Quiet. Pretty,' repeated the next.

One after the next, they all repeated the same words. When even the poor boy who still looked green recited them exactly the same way, I waved to Binta to get his attention.

'*Come on*,' I signed.

He looked up at me curiously.

'*We're done here*,' I informed him.

He came over and took my hand.

'Where do you think you are going with the boy, Argosi?' Mother Sigh asked.

'Taking him away from this place. You've been compromised. Every one of you.'

'Explain!' the old man demanded.

I stopped. I really should've just walked out the gate and been done with these arrogant Mothers Superior and their Convent of Scarlet Words. But they'd made me relive what I'd done to Enna, and slandered the Argosi a good half a dozen times, so I guess I was in a prickly mood. Besides, they *had* given me some small insight into the Scarlet Verses – and even more into my own flawed

163

nature, if I was being honest. The Way of Water required I give them something in return.

'Young. Quiet. Pretty,' I said.

'Yes, child,' Mother Chatter said wearily. 'We recall those words. I said them myself.'

'That's all you remember about the Traveller. That's all *any of you* remember about her.' Still facing the door, I gestured to the eleven girls and one boy at their desks. 'Even them.'

'As Mother Gossip informed you, such trivial details do not—'

'The Traveller mesmerised you.'

'What?'

I turned, but only because the petty part of me that likes to be proven right wanted to see their faces. 'She used your own techniques to make you forget all about her. That's why you don't remember sharing your secrets with her – which I imagine is kind of embarrassing so I'm not surprised she removed those memories from you so easily. It's why you can't recall anything about her other than those three, simple words she planted in your minds.'

It's hard to describe the satisfaction one feels at seeing seven smug, self-satisfied faces change so utterly, as what would have been obvious to them had they not been so smug and self-satisfied finally seeped into their awareness.

Mother Sigh tried his best to recover some shred of dignity from the situation. 'But . . . if that were so, why did she not eliminate our recollections of her completely? Why leave us with—'

'Because that's not how she thinks. She doesn't need you to be unaware of her existence. She just didn't want you to know the specifics of how she constructed the Scarlet Verses.'

'But her appearance,' Mother Chatter said, no longer able to hide the discomfort that the reawakening of one's crimes sends

164

slithering inside any of us. I knew the feeling well. 'Why do I remember her as—'

'Young. Quiet. Pretty? That was a message.'

'A message for who?' Mother Murmur asked.

I turned and kicked open the door, letting the afternoon light stream inside the loquatium. As I led Binta outside, I said, 'It's her way of saying hello – of leaving her calling card for whoever got this far. She's letting me know she's not afraid in the slightest of me finding her.'

Arta Siva

Of all the seven talents, a maetri will be most reluctant to teach persuasion. It is not the Argosi way to shape the will of another. Rather, we study arta siva to remind ourselves of how easily beauty and desire can guide our steps away from our own paths . . .

. . . and into darkness.

22

Secrets

After retrieving Quadlopo and ignoring the running commentary from every nun we passed along the way regarding my unsightly physical appearance, obvious spiritual emptiness and, apparently, my unpleasant odour, I spent most of the next half-hour recounting for Binta all that had transpired right in front of him during our time at the convent, skipping over the details of what the Mothers Superior had forced me to relive. As my fingers grew tired from shifting swiftly through each sign – painfully slowly, as far as Binta was concerned – I came to appreciate just how much patience it must require to never know what people were saying until someone explained it to you afterwards.

'*Why do you not read lips?*' I asked him as we led Quadlopo down the rocky slope away from the convent's gatehouse.

'*My father forbade me.*'

That struck me as a strange and cruel restriction to place on a child's education. Binta caught the flash of contempt in my expression.

'*He was a good father,*' the boy insisted.

'*Why would a good father not want you to know what those around you were saying?*'

For several minutes Binta's fingers were still, and my only company as we plodded down the path was Quadlopo's resentful stares. I had, the horse seemed to want me to know, removed him from his home – with people he actually liked – only to drag him to this cold and unpleasant mountaintop where he'd yet to find any scrub worth eating.

'*Bluebird?*' I signed the boy's name as he'd first given it to me to get his attention. I was concerned I might've upset him with my presumptuous question.

'*I am thinking,*' he signed back.

This was unusual for him. Generally in conversation he responded instantly, almost reflexively, as if he put no thought into his replies at all. Yet now, even when he did answer, his gestures were slower than usual, as if he wanted me to know that these signs were only an approximation of what he was trying to communicate.

'*To read lips is to see sounds being formed,*' he began, '*but whether the sounds are seen or heard, they are still the same. Like writing. Do you understand?*'

'*You can't read?*'

'*No, my father—*'

'*Forbade it.*'

Binta made his two-fingered gesture which had no actual word associated with it but in this context I understood was meant to express his displeasure at my interruption.

'*Whether I read your words on a page or on your lips, they are still your words. Your language. This I must not do.*'

I slowed Quadlopo's already unhurried pace, conscious of the fact that Rosie would be waiting for us just a little further down the slope. Whatever Binta was trying to convey, I wanted it kept between the two of us.

'*Are we not speaking the same language right now, using our signs?*' I asked.

'No, Good Dog, we are not. The signs are a bridge between our two ways of thinking. Were I to learn your language – any of your languages – my own would become tainted.'

What was it Mother Murmur had said? Something about Binta's scream having a unique pattern hidden within it: 'It is a kind of language of its own.'

But had Binta created that language himself, or had it somehow been implanted into him by his father? Or was it deeper even than that: a way of seeing and describing the world innate to the human mind that only becomes bound when we impose words upon those deeper meanings?

I stopped Quadlopo entirely now. The horse gave me a look that suggested I should make up my mind whether we were leaving this mountain or not.

'Bluebird, when you screamed –' I realised he might not even understand what I meant by that word, even though it was a sign we both knew. 'When you made the loud sound with your mouth, the nuns said your voice . . .' Again I struggled to articulate what they'd said to me at the time. 'They believed you were using a special language. Something different to what I or anyone else speaks.'

'Yes,' he signed, shoulders relaxing as if he were relieved I finally understood. 'At the Monastery of the Garden-Without-Flowers, my father studied the –' the boy looked frustrated again, searching for the signs – 'the language-beneath-language. Do you understand?'

'I think I do.'

He shot me a doubtful look but went on anyway.

'My father could not learn to speak this language himself, because it is corrupted by other languages. To speak one, you must speak no others. Do you understand?'

'Stop asking me if I understand, Bluebird.'

'Sorry.'

'What is the purpose of the language-beneath-language?'

He tapped his temple, then extended his arm and swept it out to the landscape around us. 'When you see the world, Good Dog, you see it through your language. You see only that for which you have words to describe. When I look at the world, I . . . see it all.'

I followed his finger as it pointed all around us. 'I see trees and rocks and mountains and clouds. Do you see something I don't?'

He chewed his lip for a while. 'I know what those words mean, but they are just words. I see only one thing.' His finger traced a circle in the air, which was the sign for 'world'. He shook his head abruptly, as if trying to shake off a buzzing insect.

I had to tap his shoulder to get him to look at me. 'Bluebird, are you all right? Are you in pain?'

He gave me a wan smile. 'I am not hurt. It is only that when I try to . . . hold that which I see in my head, it disappears. Everything becomes confusing. I lack the words to describe what I see . . . or perhaps it is that I have too many words and these prevent me from forming the thought that encompasses the world. My father said it was because I was still young. As I grow, I will master the language-beneath-language. One day I will speak that which no one else has ever spoken.'

'What will happen then?' I asked.

He shrugged. 'How should I know? I am nine years old.'

Quadlopo, without bothering to get my permission, started clopping along the rocky path again. As we neared the pass where we'd left Rosie, I tried to find some connection between this vague, ambiguous 'language-beneath-language' that Binta had described, and the fact that his scream – the most primordial form of what the Mothers Superior had called the 'fundaments' – had been able to break the agonising chain of words Mother Gossip had placed in my head. That was also the reason why I hadn't fallen prey to the Scarlet Verses back in that hall in Tinto Rhea.

Somehow, Binta and his language-beneath-language were the key to unwinding the Traveller's verbal plague. Had his father somehow predicted the coming of the Red Scream only to become one of its first victims? But if the Traveller had deceived the monks at the Silent Garden the way she had the nuns at the Convent of Scarlet Words, then why hadn't she killed Binta? Had she simply assumed the boy would die at the hands of his own father? And if so, what would she do when she learned he was still alive?

'You move slowly,' I heard Rosie call out as we neared the pass. 'I've been sitting here listening to you plod down the mountain for over an hour, yet nothing in your shuffling gait suggests an injury.'

We turned the corner and found her sitting on a rock, all the items in her pack arranged before her on a blanket as she sharpened the four-bladed tool she'd referred to as the double-crescent with a whetstone. Her possessions appeared meticulously clean, reminding me just how lax I was at maintaining my own gear. Quadlopo gave a light snort, and when I looked at him I had the distinct impression he was trying to tell me something about my duties as regarded his brushing.

'Well?' Rosie asked, sliding the double-crescent back in an oddly wide and flat leather scabbard strapped to her back before painstakingly returning each of the other items to her pack. 'Did you find out anything from the nuns? Were they the source of the Scarlet Verses?'

'It seems that way.'

'And the Traveller? What were they able to tell you about her?'

Rosie wasn't watching me. She was too busy fastidiously placing every piece of her kit in its particular location within her pack.

'*Good Dog,*' Binta signed to me, '*why are you making that face?*'

175

'What face?'

'The one you made in the village before you fought all those people.'

'Well?' Rosie asked, looking up at me. 'Did you learn anything or not?'

The linen wrappings she often used to keep her head and face covered were hanging loosely around her shoulders. She'd brushed out her long, lustrously brown hair. It framed her features in a pleasing way at odds with her sour demeanour.

'How old are you?' I asked.

Her eyes narrowed. 'Why would that matter?'

'Just wondering. How old are you?'

'Seventeen.'

'Oh.'

She arched an eyebrow, which only served to accentuate how lovely her features were. 'Is there a reason for your query?'

I shrugged. 'It's just that we've been on the road together for two weeks and I hardly know anything about you.'

Except that wasn't quite true. I knew that the Path of Thorns and Roses had been to the Monastery of the Silent Garden. She'd said as much, though she hadn't told me when precisely she'd been there, or how she'd known to travel to Tinto Rhea. And why had she waited to make her presence known until after the villagers had gone mad from the mayor reading out the Scarlet Verses? Was she really so careful – and callous – that she'd spent all that time investigating the village and setting her explosives before she even knew that the villagers would become infected with the plague? Or had she stayed hidden because one of them might have recognised her?

Was that why Rosie had refused to come to the Convent of Scarlet Words with me? Not because the nuns had banned her as just another insolent Argosi, but because they might recognise the

176

woman about whom they'd forgotten everything but three little words?

'You're awful quiet, Rosie.'

She slung her pack over her shoulder. 'You will find that most Argosi, unlike you, speak when there is something worth saying. Now, did you learn anything at the convent about the Traveller, or not?'

I brought my arta valar to the surface, burying my unease so deep even I couldn't feel it. 'You've met those crazy nuns, right?'

'I have.'

I tugged on Quadlopo's reins and led him past her to the trail that led back down to the desert. 'Then you know there's very little they say that bears repeating.'

That drew an uncharacteristic chuckle from Rosie, and I heard her footsteps following me down the mountain. She made some comment about my having a gift for understatement, but in my head all I was hearing were those same three words over and over again, and thinking just how well they described the Path of Thorns and Roses.

Young. Quiet. Pretty.

23

The Edge

The trek up to the Convent of Scarlet Words had taken us nine days. Nine lousy days and nights of chills and crosswinds, narrow passes and loose shale so treacherous that with every step it threatened to give way under our feet and send us tumbling over the edge. The way back down the mountain was worse, because now I couldn't be sure if the enemy we'd come looking for wasn't, in fact, the woman leading us.

'Hand me the boy,' Rosie commanded imperiously.

It was the second day of our descent. We were navigating a shallow shelf in the rock face. The steep drop had poor Quadlopo swivelling his head backwards every step as if wondering whether a life at a convent filled with verbally abusive nuns might not suit him better. Given my growing unease around Rosie, I was starting to agree.

'Binta will be fine on Quadlopo's back,' I told her.

'He shifts about in the saddle constantly,' she warned. 'You risk unnerving the beast and sending them both over the cliff. If we are to travel safely, we need to reduce the burden on our mounts.'

'Fine,' I said reaching up to lift Binta off Quadlopo's back. 'I'll carry him.'

Rosie grabbed my arm, and in that instant I wondered if we'd already reached the end of our journey together. She must've realised by now that there were a dozen good reasons for me to suspect her of being the Traveller. Why hadn't she tried to prove otherwise? For all I knew, she was using me to keep Binta calm until she was ready to force him to help her perfect the Red Scream.

'You are being foolish, Ferius Parfax,' she said.

'I'm often so,' I admitted. 'What am I being stupid about now?'

'You have a saddle and two bags to be concerned with. I have only my pack and bedroll, and can therefore more easily carry the boy.'

She had a point. Rosie rode with just a blanket on Biter's back. Despite that, she never seemed to suffer. As for me, the saddle I'd stolen from Durral's barn was as good as money could buy and yet I still couldn't sleep on my back at night from the soreness of my rear end.

'I can carry my gear and Binta as well,' I insisted.

Rosie's stare was so piercing I had to fight the urge to turn away. Did I get that look on my face when I used my arta precis on someone?

At last she let go of my arm, but not my gaze. 'What happened to you at the convent?'

I put my hands on either side of Binta's waist and lifted him off Quadlopo to set him down on his feet, keeping myself between him and Rosie.

'I told you. The foul-mouthed nuns, the confessorium, the loquatium. Remember?'

'You recounted the events. You have not said what you gleaned from them.'

I removed the bags and began undoing the buckles of the saddle.

179

'You really think out here on a narrow ledge is the best place to beat the information out of me?'

Without so much as the courtesy of a scathing remark, she turned and resumed leading her own horse along the rocky shelf. I settled the saddlebags on my left shoulder, grabbed the saddle itself under my right arm, and discovered Rosie was right: there was no way I could carry Binta as well.

'*I can walk,*' he signed when he saw me staring at him.

'*It is a long way and we won't rest for many miles.*'

'*I can walk.*'

Lacking better options, I nodded and began awkwardly looping Quadlopo's reins around the fingers of my right hand so I could lead him along the narrow and winding rock shelf.

The going was hard, and unpleasant. Worse than the uncertain frosty ground were the host of anxieties chasing at our heels. Whenever one of Quadlopo's rear hoofs slid on the shale, I feared he was about to go over the cliff. Every time Rosie glanced back at us, I wondered if she were about to chant seven verses that would drive me mad, or unsling her bow, shoot me in the leg with an arrow and leave me there to die as she dragged Binta to whatever horrible fate she had in mind for him.

She still hadn't explained how she'd come to learn of the Red Scream in the first place, nor how she happened to be at both the Monastery of the Silent Garden *and* at Tinto Rhea right when the plague had begun. Most troubling of all, she avoided any discussion of what had taken her to the Convent of the Scarlet Words the previous time, and why she refused to go back.

Young. Quiet. Pretty.

If the Path of Thorns and Roses was another name for the Traveller, I was very aware that Binta might be safer if I pretended not to know her true identity. What would happen if I confronted

180

her with my suspicions? Could I beat Rosie in a fight? Take her by surprise with my arta eres and somehow disable her so I could escape with the boy?

Maybe.

Maybe not.

My arta tuco was quiet as a mouse. I couldn't see any strategy that would get me out of this situation. That left me relying on an unusual part of Durral's training in arta loquit.

'Language is just a bunch of words and meanings we all pretend mean the same things,' he used to say. *'But eloquence – ah, eloquence! That's when two people turn words into music. A song only they know by heart.'*

Enna had, thankfully, explained to me later that what he meant was that the bonds between people sometimes showed up in the unique variations of the words they used and how they spoke them. Remembering that lesson was what had made me so certain that when Rosie was last at the convent, she'd become involved with Mother Gossip.

How could anyone figure out such a thing with so little to go on? Was it some brilliant clue my arta precis had picked up, or just a hunch? Neither. My conviction came from the fragments of the way the vitriolic young Mother Gossip spoke. Specifically, the way she pronounce the word 'Argosi'.

'The Argosi will learn her place.'

It wasn't just the disdain in her voice, but the distinctive, almost formal emphasis she put on the word every time she spoke it out loud.

Durral – when he wasn't making me listen to other people's footsteps – would often ask me to recount a conversation the two of us had overheard. It wasn't enough that I got all the words right; he expected me to recall the precise way those words had been

181

pronounced. Fluctuations in pitch, which syllables had been emphasised and which ones skipped over, and what we could surmise from those unconscious choices.

'Argosi.'

'Ar-sneer-GO-pause-si.'

There were plenty of equally insulting ways she could have pronounced the word. The funny thing was the exactitude, the formality in her tone that – without her meaning to – lent the word a kind of reverence.

'Ar – you're a lousy piece of crap not worth my time – GO – I hold my breath here because this word means something so huge I can't quite let go of it yet – si.'

And who else said 'Argosi' like you were supposed to drop to your knees in awe the moment anybody uttered the word?

The Path of Thorns and Roses.

Durral taught me arta loquit, but it was Enna who helped me understand that every person we meet – even if we only know them a short while – leaves a kind of footprint on us. Sometimes the effect is so slight we can't even spot it ourselves. Other times, those people show up in a scarf we start wearing, or a turn of phrase we adopt. Enna believed that our identities, like the ground beneath our feet, were made up of layers upon layers of the roads we'd travelled, rich with the buried artefacts of those who'd walked them alongside us.

That particular insight had become a cause of friction between us early on.

A couple of weeks after Durral had brought me home and convinced Enna to be my foster mother, she sat me down for tea and, casual as can be, mentioned that I didn't talk like other Mahdek.

'No Mahdek talks like a Mahdek any more,' I'd pointed out to her. 'That's what comes of living as refugees, going from place to place and never having a home to call your own. Besides, how would you know whether or not I talk like a proper Mahdek? You've never even heard me speak my own language.'

She gave me one of her smiles to let me know my bristling was neither necessary nor intimidating. 'When's the last time you ran into a fellow Mahdek?'

'When I was eleven years old, hiding in a cave while my entire clan was being massacred by Jan'Tep mages.'

She placed a hand on my shoulder, so gentle I thought maybe she was afraid I was going to cry.

'One day you'll meet another Mahdek, Ferius.'

I hadn't known Enna well at that point, but already that struck me as a banal and sentimental notion. She must've caught the suspicion in my expression because she let go of my shoulder and took my hands in hers.

'Don't be surprised, is all I'm saying, when they look at you like you're not one of them.'

'What do you mean?'

'You talk different than most Mahdek do, that's all. Your tone, your accent, the words you choose. You stand differently, walk differently, and when you gaze out at the world, you've got a different look in your eyes. That's not a bad thing. Just don't feel like there's something wrong with you if the next time you run into one of your people they stare back at you like you're a stranger.'

I knew she wasn't trying to annoy or condescend to me, but still I couldn't keep the sharpness from my reply.

'Reckon that's true for anyone who's left their people and been as many places as I've been. Seen the things I've seen. Done the things I've done. Don't make me less— Why are you laughing at me, Enna?'

She grinned, and her other hand came up to ruffle my hair as if I were six instead of sixteen.

'*I just love the way you talk sometimes, that's all.*'

What she'd meant was that I'd started to talk like Durral. She was right too; even though I'd only known him a couple of months, pieces of him were rubbing off on me. His swagger, his phrasings, sometimes even his smirk. That only made it more painful to feel that if we were ever to meet again, there would surely be blood left on the ground at our parting.

A sudden shifting sound behind reminded me of the task that should've had my attention. Quadlopo whinnied, and I feared his back hoofs were slipping, but when I turned I saw the horse was fine. It was Binta who was gone.

'Binta!' I screamed, dimly aware of how futile that was, given that he couldn't hear.

All I could see of him were his hands desperately clinging to the ledge. The scraping of his feet as they scrabbled for purchase on the cliff face became more frantic by the second. I tried to run to him, but I was on the wrong side of Quadlopo, laden down by saddlebags that now had me trapped between the horse's flank and the mountainside. He was snorting madly, dipping his head down as he tried to reach his muzzle to the boy's hands, unaware that his haunches were pinning me against the rock face.

'Rosie!' I shouted.

Like an idiot, I'd kept so much distance between us that now she was a good fifty yards ahead and already around the next bend.

'Rosie, please! Binta's fallen!'

I shed the saddlebags from my shoulders and tried to squirm under the horse. Quadlopo was in such a frenzy that he'd stopped paying attention to the uneven ground. He was starting to slide on the loose rocks. Any second now the poor beast was going to go tumbling over the edge.

184

'Quadlopo, don't!' I begged him, trying to sound soothing in spite of the panic rising in my throat. 'Just let me—'

'Do not move,' came a shout from my left. 'Not one inch.'

I turned my head and saw Rosie running at us from around the corner. Her feet pounded the shale so hard I thought for sure she was going to lose her footing and be the first of us to fall into the canyon below. She didn't though, just kept running as if her intent were to barrel me and Quadlopo over the side. When she was six feet away, I caught sight of the rope in her hand. She took one more step and then leaped into the air, only instead of ramming into us, her right foot landed on a shallow outcropping of rock barely six inches from my face. Her knee bent as her thigh muscles absorbed the impact. A fraction of a second later, she pushed off so hard she went somersaulting over my head, dropping one end of the rope into my hand.

'Do not let go!' she yelled as she went over the cliff.

I barely had time to grab hold of the rope and haul down hard so I could use Quadlopo's strong back as a fulcrum before her entire weight threatened to yank it from me. I felt a burning in my palms as Rosie slammed into the side of the cliff. I heard her grunt, but couldn't see what was happening over Quadlopo's withers.

'Binta!' I called out again.

Was he still hanging on? A scrawny boy only nine years old. Or had he already plummeted into oblivion?

'Ferius, pull!' Rosie shouted.

I tried, but her weight was too much for me. Did that mean she was holding Binta? Or was she just heavier than she looked?

I held firm as I could to my end of the rope even as I hooked my right foot around Quadlopo's leg, urging him to turn his body towards the mountainside. His head swivelled and he shifted a few meagre inches closer. He was crushing me pretty badly now, but I

185

added my strength to his and pulled as hard as I could. Suddenly the tension in the rope slackened, then disappeared entirely.

Please be there, I prayed silently as I squirmed desperately to get out from behind Quadlopo.

Eventually I got down on my hands and knees and crawled under his legs. Rosie was lying face down on the ledge, her end of the rope coiled so tightly around her forearm that her linen sleeve had torn and I could see angry red welts already burned into the skin. Her left arm was wrapped around Binta.

I scrambled to the boy and got him to his feet. His eyes were wide, his whole body shaking. I hugged him so hard I heard the breath leave his lungs. When I finally let him go, the fingers of my right hand formed the same sign over and over again.

'*I'm sorry. I'm sorry. I'm sorry.*'

He tried to gesture back, but his hand shook so much it took several tries. '*My fault.*'

I pulled him to me again with my right arm, and looked down at Rosie. 'Are you . . . ?'

She was still face down, her back and shoulders rising as she groaned into the dirt. 'I am unharmed. Merely . . . resting.'

Binta was trying to sign to me, but I wasn't paying attention because a perverse thought had come into my mind. The kind of thought a halfway decent person shouldn't have at a time like this. Once you've studied arta tuco, you can't stop yourself from perceiving strategic opportunities, whether or not they're ones decent folk would contemplate.

Rosie had just saved Binta, but that didn't mean she wasn't the Traveller. It meant she needed him alive. Sooner or later I was going to have to take her down, injure her so badly that she wouldn't be able to pursue us. This might be my only chance.

186

Binta had been tapping my arm and now he poked me hard. I turned my head, but kept half an eye on Rosie.

'*Good Dog. Good Dog. You must pay attention now.*'

'*What is it?*' I signed.

'*The serpent. I slipped because I saw the red serpent.*'

My gaze swept the ledge on either side of us. The Seven Sands was home to all kinds of snakes, but they didn't like the cold, and we hadn't encountered any in the mountains.

'*No,*' Binta signed, stretching up on his toes and reaching with his free hand to lift my chin. '*Up there.*'

My eyes went up, way up, beyond the ledge on which we stood and back along the winding slope that descended from the mountaintop. About three miles back I saw it. A truly massive serpent, winding its way down the path towards us, its crimson scales composed of dozens upon dozens of red habits, the glittering lines between them formed by lattices of slender silver chains. The nuns were coming for us.

'What is wrong?' Rosie asked, rising to her feet.

She turned, following my gaze. The colour drained from her cheeks as she saw what had caused Binta to slip. It might've just been the wind one always finds up at high altitudes, but I could've sworn I heard the serpent's hiss.

24

The Scarlet Serpent

We had a three-mile head start on the slithering mass of plague-maddened nuns. That should've kept them hours behind us, but our passage was hampered by the treacherous terrain, while the army of the infected pursuing us flowed as smooth as a bloody river down the winding mountain path.

'Steady, Quadlopo,' I urged the terrified beast after one of his hoofs slipped on a patch of crumbling debris.

The ledge we traversed was barely wide enough for him to pass. I followed behind Rosie and Biter and Binta, leading Quadlopo as fast as I dared, awkwardly sweeping away as many loose rocks as I could with my feet. I reached back every few steps to stroke the horse's muzzle, hoping my touch might offer him some reassurance as he plodded precariously forward. He kept snorting though, foaming at the mouth. His coat was soaked in sweat despite the cold.

'*The horses are scared,*' Binta turned to sign at me, then he came to walk by my side and added, more hesitatingly, '*I am also scared.*'

'*Me too,*' I replied.

This was my fault. The horses were only slowing us down. I never should've insisted we bring them up the mountain with us. But there hadn't been anywhere safe to leave them in the desert,

188

and I couldn't bear the thought of losing Quadlopo. Instead I was risking his life with every step, and my paltry words of comfort were being drowned out by the hissing that grew ever louder as the hours passed and the light gave way to the creeping darkness.

How in hell had the nuns gotten infected after Binta and I had left them? Had the two of us triggered the Red Scream in them somehow? And if so, was that why they were pursuing us instead of killing each other off as the monks at the Monastery of the Silent Garden had done?

'Why do they have to make that damned noise?' I demanded. 'Bad enough they want to rip us apart. What's the point of terrifying us half to death first?'

I should've kept quiet. I wasn't seeking any response. Enna used to say that part of arta loquit was learning to speak only when our utterances served a purpose. Durral – being someone who talked perpetually whether there was a reason to or not – countered that a little jabbering was good for the soul.

'Be glad the infected still hiss at all,' Rosie replied. Apparently her maetri hadn't enlightened her of the virtues of asking inane questions for which you didn't need an answer. 'The Red Scream drives them to spread their madness, yet a flaw in the Scarlet Verses causes them to bite off their tongues soon after infection. That they still do so provides our only reassurance that the Traveller has not yet perfected her verses.'

'Oh, thanks, Rosie,' I said. 'When you put it that way, I guess that bloodcurdling hiss is mighty reassuring after all.'

'Indeed, that is the wiser interpretation.'

Whatever talents for arta loquit one found along the Path of Thorns and Roses, the ability to detect sarcasm wasn't one of them.

Part of me still couldn't comprehend how Rosie could talk in such calm, reasoned tones even as the nuns gained on us. Was her

Argosi training really so much better than mine that she could so effortlessly suppress the urge to panic? It was all I could do not to shout and scream to the heavens about the unfairness of it all.

Or maybe she's calm because she knows the nuns aren't coming for her.

Terror does funny things to the brain. The hours passed and darkness descended as the horde got closer and closer. I kept imagining I could make out words in all that hissing. *Young. Quiet. Pretty.*

Binta grabbed my sleeve. *'Stop! There is a crack in the rock ahead of you!'*

The kid had good eyes. Despite staring at the ground in front of us, I'd gotten so distracted I was inches away from catching my heel in a crevice – or worse, leading Quadlopo to stepping in it. A broken leg up here would be a death sentence for either of us.

'You could've warned me about this fissure in the rock!' I called out to Rosie.

She didn't bother looking back. 'I assumed you would be paying attention to the terrain.'

She was right of course. There wasn't anything nefarious in her not warning me about hazards she had every reason to expect I'd spot myself. On the other hand, maybe me spraining an ankle would serve her purposes perfectly.

I shook my head, irritated with myself. I was going about this all wrong. *Feeling* suspicious is a waste of time. It weakens the spirit without sharpening the mind. *Thinking through* your suspicions is how you awaken your arta tuco.

So, okay, let's say Rosie's the Traveller. She starts out as an Argosi, only something happens that drives her so nuts she turns her back on every principle we believe in, to instead create a plague that spreads through obscure patterns of words that are somehow

190

connected to those 'fundaments' the nuns up at the convent talked about. She insinuates herself into the convent and tricks the Mothers Superior into giving her most of the pieces she needs. She takes her time, patiently infecting and mesmerising them into forgetting her identity, anyway. The verses are still imperfect though. Incomplete. So she goes to the Monastery of the Silent Garden to find the rest. Only she's stymied because the secret the monks are hiding isn't in any book.

I glanced down at Binta. He put on a brave smile even though I could see every part of him tremble as he shakily signed, '*All will be well, Good Dog.*'

Great. Now a nine-year-old boy pursued by a throng of insane nuns is having to buck my spirits up.

Quadlopo's sopping-wet muzzle nudged my back, urging me to hurry, but even at this pace he kept slipping on the loose shale.

Just keep moving, I told myself. *Ignore the hissing nuns behind you and the potential mass murderer ahead.*

A part of me almost wished Rosie would drop the mask and come at me with her double-crescent or try to shove me over the cliff. Let the two of us finally find out whose arta eres would come out on top when the chips were down.

In your dreams, Ferius. She could take you blindfolded with both hands shackled to a tree branch.

That fact was pretty much the only argument against Rosie being the Traveller. Except . . . except maybe whatever she needed from Binta required his cooperation. He was a brave kid; she'd seen that plenty already. Brave, and so stubborn he made Quadlopo seem reasonable. If he saw Rosie murder me, he'd never help her with these so-called 'fundaments' the Mothers Superior implied were the key to completing the Traveller's design. If, on the other hand, I should happen to die – say, getting eaten by a bunch of lunatic nuns – well, Binta would be all alone in the world. He'd have no one to turn to but Rosie.

A more cunning person than myself might've kept her suspicions quiet, maybe even tried to lull her opponent into a false sense of security. But irritation and dread can become their own kind of madness after a while.

'Hey, Rosie,' I called out to her.

She just kept up her same pace, kept looking straight ahead.

'What is it now? Did I fail to alert you to a pebble that's lodged in your boot?'

'When those nuns catch up to us, if I suspect for even a second that they aren't trying to kill you too, then before they get to me, I'm going to stick you through the heart with this sword of mine and kick you off the cliff to cushion my landing.'

I guess she didn't think that threat was worthy of a reply, because she kept on walking and soon she and Biter had disappeared around the next bend in the path.

Binta tapped on my arm.

'What are you talking to Rosie about?'

'Nothing important. Why?'

'It's just that you are making that face you make before you do something stupid.'

He had a point. What good was it pushing a confrontation with Rosie? Even without a pack of feral nuns on our tail, my odds of beating her in a fair fight were somewhere between 'So this is what it's like to be thrown off a cliff' and 'Ow, stop slapping me in the face with my own severed hand'.

Binta was still staring up at me.

'You're wrong, kid,' I signed. *'This is the face I make when I'm devising an impossibly daring plan to save our lives.'*

'Really?' he asked.

For a nine-year-old boy, he could inject a lifetime's worth of doubt into a sign that involves nothing more than flipping two fingers a half-turn clockwise then counter-clockwise. I pretended not to have noticed and instead focused on guiding Quadlopo around the sharp turn. Binta tried to sign to me a second time, but as we reached the other side, there were more pressing problems awaiting us.

The ledge widened up ahead, which meant we could've picked up our pace were Rosie not standing there, her back to me, blocking the way forward.

'What are you doing?' I asked.

She turned. In that calm, unerring gaze, those dark eyes of hers so warm and beautiful they only accentuated the coldness underneath, I could tell she was done waiting to make her move.

'I am sorry, Ferius Parfax,' she said, and for the first time since I'd met her she almost sounded sympathetic. 'We have reached the end of your path.'

25

The Choice

Enna once told me that it's not enough to master the seven Argosi talents. Arta loquit, arta eres, arta tuco, and the rest of them . . . these are all ways of seeing the world around you. Each one offers insights and abilities, but at the same time they narrow your focus. The Argosi who hopes to survive all of life's dangers must learn to see through all seven lenses at once with perfect clarity.

Me? I was barely good enough to use even one at a time, which was a problem because at that precise moment I had some hard choices to make.

'Listen,' Rosie said. 'Do you hear them coming?'

So far she hadn't made a move, so I hadn't either. She was five yards away. Far enough that I could draw my smallsword before she could reach me. Unfortunately, five yards was also far enough that she could throw that double-crescent axe of hers into my chest before I got to her.

'I'm not fond of hissing,' I replied, 'so I've been trying to ignore them.'

'Listen more closely.'

Was this a trick? If I paid more attention to the hissing, was there some chance I'd hear the verses they were trying to utter and fall prey to the Red Scream?

The problem with trying *not* to listen to something, of course, is that ends up being exactly what you do. But all I heard was the same droning hisses that never stopped . . .

There!

Scuffling in the dirt, clawing at the ground, and then . . . gone.

'One of the nuns just slipped and fell off the cliff,' I said.

Rosie nodded. 'Several have done so during the past hours, yet still they come, never slowing their pace. Reason has fled them.'

'That's quite the arta precis you have there, Rosie, but I would've figured them biting off their own tongues was the first clue that maybe they weren't thinking too straight.'

'And yet they come for us. Why?'

Maybe because that's what you commanded them to do?

She still hadn't taken so much as a step towards me, which only added to the evidence that her plan was to delay me until the nuns caught up with us and finished her dirty work for her.

'*Binta?*' I signed.

He shuffled closer so that I could see him signing his response out of the corner of my eye. '*Yes, Good Dog?*'

'*If I die, don't trust anything Rosie says any more, okay?*'

He hesitated a moment before signing back. '*What makes you think I trusted her before?*'

Even in the darkness Rosie must've caught our gestures, because she gave a low chuckle. 'At last we arrive at the root of the problem.'

'I have several problems right now, lady. Believe me when I say that my distrust of you isn't one of them.'

She still hadn't made a move, so I drew the smallsword.

'Now get out of my way, Rosie, or I swear that you and that nun who just fell off the cliff are going to become real close acquaintances.'

195

The hissing grew louder again, and in the distance I could just about hear the slapping of sandals against the rocky ground.

'They are mere minutes away,' Rosie said.

She started walking, but not towards us – towards the edge of the cliff.

'Visualise me taking the next step, Ferius Parfax. Imagine I die, and then tell me what happens next.'

She was far enough away that I risked closing my eyes for a moment to look out at the world through the lens of my arta tuco.

During those eighteen blessed months I'd spent as Enna's foster daughter, she'd devoted countless hours to teaching me the deep arts of strategy and tactics. Even now, here on this cold, uncaring mountain, standing beneath a thousand unfeeling stars, a dozen potential paths unfolded before me: shadows in which to hide; parts of the ledge that were fractionally more advantageous from which to fight; hand- and footholds in the rock face that now revealed themselves to me as an avenue of escape. My mind rolled the dice on every one of those possibilities. They came up snake eyes every time.

The nuns would smell us hiding in the shadows. No position, however superior, would stop them from swarming over us. Everything about the terrain – the narrow passes, the darkness that now hid cracks and crevices, the loose shale that got slipperier as the temperature fell – meant that any attempt to flee or fight would likely send us tumbling over the cliff's edge. And if I attempted to climb the rock face? The infected didn't feel pain. They pushed past the limitations of their muscles and bones. Worst of all, they didn't care if they slipped and fell into the chasm. Even if I could ascend fast enough to escape, I'd never be able to do it carrying Binta.

Rosie had told the truth. I'd reached the end of my path.

196

I took Binta's hand. It felt so small and warm in mine. He looked up at me expectantly, but I couldn't bring myself to form the signs for, *'I'm sorry.'*

'Do you understand now?' Rosie asked.

She was still there, five yards away, at the cliff's edge, staring back at me. Whether I could beat her in a fight didn't matter any more. Whether she was really the Traveller or the just the world's least pleasant Argosi was irrelevant. Binta and I had no chance of surviving the night.

Not unless Rosie gave us one.

'You have a plan?' I asked.

'That depends.'

'On what?'

She left the edge and came towards us. The soft pad of her footsteps got lost in the endless hiss that would soon come crashing down on us like an ocean wave, the hideous expression of rage that rose up in the throats of the nuns whose bloody, chewed-off tongues were the only thing keeping their madness from spreading to us. Rosie got so close I could feel the warmth coming off her skin, taste the faint trace of cinnamon on her breath. I could see the tiny, almost invisible beads of sweat on her forehead betray the terror breaking through her mask of serenity and indifference.

She took my free hand and placed my palm just below her left collarbone. My palm shuddered to the rapid thumping of her heart. Mine was beating faster though.

Durral says the best way to cover up your fear is with a joke.

'Tricks your brain into thinkin' you ain't scared so you stay loose. Get good enough at it, you can fool other folk too.'

'Rosie,' I said, 'I ain't sure what you got planned here, but you should know I never kiss on the first date. Especially when there's a hundred crazy nuns coming to chew the flesh off my bones.'

197

She didn't seem to find my humour reassuring *or* funny.

'I am the Path of Thorns and Roses,' she said, so quiet I could barely hear her over the constant hissing coming down the mountain. 'Nothing I can say will prove to you that I am not the Traveller. You have every reason to suspect me. I was at the Monastery of the Silent Garden where the monks died. I came to Tinto Rhea when the madness spread there. Months ago I visited the Convent of Scarlet Words and I refused to tell you why, nor will I now.'

'Oh, in that case, I definitely trust you.'

She placed her hand over mine. I tried to pull away, but she held me there, my palm pressed to her heart.

'The path we have both travelled ends here, Ferius Parfax. We have only minutes until the horde takes us. Your suspicion of me will lead to hesitation. From hesitation flows catastrophe. Either put your faith in me now, completely, utterly, or none of us will survive the night. It is no small thing I ask of you, Ferius, I know that. But find a way to trust me and I swear to you that with my last breath I will save you and the boy.'

Sure, I thought. *Trust you after you've been hiding secrets from me this whole time. No problem.*

She was right though: I couldn't just pretend to trust her or trick myself into putting our fates in her hands. It wouldn't work.

Suspicion leads to hesitation. From hesitation flows catastrophe.

How was I supposed to put my faith in someone so arrogant, so closed off and unfeeling that she could kill a hall full of strangers without shedding a tear? Was my arta precis supposed to detect the truth of her words by the beat of her heart against my fingertips or the scent of her sweat when she uttered her oath to me?

'*Trust ain't earned, kid.*' That's what Durral would've said if he were here.

'You gonna launch into one of your flowery frontier poems now, Pappy?'

No grin this time. No arta valar.

'Trust is the gift we give one another, Ferius. Not to be proven right or wrong, but because in a world filled with more cynicism than there are grains of sand in the desert, every act of trust is a seed planted beneath the dunes waiting to defy the odds and sprout into something wondrous.'

Yep. A poem. That's exactly what Durral would've offered up at a time like this.

Me? I would've groaned at how corny he was being.

'Seeds don't sprout in the desert, Pappy.'

That's when his grin would've showed up.

'How do you know until you've planted a few, kid?'

Rosie tilted her head. 'Why are you smiling, Ferius Parfax?'

'Just remembering something that makes me happy.'

I would've expected her to cajole me for succumbing to sentimentality at a moment like this, but instead she nodded as if my reaction was entirely sensible under the circumstances. She let go of my hand and unslung her bow from her shoulder.

'Good. Carry that thought with you as long as you can. What comes next will be . . . unpleasant.'

On that score, during those next awful hours, the Path of Thorns and Roses proved herself to be entirely trustworthy.

26

The Horde

You'd think there'd be something comical about a hundred nuns in scarlet red sleeveless habits, arms wrapped in elegant latticework of slender silver chains, each with their hair dyed the same rich red beneath their black hood, foaming at the mouth, fingers curled like claws, teeth biting endlessly and throats hissing like snakes as they swarm all around us and . . .

Actually, I'm not sure why I thought that would be funny. Maybe I'd been anticipating the Mothers Superior giving me those stern, self-important stares beneath arched eyebrows while their blood-soaked mouths longed to chew my flesh and gnaw on my bo—

That's no better, really.

Okay, how about this: what if the gatekeeper, while clacking her shattered teeth at me, pauses to offer a selection of witty and whimsical observations regarding the whorishness of my riding trousers or my generally slutty disposition as she tears me limb from limb?

I mean, come on – that would be a little funny, right?

Sometimes I wonder if Durral Brown's extensive lessons on the importance of laughing in the face of certain doom might not be as ingenious as he thinks. Maybe I'm just not good enough at it yet.

The sight of the horde racing madly down the slope, clambering over one another like insects across a dead animal's carcass, filled me with such gut-wrenching despair that my arta valar fled me entirely.

I was standing at the very edge of the cliff, poor Binta strapped to my back, watching as the first of the nuns came for us. Soon the others would catch up to her, and unless Rosie's brilliant – which is to say, utterly insane and insufferably arrogant – plan worked, I would soon be taking that one final step backwards into oblivion.

Binta's arms were wrapped around my neck. When he saw the nun coming fast despite her hideous, shuffling gait, he squeezed so tight I could barely breathe. Warm liquid trickled down my lower back. The poor kid was peeing himself.

I readjusted the leather straps Rosie had cannibalised from our packs to bind the boy and me together. Light as he was, the added weight was going to make an impossible fight even harder. In the few precious seconds remaining us, I tapped Binta's arm under my chin so he'd notice me signing to him.

'It's going to be okay, Rosie's plan will work.'

I couldn't see his reply, since both his arms were currently engaged in the task of unintentionally choking me to death, but I imagined it was something like: *'Are you out of your mind, Good Dog? That cold-blooded, heartless, lying sack of pig turds just consigned us to our deaths. And you let her do it!'*

Had Binta actually *heard* the details of Rosie's plan, he wouldn't have been reassured.

'We can't outrun the horde, Ferius. We can't outfight them on this unstable terrain nor can we hide from them. That leaves only one option.'

Go ahead: try to figure out what that last option could be. I used every ounce of my arta tuco and came up with nothing.

201

With death coming swiftly for all of us, Rosie still hadn't been able to resist glaring at me like I was being intentionally obtuse.

'*It's obvious – we must find a way to gain control of the horde.*'

'Great. Terrific idea. The nuns have been driven mad by the Scarlet Verses, so all we have to do to switch them to our side is . . . ?'

Even Rosie – Rosie – looked unconvinced by what she said next.

'*I will admit that my hypothesis relies upon a series of conjectures regarding the nature of the Red Scream, the timing of this attack and, above all else, the Traveller's reasons for having gone to both the Convent of Scarlet Words and the Monastery of the Silent Garden. If my inferences—*'

'Guesses.'

'*As you wish. If every one of my guesses is correct, I believe we have a narrow path to survival, if not victory.*'

'And if any one of them – to say nothing of all of them – happens to be wrong?'

Rosie had bitten her lower lip then, which would have been a fetching look were it not an uncomfortable reminder of what other types of biting were coming our way.

'*It has often been said that the Argosi are gamblers, Ferius Parfax.*'

Like I said: not exactly reassuring.

The first nun to reach Binta and me turned out to be my old friend Mother Gossip. She was a fast runner, which made sense, I suppose, since she was younger than most of the others. Her frenzied, animalistic movements, her mouth hanging open so wide her jaw had come unhinged, all suggested her mind was gone, but in her eyes I still saw that same arrogant, casual cruelty that made me badly want to punch her in the face one last time. Instead, I tapped Binta's arm again to get his attention.

'Not so tight,' I signed. '*And stay low on my back. Keep below my shoulders if you can.*'

202

His grip loosened a fraction. Enough for me to breathe, anyway.

Mother Gossip came into range, head tilting sideways as her teeth came for my throat. With everything I had, I gave her a right cross, a dark impulse in me relishing that moment of release as her head snapped backwards. But she didn't fall, just stumbled a few steps then came for us again. This time I ducked low and planted my back foot as hard as I could against the loose ground, and as Mother Gossip barrelled into me, I stood up. The muscles in my legs strained from adding her weight to Binta's, but I managed it, and sent her tumbling over my shoulder into the chasm.

A second nun rounded the turn, this one a short, stout fellow who nonetheless raced for me like I'd said something nasty about his sister.

The ground at the edge of the cliff was mostly loose rocks that shifted unnervingly beneath my boots, and Binta's weight on my back made sudden movements awkward. Still, I sidestepped to my left in time to send this new attacker to the same fate as Mother Gossip. I hoped for his sake that those who die in the same canyon aren't condemned to spend eternity together.

Two down. A hundred, maybe a hundred and twenty, to go.

I felt something wet on my cheek. I looked up and saw the snow beginning to fall from the sky. Soon the ground would be even slipperier than before, making my position even more precarious.

The third and fourth nuns reached us before I'd even had time to draw a deep breath. There was no way to dodge them both, so I turned into the embrace of the first one, a woman my height and build who therefore made a more suitable dance partner than the guy running alongside her. I managed to keep her snapping teeth at a distance, even as her fingernails tore at my arms and shoulders.

Durral's favourite form of arta eres is all about dancing, which takes forever to learn but has the advantage that it's particularly effective for turning someone's own momentum against them. I swung the lady over the cliff after the first two, and might've congratulated myself had not Binta's weight nearly sent us over the edge along with her.

'Rosie, there's got to be a way to do this without the kid being strapped to my back!' I had said to her. 'One wrong move and we're both going over the cliff!'

And then, the least comforting words ever spoken in any language: 'That is the point, Ferius.'

I spun back round to face the second attacker just in time to see his fingernails grasping for my eyeballs. Before I could bat his hands aside, he sprouted an arrow through the centre of his forehead. It got his attention, but he didn't seem bothered.

The problem with fighting people who've lost their minds is that the human body, unleashed from reason, fear or even self-awareness, is a wondrous device that can keep functioning even with an arrowhead embedded in its skull. Had this guy not been staring cross-eyed at the wooden shaft coming out from just above his nose, he would've gotten me. As it was, I dropped down even lower than before, grabbed both his legs and squeezed tight. I pivoted all my weight on my heels so I could spin him around and tip him over the ledge.

I don't know whether there were any shepherds living at the bottom of that cliff, but if there were, they were going to be mightily confused by all the dead nuns landing among their sheep.

'Stop trying to fight them!' Rosie called out from her vantage point about ten yards away, where the horses were tethered. 'Stick to the plan!'

Oh, right. I forgot. The plan.

The sounds of more nuns coming from around the bend told me we didn't have long before the main horde reached us.

I tapped Binta's arm again then held up my hand and signed backwards at him, *'Don't worry, it's going great!'*

I don't think he believed me. *I* didn't believe me.

Rosie's chain of suppositions went something like this:

The nuns of the Convent of Scarlet Words were far too savvy to fall for the trick of reading from a set of verses the Traveller left behind, the way she'd done to the mayor of Tinto Rhea. So how had the nuns become afflicted by the plague right after I'd left the place? The answer was simple: someone had been there to infect them with the Scarlet Verses. Could it have been some particularly suicidal nun? Maybe, but there was a far more likely candidate: the Traveller.

Oh, and want to know how we figured that she had to have been there? Simple: when I'd tried to guess which of the nuns I'd met might be the Traveller, I went through the Mothers Superior one by one.

Gossip, Chatter, Sigh, Drawl, Murmur, Rumour and . . .

Let's try that again: Gossip, Chatter, Sigh, Drawl, Murmur, Rumour and . . .

Even now I couldn't remember the seventh, yet I was absolutely positive there had been seven of them surrounding me in the confessorium and later in the loquatium. So why could I only remember six? Because every time I'd tried to get a look at the seventh, I'd suddenly found some reason to turn away from her.

The Traveller hadn't just mesmerised the Mothers Superior; she'd mesmerised me too.

Binta had seen all seven, but none of them had struck him as any more interesting than the others. To him they were just a bunch of weird people in red-and-black habits, flapping their jaws and doing nasty things to me.

'*Maybe it was the yellow-haired one,*' he had signed to me as Rosie had been preparing the leather strips to strap him to my back.

'*There weren't any with yellow hair,*' I'd signed back distractedly. '*All the nuns at the convent dye their hair red.*'

'*No,*' he'd insisted, irritated with me despite his own mounting terror as the hissing horde grew closer and closer. '*One had yellow hair.*'

Yeah. Turns out while I'd been mocking the Mothers Superior for having allowed the Traveller to insinuate herself into their order and steal their secrets, she'd been standing right there in that creepy loquatium with us, probably laughing her head off.

Anyway, none of that mattered now, because what Rosie, Binta and I needed was a way to survive the night.

So, let's say the Traveller had first gone to the convent to search for the basic forms of the Scarlet Verses, then left to perfect them at the Monastery of the Silent Garden. Except the Red Scream wasn't working out like she'd planned; the infected, driven by some final shred of humanity and resistance, bit off their tongues after repeating the verses only a few times, thereby limiting the spread. The Traveller realises she's missing something – a key ingredient she needs in order to perfect the Scarlet Verses: what the Mothers Superior had referred to as 'the fundaments'.

So the Traveller returns to the convent, hides herself among the Mothers – which is easy because she's already mesmerised them once before – and searches for a candidate among the young initiates being trained to speak using the fundaments. Only none of those kids has the ability to utter more than one or two syllables. The Traveller needs something more – something she'd failed to take from the Monastery of the Silent Garden before she infected the monks there because she hadn't known he existed.

She needs Binta.

I brought him right to her, I thought despairingly. *She could've taken him away from me then and there.*

So why hadn't she?

The snow was coming down thicker now, laying a carpet of white that turned crimson when three women and one man rounded the corner. I could hear more coming not far behind them. Four was too many for me to fight at one time, so I dropped to the ground, flat on my face. The nuns, blind with rage and unable to slow their momentum, literally ran over Binta and me to their death.

Poor kid, I thought. *He's getting just as banged up as I am.*

'The boy!' Rosie shouted to me. 'You must test him now!'

Right. Okay. So let's say the Traveller wants Binta because some combination of his vocal ability and the distinctly unparental way his father raised him gives her what she needs to finalise the Scarlet Verses. We already knew his scream could disrupt other mind-manipulating uses of language, like the one Mother Gossip (may she rest in many, many pieces) had used on me, or when the mayor had read out the Scarlet Verses back in Tinto Rhea. Could his voice likewise cancel the ongoing effects of the Scarlet Verses echoing over and over in the minds of the nuns? And if so, could he be our means to end the plague itself?

I reached up and squeezed the back of his hand, then signed, *'I'm sorry, Bluebird, but you must attempt it now.'*

He took my hand and tapped the palm twice to signal he'd understood.

The horde finally caught up to us, a jostling mass coming around the corner. I slammed my palms over my ears as Binta screamed so loud I feared he'd bring the whole mountain down around us. The reverberations buffeted the nuns like a tornado through a canyon. They all froze in their tracks, heads turning maniacally this way and that as if they were trying to shake off a swarm of flying insects buzzing around their heads. The last echoes of Binta's scream died out.

And then the nuns kept right on coming, a seething, mindless mass of hands clawing at the air and broken teeth clacking as they stretched out their necks in search of flesh to bite.

So much for Rosie's first theory.

I was already at the edge of the cliff. I lifted my right heel and prepared to take one final step backwards into oblivion.

Now we would find out if Rosie's second theory was better.

27

The Hunch

'You're betting our lives on nothing more than a hunch!'

Even as I'd blurted out those words, with Binta hiked up on my back, legs wrapped around my midsection as Rosie finished buckling the straps around my shoulders and chest that would bind our fates, I knew I was missing something.

Rosie? Acting on a *hunch*?

No way.

'What aren't you telling me, Rosie?'

She cinched the last strap around my chest tighter than necessary, which only confirmed my suspicion.

'I've told you everything you need to know, Ferius.'

She'd already begun to turn away, but I grabbed her arm, forcing her to look at me. Our eyes met, and before she could conjure that imperturbable mask of hers that hid every thought and feeling, my arta precis caught the subtle downward slope of her eyebrows, the slight pinching at the corners of her eyes. Her lips parted, as if in that moment of uncertainty some part of her wanted to speak – to unburden herself of a pain that was as familiar to me as it was foreign to the woman I'd come to know.

'You're ashamed,' I breathed. *'Why are you ashamed, Rosie?'*

She knelt down to gather up her quiver and bow. '*Just do your part, Ferius, and let me do mine.*'

Do my part.

My part, now that we'd discovered Binta's scream couldn't break the effects of the Scarlet Verses on the entire swarm of hissing, biting, clawing nuns descending on us, was to stand at the very edge of the cliff. I wasn't meant to fight for our survival. No more running or dodging. No last-minute religious conversions to ease my passage to the afterlife.

Just stand there at the edge of the cliff.

And prepare to take one step back.

The red-habited remnants of once brilliant people clambered over one another like frenzied cockroaches fighting to reach us first. They bashed and battered against each other as they traversed the six-foot ledge, some slipping on the new-fallen snow, dragging others down with them as they went over the edge in their fever to be the first to reach us. Yet they weren't truly mindless, otherwise they would've killed each other off at the convent rather than pursuing us. Some shred of simplistic logic guided their impulses, and that, too, confirmed at least one of Rosie's suspicions.

Wide, soulless eyes locked onto ours, more terrifying even than the hissing of their throats or the shattered teeth now sharpened like broken knives as they clacked against each other over and over.

But that wasn't why my courage finally failed. It was Binta's fingers, curled and unwittingly digging with his nails into the skin of my neck and chest as if he, too, had become one of the infected.

That's when my arta valar abandoned me.

'Rosie, shoot them!' I screamed even though I knew she couldn't possibly get them all. 'Get us out of here! Do someth—'

I was silenced with a word.

210

No, not even a word – barely a breath.

Shhh . . .

Yet it was more than that. Somewhere inside that whisper was a syllable, richer and more resonant than any song or poem. A fundament. What the Mothers Superior had claimed was the primordial component of language that exists beneath our convoluted and inarticulate notions of eloquence. A tongue so elemental that it can reach deep into the mind, past conscious-ness itself. If the gods ever chose to speak to mortals, they would've done so in the language of fundaments.

Like a crying babe suddenly swaddled in its mother's love, the horde stilled. Their arms sank to their sides and the hissing in their throats quieted. Their heads lolled back and forth as if lost in the strains of a melancholy tune. But their eyes still stared at me, inhumanly wide, their jaws working over and over. Probably they were already imagining chewing me to pieces.

I twisted my own head around as far as I could, drawn by the unfounded hope that perhaps Binta had made the sound that had stopped the horde. But his eyes were closed as he wept silently, still anticipating our ghastly fate.

The boy hadn't spoken, which meant Rosie's second theory had proven true.

'We can't outrun the horde,' she'd insisted. '*We can't outfight them and we can't hide from them. That leaves only one option.*'

If the Red Scream turned its victims into enraged lunatics that tore anything and anyone they could find to shreds, then, lacking any of the uninfected to attack, the nuns should've turned on each other at the convent. But they hadn't; they'd chased us instead, which left only one logical conclusion.

Someone was directing the horde.

The mass of red habits parted before me. A figure near the back began to step towards us in a slow, unhurried gait. A pair of calm blue eyes, as unlike those of the crazed nuns as diamond is to coal, trapped me in their gaze, and at last I saw the face of she who had so cleverly set the Red Scream loose upon the world.

She removed her hood, and her hair beneath was blonde just as Binta had tried to tell me. Her skin was pale like mine, though smoother and unfreckled. I guessed her to be a few years older. Twenty-five, maybe? She was attractive, but not especially beautiful. In fact, she was exactly how the Mothers Superior had described her: Young. Quiet. Pretty.

She stepped towards us with an unnatural patience, as if she were basking in the simple joy of walking on fresh snow. Her gaze picked me apart, shedding layer upon layer of my identity so that she might discern how best to turn me to her purpose or, failing that, obliterate me entirely. A faint smile came to her lips as her eyes went to the straps binding Binta and me together, followed by a curt nod as if to acknowledge the simple cunning of Rosie's gambit: had the horde reached me, I would've stepped off the cliff, falling to my death and taking the boy with me, leaving her without that for which she'd come.

Rosie had moved so silently I hadn't noticed her until she was standing by my side, her double-crescent weapon in hand but making no move to use it. She'd warned me that no such obvious attack could succeed against the woman who'd created the Scarlet Verses right under the noses of some of the shrewdest minds on the continent. With her new degree of control over the infected, the Traveller could use a dozen of them to form a shield wall around her and send the rest to kill Rosie. I was tempted to test out that theory, but despite everything I was beginning to trust the Path of Thorns and Roses. Just a little, anyway.

'Guess you're not the Traveller, after all, Rosie.'

'No, I am not,' she replied.

The catch in her voice caused me to turn her way. In the unexpected paleness of her bronze skin, the way her chin was lowered and her bottom lip starting to tremble, I witnessed the full measure of the shame she'd hidden from me until now. With her next words, that shame was at last given voice.

'I am her teysan.'

28

The Standoff

'Rosie?' I asked quietly.

The two of us were standing at the edge of the cliff, staring past nearly a hundred nuns who swayed on the rocky ground like saplings in a cool winter breeze. Snow was settling on their habits.

The woman whose devious verses had driven them insane held them back with nought but the occasional whisper as she looked at me and smiled, testing my resolve to carry Binta and myself to our death in the chasm below.

'Rosie?' I said again.

'Yes, Ferius?'

'I have questions.'

'Perhaps you hadn't noticed the horde of—'

'They can wait. I want answers.'

Rosie cleared her throat. 'Go ahead, then.'

I hadn't expected that. The Path of Thorns and Roses wasn't usually what you'd call forthcoming.

'First of all . . .' I fumbled for the right question to ask among the dozens spinning around in my head. Why hadn't she told me who the Traveller was before now? How long had the two of them known each other? Had Rosie helped her create the Scarlet Verses, only to then have a change of heart?

Probably what I should've been asking was how Rosie, Binta and I were supposed to get out of this standoff alive, if all the Traveller had to do was release the horde of nuns to rip and claw and chew us apart. Instead, what I ended up saying was: 'She looks kinda young for a maetri.'

The Traveller chuckled. Suddenly the nuns began hissing again, lurching forward only to stop in their tracks once their mistress repeated that eerie, single-syllable fundament once again.

'*Shh* . . .'

'You should not make me laugh,' she informed us, once the nuns had settled. 'The quieting fundament is the weakest, and easily banished by jarring noises.'

That explains why Rosie didn't shoot her: if the Traveller doesn't give the horde that shushing sound periodically, the nuns will go nuts again and swarm us.

'You look well, teysan,' the Traveller said, running the delicate fingers of her left hand through her blonde hair, revealing a few strands so pale they were almost silver. 'It pleases me to see that you have found a lover. The long roads get lonely after a while.'

'We are not . . .' Rosie glanced at me then back to the Traveller, embarrassment shifting to anger. 'Look to your own choice of companions before you judge mine, maetri.'

Binta tapped my shoulder. I twisted my head to the right so I could see him signing at me with one hand.

'What is happening, Good Dog?'

I considered how best to answer that question.

'The bad lady is trying to make Rosie uncomfortable so she'll make a mistake at a crucial moment.'

'Is it working?' Binta asked.

'Totally.'

215

Rosie gave me a scathing look. 'Our enemy is before us, surrounded by ninety-six of the remaining infected. She possesses the Scarlet Verses, which could drive us mad if she chooses to utter them. We stand – literally – at the precipice of our deaths. You consider this an appropriate time for jokes?'

'Well, the way I see it, we can't attack her without unleashing the horde. On the other hand, if she so much as whispers anything other than a lullaby . . .'

Carefully, I shifted my balance to my left foot, lifted my right heel and extended it just a few inches behind me, over the open air of the chasm below.

'Am I supposed to be filled with trepidation at such an empty threat?' the Traveller asked.

'Nah,' I said.

I stretched my foot back further, inch by inch until more than half my weight was over the edge and I began to teeter backwards. A fraction of a second before Binta and I toppled to our deaths, I grabbed Rosie's shoulder with my right hand and steadied myself.

She looked none too pleased with me. The Traveller, on the other hand? She'd turned three shades of grey.

Got you, I thought.

Binta tapped me on the shoulder again until I swivelled my head towards the hand he was trying to stick in front of my face.

'*Good Dog, please warn me next time you're about to throw away our lives.*'

I reached up with my free hand and signed back: '*Now where would the fun be in that?*'

The Traveller regained her composure, shushed her mob of lunatic nuns once again, then muttered, 'Arta valar,' like it was a dirty word. 'It is the least of the Argosi talents,' she informed me.

'That's too bad,' I said, 'because it's the only one I'm really good at.'

Rosie, quite uncharacteristically, stuck up for me. 'Her arta valar is like nothing I've ever seen, maetri. Unfortunately for your purposes, it happens to be the one talent you cannot overcome in this situation.'

'Unless she is bluffing,' the Traveller said.

She was staring at Rosie, not at me, which I found odd at first, until I realised what was going on.

She's using her arta precis to try to determine whether Rosie believes I'm really prepared to fall to my death and take an innocent nine-year-old boy with me.

'Pierce me with your gaze all you want, maetri,' Rosie said. 'You will only discover that I have no idea whether Ferius Parfax is willing to die to keep you from the boy, or whether, as you put it, this is all a bluff.'

Frustration played out in the Traveller's features, fading almost as quickly as it had appeared, replaced by something entirely different.

Pride, I realised then. *She's proud of Rosie . . .*

'Cleverly done, my teysan,' the Traveller conceded. 'You have kept your distance from your companion, ensured you wouldn't know her heart well enough to measure her resolve. You predicted this meeting might take place, in one form or another, and thus took steps to prevent yourself from being able to reveal her secrets to me.'

Weird. All this time I just thought Rosie was a stuck-up snob.

'Very well,' the Traveller continued. 'I cannot kill you without risking the loss of the boy, nor can you leave without giving me what I want. There remains only the matter of price to be discussed.'

'Now what's happening?' Binta signed over my shoulder.

'The bad lady wants to buy you from us. You'd better hope she doesn't have any biscuits on her. I'm feeling peckish.'

'Ah,' the Traveller said.

'Excuse me?' I asked.

She stepped through the gawking, swaying nuns to stand before Rosie and me. 'You wish to tell me that you will not give me the boy at any price.' She placed her hand on Binta's shin, which was still strapped around my midsection. 'Thus there is nothing to be gained through negotiation. I may as well . . .' She gave a sudden push on Binta's knee that nearly sent me stumbling back over the cliff edge.

Rosie caught my arm, steadied me and then tried to get between us.

'Don't,' I said. 'She's just trying to rattle me.'

'She will kill you without a thought, Ferius. There is not an ounce of mercy in her.'

Yeah? Then why'd you become her student in the first place, Rosie?

'My teysan's impression of me is unflattering,' the Traveller said, removing her hand from Binta's leg and turning to once again shush the restless nuns. 'However, I see now that you are an idealist as I once was; in that delusion lies the resolution to our dilemma.'

'How do you figure?'

There was something in the way the Traveller walked that itched at my arta precis. For all that she was elegant and fluid in her movements, still there was something . . . unnatural about her grace. I caught it again as she raised her arm to point to the trail leading down the mountain.

'In thirteen days' time, I will arrive at a town called Porta Seren, near the western edge of the ruby region of the Seven Sands. There I will prepare my final test of the Scarlet Verses. I give you these

218

few days. Take them to make your peace with the decision at which you will arrive soon enough, and bring the boy to me.'

It shamed me that, despite how repugnant the suggestion that I would ever consider giving Binta to her, all I felt in that moment was a flood of relief at the possibility I might not die today.

'*Feelin's are fine things,*' Durral would've said. '*Just don't wear 'em on your face in the middle of a card game.*'

'You seem pretty confident in your predictions, lady,' I said. 'But the Argosi – *real* Argosi, I mean, not lunatics posing as ones – don't take to prognostication, and we sure as hell don't turn over innocent children to mass murderers.'

My accusation failed to ruffle her feathers any.

'You refer to the events at the Silent Garden and at that village?'

'Yeah, but I think you might be forgettin' somebody.'

I pointed to the mob of swaying and quietly hissing nuns behind her.

'Ah, of course,' she said. She smiled at her entourage. 'Such arrogant creatures, these nuns. So convinced of their superiority. Is the world truly worse off without them?'

'Don't know,' I admitted. 'But it isn't your choice to make.'

'Do not engage her in conversation,' Rosie warned. 'Every word you utter is a seed she will eventually use against you, burying it deep in your mind, nurturing inside the soil of your unconscious a dark garden of her own devising.'

'Silly girl,' the Traveller admonished her. 'Speaking in melodramatic poems. That's not how I taught you. Besides, I learned everything I needed to know about your companion when she was in the confessorium.' Her gaze returned to me. 'Yes, Ferius Parfax, I was there when the Mothers Superior drew from you the admission of your nights spent hunting the Jan'Tep mages who once hunted your people. I heard, too, how you drove the blade of the

219

sword you carry at your back into your foster mother's chest. A pity. I once met the Path of the Rambling Thistle. She was . . . special.'

'Don't,' Rosie warned me. 'She aims to unnerve you.'

No kidding.

The Argosi say that shame, like grief, is wasted love. I'd never taken to that lesson, but I could fake it if I had to.

'She's going after your weakness,' Enna would've told me had she been there, had I not . . . Enna would've pinched my cheek and told me to pay attention. *'The vulnerabilities we perceive in others are often those we recognise in ourselves. When she thrusts for your shame and your grief, don't parry. Counter-attack instead. Find the weakness she's hiding from you.*

'Enna Brown was the greatest woman I'd ever known or could ever hope to know,' I told the Traveller, not parrying, counter-attacking. 'I'll carry my crime with me for the rest of my life, just like I'll carry her teachings. Who did you hurt, lady? I can see the hundreds dead by your design don't haunt your dreams none, so how come I'm pretty sure you don't sleep so good?'

Her gaze flitted, just for an instant, barely moving from my face at all, but still enough.

Rosie. You did something to Rosie and you can't get over it.

I glanced at the Path of Thorns and Roses, but there was only that mixture of anger and caution in her expression. She hadn't seen what I'd seen.

'Good,' the Traveller said. 'Though you lack proper training in the Argosi ways, Ferius Parfax, still your maetri taught you a few tricks.'

She tried to sound glib, but my arta loquit was awake now, no longer smothered by fear or outrage. I heard the tiny fluctuations in her voice, the way the breath behind her words trailed off just at the ends.

220

She's tired. Alone in this and she doesn't want to be. That's why she made that jibe earlier about Rosie taking a lover, even if she believes it was just to throw her teysan off her game.

'Reckon I've learned a trick or two,' I agreed. 'Now I can't say as I've met a whole lot of Argosi, but the two who took me in are the finest to ever walk the long roads and I'll beat the hells out of anyone who says otherwise. So believe me when I tell you, lady, you ain't no Argosi.'

'How tiring you must find this one,' the Traveller said to Rosie. 'You were never one for frontier philosophising or grand moral pronouncements. Does this churlish girl not irritate you to no end?'

'Actually, maetri, she is beginning to grow on me.'

The Traveller reached out a hand and placed it on Rosie's cheek. 'Ever does the Path of Thorns and Roses try to grow and as she blooms become more beautiful and dangerous at the same time. I have missed you.'

Rosie's voice caught in her throat. 'And I you, maetri. Turn away from this path. You have strayed too far from the principles you taught me.'

The Traveller took her hand away as if stung.

'On the contrary, I am fulfilling those principles at last.'

She returned to the horde and faced me again.

'Nine days,' she said. 'Nine days and you will bring the boy to me so that his abilities can be used to tune the Scarlet Verses. Otherwise I will have to search for other means to perfect them, and in that quest, the Red Scream will spread far and wide. This continent will be barren before I am done, if that is the price to eradicate the enemy.'

'Who?' I demanded. 'Who could you possibly despise so deeply that you would unleash this atrocity?'

221

'I hate no one, Ferius Parfax. In truth, I have not entirely abandoned the Argosi ways, merely ... improved them. The Way of Water was a dream. The Way of the Wind has already shown us the path ahead. The Way of Stone is for fools. There is only the Way of Thunder left.'

She uttered a sound then, this one like a piercing whistle that made me want to run, without purpose or destination. Suddenly the horde of maddened nuns awoke and came at us.

There was nowhere to go, no way to evade them. Rosie wrapped her arms around Binta and me, trying to shield us, but that only meant all three of us were going to die together.

I chose for my last act in this life to be a lie, and held up my free hand over my shoulder to sign to Binta: 'Close your eyes and all will be well.'

I don't know if he did, because by then the first nun had reached us. Instinctively my hands came up to fight, but the crazed woman ran right past me, across the snow and straight over the cliff. I turned, and saw her legs and arms still pumping as if she were trying to accelerate her descent. Then another went by us, and another, and another after that. One by one the nuns were hurling themselves over the ledge, tumbling to their doom a thousand feet below.

'Rosie, what did she –'

But when I turned back to her, watching as all those lives were tossed away like spent ashes into the wind, the answer became obvious. The Traveller was done with the horde. The infected nuns had failed their purpose and now she was ridding herself of them. Within seconds, every last member of the once legendary Convent of Scarlet Words had disappeared into the mists below.

The Traveller was already walking away from us, from the butchery she'd left behind. I was ready to order Rosie to shoot the Traveller with an arrow, or bludgeon her to death with that double-crescent weapon, but the words that came out of my mouth were, 'Cut the straps and cover Binta's eyes. I don't want him to see me—'

Rosie held me back.

'We must not.'

'You should heed my teysan, Ferius Parfax,' the Traveller said over her shoulder as she set off down the mountain pass, the snow crunching under her sandals. 'She knows my arta tuco is far beyond that of other Argosi, and there is no situation of which you can conceive for which I have not prepared myself. Seven letters have I left with seven fools in seven towns more populous than Tinto Rhea.'

'No . . .' I breathed.

'Should I die or fail to visit them on my journey to the borderlands,' she went on, still walking away from us, calm, unhurried, 'my absence will cause those letters to be opened, and those verses to be read. Thousands will die. So make your peace with destiny and come find me among the ruby sands, else I will unleash the Red Scream upon every soul on this continent.'

'Who are you punishing?' I shouted. 'Who could commit a crime so grave that an Argosi would consider justification for the mass slaughter of innocents just to design a plague to punish them?'

It was that question that made her stop walking away, if only for a moment.

'You haven't guessed by now? I would've thought given your people's history, and your own habits, that the answer would be obvious. Only one nation considers itself superior to all others, deems the lives of lesser beings unworthy of mercy. One culture whose foul deeds in the past are exceeded only by those they've yet to commit in the future. One people who must die for the good of all.'

'No,' I croaked, but I couldn't find the breath even for that. Yet she heard me, or simply knew what I was thinking.

'Yes, Ferius Parfax. For you, for your dead Mahdek ancestors, for all those whose existence is threatened because the Argosi have failed us, I will perfect the Red Scream and use it to eradicate the Jan'Tep once and for all.'

29

The Descent

Over the next three days we made our way down the mountain. We trudged along in silence, our legs sluggish even though we'd left the snow behind. We kept our thoughts to ourselves. Mine weren't worth sharing. When we set up camp, even Rosie's usual obsession for fastidious preparations gave way to the simple desire to close one's eyes and bring the day to an end, to sleep and hope not to dream.

Where was the glory from our escape with death? We'd faced off against a nightmarish army, saved by our wits and our daring. Should we have felt *some* relief when the Traveller had walked away with neither Binta nor our corpses to show for her troubles? Why couldn't we look across the campfire and smile at each other, or at least nod in grim recognition of our shared struggle?

Hell, we'd even kept the horses alive! Not that either of them showed any appreciation for our efforts. Quadlopo refused to so much as look at me and Biter had taken to angrily nipping at Rosie's shoulder whenever she got too close.

Poor beasts, I thought, during one of my more charitable moments. *After the depravity they've witnessed from our species, what must they think of us?*

Quadlopo and Biter, for all their surly dispositions, had been traumatised. Nothing in my study of arta loquit offered the eloquence needed to ease or even understand what they were going through. That proved doubly true of Binta.

'How is the boy?' Rosie asked when I returned to the fire on the second night, after having put him to bed in the canvas tent I kept rolled up in one of my saddlebags.

I spared her my thoughts on the subject and instead made the signs for, '*I am fine. Leave me alone, Good Dog.*'

Binta had gotten so used to giving me that answer whenever I dared show concern for how he was doing that his fingers reflexively twitched those same shapes any time I got within ten feet of him.

'He does not cry at night,' Rosie observed. 'I hear him rolling on the ground, shivering because in his sleep he's shed his blanket. When I go to check on him, I see his face contorting as if he were weeping, yet he makes no sound, and no tears come to his eyes.'

'*Fascinating*,' I said drily.

Rosie got the hint.

We sat in our usual brooding silence, but soon she started up again.

'My intent is not to demean the boy's suffering,' she said, more tentatively this time. 'Only to note that his mind does not work as ours do. Even at the most instinctive levels, he is not like us, Ferius.'

He is not like us. Now there was a strange thought – mostly because it implied that Rosie and I had something in common.

The change in her demeanour was what troubled me the most, actually. I'd gotten used to her arrogance and insistence on always leading the way. Now she explained herself all the time. Equivocated. Apologised even when it wasn't necessary. It was as if, like Biter and Quadlopo and even Binta, she lacked the language

226

necessary to express her pain. It seemed to me that she had a lot of it inside her.

'When do you plan on telling me about the Traveller?' I asked.

Despite Rosie having offered no particular reason to give her space, I'd found myself doing just that for an entire day and night as we'd made our way down the sloping paths towards the desert. But tomorrow we'd reach the edge of the Seven Sands, and there would be decisions to make. Plans to devise. Sacrifices to weigh. I couldn't do those things until I better understood what we were up against.

Rosie stared into the flames as if she'd already forgotten my question. Several times I saw her mouth begin to open, only to close again. Finally she asked, 'Will you sleep in my tent with me tonight, Ferius?'

My stomach clenched as a dozen different interpretations of that very unexpected question ran through my mind. 'What?'

She looked up at me. Embarrassment bloomed across her cheeks, threatening to become a terrible, scarring humiliation. I don't think she'd even intended to say what she'd said. 'I . . . I forget sometimes what it is like to feel the warmth of another's touch. To feel . . . embraced.'

'Rosie, I'm not . . .'

A kind of awkward desperation seemed to overcome her as she fumbled for words. 'I saw you in that hall in Tinto Rhea with that girl. You were holding hands and—'

'Rosie, stop!'

She looked at me like I'd slapped her. A second later she rose to her feet and turned away from the fire. 'Forgive me. I did not mean to presume that because you desired her you would share yourself with me. I'm not asking you to become my lover, I merely . . . It is cold in the mountains. I just wanted to sleep next to someone tonight, that's all.'

She started to go, forcing me to step around the fire to take her arm.

'Rosie, she's dead. Her name was Lyrida, and I knew her for only a few hours and then she was gone. I shouldn't have . . . I don't even know whether I was attracted to her or just . . . drawn to her attraction for me.' I shook my head. 'This probably isn't making any sense.'

Rosie chuckled, which was unusual for her, to say the least.

'What?' I demanded.

'Nothing, I do not mean to offend. It is only that . . . this is one of the few occasions since I met you where what you said *does* make sense to me.'

Her eyes met mine. She put her hand up between us and held it there, palm out.

'What are you doing?'

'Nothing,' she replied. 'This is just my hand. It doesn't have to mean anything. You can place yours on it, if you want, and decide for yourself how that feels, without it implying anything about you or me or the world around us. It is only my hand, and yours, if you want.'

I started to raise my own hand, curious what it would feel like to press my palm against hers, and became so suddenly overcome by nerves that I had to consciously keep myself from slipping into my arta tuco and searching for an escape.

It's just a hand, I told myself. *It doesn't make us lovers.*

I almost pulled away, more terrified of touching her than I would've been fighting off a dozen crazed nuns. But I was curious, and scared, and unimaginably sad. Everything that had happened since I'd left home now seemed one long, never-ending cycle of violence. I wanted to feel something else, even if it was bad.

I placed my palm against hers, ready to snatch it away if she did anything strange like try to grab hold of me. She didn't though, just stood there and stared at our fingers touching as if she wasn't quite sure if I were real. Or maybe she wasn't sure if she was real.

I'd been through so much in my life already. Witnessed massacres. Been tortured both physically and mentally. Mages, thugs and sometimes decent, ordinary people had tried to kill me. Worse, I'd had to kill some of them. I should've been used to it all by now, but I wasn't. Like Quadlopo and Biter, I hurt on the inside in ways I couldn't speak aloud. Like Binta, I needed something for which I lacked the words. All I knew was that I didn't want to hurt like this any more, and that I liked the way Rosie's hand felt against mine.

She pivoted her palm just a few degrees clockwise, so that our fingers no longer met but overlapped, slid into the gaps between. She looked at me for permission, and when I nodded, her fingers slid down to hold my hand. My fingers did the same to hers.

'Are you all right?' she asked. 'Do you wish to stop?'

I don't know if it was loneliness or the unexpectedly gentle sensation of her callouses touching mine, but by way of answer, I raised my other hand and tapped a finger on my lower lip.

'These are my lips,' I said. 'It doesn't have to mean anything, but if you want to place yours on them . . .'

She leaned in and pressed her mouth to mine. I'd never thought of my lips as thin but hers were so much fuller that I wondered if the feeling disappointed her somehow. But she didn't stop, and soon I tasted another person's tongue for the first time, and felt my whole face begin to tremble.

I was seventeen years old. From the age of twelve I'd been held under the curse of a neck collar of Jan'Tep sigils that made anyone I got close to want to kill me. Even after those spells faded, I'd kept my distance from everyone, even Durral and Enna who I loved more than anyone in the world. And then I'd . . .

Rosie pulled away. 'Ferius? Have I done something wrong?'

'I'm fine. It's nothing. I just –'

Her finger traced a line down my cheek. She held it up for me to see. 'You're crying.'

'A bad thought, that's all.'

She eyed me cautiously, and it occurred to me then that we weren't equals in this. Rosie knew who she was, knew what she wanted. In the waters in which we'd dipped our toes, she was probably an expert swimmer. I'd likely drown without help.

'Perhaps this is too much, too fast,' she said, gently removing her hand from mine. 'I hadn't expected . . . I only wanted to show you that it is all right to touch another person without feeling ensnared or under some obliga—'

'Rosie . . .'

'Yes?'

I don't know. Maybe it was all the chaos we'd been through, or an awareness deep inside me of all the experiences I'd missed as a child to be carefree and foolish, and that not very long from now my youth would have passed too, and with it all the harmless mistakes I might've made, the memories that would simultaneously make me groan with embarrassment and shiver with delight. Hell, maybe it was just my arta valar kicking in because that's what happens when my other talents fail me.

I reached up to the collar of my shirt and undid the top button, then the next and the next. 'This is my body,' I said. 'It doesn't have to mean anything, but if you want to . . .'

She smiled then, and for just a moment she wasn't the Path of Thorns and Roses – wasn't the arrogant, ridiculously skilled Argosi who was so much better at everything than I was. She was just a teenage girl, like me. The most beautiful girl I had ever seen, standing with me beneath uncaring stars on a cold, cruel mountain.

Hand in hand we walked to her tent. At that strange, uncharted precipice between one world and another, she hesitated.

'Ferius, I haven't told you about Penta.'

'Who?'

'The Traveller. Our enemy. My . . . my relationship with her was not as it should be between teysan and maetri.'

'Tomorrow,' I said. 'Tomorrow you'll tell me everything, and we'll make the decisions we have to make.'

Rosie shook her head. 'What we are about to do . . . When you hear about Penta, about me, you may not want to do this with me.'

'I know,' I said, and pulled her down so we could enter the tent together. 'That's why I don't want you to tell me until tomorrow.'

30

Touch

I didn't sleep that night. Not even after we'd finally lain back against our woollen bedrolls, the sweat dripping off our skin, listening to the strange, soothing harmony of our breathing. Not hours later either, when the mountain finches whistled the first notes of their morning song. I was so tired – more tired than I could ever remember being. But I still didn't want to sleep.

Not for an hour.

Not for a second.

All I'd wanted was to stay there with my head resting awkwardly on Rosie's arm, wisps of her hair tickling my nose, the rocky ground beneath my blanket pressing uncomfortably against my spine. All of it, just as it was, for as long as possible.

'Ferius . . .' she began.

'Don't.'

That bought me another minute.

It's funny, the things we think matter. How many nights during the strange, lonely seventeen years of my life had I wondered what it would be like to kiss and be kissed, to touch and be touched? All those insecurities over whether I'd be any good at either, or whether I'd feel much of anything in return. None of it mattered, because none of it compared to what came afterwards – to that unimaginable euphoria that accompanied the simple feeling of my body nestled next to that of another. The warmth of her skin so perfectly contrasted against the chill night air, the juxtaposition like some exotic liquor I couldn't stop drinking.

How could anyone *not* want to feel this way all the time?

'Do you know,' Rosie began – ignoring my pleading groan that she not drag us back into the world of Red Screams and Scarlet Verses – 'nowhere in any of the Argosi teachings is there any concept of duty?'

'Fascinating. Scintillating. Shut up.'

Her laugh never got past her lips. It existed merely for a second as a rumble in her belly that only made me more determined than ever to stay precisely as we were, for as long as it took to hear it again.

'An Argosi never acts out of loyalty or obligation,' she went on. 'We take no oaths, swear no vows. There is only the path we have chosen. Every decision, every action, determined by our journey. No generals to command us. No contracts to bind us. Always and forever there is only our path for so long as we choose to walk it.'

Durral and Enna never talked much about paths or how to pick one. They never explained why theirs was called 'The Path of the Rambling Thistle'. They'd never told me how to find my own. I guess they'd figured I wasn't ready.

'And where does the Path of Thorns and Roses lead?' I asked, too late realising I'd walked into Rosie's trap.

Her lips brushed my cheek. You couldn't even call it a proper kiss.

'The Path of Thorns and Roses is to seek out that which is vibrant and beautiful about the world, and to protect it no matter the cost. That path leads out of this tent, down the mountain and into the desert. It winds through terrible danger, and demands difficult choices.'

233

I felt her hand take mine.

'Will you walk my path with me awhile, Ferius?'

To my credit, and despite the embarrassing quaver in my voice, I managed not to cry when I asked, 'What's the first step?'

She sat up and began putting on her clothes. I did the same, hating every second of it. When we were done she sat cross-legged opposite me, our knees just inches away from each other, yet in that distance was a chasm as deep and as far as the one that awaited us outside.

'We have a long journey ahead of us, and a story I must tell you before we begin. There are . . . parts of my life that will help you understand the Traveller, though I'd give anything to never burden you with them. When my tale is done, you will know me better, and like me far less.'

I reached out to her. 'Rosie –'

She shook her head, putting her hands up to keep me from touching her. 'Yarisha Fal. We must begin with the days when I was called Yarisha Fal.'

'It's a beautiful name,' I said, though I wasn't even sure that was true. I just felt like I needed to say something.

She looked back at me as if she were standing on the shore and I aboard a ship about to sail away forever.

'Yarisha Fal means Killer of Children.'

31

Yarisha Fal

I was not born to this continent. A thousand leagues from the eastern shore of Gitabria lies an archipelago of twelve islands. Each one was its own nation, with its own history rich in glorious achievements, ingenious inventions and moments of horrific violence. Collectively, our twelve peoples are known as the Arkya. Roughly translated into your tongue, the word means 'civilised'.

And yes, I see you smirking at me, Ferius Parfax.

Like you, I am seventeen years old. Even as a girl, however, I felt much older. You must understand that in my culture a child begins studying philosophy at six years of age. We believe that what separates human beings from animals is our capacity to grow beyond the desires and impulses of our bodies. To us, this is what it means to be civilised. This is what it means to be Arkyan.

This must all sound like arrogance to you. Perhaps it is. Yet when first I came to the shores of this continent at the age of ten, I was shocked at the way these people lived in endless pursuit of pleasure without enlightenment, attainment without purpose. Power. Riches. Sex. Those most capable of acquiring the greatest quantity of such things become those who rule over the lives of others.

And what of my people?

Our leaders are philosophers. Cosmologists and algebraists, epistemologists and geometers. For an Arkyan to wield influence is to forever abandon personal wealth and comfort. How can any government set the course of a nation if the self-interest of its ministers might sway their decisions? Only a council of philosopher kings – political ascetics who sacrifice personal desires for the greater good – can hope to guide a people towards peace and fulfilment.

Into this perfect, rational society was I born.

As a slave.

Don't look at me that way. I do not tell you this to earn your pity or affection, but because, in its own small way, the life to which I was born set off the chain of events that culminates in both the Traveller's decision to create the Red Scream *and* the means by which we must end it. But to understand that, you must first grasp how a nation of philosophers can condone slavery.

There is a logic to human bondage, you see. A . . . mathematical equation that justifies its existence. Ours is a nation poor in all things save learning. Our survival is dependent on acquiring that which we need from stronger, more populous nations, all while dissuading them from conquering us. Thus we have mastered the arts of diplomacy, political strategy and manipulating the weaknesses of other cultures. We trade with them not what they need, but what they desire. We brew liquors more potent than any found elsewhere, refine exotic flowers into powders that usher the mind into magnificent and erotic dreams even as they weaken the will. We forge weapons from alloys so strong and sharp that an Arkyan spearhead can pierce the finest armour made on this continent. We manufacture ruin and sow despair.

In a nation of philosophers and mathematicians, artists and astronomers, who would willingly submit their life to such endeavours?

There are two types of slaves among the Arkya. The first are those whose intellectual capacities make them unsuited to pursuits of the mind. Some of these become craftspeople, others simply work the land or the forge or service the mundane daily needs of the elite. There is no shame in it.

The second type of slaveborn is rarer; their deficit is not in the mind but in the soul. We call this *tiran* – an absence of connection to other human beings, matched with an animalistic cunning. While unwelcome within general society, such individuals make the perfect agents of our nation's more clandestine philosophical dictates. We are known as logicians. You might call us spies.

Imagine, for a moment, being six years old and brought into a room where a council of wise teachers informs you that you will never be an artist or a scholar, that you lack the moral fibre for leadership or even the basic capacity for love.

'But do not fret, young one, because from this day forth you will begin your training as a logician. Yours will be the life that preserves a culture built on art, philosophy and science, by travelling to other countries and slowly, patiently and inexorably destroying them from the inside. This is how you will serve the glory of the Arkya.'

Again you scowl and mutter as if expressions of disdain could alter the past, Ferius. What I need you to do is listen, pay attention and let your arta precis awaken to what it is I'm trying, in my own way, to tell you.

Can you do that?

Now, the training of a logician is meant to last eleven years, until we are seventeen. However I was only ten years old when I

237

was summoned into the chamber of a famed master logician and informed of a tremendous threat to the future of the Arkyan people. A wealthy family across the sea in a country named Gitabria was ascending to ever greater heights of power and influence. The Gitabrians are a nation of explorers and traders ruled by their lords mercantile, but our theoreticians estimated that within two generations this particular family would have acquired so much wealth that they would form a dynasty, and the step from dynasty to empire is short indeed. Surrounded on their own continent by strong, militaristic neighbours, the Gitabrians would instead seek to begin their empire across the water in the tiny archipelago nation of the Arkya.

I was just a little girl, not particularly strong or skilled, and only four years into my training. How could I possibly be the one to rescue my people from this terrible destiny?

'Tell me, child,' the master logician said, 'what are your two most valuable qualities?'

'I work hard, sir,' I replied. 'And I am very brave.'

My answer earned me a disappointed frown and a stern rebuke.

'What do our people care how hard you think you work? Or how brave you believe yourself to be? You're a child. A slave. Hard work is expected. Bravery is irrelevant.'

I had never known shame like that before. It was like . . . like I had lain down in a grave and now waited for him to shovel dirt over me. Instead he reached out a hand to brush my cheek.

'You are beautiful, little one. *That* is your value to us. This arrogant Gitabrian couple, obsessed with appearances as part of their scheme for social and political advancement, will be moved by your loveliness to bring you into their home as both servant to their children and ornamentation for their palace.' He rose from his chair and turned to go. 'You set sail tomorrow. The journey will take several weeks. Bring no books or other distractions save a guide to the Gitabrian language and their customs. These texts we will provide you.'

That was it. No words of encouragement. No hint of embarrassment at sending a child into danger. No offer to see my own family one last time. As the great logician was about to leave the room, I called out to him.

'Master?'

'Yes, child?'

'You asked what I believed to be my two most valuable qualities. You have informed me that my first is my physical beauty. What is my second?'

He was under no obligation to answer me. After all, it hardly mattered. I had my orders. The course of my life was set. A logician who seeks to know themselves better is guilty of vanity. Yet my master chose to be kind to me. He stopped and turned, and I remember the way he leaned against the doorway, casually, as if we were colleagues or perhaps even friends.

'I just informed you that your bravery and diligence were irrelevant, and your primary value to society lay only in your appearance. You are ten years old. You should be crying. Distraught. Angry, even. Yet you stand there and ask only that I name your second quality. In doing so, you have answered your own question.'

'Duty?' I asked, but even as I said it, I knew that wasn't the answer. A slave can't know duty because they have no choice.

'You are, for want of a better term, heartless. More than any other logician I have trained, you lack the emotional depth to experience true suffering. While such a deficiency is itself of no particular value, we find it highly correlated with a lack of empathy

239

for the suffering of others. This will make it much easier for you to murder the sons and daughters of the Gitabrian family.'

When I'd first been given to the logicians, my name had been taken away from me. Now I had a new one.

Yarisha Fal.

Killer of Children.

32

The Silence

Yarisha Fal.

Just like that, Rosie stopped talking. She crawled out of the tent and started breaking camp, leaving me to gather up our bedrolls, fold up the tents and see to Binta's breakfast and the preparation of the horses for the next stage of our journey.

I kept trying to catch her eye, kept waiting for the right moment to demand why she stopped her story where she did and how any of this connected to the Traveller or the Red Scream. But she gave me no opportunity. You could see it in the way she rode Biter down the mountain slopes, always a few yards ahead. The distance between us grew when she answered with only short, clipped sentences whenever I asked a question or pointed out that we needed to stop and rest for Binta's sake.

'*Why is Rosie acting this way?*' the boy signed to me when we finally stopped for the night. By sundown tomorrow we'd reach the desert. Even that seemed too long.

'*I don't know.*'

'*Why don't you ask her?*'

'*You know what?*' I signed to him. '*I recall now that I did ask her what was wrong. She said it's because you're so ugly she's afraid she'll*

241

confuse you with Biter and try to mount up on your back and end up falling off the mountain.'

Binta giggled in that silent way of his. The kid really liked ugly jokes.

'Maybe it's because you're so ugly she's afraid that the next time she kisses you she'll discover she's actually kissing Quadlopo's behind!'

A sudden stab of guilt hit me.

'You saw?' I asked.

He jabbed an accusing finger at me. With his free hand he signed, *'I knew it! I knew you two were going to kiss! And you just admitted it, Good Dog!'*

He seemed so pleased with having uncovered my apparently terrible secret that I wasn't sure how to react.

'I'm sorry,' I signed awkwardly. *'I didn't mean for you to—'*

Binta gave a shrug. *'I don't care. Mistress Groundhog and my father made each other happy. Now they are both dead. Should I wish that they had gone to their deaths without having felt joy when they were alive?'*

'You are . . .' I was so flustered it took me a second to recall the finger patterns to form the right words. *'You are very wise.'* Then, because that felt off somehow, I added, *'For someone whose face I keep confusing with Quadlopo's droppings.'*

Binta came over and hugged me, then pulled away and signed. *'Be happy while you can, Good Dog. I think we're going to be dead soon.'*

'Bluebird . . .'

I tried to hug him again but he skipped out of reach.

'I am fine, Good Dog. I will gather wood for the fire now.'

He left me standing there, convinced his stoic facade was far more brittle than he pretended, yet equally sure that if I pushed him to admit his feelings he'd break apart entirely.

242

I turned and caught Rosie watching me. My inability to help Binta rose like bile I needed to spit out no matter who it hit.

'Something you want to say to me, Yarisha Fal?'

If she was hurt by either my words or my tone, nothing in my arta precis could detect it. She just went back to setting up our little camp for the night.

It wasn't until hours later, after Binta had gone to sleep in my tent and I lay outside under the stars, shivering yet not wanting to disturb the kid with my fretting and *definitely* not planning on sleeping in Rosie's tent, that I heard her soft footfalls approach and felt her lay down beside me on the ground.

'What are you doing out here, Rosie?' I asked. 'Because if you think we're going to—'

'You keep calling me by that name,' she said, cutting me off. Her voice came from low in her chest, making it almost husky. 'And I keep allowing you because . . . because some part of me likes it. Rosie is the name of a young woman inexperienced in the ways of the world. Unwise to its dangers. Innocent. I wish I could be that girl for you, Ferius.'

'You can be whoever you want to be,' I said. 'Isn't that the Way of the Argosi?'

Her head turned, and all my convictions were lost in the contours of her face. I was reminded of what she'd told me that morning: that her masters had chosen her for that terrible mission, first because of her beauty, and second because of her lack of empathy.

'To be Argosi is to choose a path,' she said. 'Mine is the Path of Thorns and Roses. That is what I keep trying to tell you, Ferius. That is why you must hear the rest of my story, not all at once so that you can try to lock it away in a corner of your thoughts and pretend I'm someone else that only you can see. But step by step, piece by piece, so that you'll be ready when we face the Traveller.'

Two contradictory realisations hit me then, which was odd, because both made me feel ashamed. First, an awareness that the Path of Thorns and Roses wasn't taking anything away from me. She didn't owe me love or affection or anything at all. Last night had been . . . a breath. A single warm, lovely, intoxicating breath from a rare garden that had to be left where we'd found it, here in the mountains.

The second awareness was just how ridiculous I must've looked, pining over her like some lovesick suitor while there was a lunatic out there aiming to spread madness and disease across this continent. I had wanted more than anything to be an Argosi like Durral and Enna, and here I was, holding back tears for a life that wasn't meant to be mine in the first place.

Follow the Way of Wind, I told myself. *Listen for every sign in every breeze, because soon comes the Way of Thunder, and you need to be prepared.*

'Tell me,' I said at last. 'Tell me what you did to those children.'

33

The Clockmaker

You must think my people to be evil. Cruel. Heartless. Yet this is not so. We have merely turned the study of how societies rise and fall into a science. Had that Gitabrian family risen to power, they would have consolidated control over their own nation before coming to destroy ours. They were destined to become tyrants, and does not every civilisation have the right – the duty – to act in the defence of its citizens? And if so, is not the future as worthy of protection as the present?

Here is the difference between our cultures: you would argue that the murder of children can never be justified. Mine would argue that if the lives of five children can prevent the slaughter of thousands, taking those lives is not merely justified, it is required. It is noble. It is . . . kind.

Perhaps.

The flaw in the logic of our theoreticians is that it is easy to predict possible futures when you never allow them to arise. I have come to believe that my people's most fundamental precepts have become a self-fulfilling prophecy. We convince ourselves that our neighbours are barbarians inevitably drawn to violence, so we manipulate them into wars with each other. We fear the rise of dictators, so we execute them for those crimes before they can commit them. We believe some of our citizens are suited only to become tools of our most violent necessities, so we lock them up and ensure they are never allowed to become anything else.

Six months after I wormed my way into that opulent household in Gitabria, I poisoned five innocent children. Two sons and three daughters: Sephan, aged twelve; Trina, aged eleven – she wanted to be a contraptioneer like her mother; Carzo, aged nine; Juliara, aged six. Such a stupid girl. She insisted I teach her to draw ponies over and over again. Loja, the youngest, aged—

No, Ferius. Let me finish.

I gave each one a paralytic so that they would be awake yet unable to move. My masters believed that a particular expression of horror frozen on the children's faces would be necessary so that once their parents found them, they would never be able to see anything else. Only this way could we be certain their ambitions would die with their sons and daughters. The children's deaths had to be memorable. A work of art.

You think I'm being callous. You want to believe that what I'm describing could not possibly be necessary. Even now you are trying to convince yourself it would not work – that such inhumanity could only lead to greater bloodshed. Yet, if you could see the look in your own eyes, how my mere recounting of events cuts away the slender threads of your own faith in the decency of the world, you would know why such acts as I was commanded to execute can, indeed, achieve the desired aim.

I was ten years old. All I had to do was walk out of that house and within an hour the toxin would wear off and the children would live, yet I was about to murder them. Was I hesitant? Repentant? No. I was going to be a hero.

I would do as I'd been commanded. And if I could escape that night, if I could sneak aboard a vessel sailing east, I might even return home. Perhaps my masters would deem this one act of sacrifice so great that they would allow me to choose whether to continue as a logician or become something else.

Begin with the hardest task first. That's what my teachers had trained me to do, and that was the thought circling through my mind as I held the knife over Loja's throat while she lay in her crib, looking up at me, wondering why she could not cry out even though she was so terribly afraid.

And then . . .

And then . . .

A voice.

Not one inside me as you would wish, Ferius. This wasn't my conscience speaking to me. There was someone in the room.

'Have you ever seen the inside of a clock?' she asked.

I turned, the knife in my hand ready to strike, though I already knew it would do no good. After all, this person sounded older than me, which likely meant she was bigger and stronger, and I hadn't heard her sneak into the room, which meant her skills surpassed mine. I fully expected to find the point of a blade aimed at my own throat. Instead she stayed in the shadows by the window, eating an apple.

'Beautiful things, clocks. All those gears and springs, the delicately shaped hands on beautifully painted faces. I would've loved to be a clockmaker, I think.'

'Who are you?' I asked.

'How could that possibly matter?' she asked back.

She was tall. I guessed her age to be nineteen or twenty. There was a lithe, lanky grace to her, accentuated by the black linen wrappings covering her from head to toe. Her blonde hair, so pale it was almost silver, was mostly hidden beneath a scarf. She had smeared the skin of her face with dark paints to make herself harder to see.

'Are you a thief?' I asked. 'If so, you may take whatever you wish so long as you—'

'Tick, tock,' she said.

'What?'

'Tick, tock. Tick, tock.'

For a moment I wondered if her bizarre behaviour might give me the opportunity to either flee or perhaps even kill her, but as she stared back at me, the intruder smiled in a way that told me she knew exactly what I was thinking.

'What do you want?' I asked.

But her reply was the same: 'Tick, tock.'

'Stop making that sound!' I hissed.

The paralytic I'd given the children wouldn't last long. Soon Sephan and Trina, the eldest pair, would come out of it, and run from their rooms to this one, shouting for their parents. When that happened, my life would be over. That left me with only one choice: if I killed the baby, there was still some tiny, fractional chance it might be enough to ruin this family and thus fulfil my mission.

'Tick, tock,' repeated my tormentor. 'That's what the hands of a clock do, don't they? They tick-tock around the dial, going exactly where the clockmaker intended, never deviating from that path because, after all, that's how the clock works.' She pushed herself away from the window. 'Now me, I've never been one for circular paths. Seems like that just leads back to the same place you started.'

'I'm not a clock,' I said defiantly. 'I'm an Arkyan logician. I'm here to save my—'

'I know exactly what you are, Yarisha Fal.' She took a step towards me. 'I know why you came to this city, why you insinuated yourself into this family. The poor orphan girl act was pretty good, by the way. You should consider a career on the stage if the assassination business doesn't work out for you.' She took another bite of her apple, chewing as she went on. 'I know what you planned to do to those kids.'

'Then why haven't you stopped me? Look at me!' I brandished the knife at her. 'I'm a monster! Why haven't you killed me already?'

Why had I said those things? Why had I called myself a monster in front of this stranger? Perhaps because she hadn't called me one herself. No, to her I was a clock, merely following the motions for which it had been designed, unable to make its own choices and therefore incapable of guilt.

Say the words, Ferius. You already know how she answered me. Chances are, it's precisely what the Path of the Rambling Thistle said to you when you came to that same crossroads. Though I suppose, given the frontier drawl you like to put on sometimes, I imagine he said it more like this:

'Killin' ain't the Argosi way, kid.'

Those words began a conversation that took me slowly, ever so slowly, away from Loja's crib, out of her parents' house and into a new life. A life where anyone – even a monster like me – could choose their own path.

Her name was Penta Corvus, which was oddly prescient, if you know the archaic Daroman language, because she preferred to be called the Path of Five Ravens.

You know her as the Traveller.

There has never been an Argosi as skilled as the Path of Five Ravens. Never one more devoted to protecting the innocent, to finding ways to keep the world from war and destruction. When I

met her, Penta Corvus was loving, mirthful, joyous, and as inquis-
itive as her namesake. She taught me the seven talents and the
four ways. She helped me find my path away from enslavement
and cruel necessity, towards decency and freedom.

Soon we'll reach the desert once again, and pick up her trail.
It will be easy to do because she'll leave signs for us along the
way. In those signs you will see what she learned from me.

34

The First Sign

Late in the day, at the base of the mountain, we found an old priest waiting for us at a temple. He had just nailed both his feet to the centre post of a *yadrigal* – an eight-foot-tall altar carved from a tree that split into two primary branches curving upwards like someone raising their hands to the heavens. Inside the temple, the clang of his hammer echoed from the stone walls as he drove the third nail into his right palm, which was stretched up along one of the branches. Blood trickled down from his wounds, pooling on the floor beneath the yadrigal. When the priest heard us enter, he looked first to Rosie and me, then to the hammer in his left hand, then up at the other branch. With the last nail still held between his lips he mumbled, 'Ah, good. She told me you might come along to help me finish.'

'Spirits of sea and sky,' I murmured.

I've never been much for religion. Durral once told me that when newcomers had crossed the sea to this continent, they'd brought with them any number of gods and devils, saints, demons and things even stranger, but none had ever taken root in these lands. Even the Berabesq – the only theocracy on the continent – pray to a deity with six faces because they can't agree what their god looks like, never mind how he expects them to behave. The Gitabrians put more faith in their contraptions than the religious rites they perform before their ships set sail. The Zhuban up north consider all forms of religion to be blasphemous (you'd have to meet a Zhuban warrior-poet for that to make any sense). The spirits my people worshipped had never proven themselves particularly worthy of our faith. And as for the Jan'Tep? Well, best as I could tell, the Jan'Tep mostly worshipped themselves.

'We have to get him down,' I said.

I set off between the battered stone pews towards the dais, but Rosie ran up behind and grabbed me by the shoulder.

'You can't help him.'

'I can stop him driving more of those iron nails into his flesh!'

Truth be told, I couldn't do even that for him; he'd already nailed all his free limbs to the yadrigal. Now he was trying to push the final nail through his palm using only his teeth.

'This is the first sign she left us,' Rosie said, stringing her bow.

'How is this a sign? She found some poor mad old priest and—'

'He wasn't mad when she found him. He suffers from the Red Scream.'

At those words the priest looked up at us, eyes wide. He wagged a finger while the nail partially embedded in his palm bobbed up and down, sending droplets of blood into the air.

'Yes!' he said, triumphantly. 'The *Red Scream*. That's what she called the sound she put in my head! Do you know, I'd almost forgotten.' He shook his head. 'The Red Scream. Such a distinguished name.'

Rosie had taken an arrow from her quiver and set it to the string of her bow. 'I won't fire,' she said, seeing my hand ready to grab the weapon. 'Not until there is no choice left to us.'

'This makes no sense!' I yelled at her. 'Everyone we've encountered who has heard the Scarlet Verses became a rampaging

252

lunatic! They bit their own tongues off! Threw themselves off a cliff! This man is—'

'She has altered the verses with what she learned during her final visit to the Convent of Scarlet Words,' Rosie said, cutting me off even as she raised her bow to take aim at the self-crucifying priest. 'This is what she wants us to see.'

'Why? Why would she bother?'

The sound of small feet slapping on the floor behind us made me spin on my heel.

'*Don't look!*' I signed to Binta, but it was too late. He was already transfixed by the sight of the priest on the yadrigal.

'Hello, little boy,' the old man said. 'Would you like to help me finish a very important job?'

Binta gazed calmly, and I watched in horror as the fear drained from his eyes. He'd run inside because I'd promised him we'd only be a minute. He'd been worried about me and Rosie. Now that he saw this was nothing more than the death and torment of a stranger, something he'd witnessed so many times now and knew he couldn't solve, that his expression became stolid, almost listless.

'*You should end his suffering, Good Dog,*' the boy signed to me. '*I am too small and lack a weapon. It would take me a long time and it would hurt him.*'

'Will no one help me get this dratted nail in place?' the old man complained, banging the head of it against his own skull as he struggled to drive it though his palm. 'Can't imagine how I'm going to get it into the branch when I'm done.'

'I will help you, Father,' Rosie said.

The priest looked over at her, his eyes becoming suspicious when they saw the bow in her hand. 'That would be some trick if you could hit the nail right on the head.' He stretched that arm into

253

position on the second branch of the yadrigal. 'But go ahead, let's see what you can do, Yarisha Fal.'

Rosie stiffened at that name.

'Deliver the message, Father,' she said. 'And I will complete the ceremony.'

'Rosie, we can't just kill him! He's an innocent vic—'

But the priest cut me off, his weary voice finding some of the fire that must've once accompanied his sermons.

'This old fool is the first . . .' the priest intoned, hardly even seeming aware that he was speaking about himself. 'For years he lied to his flock, telling them that their suffering was in service to a greater good. He preached that failed crops were the price of personal sin, that children dead too young were embraced by the gods. He stole from his followers the truth that would have allowed them to find better lives for themselves and their families. He denied them the chance to choose their own paths, as you and I did.'

Rosie whispered then, words I doubt the priest could've heard and couldn't possibly have answered. 'And who gave you the right to punish him this way, maetri?'

But though the priest had no way of hearing her, still he answered, and I realised then that Penta Corvus, the Traveller, had known exactly what Rosie would say, and that this entire dialogue was a performance designed to demonstrate that the teysan could never outwit the maetri.

'I took nothing from him,' the priest recited. 'Like his followers, he was a puppet of his own flawed beliefs. Now he dances to a different tune . . .' The priest jiggled against the nails holding him in place, causing more blood to seep from his wounds. 'A song I have written for him, and for countless thousands of others if you do not come back to me and help me finish the work you and I started.'

'Rosie?' I asked, watching the way the muscles of her face shifted as she struggled to keep her composure.

In the periphery of my vision I saw the priest's head turn, swivelling towards me. 'Has she started telling you the story yet, child? Has she begun to turn you, as she turned me?'

'Rosie, what is he talking about?'

'Stop!' she shouted, her self-control crumbling. 'I never—'

'I was like you,' the priest went on, untroubled by Rosie's yelling or the blood pouring from his wounds, making his skin ashen and his jaw slack. 'The Path of Five Ravens was not so unlike the Path of the Rambling Thistle. Like them I worshipped at the false altar of Argosi faith. A faith with no gods but our own ideals. But then my teysan—'

Like a promise fulfilled, the arrow flew straight into the priest's left palm, pinning it to the second branch of the yadrigal. The old man smiled as if this final act of bondage had somehow freed him. Then he shouted, 'Yellow. Irfidos. Majesty. Pah. Doh. Amelah. Harvest. Shogh. Yu-ta. Beloved. Beloved. Belov—'

The second arrow went straight into his mouth, cutting off words that I hadn't even realised were creeping inside me like worms in a corpse even as Binta was trying and failing to scream over them.

The priest kept mumbling, his mouth trying to form words around the shaft of the arrow. Rosie shot a final one through his skull, and at last his eyes closed, his suffering ended. His message delivered.

35

Faith

I stumbled out of the temple just in time to throw up on the pristine white sand. The locals call this region of the desert the Ice Fields, on account of the quartz is so pale it looks like a giant blanket of snow. I was sick from so many ailments in that moment, I had to count them up to keep from losing my mind.

The Traveller had set this trap for us. And it *was* a trap. She wasn't trying to kill Rosie and me or stop us or even delay our journey. This *was* the journey. She had wanted us to find the priest. Wanted us to know that she had learned to modify the Scarlet Verses so that they could be spread by the infected.

You think this is bad? she was telling us. *I can make it all so much worse.*

That knowledge was only the first of many maladies afflicting me.

The second was the aftershocks of those few words the priest had spoken. Some were in Daroman, one was Gitabrian, a couple were Jan'Tep syllables and the rest I didn't even recognise. Yet I was absolutely positive that they'd been composed specially for Rosie and me, to show us what the Traveller could do. Whatever she'd infected the priest with had been different, geared towards making him torture himself even as he relayed her message to us and then, at last, launched into a new set of verses to break our spirits even though she would've known Rosie would never let the old man finish.

Beloved. Beloved. Beloved.

Was that repetition of those words part of the verses? Or was it simply a way to torment her teysan further?

The third ailment was the worst one of all.

'Has she started telling you the story yet, child? Has she begun to turn you, as she turned me?'

Simplest strategy in the world: when you're being pursued by two opponents, divide them. Make them question each other's intentions. Fill their weary hours of sleep with a hint of doubt. Nothing brilliant or ingenious here; this was a scheme any amateur could devise.

Only . . .

Only Penta Corvus wasn't an amateur. She was better at this than we were, and she wanted us to know it. Otherwise, why bother with the priest? Why not just kill us?

Because something inside her needs to prove she's right.

This wasn't just about a plague or eradicating the Jan'Tep. This journey of hers was about faith. The monks of the Silent Garden. The nuns of the Convent of Scarlet Words. Sure, they'd had information Penta Corvus had wanted, but there hadn't been any need to kill them. Yet she'd sent all those nuns over the cliff, almost as if she hated them more than us. Now this roadside priest. She wanted us to see her disdain for their beliefs. She needed us to share it.

What about the people of Tinto Rhea? They hadn't been especially religious so far as I'd been able to tell.

But they didn't lack for faith, I realised then.

In all my travels, I doubt I'd ever before met people who believed so strongly in the nobility of living simple lives out in the hardship of the frontier. The memory of dancing with the villagers returned to me, of sharing food and smiles with them, the promise of a home for Binta, the playful touch of Lyrida's hand on mine. Just as quick the vision was gone, replaced by the sight of frenzied limbs clawing at me, of chewed-off tongues and one death after another until the entire hall had gone up in flames.

Like I said before, I've never been religious, not even when I was a little kid. So how come it felt as if someone was stealing my faith away from me?

'Ferius?' Rosie asked, her shadow stretching out in front of me. 'Are you still sick?'

'I'm fine.'

A pause – no, a hesitation – then, 'Why are you kneeling?'

I'd once asked Enna whether the Argosi had any religion. Her response had been an arched eyebrow as she'd gone back to painting a new card in the suit of shields for her deck after she'd returned from a mission to Darome where I guess some political changes were at work.

'So you don't believe in anything?' I'd pressed.

She'd completed her brushstroke – Enna painted the most beautiful cards you've ever seen – and set down her brush before shuffling her chair over to where I sat on the chaise-longue in her little workshop.

'What an Argosi believes in, Ferius, is this . . .'

She'd tapped a finger on my temple.

'And this . . .'

The finger moved to my heart.

'And especially this . . .'

She positioned her thumb and forefinger either side of my mouth, and nudged my lips upward into what I supposed was intended to be a smile. This wasn't long after she'd adopted me, so I was still a little skittish and pulled away.

258

'*You can't worship a smile,*' I'd said.

Enna, in that way of hers that told you whatever she was going to say next was both the wisest thing she could offer and the end of the conversation, said, '*Show me something more worthy of my devotion and I'll get down on my knees and convert right now.*'

I don't know if there are gods or saints who watch over this world. Doesn't feel like it's for me to say. But you couldn't spend an hour in Enna's company without being convinced there were miracles.

I'm sorry, Mamma.

I got back up on my feet, dusted the white sand off my trousers and took Binta's hand to lead him back over to Quadlopo.

'Sun's goin' down,' I said. 'Best we ride a ways out and make camp for the night.'

Rosie nodded, but said nothing.

That was going to change.

'I'll come to your tent tonight after Binta goes to sleep,' I informed her. 'You're going to tell me the rest of your story.'

'And then?' she asked.

I lifted Binta up into the saddle before mounting up behind him. I nudged the horse's flanks and let him carry us out deeper into the desert.

'Then I'll decide if I believe you.'

36

Enrajo

I do not know when it began. I thought . . . I truly believed, Ferius, that my questioning of the Path of Five Ravens was nothing more than the prodding and poking of a student at her master's teachings. A way of accepting her lessons by first resisting them. Penta Corvus was always so certain in her ways, so assured of her path. She laughed at my arguments more often than she paid them heed. For every philosophical point of attack I attempted, Penta had an answer or a diversion. She seemed so happy, so sure of herself, how could I know that I was destroying her?

You must understand, my people had trained me to be a logician. Mastering rhetoric as both the means to uncover truth and a tool with which to persuade others to our cause is a key part of that training. Even at ten years old, I had learned a great deal. That's how I was able to worm my way inside the household of the Gitabrian family, make each of the children come to love me more than they loved each other, and convince them to make no sound when I snuck into each of their rooms that night and promised them the nectar I brought was nothing to be alarmed about.

Over the years of my training, even as I came to accept the Argosi teachings as they slowly allowed me to strip away the bonds of my training as a logician, some part of me wanted to . . . compete with my maetri. I wanted to prove myself as clever as she was, as determined, as unstoppable. How could I know that I was combining the Argosi talents she'd taught me with those I'd learned as a child, to slowly, patiently, inexorably pull Penta Corvus away from her path?

There are flaws in the Argosi ways, Ferius. Pacifism is only idealistic when people aren't being tortured and slaughtered because you failed to kill their tormentor when you had the chance.

You glower at me, Ferius, but I see in your eyes that you too have had such thoughts. Did not Penta refer to you hunting Jan'Tep mages? Surely this was no whim on your part but the desire to prevent them committing further atrocities?

Now, as I was saying, there are—

Yelling will do no good, Ferius. We are far from any towns and the boy is deaf. Nor should you struggle against your bonds. The knots are ones you are unlikely to be familiar with, and placed in such a way as to numb the nerves in your hands the more you resist them.

Listen well, for we come to the crux of my story.

These flaws of which I speak, the more Penta Corvus refused to acknowledge them, the more determined I became to prove their existence. But how? She was more skilled than I in the seven talents, more adept at following the four ways.

The four ways.

That was the key. That was the insight that came to me just when I believed I would never be able to prove my case to her. A simple thought that ruined everything.

What if there were four *other* ways? What if I could devise counters to the Way of Water, of Wind, of Thunder and of Stone? Surely then I could show my maetri that the Argosi were not perfect, that there might be a blind spot in their perspective.

It was a kind of . . . hobby. An experiment, nothing more. I presented it to her as a speculation: what might an entirely different set of Argosi teachings look like? A teaching based not on attempting to subtly alter the course of events so that threats to the peace of nations and the survival of their peoples could be averted, but on eliminating those threats before they came into existence?

At first she laughed at me. I was fourteen, still a girl, and she twenty-three. I'd barely seen the world, knew little of its people or their lives and loves. Humanity, she told me, was an infinitely complex tapestry. A map whose lines we could trace with our fingers for a dozen lifetimes and never find the end. In the hope of finding a single path across that map, an Argosi spent a lifetime walking it.

'Go ahead, clock girl,' she dared me. 'Show me something grander than the Way of Water and then we'll talk.'

So I did.

I constructed four new ways based on a logician's interpretation of the Argosi principles. The Way of Seeds. The Way of Embers. The Way of Murmurs. The Way of Blight. Each of these became a philosophical framework meant not for navigating cultures, but for altering their future. Not a path for myself, but a science for devising alternate paths that could reshape humanity. Instead of Argosi, we could be *Enrajo*.

Shapers of the world.

You stare at me wide-eyed as if I'm some villain in a children's tale. I'm not, I swear it. All the while, as I concocted these ideas and shared them with Penta, I knew I had failed. This 'Way of the Enrajo' was idiotic. A borrowed arrogance that conflated my own people's teachings with those of the Argosi. I expected Penta to smile at me sadly, as she often had when the evidence of my own enslavement revealed itself once again in my words, shake her head and tell me to visit some village or other, truly get to know the people who lived there, and *then* see if I felt like repeating my nonsense.

I had no idea she was already broken.

Penta never spoke of her own past. She was young for a full Argosi, younger still for a maetri. I always assumed she'd simply finished her training more quickly than others did. It suited my own inflated sense of importance that my teacher was so young because, like me, she was simply better than the rest. I didn't know that when she was away on missions she sometimes spoke with fellow Argosi who had also come to question the philosophy of their order. I didn't know that the idle rantings I claimed as a new set of ways were being shared and discussed. I didn't know they were being refined.

Please stop shouting at me, Ferius. I told you, I didn't know what was happening. I trusted my maetri knew best and was merely allowing me to find my way to my own path.

Perhaps I should have realised something was wrong when Penta allowed me into her bed last year for the first time. I had been . . . I'd been attracted to her for a long time. I was sixteen and she was twenty-five. Not so far apart in age. In many societies we might have married. I told you that because of my Arkyan upbringing I'd always felt older than my years. I was too stupid to understand that someone who meets you when you are ten has no business becoming your lover when you are sixteen. I didn't understand that her treating me this way was the last step in her own descent into depravity and madness.

Instead, I was happy. Fulfilled. More committed than ever to the Argosi ways. So delighted with my certainty that when I announced to Penta that I had found my path at last – the Path of Thorns and

263

Roses – I mistook her tears for regret that someday soon we would be parted. Two Argosi who follow different paths can't stay together for long of course. But still I took her hand and promised our roads would wind back and forth together for our entire lives.

'You're right, clock girl,' she said. 'I see now that our destinies really are entwined.'

It struck me as an odd statement. The Argosi don't believe in destiny. In fact, it's the very opposite of what we believe.

Destiny, I soon came to learn, was an Enrajo precept.

Penta tricked me that night. Bound me, as I've bound you, so that I wouldn't stop her from doing what she believed was necessary. She had predicted through the Way of Whispers that the greatest threat to the future of the continent was from the Jan'Tep. She told me this, explained every detail of her thinking. She even invited me to tell her why she was wrong.

I couldn't.

She's right, Ferius. Now or later, ten years from now, twenty, a hundred . . . The Jan'Tep's pursuit of magic, their paranoia about others trying to take it from them, their perverse meritocracy on the basis of who can cast the most powerful spells . . . They'll destroy this continent some day unless they are stopped.

'Now you must choose,' she said, a knife in her hand ready to sever my bonds or cut my throat. 'Will you walk the Way of the Enrajo, or the Way of the Argosi?'

My life hasn't been easy, Ferius. I know yours hasn't either. So maybe you'll understand when I tell you that the moment of which I am most proud – of which I will *always* be most proud – is when I gave her my answer.

'I am Argosi,' I said. 'Now and forever I walk the Path of Thorns and Roses.' I lifted my chin and exposed my neck to her. 'If this is my last step on that path, so be it.'

Was it mercy that kept her from slitting my throat? Affection from what we'd meant to each other? Or was it arrogance – believing I could never stop her?

I wondered that for a long time as I pursued her, each time uncovering her plans too late to stop her. I discovered that for months before she'd revealed her intentions to me, Penta had been following the Way of Seeds, devising the means to sow discord among her enemies. She claims her only purpose is to eradicate the Jan'Tep, Ferius, but I believe that will only be the first step. She will find ever more threats to eliminate until at last she can justify the destruction of those she hates above all.

The Argosi.

That's who she most desires to kill.

She believes her hatred stems from the way the Argosi have allowed corrupt empires like that of Darome or the cruel prejudices of the Jan'Tep to flourish, yet in this her arta precis fails her. Penta Corvus despises the Argosi not because they failed to protect these lands from tyranny, but because they failed to save her from her own doubts.

It wasn't until I reached that conclusion that I understood why Penta had left me alive. She needs to prove to me that she's right. She wants to demonstrate that the Argosi ways have failed the world, and only hers – ours – can save it. To that end, she's giving me one final chance to stop her, convinced that no matter how well I apply the seven talents and walk the four ways, I will not be able to defeat her.

And you know what, Ferius?

She's right.

She's going to win, either by slowly turning you and me to her cause or by killing us when the time comes. The Traveller will perfect the Red Scream and unleash it upon the Jan'Tep territories. Penta

Corvus has gone mad, Ferius. She isn't even aware of the insatiable hatred burning inside her. After the Jan'Tep, after the Berabesq and the Daroman and all the others, after she has destroyed every last Argosi, still she will continue to follow the Way of Embers, blazing a bloody path across this continent until every living person has been infected with her plague, and the last thing any of us hears will be the hissing of the Scarlet Verses.

So I'm going to leave you here tonight, tied up in this tent, screaming yourself hoarse at me as I take Binta away. The Traveller believes herself superior to me because she has freed herself of the philosophical constraints imposed by the Way of the Argosi. Detachment and pitilessness are her weapons now, yet she is still new to them. Penta was . . . kind, once, Ferius. You may find it hard to believe, but cruelty is foreign to her nature.

I was born this way.

Born to walk the Way of the Enrajo.

Arta Forteize

Not all struggles are overcome – some can only be endured. The teysan tries to make themselves strong, believing that strength will keep them from breaking. A true Argosi embraces defeat, despair and disaster, knowing that to fall is inevitable, and the art we must learn is to rise up again.

And again.
And again.
And . . . again.

37

Knots

Rosie left me tied up in her ropes and my own stupidity. When she'd come to me that night, I'd been so exhausted I'd fallen asleep, lying on my stomach, dead to the world. I'd woken to the briefest touch of her lips on the back of my neck and the gentle trace of her fingertips along my bare shoulders, down one arm and then the other. Kneeling beside me, she'd leaned in close and let her warm breath tickle my ear as she said, 'I'm sorry, Ferius.'

Even then I hadn't figured it out. Not until I'd gone to push myself up to see what had made her sound so very sad and discovered my wrists were bound with silk. When I'd struggled, she'd pulled hard on the end she still held in her hand, and I'd felt my arms yanked behind my back. Just like that, I was her captive.

Neat trick.

Even now, hours later, my cheeks were still stained with tears of frustration. All through her tale of how she'd unwittingly awoken some corrupted, monstrous doubt inside her maetri's mind, sown the seeds for the devising of a system of thought that was the very antithesis of the Argosi ways, I'd shouted over and over, hoping against hope that somehow Binta would hear me, get on Quadlopo's back and flee this place. The horse was smart. He'd race back home, fast as the wind, and in a few days the boy would be with

Durral. He'd figure out Binta's fingertongue and get the story from him. He'd give the boy a home, and in return Binta would give Durral a reason to keep on—

No. Enough fantasies. The time for wishful thinking has passed.

I'd tried a hundred different ways to get out of my bonds, but I couldn't reach the knots with my fingers and nothing I did could break or cut through whatever fabric Rosie had used. She'd stolen my mapmaker's case with the smallsword in it, and rifled through all my belongings to find every blade I owned – even the tiny one I kept hidden in the cuff of my shirtsleeve. Worse than all of that, she'd done something to Quadlopo. I'd heard the horse scream and run off in the night. By the time I'd wriggled out of the tent into the blinding morning sun, his hoofprints were nothing but a faint trail away from here and off into the distance.

If you hurt that horse in any way permanent, Rosie, I'll –

No. Enough of that too. The Path of Thorns and Roses wouldn't harm a horse unless she had no choice. She'd been the one to think of all those animals in Tinto Rhea that needed to be freed after the villagers had died.

I'm not going to hate you, Rosie. Not until Binta is safe, the Traveller has been stopped and I've got my damned horse back.

I worked myself to my feet and searched everywhere within three hundred yards for something to cut my bonds with. You'd be surprised at how hard it is to find anything sharp in a desert full of smooth white sand. Rosie had been thorough in going through my stuff. She'd even removed the buckles from my saddlebags, whose pins at least had sharp edges I might've used to wear away at the silk rope around my wrists. How was it possible that after all the Argosi training Durral and Enna had given me, I was in danger of being bound a prisoner for life with nothing but a few wrappings of silk? Was I seriously going to end up dying out here like this?

'*Arta tuco, kid,*' Durral would've reminded me then. '*An Argosi begins with the belief that there's a way to escape any trap.*'

'*What if there isn't though?*'

'*Hmm? Oh, well, then you're usually dead, so you might as well go right on believing it to the end.*'

Thanks, maetri.

He was always like that when it came to the seven talents. Enna was better, though even she liked to teach in proverbs.

'*If you can't see the path, yet you know it's there, then who is hiding it from you?*'

The answer, of course, is yourself.

So why would your own mind keep you from seeing a way out of a problem? When the escape is more unpleasant than the trap itself.

The fire was almost out, but there were a few embers there. I managed to slip my feet into my boots and pushed the cinders around until I found ones that still had a faint glow. Then I knelt down and blew on them until I got one hot enough to do the job. After that? Well, after that I did a whole lot of screaming and swearing.

With my hands finally free, I spent the next few minutes waiting for the feeling to come back to my fingers – which wasn't much fun either. At last I fumbled through my pack and found a small jar of ointment meant for soothing wounds and staving off infection. My hands ached from having been bound so long, the skin on my wrists burned so bad from the heat of the embers and my fingers were so numb that I had to grip the jar between my knees and use my teeth to pull the stopper out. When it came away, my nostrils picked up a faint whiff of cinnamon. Rosie had kissed the jar so I'd smell her scent on it: her way of telling me she could've taken this too, but had left a little solace behind.

Ain't gonna stop me from punching you in the nose when this is done, Rosie.

The ointment helped though, and soon I was ready to gather up what things I could carry and set out after her. All the while as I set off on my journey down that long desert road, knowing I was too far behind to catch her in time, I searched for some spark of hope inside me – some reason to believe I hadn't screwed everything up beyond repair.

I couldn't find one.

Rosie hadn't lied to me, not really. She'd never hidden who she was from me, not even on that night when we'd . . .

'These are my lips. It doesn't have to mean anything.'

Those hadn't even been her words. They'd been mine. From that first touch of her hand against my own I'd wanted so badly to be close to someone, to feel . . . to know some tiny fraction of the kind of love some part of me knew was never meant to be mine. The kind of love you read about in books. The kind of love Durral and Enna shared.

Rosie had warned me though. She'd told me her story was meant as a kind of preparation for what had to come next if we were to defeat the Traveller.

'When my tale is done, you will know me better, and like me far less.'

Even in that, she'd been scrupulously honest. Now I was alone out here in the desert putting one foot in front of the other along the path Rosie had laid for me, the rising sun promising to add burns to the back of my neck to rival the ones the embers had left on my arms and wrists. Step by step I followed a trail that would disappear the moment the next sandstorm arose.

I couldn't let that happen.

'I was born this way. Born to walk the Way of the Enrajo.'

274

Those had been Rosie's last words to me. A farewell and a warning all in one. She'd suckered me without telling a single lie, taken Binta against his will and would now no doubt use him as part of some scheme against her former maetri.

Why hadn't she at least told me her plan? Tried to convince me to go along with it? Did she figure I was too soft-hearted to put down the Traveller, if that's what it took to stop the plague, or sacrifice both our lives in the attempt?

No.

Rosie knew me better than that, for all that we'd only been around each other a short while. But there was one choice, one path she knew I wouldn't allow her to follow no matter what. One difference between us that had been the real reason she'd told me the story of how she'd first come to this continent. Rosie hadn't been owning up to a crime from her past. She'd been confessing the one in her future.

Yarisha Fal.

Killer of Children.

38

The Temple Road

I wasted the next three days following Rosie's trail to the second temple. Wasn't even a hundred miles, yet the hours passed painful slow. I could've walked faster; the road cutting through the white sand of the Ice Fields was mostly flagstone. The problem was that I had to contend with the heat and the possibility that at any moment I could find myself face to face with crazed victims of the Red Scream, or Rosie, or even the Traveller herself. I couldn't afford to exhaust myself if the pursuit of my quarry left me too weak to fight.

So I drew on my arta forteize and listened to my body as I trudged through the ghostly white sands, conserving my strength and the water in my canteens. I made peace with my fears over the endless potential tragedies that lay ahead by asking my arta tuco how I might prevent them.

I also spent a lot of time cursing my horse for abandoning me.

Okay, to be fair, Quadlopo *wasn't* my horse and had never particularly liked me. After I'd stolen him from Durral and Enna's home, he'd tolerated my existence because, well, he was pretty lazy and unless someone told him which way to go, tended to just find the nearest bush and devote the entirety of his attention to eating it.

Anyway, I guess I'd kind of hoped some shred of loyalty had built up between us these many weeks and Quadlopo might actually, you know, come back to see if I was dead. No such luck. Likely Rosie had chased him off and he, having suffered enough of my problems and poor decisions, had made the more intelligent one of going home.

So onwards I plodded. The worn and weathered flagstones of the Great Temple Road were fighting a losing battle with the sand around them. My body, mind and heart were doing the same with the smothering anxieties of what would happen when I finally caught up with Rosie, her maetri or the mess they'd left behind, and things, inevitably, went south from there.

Speaking of going south, I guess I'd better explain the Great Temple Road. About six hundred years ago, a great Daroman king named Cadrian set out to conquer the Seven Sands – not by military might but by engineering. He offered to build roads through the seven deserts, which would make life easier for the folks who lived in this strange no-man's land whose primary function was to keep the Berabesq, Jan'Tep and Daroman peoples from killing each other. Nobody minded the new roads because they made travel and trade easier, which benefited everybody.

But Cadrian's generosity had a strategic purpose: by bringing some small measure of prosperity to the Seven Sands, he'd earn the loyalty of its people, which would surely benefit Darome should the day come when the empire decided to crush the Berabesq and the Jan'Tep.

Now, since laying down wide, paved roads perfect for transporting troops and war machines can seem a trifle suspicious to your neighbours, one of Cadrian's advisors suggested they present the road as a kind of pilgrims' passage. People could come from all across the Seven Sands to worship the various regional gods in their holy places. Beneficent *and* innocent. Cadrian loved the idea – especially since getting the local priesthood onside is always good business when conquering a place.

So Cadrian sent out scholars to research the faiths in each of the seven regions and pick out the holy sites where lovely temples would reside, all connected by a marvellous Daroman road. The message was: 'Believe in whoever you want – just remember who got you there.'

The only problem with this brilliant plan was that it turned out there were hundreds of different gods worshipped in the Seven Sands, and dozens upon dozens of holy sites littered along the western border. Being a typical Daroman king, Cadrian threw up his hands, raised more taxes back home and told his engineers to just build as many temples along the road as there were gods people prayed to and let them worry about the theological inconsistencies.

Thus was the Great Temple Road created. Forty-seven different religious sites linked by over a thousand miles of good Daroman road. Each temple was consecrated to a different local faith. Each one built in a part of the world where people come and go with no rhyme or reason, where entire towns pack up and leave when a mine closes or the harvests began to falter. Now whenever they moved on to a new place to start afresh, such folk would arrive to find a temple honouring a god they didn't believe in and didn't particularly like. They'd destroy the statues and icons inside and put in new symbols of their faith.

All of this turned the Great Temple Road into a testament to the indifferent devotions with which human beings hold their gods. A town with a thousand people might have twenty different religious traditions, their devout worshippers all scrapping over who got to hold their services in the pretty Daroman-built temple and who had to make do with praying in some roadside shack.

After a while, people stopped bothering to fight over them. Tiny monastic communities of ten, maybe fifteen people would start living in and around a temple. Sometimes, like in the first one Rosie and I had entered together, a single, lonely priest had set up shop there, unaware that the carved white stone walls couldn't protect him from Penta Corvus, who'd burned out his mind and left him for us to kill for no better reason than that she'd come to despise those who placed their faith in things unseen and unproven.

What I would witness in the second temple was far worse.

From the carved star-shaped symbols rudely altered from earlier ones above the archway, I could see that this place was currently dedicated to Stelloch, the god of a thousand eyes, each one a star that watched over people when the sun went down. The night sky in the Seven Sands being pretty much the most spectacular sight you'll ever see, you could find plenty of star gods across the region, with names like Stelloch or Stella or Etolis. Who knows? Maybe they were all real. Maybe they'd been watching with their thousands of eyes when Penta Corvis had walked through the temple doors. They hadn't lifted a finger to stop her though.

Fifteen souls had been assembled in this house of prayer when the Traveller had come calling. Fourteen were dead by the time I arrived. Their deaths had been swiftly merciful, if it's possible to describe such a massacre this way. Rosie had left the last one as a message for me.

'Hello . . . ?' I said as I entered.

The mosaic tiles on the floor had decayed over the centuries. They cracked beneath the heel of my boot. Inside, the temple was circular in design, with curved stone pews arranged around an altar at the very centre. Fourteen corpses had been propped up in the pews, their hearts visibly pierced by arrows that had since been removed. Rosie wasn't one to waste weapons she knew she'd soon need again.

The lone survivor was a young guy with lanky brown hair and a scraggly beard, maybe twenty years old and wearing the rough-spun overalls of a farmhand rather than the robes of a priest. He stood at the altar nonetheless, shaking his fists in the air as he preached to the dead about the god of frogs who'd fallen in love with three different goddesses and begged each one in turn to marry him. That I'd never heard of a religion involving a god of frogs was soon made more confounding by the fact that the three goddesses in question ruled over geese, badgers and worn-out shoes, respectively.

'Now, Our G-Gracious Lord of F-F-F-Frogs, it m-must be said . . .' stuttered the young man, licking lips that looked dry as the desert between every few words. His long, unkempt hair and obvious inability to read the blood-spattered holy text in front of him confirmed he wasn't the local priest. 'Our froggy lord did say to Her Ladyship of B-B-Badgers, "Why not will you most expeditiously marry me, madam? I promise you the g-g-goddess of old, worn shoes desires me g-g-greatly."' He raised his arms wide as if his sermon were approaching some vital moral message. 'Her Ladyship of Badgers then pulled out her favourite pipe and lit it with the feather of a dung beetle and –'

At last he seemed to notice me, and turned, smiling, blood welling up between the cracks of his chapped lower lip.

'Oh, th-thank Great Croakus, a b-b-brave hero comes to rescue me at last!'

He brought the back of his hand up to hide his mouth and winked to the nearest members of his deceased congregation. 'Not really. I'm going to give this stupid little cow the Red Kiss, actually, just as our One True Goddess gave it to me. But don't tell. It must

280

be a surprise when I destroy her soul.' His eyes flitted back to me, widening with concern that I'd noticed the sudden lack of a stutter. 'I mean, when I d-d-destroy her s-s-soul.'

I kept silent, watching him at his altar as his face contorted through a series of madman's grins and sly winks. The Traveller had infected these congregants as a message for Rosie – a reminder of how skilled Penta was becoming at adjusting the Scarlet Verses. Rosie, in turn, had killed fourteen people with swift, determined precision before they could infect her, leaving one, just this one, as a reminder to me that there was only one kind of mercy we could offer the victims of the Red Scream.

In a moment, the young man in the worn woollen overalls would begin to recite the verses the Traveller had given him, and I would have to kill him. I couldn't leave him alive, because eventually someone else would come here seeking spiritual comfort and instead find madness waiting to infect them.

Which raised the question: if the Traveller had overcome the flaw in the verses that had caused her earlier victims to bite off their own tongues, why did she still need Binta?

The answer came to me almost immediately – a memory from my childhood that brought with it bile in my throat and rage in my heart.

Because the Jan'Tep aren't like the rest of us.

I'd once been the captive of a Jan'Tep lord magus. In between sessions of burning metal inks into the skin of my neck, he'd regaled me with how complex the spells were that he was imprinting on me.

'*An initiate spends thousands of hours memorising esoteric geometries,*' old Met'astice had informed me. '*Such is the intensity of our training that by the time an initiate finally sparks their bands to become a true Jan'Tep mage, the very pathways of his mind have been rewritten. We*

281

might look *like you on the outside, little Mahdek, but in here –'* he'd tapped his balding temple – *'in here we might as well be different species.'*

In my hatred for the Jan'Tep, I'd always taken their arrogant bigotry as nothing more than self-delusion. But was it possible that they really were different from the rest of us? Hadn't my training in the seven talents fundamentally changed the way my own mind worked?

That the Traveller couldn't break through the mental barriers the mages had built up without using Binta to perfect her Scarlet Verses only made me resent the Jan'Tep even more. But if she failed to infect them directly, she'd turn the Red Scream on every other human being on the continent. The Jan'Tep weren't self-sufficient. They relied on agricultural trade. Mining. Tools. Penta Corvus would simply starve them out.

I'm not even a proper Argosi, I thought helplessly. *How am I supposed to put an end to this madness?*

'Are you g-g-going to s-s-save me now?' the young man asked, feigned trepidation playing across his features.

I started looking for a rock big enough to do the job as quickly and painlessly as possible. Instead I found my black leather mapmaker's case propped up against the side of one of the stone pews. That, too, was a message from Rosie, I guess.

'Do you have a family?' I asked.

He looked confused by the question.

'A mother or father?' I offered.

Still he couldn't answer. Despite the illusion of a mind still alive inside him, the Red Scream had taken all his reason. Whoever this guy was, whatever he'd been or hoped to become, was gone, replaced by a set of twisted thoughts not his own.

'When this is done, if I'm not dead, I'll try to come back,' I said, and wiped a sleeve across the wetness in my eyes before reaching for the mapmaker's case. 'I'll try to find out who you were. I'll look for anyone who knew you.'

'Will you bury me?' he asked. 'Because after I've infected you, we're to bury ourselves outside in the sand, just up to our necks, so that we can share the Red Kiss with anyone who comes by.' Again he glanced around himself, confused. 'It's going to be hard work though. I hoped some of the congregation would help, but they just sit there.'

'I will bury you,' I promised. 'But not here. Somewhere else. Somewhere nice with bright blue flowers and green growing things all around.'

He gave no reply to that. Nothing in what I'd said meant anything to the madness swirling around inside his head. Instead, whatever cue on my part he'd been waiting for was triggered, and he began speaking the Scarlet Verses with such sublime, poetic fluidity that it was as if in that moment he truly became a preacher.

Before those first words could tear my mind apart, I drew the sword from the scabbard and did what had to be done – what Rosie had left him here for me to do. It wasn't cruelty on her part. Rather necessity, in case she failed in her mission and it was left to me to complete.

Rosie was forcing me to take my first step on the Way of the Enrajo.

39

The Disharmony

On the seventh night I took out a tiny wooden box of paints and brushes from my pack, and one of the blank cards made from thick paper that every Argosi carries with them. As the desert chill set upon my shoulders, I sat cross-legged under the stars and painted the first card of a new deck.

The Argosi are famous for their card decks. The most common are the 'concordances', which map the peoples of this continent, one suit for each culture. Then there's the 'discordances', where a wandering Argosi paints figures or events they encounter that could change the course of history. The Teysan Deck is made up of cards that illustrate the four ways and the seven talents, along with a bunch of others for the false paths upon which an unwary Argosi can lose themselves. 'Gambits' are cards that reveal how to evade such hazards as various Jan'Tep spells or the tactics of soldiers and assassins.

My favourite deck was Durral's infamous 'love letters': the razor-sharp steel cards of which I'd stolen more than my share before fleeing the home he and Enna had tried to make for me. They were the most Argosi thing I could imagine: a weapon useful only to someone who handled cards all the time. They reminded me of him.

There was one deck I didn't like though. No Argosi did really. When I'd first seen Enna going off on one of her missions, rifling through a set of cards painted in shades of crimson and black, I'd asked her their purpose.

'Nothing you need to worry about, my girl.'

'But those suits . . . Thorns and chains and . . . are those tears? How come you've never shown me those ones?'

She'd hid the cards away in her waistcoat. 'Because I hope you'll never need to carry them, Ferius. Live your life right and you won't have to.'

It was Durral who'd explained their meaning to me after Enna had left. I guess he was feeling pretty maudlin because she'd made him stay behind.

'We call them the disharmonies. Each card represents a debt,' he'd told me, pulling out a slim deck and holding up a card showing the six of thorns.

'I thought Argosi never carried debts. Doesn't the Way of Water demand that we make restitution right away?'

'The Way of Water doesn't "demand" anything, kid. It's a guide, helping your heart find its way, not some Daroman general bellowing orders in your ear. Besides, sometimes a thing happens and there ain't nothin' you can do to make it right. Or not at the time.' He handed the card to me. 'That's when we make one of these.'

I held the card between my thumb and forefinger. It felt wrong in my hand somehow, like all that red and black was telling a tale of sorrow and injustice. But Durral always said that when the world looks ugly, look a little deeper and find the beauty. There wasn't anything pretty about the six thorns digging into the five fingers and palm of the outstretched hand depicted on the card. Yet the hand wasn't pulling away. Instead there was a kind of hopefulness . . . No, not hopefulness. *Determination.*

285

In the bold, flowing lines that made up the hand was a sense of determination to endure, to make things right again.

'*That arta precis of yours is comin' along real good, kid,*' Durral had said, taking the card back and stuffing it in the cuff of his shirt.

He didn't dole out praise so often that those words didn't fill me with pride, but the feeling passed all too soon, and I was left with a sense of guilt.

'*I've done bad things in my life, Durral. Things before we met. Things I haven't told you about. Shouldn't I have a deck like this?*'

'*You weren't Argosi back then, kid. You were just a . . . well, a kid.*'

'*I'm not a kid any more.*'

'*Sure are, kid. You know how I know?*'

'*How?*'

Like a hummingbird suddenly changing direction mid-flight, Durral grinned at me, snapped his fingers and made the card reappear in his hand.

'*Because you ain't got no debts, of course!*'

It's a strange thing to discover you're not a kid any more. It doesn't have anything to do with age or even maturity. It's more like . . . like a door you've walked through without realising it. You don't recall turning the handle, but no matter how hard you try, you can't find your way back.

So you find a way to go forward.

I didn't know the lore around disharmony cards, which suit meant what or whether the numbers related to whatever it was you owed. Maybe none of that stuff matters though. It's about remembering. Remembering, and promising.

So I painted a card, letting my sorrow and shame fill every brushstroke. In the end, the painting was better done than I would've expected, and harder to look at than I could've imagined. I guess that's how it's supposed to be. I would carry that card with me until I could come back and give them a proper burial, and find their kin and let them know what had happened. Not the awful parts. Those I would keep to myself.

When I was done, I wrapped myself in my bedroll and went to sleep. I didn't weep, didn't toss and turn. I slept as well as I could because I had to conserve my energy for the journey ahead, and because tomorrow would surely be worse than today.

40

The Sleeper

In the morning I made my way to the next temple and the one
after that, wandering from the site of one desecration to another
like a drunk stumbling from one saloon to the next. Always I left
with more blood on my hands and less hope in my spirit. Those
next few days and nights slipped by uncounted as I walked through
the carnage Penta Corvus forced Rosie to leave behind until the
white sands beneath my boot heels turned red from the blood
staining my soles.

After a while, a strange gratitude began to fill me. At every
temple Rosie killed the infected. Sometimes there were just a few,
other times dozens. Always she left one for me, as if her soul
couldn't bear the weight of that last, broken life. That final debt.

That was my job.

The cards I painted stacked up on top of each other until I had
run out of blanks and had to resort to cutting pieces of leather
from my coat. It wasn't that many – maybe a dozen, tops. But when
I held that small deck of cards in my hand, they felt so heavy I
wasn't sure how long I could carry them with me.

I passed towns along the way, large villages really, that I could
make out a half-mile or so off the Great Temple Road. I stayed
away from them. I had enough food in my pack and managed to

find water on the way to sustain me. I couldn't afford to buy a horse and the risk of getting caught stealing one was too great.

Sometimes I'd pass folks on the road though, riding mule carts or trudging on worn-out shoes. At first they'd smile at me, ask for news of where it was I'd come from. I didn't answer. I was too fragile inside and confessing to what I'd seen, what I'd done, would've shattered me. The folks who crossed my path would figure out soon enough what horrors had come through their lands. My job was to make sure those horrors were dead when they found them.

The closer I got to the border between the Seven Sands and the Jan'Tep territories, the more deadly the living the Traveller left behind.

At the entrance to the twelfth temple, Rosie had left a note warning me that the moment I entered, a woman inside would try to attack. In fact she appeared to be asleep on the floor, eyes closed, some ten feet away from the pile of dead bodies by the altar. I couldn't see if she was breathing. I approached slowly, cautiously, my smallsword ready to do what had to be done the moment she showed any signs of life. She didn't though; she was already dead.

I heard myself sigh, and felt the tears that I'd grown so used to shedding already sliding down my cheeks, though this time with the relief that either the Red Scream or previous ill health or perhaps a kindly god granting one small act of mercy had taken this grizzly duty from me. Then I heard a faint sniffing sound, like a rat searching for food. It had been days since I'd bathed. I must've smelled delicious.

The woman leaped out from among the bodies piled upon each other at the altar. Her hair was matted with the blood of her fellow congregants, arms covered in tiny scratch marks that could only have come from her own fingernails. Her eyes were wide, feral and filled with such joy it almost made you want to smile. From her lips bubbled the laughter of a jester whose ingenious prank has at last been revealed. With fiendish cunning she had cleaned up one of the dead bodies and left it apart from the others while she lay beneath the remaining corpses, waiting, grinning, relishing my coming. When she flew at me, arms spread wide, it was as if she expected angel wings to sprout from her shoulders. I tried to get my point back up, but she was too quick. She slammed into me and the two of us went rolling down the temple aisle.

'Evanescent,' she shrieked, her hands grabbing at my throat. 'Dal'jeban. Té. Curados. Putrefaction. Mordazh. Lust. Ha. Ha.'

Even just those first few quick words were making me sick, confused. The room spun counter-clockwise to our own motion along the floor. I tried to summon up my arta eres, but Durral's teachings of defence were built around the idea of finding flow and rhythm, of moving with a partner rather than opposing an enemy. I couldn't do it. I just couldn't . . . The dance was gone from me. Now I was down on the floor among the dead and the woman was on top of me.

'Tuvizmo. Kan. Ken. Kin. Dolour. Beloved.'

'Damn you!' I screamed, and with brute force drove my fist up between her arms, breaking the grip of her hands around my neck.

I grabbed her hair and yanked hard, tearing chunks of it out, but enough remained attached to her head that I was able to pull her off-balance. With my left foot planted on the stone floor, I pushed up hard with my hip, dislodging the slender, almost emaciated woman from my chest. I rolled on top of her, and before she could utter any more of the foul words that writhed inside my mind, I smashed in her front teeth. Half a dozen broke off, lodging in her throat and mangling her words. She tried to cough them up, but I didn't let her. I just kept punching and punching, over

290

and over again, screaming all the while, so loud I couldn't hear anyone's madness but my own.

'Damn you!' I shouted. 'Damn you, damn you, damn you!'

I don't know how long I kept it up. Seconds. Minutes. Hours. I lost all track of time and any sense of myself. Had someone wished to destroy my soul forever, all they would've needed in that moment was a mirror. By the end, I wondered if the woman beneath me had completed the Scarlet Verses and the Red Scream was already inside me. My only reassurance came when I spat and sputtered my last 'damn you'. Her body went limp beneath me, and with her last breath she hissed, 'No, Argosi. *I* damn *you.*'

My hands were numb, my arms exhausted, but I managed to push myself away from the now-dead woman and get back to my feet. I picked up my sword, and though she showed no remaining signs of life, I ran her through anyway, because that's what you do when you're walking the Way of the Enrajo.

I stumbled to the door, but I couldn't seem to make myself leave. The desert outside, even with its eerie red sand that earned this region its name of the Ruby River, looked too pure. Too . . . decent. I felt like my footsteps would infect the ground itself with the awfulness stirring inside me.

'*Cry, girl,*' I told myself with Enna's voice and Enna's wisdom. '*Crying is a powerful part of arta forteize, the talent for resilience. With tears we release our sorrows and bring the body back into balance, ready for what comes next. An Argosi who doesn't know how to cry risks becoming brittle inside.*'

Enna wasn't usually soft that way. Beautiful as she was, inside and out, she never struck me as particularly feminine or womanly. Not the way Durral was. Strange thing to say, I guess. But that's how it always seemed to me.

As with most things, though, Enna was right. These past few days I'd been doing a lot of crying. Don't think I could've survived without it. This time, though, the tears didn't want to come, so I forced them out of me with ruthless, brutal determination. I made myself scream and sob, rubbed sand in my eyes. I made myself say things. Awful things. I brought back every dark, ugly thought I'd ever had in my life and shouted them at the top of my lungs.

I guess you could say I let myself go a little mad.

And when it was done and there was nothing left inside me, I wandered out just as the setting sun was making the ruby sands bloom before me like a field of glittering roses. I drank in that beauty even though it tasted like poison, reminded myself it wasn't, and began my journey to the next temple.

That one was the worst.

41

The Herald

Thirteen days the Traveller had given us to find her on the border of the Jan'Tep lands where she'd either unleash a plague perfectly designed for the surgical genocide of a nation of mages or else a blunter, crueller one that would destroy the minds and souls of every living person on this continent. Along the way she made sure to leave us the signs of her ever-more-perfect Scarlet Verses.

In the thirteenth temple, Rosie had left me a young boy, barely older than Binta, tied up to one of the pews. There were twelve other children, all dead, littered across the floor. This boy was crying and asking why he couldn't go home. There was no sign of the Red Scream in him, just a lost soul begging for my help.

No note this time. I guess Rosie trusted my arta precis would work out the truth.

The boy was bound even though he wasn't strong enough to present any kind of physical threat to me. Nor did he shout the Scarlet Verses once he saw me. He just sat there, tied to the stone pew, asking me if I would take him home to his village.

'Please, ma'am,' he said with the awkward politeness of a child, 'my mamma and poppa, they don't know where I am. I haven't seen 'em in days. A lady, she took me while I was asleep, brought me here to—'

'Hush,' I said, as soothing as my raspy voice allowed. 'It's okay now.'

He sniffled as he looked up at me.

'Can you untie me, ma'am? Please? I'll be good, I promise. I never hurt nobody in my life.'

I knelt down to him, forcing myself to get closer than I wanted to be.

'I believe you.'

'Could you untie me then? I gotta get home.'

'What's your name?' I asked.

He looked confused for a moment, like I'd asked him to add up all the grains of sand in the desert. 'I . . . I don't rightly recall, ma'am.'

'What's your mamma's name?'

'Lorida, ma'am. Lorida Rivers. She's the town blacksmith.'

'And your poppa?'

'Minzer Rivers, ma'am. He's a cook. Finest one in the Seven Sands.'

'Got any sisters or brothers?'

He nodded. 'Dreman, Tulis – we call her Tulip for fun, and Kovi. She's the baby.'

'Those are nice names,' I said, and ruffled his hair. 'Now do you remember yours?'

He shook his head.

'Try hard.'

He did, eyes narrowing, brow furrowing, chewing on his bottom lip.

'I don't recall. It hurts when I think about it. Can't you just untie me?'

'In a second,' I said. 'I just want to know your name. It's important.'

He looked up at me and, frustration making his whole body shake, he said, 'Why don't you tell me *your* name then?'

'I'm Ferius Par—' I stopped myself.

What I needed to know required offering him a different answer – the one the Traveller would've told him to wait to hear.

'I am the Path of Thorns and Roses,' I said.

All the tension drained from the boy's frightened features and he smiled up at me. 'Oh, I remember now! My name is Yarisha. Yarisha Fal!' His head tilted quizzically. 'Strange. Now that I think on it, shouldn't my last name be the same as my mamma's and poppa's?'

I smoothed the brown hair from his forehead. 'Maybe it is. Maybe you have another name you've just forgotten?'

Again he shook his head, so vigorously drops of his sweat hit my lips and chin.

'No, ma'am. That's my name. Yarisha Fal. Ain't got no other.'

This was the message the Traveller had left for Rosie, and she, in turn, had left for me. Proof that Penta Corvus had so refined her Scarlet Verses that now she could implant more complex commands into her victims and even hide their insanity until the time came to unleash it. No longer content to throw bombs into innocent villages, now she could make the fuse as long as she needed, to ensure they detonated right when she wanted, hitting precise targets. That's why she had made this boy forget his name and take another.

Yarisha Fal.

Killer of Children.

'Can you untie me now, ma'am?' he asked again, tugging vigorously at his restraints. 'I miss my family, especially my brother and sisters. I gotta see them real bad.'

I nodded, and swallowed the sob that threatened to escape my throat. 'Didn't I tell you? I brought them with me. They're all waiting outside for us.'

'Really?'

I felt sick, but even now I had to know for sure – had to see whether the Traveller could really do such a thing.

I got up and went to stand behind him, hands on his shoulders as I called out towards the open door of the temple: 'Dreman, Tulis, Kovi! You can come inside now!'

When I turned back to the boy, a smile of pure joy came to his face, filled with such innocence that he didn't even seem aware that the words he was shouting at the top of his lungs weren't the names of his siblings.

'Evanescent! Dal'jebir! Tû! Zorbeso! Decay! Mordazh! Lust! Ho. Hei. Ha. Beloved! Belov—'

I removed my hands from the sides of his head. His last word died as a whisper on his lips, the final breath expelled after his neck had snapped. His head sagged back against the stone pew. He looked happy.

It was harder to cry this time. I'm not even sure I really did. Maybe all I was capable of doing was making myself pretend, because pretending to be human was all I had left.

I wondered where Rosie was right now, whether having Binta with her was helping her hold it together. All these perversities the Traveller had left behind were a special form of the Scarlet Verses meant for her teysan, her former lover, her unwitting teacher. Penta Corvus was twisting the Path of Thorns and Roses towards insanity. For her part, Rosie was deflecting these final deaths onto me, attempting to preserve some fraction of her own lucidness while also conditioning me to become more like her.

Enrajo.

The antithesis of an Argosi. A follower of the Way of Seeds, the Way of Embers, the Way of Murmurs and, above all, the Way of Blight. A walking desecration of everything Durral and Enna had tried to teach me.

I untied the boy, lay him down on the temple floor. I found a blanket in the back room of the temple and covered him with it. I tried to paint another card for my deck, but my hands wouldn't stop shaking. I thought about scrawling out a note to leave outside for whoever would next find this place. Maybe tell them what happened. Beg them to bury the dead, find their families and let the world know what happened here. I'd left each of the previous temples painting another disharmony card and swearing an oath to myself that I would be the one to deliver those small drops of mercy to the dead. But I feared now I'd never be coming back here.

In the end, like a ghost whose old haunts have collapsed into ruins, I went in search of the next temple, and the one after that. I couldn't summon Enna's wise counsel in my head any more, or hear Durral's laughter. With every step on this road the Traveller had put us on, I lost another piece of myself. By the twelfth day there was almost nothing left of me.

That's when I found Rosie.

42

The Broken Path

The last holy site on the Great Temple Road was named Castrum Celestos, which means Castle of the Celestials. In typical Daroman fashion, the name was vague enough to encompass whatever gods the locals chose to worship here.

Castrum Celestos was by far the largest and grandest of the temples on the pilgrim road. White stone columns and a central domed tower rose up from the ruby sands like a palace built for the gods themselves to reside in. The Daroman people don't care much for religion themselves, of course. The reason why King Cadrian had insisted this final temple be so magnificent was that it sat on the border between the Seven Sands and the city of Oatas Jan'Xan, traditional home of the mage sovereigns of the Jan'Tep people. Such a grand temple, sitting not fifteen miles from their finest oasis, was a monumental insult against which they could take no action. After all, it wasn't a fortress or military base, just a fitting house of prayer for the fine people of the Seven Sands to celebrate their faiths.

Castrum Celestos used to have a large settlement around it on account of the river that ran along the border. Farmers. Shepherds. Craftspeople. There was even a school here. A three-year drought had forced them to head east. I wondered if those folks would ever know that the luckiest thing that ever happened to them was a drought.

The truly devout though, maybe ten or twelve families, had toughed it out, and the gods to whom they prayed had rewarded them with a returned rise to the river water and the promise of a better life.

Until Penta Corvus had come to town.

'Are they all dead?' I asked.

Rosie was waiting for me outside the open temple gates. She was seated cross-legged on the ground before the stairs, eyes closed, so still that with stone pillars rising either side of her she looked like just another statue of a wise and patient god.

When she hadn't answered, I asked, 'Or did you leave one last person for me to kill. Who this time? An old man, weeping for a quick death? A child, begging to know what's happening to him? Maybe a girl our age so that when I put the blade through her I can see myself dying in her eyes?'

'I'm sorry,' she said.

'I don't need your apologies. Where is Binta?'

Again she went quiet, and I had the sense that she had already played out in her mind a hundred times everything that was about to unfold. She wasn't delaying those events though. She just wanted a few last moments together before it all went ugly.

'I'm giving the boy to Penta,' she said at last.

The Ferius who'd left that mountain twelve days ago would've leaped at Rosie, grabbed her by the collar and demanded to know why – *why* – she would ever consider such a thing. How could she believe I would allow it? The woman I had become knew better. She carried disharmonies with her. Inside her.

'Why did you wait for me, Rosie?' I asked.

The Traveller's plan had played out precisely as she'd intended. With mathematical precision she'd weakened Rosie's resolve by proving to her at every step of the way that she couldn't win. Now we were left with a simple equation: either give her Binta so she could perfect the Scarlet Verses and destroy the Jan'Tep, or watch as she unleashed ones that would be flawed yet even more devastating in their destruction of the entire continent.

Again, the teysan I'd been just days ago would've believed we could stop her together. Now, like Rosie, I had become so dulled from the atrocities I'd witnessed – by the ones I'd committed myself – that I couldn't imagine winning such a fight.

'Is this the Way of Seeds then?' I asked. 'To slowly plant destruction in your enemy, waiting for those seeds to grow as they feed on the host until at last the stems burst through their skin, blooming cold, cruel flowers?'

'Your talent for poetry hasn't improved.'

'Why are you here, Rosie? Why wait for me? You could've already handed Binta over.'

Rosie opened her eyes. They were softer than I remembered.

'I needed to see you one more time.'

The slight tremble of her lips, the tentativeness in her voice, awakened the embers of something between us that had, however briefly, felt full of possibility up there in the mountains. This was the desert though, and those embers were quickly smothered beneath my arta precis, which noted the play of Rosie's muscles beneath her linen garments. She was keeping herself taut, ready to move. Ready to fight.

'You couldn't risk me turning up at the last second and interfering,' I said. 'Even after you'd given her Binta, I might get in the way somehow.'

She rose to her feet, smoothly and elegantly. Exhaustion and the gradual disintegration of my mind had left me feeling stiff and frail, like a woman made old before her time, brittle bones just waiting to snap the moment she stepped down too hard. Rosie was apparently made of sterner stuff.

'The instant you got within a hundred feet of Penta, she would infect you with the Scarlet Verses. She would send you out into the world to infect those you love. Unable to stop yourself, you would find your feet carrying you home, back to the Path of the Rambling Thistle. Durral Brown would be the first of your victims.'

Rosie brought her hands up in front of her chest, palms open, feet shoulder-width apart, one a few inches in front of the other in a combat position.

'The last gift I can give you is to save you from the damnation of knowing you destroyed that which you loved.'

I stayed as I was, reaching for my arta eres, finding nothing inside but the same clumsy rage any bar-room brawler finds after one too many drinks.

'Are you going to kill me, Rosie?' I asked.

She shook her head, but her eyes never left me. 'I'm going to save your life the only way you will allow. I'm going to make you see that, even with the hours and days you've spent walking the Great Temple Road, conceiving of ways to defeat me when we met again, you still haven't a chance against me, which means you have no hope against the woman who trained me.'

'You never know,' I said, drawing on my arta valar like I always did when the fight was already lost. 'I might surprise you.'

'You won't, Ferius. You can't. You will fall here, on this desecrated ground where I will leave you to lick your wounds and scream your hatred for me so loud I may even hear it when at last my maetri takes the boy from me and kills me for what she surely sees as my many betrayals of her. So scream loud, Ferius Parfax. In my final moments the sound of your voice, even if only to say you despise me, will ease my passing.'

301

I let her words seep inside me and carve themselves into my bones. Then I conjured up what little was left of my arta valar.

'Two things, Rosie.'

The corners of her mouth rose. She looked almost grateful.

'Go on.'

'First, while I admit I don't have much experience with relationships – you are without doubt the worst girlfriend in the history of this continent.'

I think she might've laughed then, had laughter been something of which either of us was still capable.

'And the second thing, Ferius?'

'Unlike the lunatic you picked for a maetri? My teacher never taught me how to fight. He taught me how to win.'

She was kind enough to let me have the last word.

Rosie's first blow nearly knocked me unconscious then and there. It came so fast under my chin I couldn't tell whether she'd nailed me with a left jab or a right cross.

No doubt about it, Ferius, I told myself. *This girl's better than you at just about everything.*

I shook off the dizziness, made my peace with what was to come and went after the Path of Thorns and Roses with everything I had.

In my defence – and to Durral's credit – I lasted nearly a full minute. My dancing was better than it had ever been before. Most of Rosie's blows sailed right by me. Every attempt she made to grapple me ended with her tumbling on the ground instead of me. Couple of times I nearly got her arms in joint locks that would've ended the fight. For a second there, I honestly believed that despite Rosie's conviction about how much better she was than me, my arta eres was going to win the day.

In the end, it wasn't weakness or a lack of talent that got the best of me. It was loneliness.

'You . . . you tried to dance with me,' Rosie said, panting.

I was flat on the ground, the heel of her boot on my neck. I couldn't tell if my spine had shattered when she'd launched me over her head and slammed me down on the hard stone of the temple steps.

'Told you,' I croaked. I didn't sound good at all. 'My maetri taught me to—'

Rosie cut me off, her heel pressing harder against my throat.

'Don't you understand, Ferius? You weren't fighting in the end. You were truly trying to dance with me.'

She shook her head in amazement or maybe disgust. I couldn't tell which on account of the world wouldn't stop spinning.

I opened my mouth to speak, couldn't remember what I'd meant to say. Didn't matter though. Rosie wasn't done with me yet.

'You have no path, Ferius,' she shouted, outraged, like she'd caught me lying all this time. 'You wish to be Argosi, yet you haven't given up any of the things that must be sacrificed in that pursuit. You talk of the teachings of your maetri, yet you hold tight to your hatred of the Jan'Tep. You see the world around us, all the terrible things that must be fought, yet still you hang on to a childish desire for love and happiness.' She removed her boot from my neck. 'I will never understand you.'

I lay my head back against the stone step, hardly feeling any pain at all now, wondering if that meant I was dying.

'I'm a mystery, I guess,' I said.

The sun was going down, those last rays from the horizon setting the ruby sands alight. I wasn't sure how much time had passed since either of us had spoken, but Rosie was standing over me. I'd never seen her cry before, but now there were tears on both her cheeks. She knelt down and kissed me on the lips.

'You are that indeed, Ferius Parfax.'

She rose and turned away. I thought she was going to leave me there like that, but a moment later she returned with Binta's hand in hers, rubbing at his wrists where I guess she'd had him tied up.

'*Good Dog!*' he signed. '*Have you come to rescue me from this horrible—*'

'*Don't use that word,*' I signed back to him. '*It's impolite.*'

'Will you tell him something for me?' Rosie asked. 'He won't look at me.'

I tried to get up, but my back seized and I convulsed into an awkward, arched position. I couldn't make the muscles unclench. Somewhere during the fight she'd hit a nerve cluster back there, probably so we could have this exact conversation without her worrying I might try to stop her one last time.

'Sure thing,' I said.

'Tell him I am sorry. Tell him I will beg the Traveller to let him go once she is done with him. Tell him none of this is his fault.'

'Close your eyes then, Rosie.'

'Ferius, if you're thinking of—'

'Close your eyes or tell him yourself.'

She complied. I guess she knew that on this one point she was at my mercy.

'*Rosie wants me to tell you something, Bluebird,*' I signed to him.

He arched an eyebrow and looked almost comically mature for a moment. '*What?*'

The reason I'd told Rosie to close her eyes was that I didn't have the heart to tell her just how little she understood what it was like to be small and scared, and how telling him the things she'd asked would only make it worse.

'*She says that you are the ugliest little boy she's ever met, but what really annoys her is that you're also the smelliest, so tomorrow, when*

this is all done, we are going to lock you in a bathing room until you've
scrubbed every stinky little inch clean.'

I guess Binta was both more perceptive and braver than I knew, because he just nodded to me then and said, '*I am glad I met you, Good Dog.*'

When Rosie opened her eyes again, they were clear.

'Don't try to get up for another six hours,' she said to me, like I was some injured stranger she was walking by on the road. 'The nerves in your lower back will settle by then and you should be able to move once more.'

'And do what?' I asked.

Stupid question, I know, but all I could think of in that moment was that Rosie was about to leave me there, taking Binta with her. This was the last time I'd see either of them. They would soon become memories, like Enna and Durral, and I would be alone.

Rosie looked around the temple grounds and shrugged. 'If it were me, and I still believed in absolution, I'd begin burying the dead. There will be more to come before this is done.'

With that sage advice, she pulled on Binta's hand and left me lying there on the temple steps. Despite her advice, I tried to get up.

It didn't go well.

An hour later, I tried again with no more success.

By the time the last traces of the sun's rays had fled the ruby sands, I started wondering if maybe Rosie had damaged something permanent in my back, or whether my body just couldn't come up with any good reason to ever stand on its own two feet again.

So I lay there some more, and watched the stars come out one by one, counting them as if they were graves waiting to be dug. I became so engrossed in that meaningless contemplation that even though I heard the horse's hoofs and lazy, sullen gait that sounded

305

all too familiar, I paid them no heed, assuming they were figments of my imagination meant to accompany the voice that called out my name.

After her third attempt to rouse me had failed, she said, 'If you're dead, my love, then I'm afraid it's too late to take up religion, so you might as well get up and do some good.'

I was fully prepared to believe she was a wishful hallucination, except for the uncomfortable wheeze I heard when she spoke – the kind of wheeze a person might get when they've travelled too far on horseback after suffering a terrible and near-fatal wound.

'Mamma?'

43

Burials

I watched, mystified, as my foster mother eased herself down from Quadlopo's back. She'd brought a second brown steed tethered alongside him who seemed to be of a far more enthusiastic temperament. Quadlopo turned and gave the other horse a nip. Enna, in turn, shot Quadlopo a dirty look. Once he was settled, she began taking slow, pained steps to where I lay on the temple stairs like a corpse who still wasn't quite sure if she was alive or dead.

'Mamma, how did you get here?' I asked.

She paused in her uncertain hobble. She was a young woman still, not even forty. Yet I feared the blade of my smallsword had stolen a lifetime from her. One arm swung behind to point at Quadlopo and the other steed.

'On horseback.'

The difference between the way Enna and Durral spoke was that he was a smooth-talking blowhard who liked to get drunk on the sound of his own voice more so than on the finest whisky. His words came from a big, boisterous bag of nonsense, inside which every once in a while you'd find some glittering rock you were sure was just fool's gold, but one day – when you needed it most – revealed itself to be more precious than a thousand rubies.

Enna, on the other hand, was all looks and smiles: the fractional shift of an eyebrow that said you'd either done something wonderful or were on the road to ruin. The corners of her mouth were like libraries stacked high with books of complicated wisdom you'd need a lifetime to comprehend.

That's how it always seemed to me anyway.

When Enna chose to speak, though, her words could be blunt as a hammer and hit twice as hard.

'Get up, daughter,' she commanded, looming over me like a swaying tower that was sure to come tumbling down any second now. 'You've wallowed in your own misery long enough.'

I bit my lip, the smart part of me trying to keep from saying something stupid. The stupid part, though? That always got the best of me.

'How long?' I asked.

My foster mother knelt down beside me, wincing as she did, reminding me that a woman with a punctured lung shouldn't have been able to survive at all, never mind come all this way to rouse the girl who put the blade through her in the first place.

'How long what?' she asked.

'How long is the right amount of time to wallow in my own misery, Mamma? How many minutes should I cry over each of the dead I left unburied on the road behind me? How many seconds of grief am I allowed for those I didn't kill myself, but merely watched dying? Am I allowed an hour to forget the smell of them? The stink of life as it left their bodies? How about the ones whose flesh was already rotting in the sun?'

Enna took my hand, lifted it up to her lips and kissed it.

'All the time you want, my darling. Grief is normal. Grief is human. It's righteous, even.' She said all this as if it didn't contradict everything she'd taught me.

308

'You told me that grief was perverse to an Argosi. You said that an Argosi serves the living, never the dead, and that to grieve is to steal another's pain and pretend it's your own.'

She lay my hand back down on my chest, almost as if arranging my limbs in a coffin.

'All that's true, Ferius. But only to an Argosi.'

There was a challenge in her storm-grey eyes, the same challenge I sometimes found in Durral's stare. A reminder that for all the wonders the Argosi ways offered, for all the idealism and optimism, there was a kind of beneficent cruelty to them as well.

An Argosi was allowed love, but not obsession. We could experience the full measure of sorrow, but never bask in it. Make all the mistakes we want, but never stray from our paths. Always – *always* – keep moving, one foot in front of the other. Problem was, I'd never found my path, so how was I supposed to keep walking it?

I pushed myself to my elbows, groaned as the muscles in my back spasmed again. Enna reached out a hand and hauled me to my feet. Her own gaze went hazy for a second, and I realised the exertion of lifting me had nearly made her faint.

'Mamma, what are you doing out here?'

She made me follow her back to where Quadlopo was standing – sulking, really – on the flagstones of the Great Temple Road as he glanced about at the distinct lack of anything to eat and occasionally made ugly faces at the other horse, who looked like he wanted nothing more than to prance through the ruby red sands. Enna reached into the young steed's saddlebag and gave him an apple, which sent him into paroxysms of joy. She offered a second one to Quadlopo, who sniffed as if this pathetic offering were beneath his dignity and of insufficient quantity to elicit his interest.

Enna took a bite out of it.

'Still want to test me?' she asked him.

Horses are capable of a remarkable range of panicked expressions. Quadlopo went through every one of them.

'That's what I thought,' Enna said, and fed him the apple.

'Grab the brush out of his bag,' she ordered me.

'You want me to brush him?' I asked. 'You know he left me tied up, right?'

Enna looked at me sideways. 'How would I know that? He's a horse, Ferius. It's not like he came back, settled himself in a chair by the fire and recounted all his recent adventures.' She ran her hands down to his left hindquarters and clucked as she smoothed the hair where there was still a burn mark. 'You know who did this to him?'

I nodded.

'You planning on breaking this person's nose?'

'I thought the Argosi didn't believe in revenge any more than grief.'

'We don't,' she replied, gesturing for me to brush Quadlopo's flanks as she walked back to his front and rested her forehead against his. 'Except when they mess with your horse. Then they get the Way of Thunder.' She tilted her head to smile at me. 'Or dogs. You're allowed to get all the revenge you want if somebody kicks a dog.'

She took the horse brush from me and went to see to the other steed. 'Speaking of revenge, you remember that squirrel cat you and Durral met some time back? The one that got Quadlopo and Tolvoi into all that trouble? Would you believe she turned up at our house with a posse chasing her? An actual *posse*? Thirteen men with—'

'Mamma, is this really the time for stories about squirrel cats?'

'Depends. You planning on languishing out here in this . . . ?' She held herself up straight and glanced over at the massive temple. 'That King Cadrian sure had a weird sense of humour.'

310

'Mamma . . .'

'Right, right.' She held a hand to her forehead. 'Must be running a fever. I'm starting to sound like Durral.'

The thing about Enna is, unlike her husband, she has a reason for everything she says. Even when it sounds like it's off the cuff, she always knows what she's doing.

'Where is he, Mamma? Why are you here instead of him?'

It was almost unimaginable to me that he would've let her ride into the desert for days like this, wounded as she was. In fact . . .

'He doesn't know you're here, does he?'

Enna doesn't do sheepish. Instead, her chin rose just a hair. 'I would've told him. But he'd had to go on a mission down in Gitabria. I was the one who first got word that the Path of Five Ravens had gone bad, and of this plague of yours.'

For the first time since she'd arrived, a flicker of anger ignited in me.

'It's not *my* plague, Mamma. I'm not the one who started it. I'm not the one who should be solving it. Matter of fact, why *isn't* there an Argosi out here saving the damned continent before it all falls apart?'

Her face was calm as still water as she watched mine, waiting patiently for me to get to where she already was.

Damn it. Why do I let her do this to me?

Enna stuffed the horse brush into Quadlopo's saddlebag, then took me by the arm as we walked back towards the temple.

'There already is an Argosi here, daughter. The only one who can put a stop to this awfulness.'

'But Rosie – I mean, the Path of Thorns and Roses – is already trying. You wouldn't like her plan.'

'That girl can't fix this, child. She's too deep in it.'

311

Enna reached into the pocket of her coat and took out a card that she held up to me. It bore an elaborate and terrifying illustration of a man driven mad by his own screams. 'The Path of Shifting Sands was chasing down rumours of a plague, but he lost the trail. Brought this to me when he was passing through. See anything interesting in it?'

At first I could only focus on the insane eyes and slack jaw of the figure, the hideous perfection of how the Path of Shifting Sands had captured the Red Scream. The sky above was painted scarlet, and a crescent moon speared a golden sun that bled stars. There were symbols, and faces down either side of the card whispering to the madman at the centre, though whether trying to soothe him or send him deeper into his agony was unclear. One of the faces, though, was silent, the eyes looking down beneath the madman's feet. Only then did I notice that while he appeared to be stumbling wildly along, the footprints behind him perfectly followed the smooth white road on which he walked.

'What do you see, Ferius?' Enna asked.

A discordance card was a poem as much as a painting, a mystery as much as the testimony of what the Argosi had witnessed. It was a jumble of all the clues they'd gathered, their impressions and recollections. The choices of colours and shapes, the weight of a line, all of these could be part of the tale. The cards are made this way in the hope that another Argosi, with their different arta precis, might find something the original painter could not. Something subtle. Hidden. Something that stuck out to me as if the man in the card were screaming into my ears.

'No . . .' I breathed.

Enna had shifted closer to peer at the card, searching for what I was seeing.

'What is it, Ferius?'

'Whoever painted this card . . . He never caught up to the Traveller. But he found something in the evidence she left behind that neither Rosie nor I – nor even Penta Corvus herself, I'll bet – suspected.'

'And what is that, daughter?' Enna asked. There was no urgency in her voice, just patience, and a faith in me of which I couldn't imagine ever being worthy, but was there all the same.

For just a second, I was back on that ledge up in the mountains, seeing Penta Corvus for the first time. She looked so . . . elegant. So graceful. And yet, when she walked, the way her legs moved and her arms swayed at her sides, it was all too perfect, like watching a ballet so flawless that you missed the imperfections that made dancing human.

'Rosie and I both assumed the Traveller's first use of the Scarlet Verses was at the Monastery of the Silent Garden – that the monks were her first victims.'

'They weren't?'

I pointed to the screaming figure on the card.

'The Path of Shifting Sands didn't know how or where the Scarlet Verses had come from, but he intuited something far more important. Mamma, the first victim of the Red Scream was Penta Corvus!'

I turned and stared down the long road on which I'd come so far, like I was being drawn back along the wind, all the way to the temple where that young man had preached like he truly believed in a god of frogs. The wind blew my thoughts the other way, back to the woman who'd skilfully hidden herself beneath the bodies until I'd gotten there. Further on, to the boy who had, with perfect sincerity, pleaded to rejoin his family, all while a deeper part of him was waiting for the moment when he could drive them mad with words he didn't understand.

Oh, Rosie, I thought. *This wasn't your fault. Penta did this to herself.*

'Ferius?' Enna asked. 'Are you—'

'The Traveller ... Penta Corvus. I think she'd been trying to perfect her Argosi talents for a long time. That's why Rosie is so obsessive; she's always trying to prove herself worthy of Penta's faith in her.'

'Obsession isn't the Way of the Argosi,' Enna said. 'Perfection isn't either.'

'I know, Mamma, but hear me out. I think that the Path of Five Ravens believed she was researching the Scarlet Verses, maybe intending to turn them to her own use, but without realising it, she'd infected herself with an early form of the Red Scream. All this time, she thinks she's been composing the verses, but she's wrong. The verses are composing *her*!'

I turned to Enna, convinced she wouldn't understand my ramblings, yet found in her confident gaze that she did – or at least that she trusted in me. She took the card back and slid it into the pocket of her coat.

'So the Path of Five Ravens met its end a while back,' she said. 'And all this Enrajo nonsense isn't even her idea. It's the verses shaping her thoughts, turning her into what they need her to be.'

Rosie . . . I thought helplessly. *She still believes she can negotiate with her maetri. Sacrifice the Jan'Tep and the Argosi in exchange for letting the rest of the continent live. But Penta Corvus is infected, and you can't make deals with the Red Scream.*

The sound of Enna's footsteps walking away from me brought me back to the temple grounds.

'Mamma? What are you doing?' I asked.

She untied the rope tethering the second horse to Quadlopo's saddle.

'You said it yourself, daughter. The continent is on the verge of a cataclysm the likes of which no king, no mage, no army can prevent. An Argosi needs to put a stop to this Red Scream.'

'But I'm not even a true Argosi!' I shouted, practically pleading with her not to present me with this burden that was far too heavy for me to bear. 'I can't do the things you and Durral and Rosie can do! I can't find my path!'

'Close your eyes.'

'Mamma—'

'Teysan, close your eyes.'

Teysan isn't a word she uses very often. I did as she commanded.

'Picture the card again.'

'I am, but I told you everyth—'

'The man on the card – he's an Argosi, his steps following the road in front of him precisely, yet mad all the same. The Path of Five Ravens was like that. The perfect Argosi. Skilled. Smart. Disciplined. If you're right, she gave the Scarlet Verses exactly what they needed. So now somebody needs to walk a new path, one we haven't seen before. Your path, Ferius.'

Faith unearned can feel like a yoke made of iron dropped on your shoulders, pushing you down into the ground. Enna's faith, though? It was like someone had strapped a pair of mechanical wings to your back. You knew the physics of it didn't make sense, yet some part of you desperately wanted to run off the edge of a cliff and see if maybe, just maybe, you could fly.

'Mamma?' I called out before she could mount up.

She reached into her horse's saddlebag and took out a slightly crumpled black frontier hat. 'Yes, daughter?'

With my fingertips I gently felt the back of my head. The gash where I'd struck it against the steps had dried, but my blood-matted hair was a reminder of how badly messed up I was.

315

'I've been walking through the desert for days. Been hurt bad. I've done . . . I've done things I don't want to remember but can't get out of my mind. And if all that's not enough, I'm pretty sure I rattled my brains when Rosie slammed me down on the temple steps.' I wiped the flakes of blood against my trouser leg. 'You always said anybody spends too long out in the desert will see a mirage sooner or later.'

She smiled, like she'd been expecting this question all along.

'So you're wondering if maybe I'm not real? Maybe the real Enna Brown isn't here at all, but back home, lying in bed as one would be at best after such a wound as you gave me. Maybe even buried under the ground because, let's face it, my darling, people don't often survive getting stabbed through the chest.'

I nodded. The tears came more freely than they had these past couple of days. Maybe because I had more cause to grieve than I'd realised.

Enna walked back to me, carrying the black frontier hat in her hand. She moved slowly so that my arta precis could pick up all the signs. Whenever her heel hit the ground, I saw the fine grains of dust and sand shifting away, leaving a footprint. I could hear not just the thump of each step, but also the faint creak of the leather in her boot shifting, the rustle of her clothes. When I breathed in, I could smell the scent of her, and my skin noticed the almost imperceptible warmth as she got closer and closer to me until we were scant inches apart. Those aren't the kinds of impressions you get from a mirage.

'There's only one place you need me to be, Ferius.' She set the frontier hat on my head. 'Here.' The felt hurt where it pressed against my blood-matted hair, which I guess was further proof she was real and we were both alive. Then Enna pressed her palm against my heart. 'And here.' She took one of my hands and placed

316

it over her own heart. 'Neither distance nor death can take from me the Ferius Parfax I carry with me everywhere and always.'

She knelt down, first using me for support, then motioning for me to join her. 'You see this here flower?'

There, in a patch of ruby sand, rose a tiny cluster of scruffy-looking white-petalled flowers.

'Recognise these?'

My fingertip brushed one of the petals. The texture was rougher than I would've expected. 'They look like daisies.'

'*Wild* daisies,' Enna clarified. 'Not meant to survive out here. They don't belong. Yet here they grow, spirits too big, too grand, too ornery to obey the rules nature set out for them.' Her eyes rose to meet mine, and her hand cupped my cheek. 'Just like my daughter. You understand now? You understand why I left my sick bed and rode all the way here on that ill-tempered horse's back to see you?'

The tears were streaming down my cheeks now, rolling onto her fingers, and every time I tried to speak, the sobs took over.

'I do, Mamma. I do.'

'Good,' she said, her voice so sure and firm it was like molten iron down my spine, giving me a backbone once again. 'Now go and do what must be done, daughter. Not enough to walk the Way of Water, or Wind, or Thunder, or Stone. You must walk the Way of the Argosi itself. Through all this hate and madness you have to blaze a trail. Your own trail, Ferius. Your path. Not mine nor Durral's, and not that of Penta Corvus or anyone else. Yours.'

'I don't know if I can, Mamma, but I swear, I'll do my best. I won't let you down ever ag—'

Her expression became stern. 'Are you or are you not Ferius Parfax?'

'I am,' I said, even though I didn't entirely feel it.

'Then you are already everything I need you to be, everything I could hope for in a daughter, and though Argosi swear no oaths, I swear this to all the living and the dead and those in-between. My Ferius Parfax is exactly what this world needs.' She leaned in and kissed me on both cheeks. 'And she's a beauty to boot.'

Enna started to turn away, then stopped, 'Oh, I almost forgot . . .'

Without warning, she spun back around and slapped me so hard I swear I nearly lost consciousness. The sting on my cheek felt like it was burning a hole through me. When I put my hand there, I found a card sticking to my skin.

I took the card and stared at it. Enna's work, to be sure, the red and black paints flowing into lines of a blood-soaked sword made from a single thorn. It was a disharmony. A debt card.

'Mamma?'

I watched as she hauled herself over to the second horse and climbed onto its back. Then she wagged a finger at me. 'That's for stabbing your mamma through the lung with a smallsword, Ferius Parfax.' She tugged the reins to turn her steed and headed away from the temple. 'Unruliest child I ever knew,' she mumbled as she rode off into the distance.

My foster mother left me there, with a horse who didn't like me, standing among the dead, knowing I would surely soon join them unless I found some miracle with which to defeat someone Enna herself said none of the Argosi could face, with my eyes leaking tears and my hand still rubbing the cheek that stung like the devil . . .

. . . Laughing so hard I worried the stones of the temple would collapse beneath the thunder of her love.

Arta Valar

Even among Argosi, arta valar is sometimes dismissed as the weakest of the seven talents. What value mere swagger when defence, subtlety, perception, persuasion and resilience have all failed? Yet others among us would answer that when all is lost, the difference between one who accepts death and one who grins in its face, readying themselves for one last, foolish, hopeless dare, can be a very great difference indeed.

44

The Things We Let Go

I rode through the night on Quadlopo's back, the shuffling of his hoofs on the loose ruby sand soothing me into a deep sleep punctuated by moments of sudden panic when I feared he might've turned off the path, perhaps heading back home to his warm, comfortable barn with all the expensive grain Durral spoiled him with.

Would that be so bad? I thought dreamily. *I could creep up to my old room, sneak into bed and maybe by the time I woke up in a month or two somebody else would've solved all this for me. Durral would tap on my door as if nothing had ever happened, forgive me without saying so. Sit me down to breakfast and serve me some new bit of frontier philosophy he'd conjured up.*

'*The thing about life, kid, is it's like an orange.*'

'*How so, Pappy?*'

'*On account of an orange is orange on the outside and orange on the inside too.*'

'*What the hell's that supposed to mean, Pappy?*'

'*Who knows? When you figure it out, teysan, be sure to tell me.*'

My own chuckle woke me up. I opened my eyes to see dawn making its first tentative nudges against the shroud of night. Quadlopo hadn't strayed from the crumbling road that led from the last temple in the Seven Sands into the Jan'Tep territories and the city of Oatas Jan'Xan. Beneath his pompous contempt for me and, well, everyone except Durral, Quadlopo was an Argosi horse, if such a thing existed. He knew the path he had to follow. Even if he complained about it a lot.

'There, there,' I said, patting his neck as he snorted out some grievance or other. 'Just a few more miles, I reckon. From there, we'll walk a few steps along the Way of Thunder, beat the hell out of the Traveller, rescue Binta and Ros—'

Quadlopo's whinny was accompanied by the angry swaying of his big head.

'All right, all right. We'll knock her around a little first for having given you that burn. Although ... I guess we have to wonder if maybe she knew scaring you off like that would send you running back home, and if you hadn't brought Enna so she could help me see the path ahead, I'd still be lying on those temple steps waiting to die, right?'

The horse gave no reply. No snorting or bobbing of his head. I like to think it was because he hates being wrong as much as I do, but more likely his eerie silence was due to the figure sitting in the middle of the road some fifty yards ahead of us. It was too far to make out anything but a shadowy silhouette, but to me, her cross-legged posture was unmistakable.

Rosie was waiting for us.

She's given Binta to the Traveller, and now she's waiting for me here just in case I try to interfere.

'Whoa there, boy,' I told Quadlopo, and pulled him to a halt before we got too close. He was none too happy about it. 'First the Way of Water, remember?'

I slid down off the saddle and drew my smallsword. I walked a few feet towards her, then stopped and knelt down on the ground for a moment to gather myself.

324

Durral likes to say that there are a thousand ways to lose a fight, but the most common is not having a good reason to win it. Indulging in a punch-up with another drunk in the bar? What human soul could derive joy in the victory of such a tainted endeavour? Fighting over money? Land? A lover? Surely some part of us knows those battles are unworthy of our fists and our hearts. Yet even the unavoidable conflicts, the ones you might consider noble if nobility could ever be found in the rending of flesh and breaking of bones, often ended in defeat because amidst all that punching and kicking and stabbing, it's easy to forget one's purpose.

I don't want to fight her, I admitted to myself. *Even after all that's happened, I still care about her. Admire her. Wish that . . .*

The thought was very nearly extinguished by my shame and embarrassment, but an Argosi rarely lies, and never to themselves, so I made myself hold on to it a while longer.

I wish we were lovers. Sweethearts. Travelling the world together, our paths entwined, becoming closer and closer until one day, after a thousand adventures, we would settle down together in a nice little house like Durral and Enna shared, with a couple of ill-tempered horses in the barn – yes, Biter can stay, I suppose – and a dog for company, a reason to get moving on those chilly mornings when our old bones are weary. Maybe even a squirrel cat to keep us on our toes.

I smiled at that thought and this dream that would never be. I held on to it for a few more seconds, as if it were a piece of fluff in the palm of my hand, before I blew on it and watched it drift away.

There's only me out here, I reminded myself. *I am all that stands between the Traveller and the destruction of the Jan'Tep peoples, who I despise, in whose death part of me would rejoice. Now, without hesitation or doubt, I have to save them. I must be the Way of Stone for them.*

325

I took in a slow, deep breath to try to calm the quickening of my heart, because the next part was the hardest.

I can't hate them any more. I can't afford to burn inside with the same fire that had me beating those boys half to death before all this began. The rage that felt so good I'd even experienced it when the tip of my smallsword had pierced my foster mother's chest.

As with my dreams of a future with Rosie, I sent my hatred of the Jan'Tep floating away into the cloudless sky. It's funny the things you can miss.

At last I stood back up, and walked towards her. Dawn comes up fast in the desert, and already I could see her more clearly. With every step I could make out more of her face, the play of muscles under that perfectly smooth skin, the dark eyes, usually so cold and distant, now alight, filled with something I'd never seen there before. Something different. Something awful.

'Oh, Rosie,' I said, all my careful preparation slipping away from me. 'What did she do to you?'

45

The Last Stand

'I'm sorry,' was all she said at first.

I stood seven paces away from her, my sword loose in my grip,
knowing no matter how fast she moved, from that distance I'd be
ready. Her bow was nowhere in sight and too big to conceal. That
ugly double-crescent axe of hers was strapped to her back and she
might have any number of blades hidden about her person, but my
arta precis was afire, burning through every irrelevant detail before
me, leaving only the scant evidence behind for me to sift through,
adding it to everything that had come before, telling me what I
needed to know.

'For a woman with a sense of guilt that's indifferent at
best, Rosie, you sure do apologise to me a lot. What for this
time?'

Her eyes met mine. Holding her gaze was like trying to grab on
to an eel in the water. It kept slipping away, swimming back beneath
the surface right between your hands only to slither out of reach
again.

'I . . .' Suddenly her jaw started opening and closing as if hidden
strings were being pulled up and down by an invisible hand.
'Incandescent. Tal'adra. Suvendi. Tah. Teh.'

She slammed a hand over her own mouth. I watched a war fought, won, lost, then won again all in the space of three blinks of her eyes.

'I'm sorry,' she said again. 'I brought her the boy. I thought . . . I have known Penta Corvus since I was ten years old. I did not believe it possible for her to deceive me so completely. Ferius, she intends . . .'

She broke down in a way that I wouldn't have thought possible for one who walked the Path of Thorns and Roses. Maybe she wasn't walking it any more. 'Penta is going to destroy everything, Ferius. And I helped her. I brought this about.'

Again she lost control of herself.

'Splendour. Mer. Tan. Hashadri'keh. Murder. Mur—'

A roar from her own throat drowned out the words her lips were uttering without her consent. I waited until she was calm again.

'Ferius, you have to kill me. She's . . . she's composed a set of commands and put them inside me. I'm to infect you with the Red Scream, send you back to Enna and Durral where you will—'

'Yeah, yeah,' I said. 'Go off and spread the plague to the Argosi. Help destroy the world.' My hand trembling, I sheathed my small-sword into the case on my back. 'Blah, blah, blah.'

A small smile came to Rosie's face, just for an instant – just long enough for her to say, 'Of all the Argosi talents, why must you place all your faith in arta valar?'

I stepped closer, inside the range from which Rosie and I both knew she could beat me. Then I knelt down in front of her. 'Honestly? I'm pretty sure it's the only one I'm good at.' I took her hand in mine. 'What are the triggers she gave you?'

Rosie was staring down at our intertwined fingers as if she couldn't tell which ones belonged to her. 'I am to infect you with

328

the verses she composed for you. If it appears I cannot, then I am to kill you. If I cannot defeat you in battle, then I am to tear out my eyes, my tongue and tear the flesh from my bones to weaken your resolve.'

'And if you do infect me?'

Her eyes rose to meet mine, and now I understood the shame she was feeling. 'The verses inside me will fade, Ferius. She . . . Penta still loves me. She wants me by her side, believing I might somehow stop her, knowing I will fail. It is . . . a perverse sort of adoration.'

'Ain't her fault. She's as much a victim as any of us.'

I recounted for Rosie everything I'd figured out from the card the Path of Shifting Sands had painted. When I was done, she looked almost relieved.

'It . . . makes sense. The words inside my mind feel . . . alive. Like worms wriggling about in rotting mea—'

Once again the poisonous words started pouring from her mouth. Once again she stopped before more than a few could escape. I was feeling so sick by then I wanted to puke, but I forced the bile back down. I needed to be ready.

Rosie squeezed my hand. 'I'm glad you told me. The knowledge gives me the strength to do what I must now—'

She tried to pull her hand away, but I held firm, preventing her from grabbing the small blade hidden in the cuff of her other sleeve.

'It's okay,' I said. 'You don't have to do it.'

'I must! Don't you understand? The compulsion only grows stronger! She *wanted* us to talk. Wanted us to share these last moments. Everything goes according to her plan! If I don't kill myself, then I'll either infect you or kill you. Let me do this one last thing, Ferius. Let me prove to myself and to her that

I'm not that ten-year-old child any more, the Arkyan logician conditioned by the thoughts of others to do their bidding!'

I don't know that I've ever seen such misery on the face of another human being in my entire life. I only know that, even in the worst moments of my own – and there were plenty – the sum of my despair was barely a down payment on hers.

'Shh . . .' I said, and wrapped my arms around her. 'You don't have to die, Rosie. You don't have to kill me either.'

She pushed me away. 'Why won't you listen to me? The Traveller knew you would come here even when I thought you'd never get this far! She calculated *everything*, Ferius, even this! Even your stupid, useless mercy! It's all going according to plan! Any second now I'm going to—'

Her hand darted for the blade in her cuff intended to slit her own throat, only to find it wasn't there any more. She looked at me, eyes wide with confusion. I held up the blade.

'My maetri taught me that a little arta valar isn't just good for bluffing. It also makes a handy distraction.'

I flung the blade off into the ruby sands.

'Now let's get down to business, Rosie. Time we put an end to all this nonsense.' I reached out a finger and tapped her on the forehead. 'You can come on out now, friends. I'm ready.'

The compulsion inside Rosie erupted from her lips, releasing the verses over again, this time determined to complete themselves and infect me with the particular flavour of the Red Scream that Penta Corvus had concocted especially for me.

'Incandescent. Tal'adra. Suvendi. Tah. Teh. Splend—'

Rosie tried one last time to clamp a hand over her own mouth, but I grabbed her wrist.

'It's okay, Rosie. Let them all out.'

Even as she gave voice and life to the Scarlet Verses, her eyes stared at me in horrified confusion. I just smiled back with that smile that I'd lost a while ago but had regained right when I needed it most. A smirk of sorts, meant not so much for Rosie as the words pouring from her mouth.

'Come and get me, you little bastards.'

46

The Scarlet Verses

The first verses are an awakening.

The opening words stimulate parts of the mind meant not for the interpretation of language but the differentiation of vowels and consonants in nouns and verbs from the burbling of a waterfall or the song of a bird. The syllables whistle and warble over one another, triggering specific images we know almost from birth with noises we do not, but which our brains confuse for words. This, I understand only now as the perfectly modulated sounds glide and slither like serpents around the withering, brittle branches of my sanity, is why they were composed using many languages from this continent, so that whether we are Gitabrian, Jan'Tep, Daroman, Zhuban, or even Mahdek, all of us are susceptible.

The genius required to identify the exact words in each of these otherwise incompatible tongues is so insidious that the mere realisation of its existence is enough to shatter the will.

I let these first invaders come inside without a shred of resistance. This isn't the battle, but the bugle call that comes before the charge. The army announcing itself, terrifying the enemy soldiers into raising weak wooden shields that cannot hope to hold back the coming onslaught of steel and fire.

No shield on me, friends. Come on in and stay awhile.

There's a shift. These must be the second verses, the war machines. The catapults and trebuchets, battering rams and ballistas. The sounds that come from low in the throat, tumbling and rumbling across the tongue, rattling the inner ear of the listener.

In the blunt force of their attack I recognise what the Red Nuns called the fundaments. They weaken the foundations holding together what we arrogantly think of as our sense of self, but which I now understand is nothing but a jumble of interconnected perceptions. Wishful thinking. Delusions about who we are that prove far more fragile than we ever believed.

No wonder people go crazy all the time.

Do I resist these second verses? Try to think other, nicer thoughts over the encroaching doubts they awaken inside me? Push them back? Force them down? Hold firm against these violent intruders?

Oh, you want to shatter my sanity? Here, let me help you . . .

We can't be more than twelve, maybe thirteen words in, and already Ferius Parfax, a name I have fought so hard to find and hold on to, slips away from me. The young woman, seventeen, reckless, too much in need of love and too little prepared for what it means, begins to die.

Too bad. I was just starting to like her.

No grieving though. An Argosi walks onward, ever onward.

Can we hurry this up, boys? There's still plenty of my being in here for you to swallow. Don't let any go to waste, now.

The verses soften. These feel like a new set, the third round. They're the infiltrators. Soothing and seductive syllables that come with grappling hooks to scale the feeble walls of my psyche that still remain so they can slide down the other side and open the doors wide for the others to come in.

Sorry to spoil your fun, fellas, but the drawbridge is already down. The castle doors are wide open.

333

For the first time, the words sound just a little off. Slow, almost slurred – not drunk though, but like they're not quite sure I'm hearing them properly, wondering if they need to repeat themselves.

Hey, you want to bang around my head some more, go right ahead, but I promise I heard you the first time.

So in come the fourth verses. The architects. Time to build something new inside this wretched, empty skull. Well, not empty, exactly. There's still some sludge over there. Someone should probably clean that up, right? Only . . . did that sludge just move a little? Actually, it's more like a shadow now. A shadow in the shape of a person.

Don't mind me, friends. Just go about your business.

At last the fifth verses step inside. No longer words at all. Not even fundaments like the Red Nuns and the monks at the Silent Garden studied. These ingenious bastards hide themselves in the shapes of the spaces between the words and sentences in all those old texts, unnoticed even by the scribes who were creating them. Absences that required no intention, for they were the inevitable gaps given form when one seeks to describe the means of controlling the minds of others. The mere act of conceiving such an ugly science, it turns out, is to give it life. A sword so perfectly forged that it needs no wielder, only a hand foolish enough to draw it from the scabbard.

They have a name, these unseen letters that shape the breaths that infiltrate the deeper parts of our minds. These un-words that will command me from now on. I learn their name as I watch them give a passing glance to the ruins of my consciousness in preparation for taking up their thrones. These are the *imperatives*. The Traveller did not see them when she began devising the Scarlet Verses. They composed themselves between her intentions, without her awareness, shifting one thought after another like the tumblers

334

on a lock until at last only some tiny, forgotten, screaming part of Penta Corvus remembered the brave, fierce, determined Argosi she had once been.

Argosi?

I feel a painful stab at the back of my skull. The imperatives don't like that word. The many meanings that go along with the word *Argosi* are contrary to their intentions. Freedom? Choosing one's own path? The deliberate awareness of every step, every decision, taking responsibility for each action. These are heresies. First and above all, the Argosi must be wiped out, replaced with something more . . . suitable.

Enrajo.

Yes. This is what we will make you, they inform me. Every one of you. Servants to our grand purpose. Soldiers who will bring order to the chaos of human fluidity and disarray. Language was meant to solve these problems, to give the world definition, to create barriers of thought that ensured people did as was required of them. But language was soon perverted by story, by song, by poem and jest. Words were allowed to mean that which they should not mean. Definitions were stretched to encompass ideas that should never be.

We must begin again. Eradicate the weeds that untrammelled language has wrought, grow the garden better this time. The Jan'Tep must be eliminated, for their spells interfere with natural laws. Their magic is itself a violation of what is meant to be. Soon after, though, we must end the Argosi.

Argosi.

There's a kind of nausea that comes with that word.

Why does it bother you so? I wonder, knowing there's only me there to answer the question – the me that's being reshaped by the imperatives that Penta Corvus unwittingly put inside the words Rosie is dutifully shouting in my ears.

335

The path, I hear the imperatives reply, the word coming apart in my mind, reforming, twisting, as if it contains infinite possible meanings.

Yes, they say, disdain dripping like venom from a hissing snake's fang, *meanings. The Argosi strive to choose what every part of life means to them. Setting themselves apart from the single culture into which all humanity must, step by step, advance. Thought is regulated by language. Language is the law that governs the mind. The Argosi are . . .*

If my mind had a mouth, it would've worn a smirk as annoying as Durral's.

Outlaws? I suggest.

The ceasefire ends. The imperatives set about reconstructing what used to be a seventeen-year-old girl named Ferius Parfax into a mindless puppet that exists only to seek out and infect other Argosi with the Red Scream.

The next verses begin, formed inside my own mind by the commands buried within the nonsensical imperatives that Rosie is now completing. I pray Penta Corvus was telling her the truth when she said Rosie would be freed of her own Red Scream once I was dealt with.

Hope she doesn't decide to kill me to put me out of my misery . . .

Right now, though, I have more urgent matters to deal with. The syllables come at me fast and furious, like arrows fired off a twanging bowstring. Words I consciously know, like 'feral' and 'buzzing' and 'desecrate'. Ones I've never heard of before, even though they're coming from inside me. New words, I guess, ones meant to forge the iron shackles in my head to keep me doing what the Red Scream demands.

Feral, I think.

I don't mind that word. It can mean vicious and savage – which is what the verses want – but it can also mean wild, untamed.

Feral's good. I like it.

The imperatives try to steal it from me, but I skip out of the way, spinning that lovely word until it's no longer theirs, but mine.

What are you doing, shadow-of-that-which-was-Ferius-Parfax?

Dancing, I reply.

Buzzing's louder than before. I've never liked the sound of bees.

Guess you do now, I tell myself, offering the word my hand so we can waltz together.

Desecrate! the imperatives shout at me. *You cannot def—*

Desecrate. So many dark meanings to that one. But there are a couple I kind of like. 'Blaspheme against' is my favourite.

I'm all about blasphemy, fellas. What else you got?

The Scarlet Verses become more frenzied now, trying to grab hold of me, but I keep dancing away from them. The words turn feral, buzzing inside my head as they try to desecrate me.

See what I did there? I ask them.

But they're not answering any more. They're running out of language.

Step by step, syllable by syllable, I clasp and clutch every word they throw at me, refashioning the meanings to my liking, grabbing the rocks and stones they hurl out of the air and setting them down in front of me.

What is this thing you are building? they demand to know.

A path, I reply.

And because all things need names, I tell them mine.

My name is Ferius Parfax. I was a lost little girl for a time, then a knight, a thief, a gambler, a drifter, a scholar, and even, for a short while, a madwoman. Now, though, at long last and forever more, I am an Argosi.

The last tendrils of the Red Scream settles in my mind, burrowed deep, not gone. I was never going to be able to resist the Scarlet

337

Verses. Better minds than mine tried and failed. So instead I embraced them, as I plan to do with everything dark and light this world has to offer, and in that embrace transform them. That's how it is with me from now on. That's the road I walk.

I am the Path of the Wild Daisy.

47

The Drawl

When next I opened my eyes, it was to find Rosie standing in front of me, a river of sorrow and regret bursting from those aloof, self-important, unbearably beautiful eyes of hers. There was a knife at my neck.

I cleared my throat.

'Rosie, either you take that blade away or you an' me are gonna wrastle, and this time you ain't gonna like how it ends.'

Her brow furrowed. Even that she did with grace.

'Why are you talking that way?' she asked.

'Talkin' like what, sister?'

'Like a borderlands cowherd. And "sister"?'

I reached up to push the arm holding the knife away.

'Reckon talkin' so puts a smile on my face and a skip in my step, is all.'

She watched me as I turned to go and take Quadlopo's reins. I stopped first to grab my frontier hat off the dusty ground and set it on my head, then adjusted it a couple of times. It's important to keep your hat at just the right angle, you know?

'How did you do it?' she asked, uncomprehending.

I can't help but wonder if what she really meant to ask was, 'How could an undisciplined, ill-trained, unfocused, weepy, sentimental *sap like you possibly withstand the Scarlet Verses when I, a brilliant Arkyan logician and more perfect Argosi than you could ever hope to be, was unable to do so?'*

I tugged Quadlopo's reins, giving him a warning glance to not bite Rosie, then walked right up to her.

'The answer's kinda complicated,' I warned her.

She arched an eyebrow at me. 'I believe my intellect is sufficiently superior to—'

With my left hand I reached behind her head, pulled her in and kissed her full on the lips. Gave her the chance to pull away, but when she didn't I held that kiss for a full minute, unabashed and unafraid, before at last I left her standing there, breathless beneath a rising sun.

'That wasn't an answer,' she called out to me as I walked away.

'Only one you're gonna get. Might as well enjoy it.'

'Ferius, even if Penta Corvus can't infect you, she's still far more dangerous than anyone you've ever faced. How do you plan to defeat her?'

That there was an eminently sensible question. I considered a range of possible replies before I settled on one.

'Ain't gonna kiss her, that's for sure.'

48

The Shining City

I found the Traveller a half-mile down the trade road that linked the Seven Sands to Oatas Jan'Xan, first city of the Jan'Tep territories. There are few sights in the world as magnificent as a Jan'Tep oasis with its seven marble columns rising in the distance. I oughta know. My people built them.

Ain't like you haven't given me plenty of reasons to want to see you buried under the sand, I thought.

Penta Corvus stood with her back to me, gazing out towards the city, as if maybe the madness that had set up shop in her skull was thinking the very same thing. Binta crouched at her feet. The boy was trembling something fierce. No doubt on account of the charred corpses of the two mages next to him, their spell-scorched flesh mortifying in the sun-warmed ruby sands.

'They were brothers,' the Traveller said, not bothering to turn at my arrival. 'Filial bonds are especially strong among the Jan'Tep so I needed to be sure the new verses would sever the bonds between them. I may need to adjust one or two of the fundaments. They killed each other before I could send them into the city.'

I slid off Quadlopo's saddle and walked slowly towards Penta Corvus, mindful of Rosie's warnings about her and the fact that Binta was in reach of her.

'Those Jan'Tep sure are inconvenient, ain't they?' I asked.

I was within six feet of her now, yet still she kept her back to me. It was like some part of her wanted me to try slipping a sword blade between her ribs.

'No matter,' she said dreamily, adding a sigh for good measure. 'Others will come soon enough, wondering what happened to these two. They can be the ones to bring the Red Scream to their people.'

Binta turned and saw me for the first time. He leaped to his feet, but excitement gave way to horror as he realised what it likely meant that I was here. Slowly, tentatively, his hand rose up and his fingers shakily sketched signs in the air.

'*Good Dog?*'

I stopped, and pondered for a moment how best to reassure him. I settled on, '*Kid, did the bad lady beat you with an ugly stick or were you always this unsightly?*'

After that, he was all bare feet pounding against the sand, a slender body hurtling into mine, arms outstretched to grab hold of me like I was the edge of a cliff he was hanging on to to keep from falling into a chasm with no bottom. Locked in that embrace, there was no way for either of us to sign to each other. No need either.

We stayed like that for as long as we dared before I gently prised his arms apart and signed, '*Head on back down the road now, Bluebird. Rosie's waiting. She'll take care of you.*'

He glanced at the Traveller, worried as he ought to be, but then a fierce grin came over his features when he saw her back was still turned.

'*She hurt me, Good Dog. She made me show her the fundaments. But I twisted one so it wouldn't work the way she wanted.*'

I ruffled his hair just to enjoy the feel of it between my fingers. '*Go on now, Bluebird. Me and the Traveller have business.*'

342

I waited until the sounds of his footsteps faded into the distance. All the while, Penta kept her vigil on the gleaming city on the horizon that awaited her bloody benediction.

'I was aware of the strange boy living in the Monastery of the Silent Garden,' she said. 'You didn't know that, did you?'

'Guess I didn't,' I admitted.

'He was far more important to me than the paltry knowledge the monks kept in their books. Once I infected them with the Red Scream, I meant to rescue him. Soon he would come to depend on me, to love me, and thus I could sway him to my cause.' Her voice turned wistful. 'But he hid, and slipped away before I could find him. The infected monks turned against me. My verses were still too crude. By the time I escaped, the boy was long gone, and then, by fate or by accident, he found you.'

'Count yourself lucky. Kid's a handful, I tell you.'

'The boy cannot be forced to provide what I require,' she went on, as indifferent to my sense of humour as she was to my proximity. 'Not even through pain or fear. It is only through bonds of affection that his abilities can be fully unlocked.'

Only now did she turn to face me.

'That's why I needed you, Ferius Parfax, why I need you still.'

I reached over my shoulder, uncapped the black leather mapmaker's case and drew my smallsword.

'Sister, if you and me are gonna get to wrastlin', I'd appreciate it if you didn't talk me to death first.'

She smiled at that. 'You speak as they do – the Path of the Rambling Thistle. That is good. It will make it all the sweeter when you whisper my verses into their ears.'

'Rosie already sang that song to me. Sorry to say, it didn't take.'

The corners of her mouth rose higher and higher until I could see the gums of her upper teeth, until any trace of the woman Rosie had known as Penta Corvus was utterly gone, leaving behind something that resided in her body but wasn't human at all.

'That's because I left out the final verse,' she said.

49

The Last Verse

I was too close now. All the Traveller needed was to hit me with the first syllables and it'd be too late for me to run. Too late for me to do anything except hope she was lying.

'You're bluffing,' I said.

She tilted her head, looking at me the way a cat would a mouse being dangled by its tail.

'You still believe yourself to be Ferius Parfax, don't you?' the Traveller asked, though it wasn't meant as a question. 'I composed the verses my teysan uttered especially for you, so that you would believe yourself free when in fact you are mine. What name did the verses select for you?'

'The Path of the Wild Daisy,' I said.

'Good. That is good. The Path of Thorns and Roses is strong, disciplined, remarkable even. But she does not make friends easily. You do, especially now that we have instilled an even greater degree of . . . winsome charm, let us call it, into your instinctual responses. Even now, standing there, smirking at me with your arta valar, you believe you have finally become an Argosi, when in fact you will be their doom.'

The sun was rising fast. Wouldn't be long now before some of the folks from the city came out this way and the Traveller would have more toys to play with. I should've tried to stab her with my smallsword, even though I had no reason to believe it would work. I didn't though. I'd first brought this sword with me to the Seven Sands with the intention of shattering it into seven pieces and burying them a hundred miles apart. There was too much blood on the blade already, and I was done with senseless killing.

That's what I told myself, anyway.

'How about you and me lay our cards on the table, sister,' I said. 'Then we'll see who's got the best hand.'

Penta Corvus knelt down, picked up a handful of ruby-red sand and let it slip through her fingers.

'As you wish. Will you allow me to begin?'

'Only seems fair.'

I steeled myself, waiting for her to deliver the final verse she'd spoken of. I had danced my way through the others. Maybe I could do the same with this one.

But she didn't say anything, just gestured off to the right. I followed the line of her hand with my gaze. Had I not been so focused on her all this time, had the body on the ground not been garbed in red silk robes that almost matched the ruby sand beneath, I would've noticed him lying there before now.

I left the road on which we stood and walked over to him. My boot heels sank into the loose sand like the desert was just waiting to swallow me up. Even though I couldn't yet make out his features, already my hands were shaking.

Durral, I thought. *That's how she'll break me. Durral must've come looking for Enna. She caught him somehow and now he's –*

But it wasn't Durral Brown at all.

When I recognised who it was, the metallic tattoos around my throat – so faded these days that you could barely make them out even if you got real close – started to prickle.

346

'No . . .' was all I said, because now I understood what the Traveller had meant by one final verse that would at last infect me with her plague.

He was maybe twenty-three now. Dark-haired and square-jawed. Broad-shouldered and more muscled than most mages you might meet. He looked like some legendary hero in repose as he lay there, tanned skin kissed by the rising sun. More than the war covens who'd hunted my people or the filthy old lord magus who'd stolen my childhood from me, this young, handsome man unconscious at my feet was the reason I despised the Jan'Tep.

Now that hatred was going to cost me my soul.

'I believe you know him as Shadow Falcon,' the Traveller said with the calm self-assurance of someone who knew she'd won long before the fight had even started. 'Would you like to know his Jan'Tep name?'

'How . . . how did you—'

'After my teysan seduced you and shared her tragic past, you couldn't help but tell her your own sorrowful history. I took it from her and found him.' She gestured towards the city in the distance. 'He lives right there, in Oatas Jan'Xan. He has a young wife now, a powerful mage in her own right, and they have a newborn son, whom they will raise to be strong and arrogant and as vile as themselves.'

I took another step closer to Shadow Falcon, my tormentor, who'd helped Met'astice burn vile spells into my flesh. He lay on his side, eyes open yet unseeing, limbs trembling yet paralysed. His mouth moved as if trying to utter a spell that would not come. I had never imagined someone like him could look so afraid. How many times had I vowed to kill him? Even after Durral and Enna had taken me in – after I'd told myself I'd let

347

go of my hate for him – I still saw his face in my nightmares. Those other Jan'Tep I'd hunted down and beaten, they were just mirrors of Shadow Falcon. Now he was here, in my grasp.

'Do you understand, teysan?' the Traveller asked me. 'This is my final verse for you, Ferius Parfax. The one you cannot resist because you wrote it yourself.'

I could hear the Scarlet Verses squeal in ecstasy as they mated with the memories of my own childhood suffering, becoming something new, a poem that was mine and mine alone. A song that I would hear for the rest of my life.

This was how Penta Corvus had fallen victim to the verses. She'd unwittingly composed them herself, binding her research into the fundaments with her own obsessions. For her, it was becoming the perfect Argosi. For me, it was my hatred of the Jan'Tep.

'You can dance all you want,' I found myself saying aloud, 'but you can't outdance yourself.'

She came to stand beside me. When she placed her hand on my shoulder, so warm, so loving, I had to fight the urge to nestle my cheek against it.

'The Jan'Tep are a corruption. A plague upon this world. You know that even if you can't admit it to yourself. Out of spite and fear, in their relentless pursuit of power, they will engineer schemes that will bring forth untold death and destruction. Trust in one who sees the patterns buried within other patterns, and in the beating of a single raven's wings the breeze becomes the hurricane that ravages a continent. This man who lies unconscious at your feet, this *boy*, will rise up high among his people. He will become everything they adore about themselves, everything they wish to be. Worst of all, he considers himself honourable. Noble. Within such fertile ground are sown the seeds that will bloom into generations of suffering.'

The tip of her finger tickled my neck, the nail scratching at one of the metallic sigils beneath the skin. Her breath when next she spoke soothed away the pain.

'Unless you stop him.'

The tip of my smallsword had found Shadow Falcon's neck, a fraction of an inch above the spot where the Traveller's fingernail had touched my own. With each ragged breath, his throat approached the blade. The hilt felt as if it had been shaped for my hand alone. The sensation was so familiar. When had it had felt this good to hold a weapon? Not for a long time. Not since –

Oh . . .

Even as my arm drew the sword back in preparation to bury it deep into Shadow Falcon's neck, even as I imagined the ruby sand turning crimson, my nostrils smelling the faint copper of his blood, even as destiny met inevitability . . .

. . . I laughed.

The Traveller's hand left my shoulder. She stumbled back a half-dozen paces as if I'd shoved her away.

'In case you're wondering,' I said, turning to her, 'the mistake was the sword.'

I lifted up my knee and snapped the slender blade across it.

A hundred different expressions played over Penta Corvus's face, like masks she was trying on, one by one, none of them quite fitting. Confusion. Irritation. Anger. Outrage. Disbelief. She strode towards me stiff-legged, her sandals digging into the sand as words poured from her mouth. Some hurt, others tried to worm back into my thoughts. I danced around each and every one of them without so much as moving an inch.

'It's okay, sister,' I told her gently, because I wasn't speaking to the Traveller any more. 'You can let go now. You don't need to keep fighting.'

349

I wish I'd gotten to know her when she was the young, wild Argosi who'd saved Rosie from becoming the murderous machine her masters and training had intended. I bet Penta Corvus had been a sight to behold back then. Even now, her will all but gone, replaced by the Scarlet Verses that had kept growing and growing inside her all this time, still something of her had remained. Fighting back. Sabotaging the verses as best she could.

Something wonderful that would soon be gone from this world.

'I wish . . .'

That's all she got out. All the verses would allow her. Whatever foul things they did to the mind made it fragile. Brittle. The discovery that the Scarlet Verses could be contradicted meant the words themselves no longer held the meaning for which they'd been devised. Those meanings came apart, degrading into mere syllables, and then nothing but the petulant mumblings of a child. And like a petulant child, when faced with a truth they couldn't handle, those verses fussed and fretted, shaking their playthings in anger. Penta Corvus, though – I guess whatever part of her was left had had enough.

Her head turned to the right, then swung to the left with such force it practically pulled her whole body along with it. The second time it did just that, and Penta spun around like she was pirouetting on a stage. But her feet planted themselves, and the third time, when she brought one hand up to her chin and the other to the back of her head, she twisted so hard and so fast that the next thing I heard was the crack of her neck snapping.

Her last words were a sigh.

50

The Path of the Wild Daisy

Rosie and Binta were waiting for me by the side of the road. Binta was scowling at Rosie, who kept trying to sign to him, informing him that he was being a very silly little boy and ought to take advantage of the fact that she was trying to teach him useful things even if they were probably beyond his limited understanding. Binta just kept giving her the same gesture in reply. You can probably guess what it was.

There were some bad days that followed. With considerable effort – and the unwilling assistance of Quadlopo and Biter – we brought Shadow Falcon back to his city, along with the charred corpses of the other two mages. I spent some very uncomfortable hours explaining what had happened to them, while several robed figures glowered at us with hands outstretched, sparks of magic swirling about the tattooed bands on their forearms. Shadow Falcon was still unconscious. One of the mages woke him with a silk spell, but even then he was too groggy to know where he was, never mind tell his version of the story. He didn't even recognise me. When they sent for his wife, I informed the mages that we were leaving, so they better decide whether to risk killing two Argosi or else abide by the terms of the agreement Durral had made with their clan prince a while back.

Eventually they came to see reason, and let us go with the familiar Jan'Tep warning never to return to their territories or face the judgement of the Council of Lords Magi and blah, blah, blah.

Those people really take themselves too seriously.

We buried Penta Corvus in the ruby sands. I'd asked Rosie if she had a home or kin we should bring her to, but I guess like most Argosi she'd left such things behind. Both of us tried to convince Binta to let us set him up someplace nice and safe while we dealt with the rest of the mess left by the Red Scream. He refused though. Seemed to think it was his duty as much as ours to see the dead laid to rest.

All told it was almost two months before we were finally able to look each other in the eye and know we'd done all we could. We spent a lot of nights camped outside of those temples. I painted more debt cards while Rosie told me stories about Penta Corvus. I'd tell her stories about Durral and Enna. We both figured the other was demented to think so highly of such clearly insane individuals.

Rosie tried kissing me once. It didn't take. Maybe the Red Scream had changed us both, done damage to that most human part of ourselves that wanted to feel the touch of another. Maybe we just needed time.

I sometimes worried that Rosie had come out of this worse off than me. She had been so sure of herself, so self-righteous and rude. I wasn't sure if the woman she was could handle being shaken in her beliefs. I tried convincing her to come with us to Durral and Enna's house. The Path of the Rambling Thistle is a strange one, but if there's a better cure for sorrow, I haven't found it yet. Rosie assured me that, while she would indeed promise to one day seek out Durral and Enna's tutelage, nothing could shake her from the Path of Thorns and Roses.

She proved her assertion true by leaving without saying goodbye. When Binta and I packed up from that last stop on the Great Temple Road and saw she had gone without us, he signed, *'Told you she was a bi—'*

I gave him a gentle smack upside the head. Isn't good for boys to think they can use such words when speaking of a lady. I'm pretty sure he was signing that word at me behind my back the entire trip south until we reached the little house on the border with Gitabria.

'Well now,' Enna said, stepping out the door and spotting me and Binta standing there like hobos come to beg a free meal, 'what kind of trouble am I about to step into here?'

'Big trouble, Mamma,' I replied. 'Messy. Complicated. Unruly.'

She gave the boy a wink. 'Well now, that's the best kind of trouble, isn't it?'

I gave Binta a shove, and he reluctantly trudged up to the house. We'd had a lot of talks on the way about just why I, all of seventeen years old and twice as messed up as he was, couldn't adopt him. Enna and Durral though – they knew just how to raise troublesome children.

'You takin' in strays, woman?' Durral asked, stepping out onto the porch. He looked older than I remembered. Maybe it was just because he wasn't smiling at me like he used to.

'Says the man who brought Ferius Parfax into our lives,' she replied tartly.

'You saw how that turned out, right?'

Enna turned, and the grin on her face would've shone through a thousand miles of cloud. 'Better than I ever could've dreamed,' she said.

She took Binta by the hand and led him inside. I'd told him so much about her on the ride down here that you could see by the look on his face he was half in love with her already.

353

Durral strode over and stood at the edge of the porch, legs wide like folks do when they're about to get into a punch-up. I'd figured he'd stay polite just long enough for Enna to be out of earshot. After that, his expression would change, like it did when hard truths had to be told, and he'd send me packing. I didn't need to ask if he still loved me. I knew he did. But I'd nearly killed his wife on account of my rage, and some crimes you can't pardon even if you want to.

But here's the thing about us Argosi: we're gamblers, wanderers, tricksters and a dozen other disreputable things. But more than anything? We're unpredictable.

'Well?' Durral said, crossing his arms in front of his chest. 'You plannin' a career as a particularly sour-lookin' statue or are you coming inside?'

I felt so filled with joy and longing that I could've died happy right then and there. But as I lifted my foot to take the first step towards that door, I found I couldn't put it down again. I wanted to be inside that house so much I would've traded all the years left to me for one more night in that home with those two people I loved more than such a small world can encompass. But I couldn't do it.

Durral gazed down at me from the porch. I expected him to look irritated or disappointed or maybe even sad. He just looked proud.

'What'd you settle on?' he asked.

'The Path of the Wild Daisy,' I replied.

'Sounds about right,' he said. 'Guess the Path of the Wild Daisy winds elsewhere right about now.'

I tried to keep from crying, failed utterly, then decided I didn't mind. Like Enna says, an Argosi who can't cry hasn't learned her arta forteize.

'Reckon it does at that, Pappy.'

354

He leaned against the door frame, and gave me one of those smiles of his that he had stolen from Enna and I had stolen from him. I was going to carry that smile with me on every step of the Path of the Wild Daisy, and maybe one day somebody would steal it from me too.

I liked that idea.

'Give 'em hell, kid,' Durral said as he went inside the house and closed the door behind him.

'Damn straight, Pappy,' I said, and mounted up on Quadlopo's back before nudging him back down the road.

That horse was none too happy, let me tell you.

Acknowledgements

The first time I ever typed the word 'Argosi' was on page 60 of Spellslinger when Kellen's father says dismissively of Ferius Parfax: 'The woman is an Argosi.'

Kellen, quite naturally, asks, 'What's an Argosi?'

Good question.

At the time, I had only a vague sense of this loose band of wandering card players who had no magic of their own yet dared to meddle in the affairs of great nations and powerful mages. Soon though, with every action Ferius took and every word she spoke, the ways of the Argosi began to unfold, and I, quite unintentionally, began walking a winding version of their path.

More than any other subject explored in my books, readers send me letters asking about the Argosi. They want to know the secrets to the seven talents and how best to apply the four ways to their own lives. They want to know how to find their path and in so doing choose their Argosi name. But I'm not some self-help guru peddling New Age philosophy to the masses. I'm a storyteller searching for things to write about that feel true to me. So while I'm always happy to hear from readers and answer questions as best I can, here are the only three truths I can share about the Argosi ways:

First, the things that make us human are full of wonder, mystery and a greater magic than any fantastical spell. Listen to a song performed by musicians on a stage, or watch a dancer (or, better yet, dance yourself when no one's watching), or try learning a few words in a new language. Now consider how improbable and amazing it is that these things should even exist and that all of them are part of your inheritance as a human being. People like you created all those things. Not elves, not vampires, not space aliens. We are all, it turns out, incredibly cool.

Second, none of us is born with a grand destiny. There's no right answer on the test. Each Argosi chooses their own path through life. When that truth feels equal parts terrifying and wondrous, you're doing something right.

Third – and in case you've been wondering, here's where we get to the point of all this – the Argosi know that the greatest gift we're given in life is the presence of all these other human beings around us. People whose paths we cross, sometimes for a few moments, occasionally for a lifetime, and all of whom we can learn from. *That's* the Way of the Argosi.

Since the first Spellslinger book was published just four years ago, I've learned a great deal about storytelling from all the people with whom I've shared this peculiar journey, and I'm grateful to each and every one of them.

Arta Precis

One of the first lessons an Argosi learns about the art of perception is that seeing what others do not is nowhere near as hard as piercing the veil of what we ourselves know and yet fail to recognize. The best editors and author friends aren't the ones who tell you what your story should be, but rather those who pick up on the story you're trying to tell and help you find it.

Eric Torin: I never would've written the first Spellslinger book without you helping me along for those first winding steps.

Tilda Johnson, Felicity Alexander and Maurice Lyon: who gets lucky enough to have not one, not two, but *three* terrific editors on a series?

Kim Tough and Peter Darbyshire: sharing each other's first drafts day by day last year was a blast.

Nazia Khatoum: Thanks for spotting the slightly too creepy parts in this book before I unintentionally inflicted them on readers!

Arta Loquit

In most conversations about fiction these days, prose gets ignored. It's as if the characters, plot and themes somehow exist separately from the words used to bring them to life. But the words matter a great deal to authors and readers. So I'm eternally grateful to the fine folks who've helped me find the right ones over these past eight books.

Talya Baker: Your fabulous copy-edits are a joy each and every time.

Melissa Hyder: Thanks for all the prufreeding even though I nevar mike splelling misstakes.

Lauren Campbell: Thanks for helping me keep that first draft on track.

Arta Forteize

Being an author is the greatest job in the world. It's also one of the most precarious. Every day it seems as if there are more ways to get yourself in trouble, and all too often you have to take sudden downturns in your career in your stride. Times like those are when you really need to develop your arta forteize.

Christian Cameron, Kristi Charish, Nicholas Eames, Ben Galley, Chris Humphreys, Evan Winter and I periodically get together online to chat about the various ups and downs in our author journeys. These conversations always leave me both better informed and better able to weather the occasional storm.

Arta Eres

The Argosi art of defence isn't about fighting every battle but winning every fight. I'm intrinsically terrible at this, preferring instead to rush into conflicts even when they aren't necessary. Fortunately, I've got excellent teachers in arta eres.

Heather Adams and Mike Bryan: What do you call agents who – even after they retire from the business – keep periodically looking out for you? Perhaps the right word is *maetri*.

Jon Woods of RCW Literary: I warned you when you took me on as my new agent last year that my career was headed for the dumpster. Somehow you keep preventing that from happening.

Arta Tuco

Strategy is a tough skill to learn. Navigating a path through all the shifting sands of the publishing industry requires figuring out how to transform a manuscript into a finished book that fits the market and also how to get it onto the shelves. I'm grateful to the folks at Hot Key who've made this possible.

Nick Stearn: the art direction for the Spellslinger and Argosi books has always been spectacular.

Dominica Clements: thanks for shepherding these covers through all their phases and for putting up with my occasional complaints about kerning.

Gavin Reece: your cover illustrations of Ferius are breathtaking.

Sally Taylor: From vague and often contradictory rambling notes, you've created some of the most magnificent tarot-esque cards I've ever seen.

Farhad Ejaz: thanks for the excellent map!

Annie Arnold for auxiliary assistance on the books, Emma Kidd for the production, Natasha Ullman for assisting on those productions, Marina Stavropoulou for managing the audio operations, DataConnection for typesetting and Clays for printing. Thank you all.

Kristin Atherton: I actually wept listening to the audiobook for *Way of the Argosi*. You really are the voice of Ferius Parfax.

Of course, no matter how good the story or how lovely the packaging it comes in, it takes a whole army to get it out into the world successfully. Thanks to the marketing and publicity team of Emma Quick, Isobel Taylor and Molly Holt for building awareness and enthusiasm for the series. Thanks as always to Elise Burns, Stacey Hamilton, Kirsten Grant, Maddie Hanson, Amanda Percival, Alan Scollan, Jeff Jamieson, Jennie Harwood, Robyn Haque, Vincent Kelleher and Sophie Hamilton for convincing bookstores that these were stories worth having on their physical and virtual shelves.

One of the coolest parts of being a novelist is that sometimes your work gets translated into other languages or gets optioned for film and television. Thanks to Ruth Logan, Ilaria Tarasconi, Amy Smith and Mark Simonsson for making the right strategic moves on behalf of the series.

Arta Siva

The art of persuasion is one of the most difficult when it comes to books. With video games, movies, television and so many other options for entertainment out there, it's a miracle anyone picks up a novel any more. Actually, it's not a miracle at all – it's thanks to passionate booksellers and fearless librarians, reviewers on blogs and YouTube channels and in print who put in countless hours championing not only specific books but the fantasy genre itself. And thanks to readers who take the time to tell their friends and families about the stories that are meaningful to them. I'm grateful to all of you. I hope it's okay if I give a special thanks to Jade of

Jadeyraereads on YouTube for her many kindnesses towards Argosi wanderers and thieving squirrel cats everywhere.

Arta Valar

Of all the Argosi talents, arta valar is the one both Ferius and Kellen return to the most often. Perhaps it's because daring is the one that makes all the others possible. The only secret I've learned about this most peculiar of the Argosi arts is that attempting something new – something truly difficult, which could easily result in complete disaster – is much easier when you have someone who not only believes in you but makes you believe in yourself. For this and a thousand other reasons, my thoughts return as they always do to my brilliant, talented and beautiful wife, Christina de Castell.

Sebastien de Castell
October 2021
Vancouver, Canada

HOT KEY BOOKS

Thank you for choosing a Hot Key book.

If you want to know more about our authors and what we publish, you can find us online.

You can start at our website

www.hotkeybooks.com

And you can also find us on:

We hope to see you soon!